## Well written historical fiction
* * * * *

This book was written with so much detail that it seemed like you were there.

## All the feel!
* * * * *

This book stays with you long after you are finished reading, keeping you feeling all the feels! Each character is written in such a beautiful way that you feel like you know them, with enough detail to understand them but also room for your imagination to complete each character too. Maddie Pearl's journey is not an easy one to read, BUT it is certainly not one that should be missed. While this is historical fiction, I'd venture to say it will resonate with some who lived through this time in history. It was incredibly hard to not finish this story in one sitting!! I'm eagerly awaiting the next book in the series!

# MADDIE PEARL

❖ ❖ ❖

## *SOUTHERN GIRL*

# MADDIE PEARL

❖ ❖ ❖

## *SOUTHERN GIRL*

Tracy & Norris,
I hope you enjoy getting
to know maddie Pearl
as much as I enjoyed
creating her!

### Jack Jenkins

*Jack Jenkins*

march 2023

Published by Jack Jenkins
In collaboration with Kindle Direct Publishing and Amazon

# MADDIE PEARL – SOUTHERN GIRL
## by Jack Jenkins

First Edition 2022
2 3 4 5 6 7 8 9 10

*Dedicated to Mary Charles,
my best friend and co-conspirator
over forty years now*

# Preface

A close friend's mother, Ruth, passed away expectedly after a long but ordinary life in eastern North Carolina. I knew her story, or so I thought, and stood perfunctorily at the graveside "listening" to the preacher while actually watching two squirrels playfully chase each other around an ancient oak. Somewhere in reverie, something external caught my attention.

"What'd he say?" I asked my wife Mary Charles, but she summarily "shushed" me.

Now tuned in, I heard an amazing story of a woman I'd known my whole life but really knew not at all. Later that night, I re-read her obituary. Like most, it was short, factual, and dry as unbuttered toast. She lived, worked, married, had a son, and died survived by....

The disconnect piqued my interest, so I began reading obituaries daily. Most mirrored the aforementioned. Even the long ones, typically about some civic leader, devolved into superficial lists of club memberships, financial conquests, and silly statements of how he adored "his" ECU Pirates or loved golf, fishing, and hunting in Canada. Perhaps we expect too much from a life's short synopsis buried in a dying newspaper, but surely there's more to our stories than the daily obit drivel. I am hopeful this series illustrates that point in an entertaining manner.

For a time, I considered writing Ruth's biography. Quite honestly, the research was beyond my interest span. So I opted for this, a work of fiction. Aside from a few unavoidable overlaps (each is a woman from eastern North Carolina, for instance), there is absolutely nothing herein that intentionally reflects the actual life of my friend's mother.

The fictional heroine, Maddie Pearl, grew up dirt poor in the Jim Crow rural South. The stench of that era permeates today. For accuracy and by necessity, racial slurs and depictions of segregation, white power, blatant discrimination, and abject ignorance pervade. Please do not hold that against me personally. Much of what's written reflects a culture and mindset deeply detestable to all sensible people, including me. But to sugarcoat with vague references, glossy overviews, and veiled words without letters (n.....) serves no purpose beyond catering to those who distort history through pretense, book banning, and whitewashed curriculums.

This is the first book in the *MADDIE PEARL* series. Because Maddie Pearl's fictional life is so rich and full, one volume proved far insufficient. The series is chronological, beginning with her birth in 1922 and covering American history from the Great Depression to World War II, McCarthyism, the civil rights movement, and even the Beatles' first appearance on *The Ed Sullivan Show*. It is an American story that reflects much of what is right and wrong in this country, not only in days gone by but generationally to the present.

Before concluding, I want to thank Mary Charles for all of her help and support in making this possible. Aside from giving me constant encouragement, she added tips and observations about the story that proved invaluable, helped edit numerous rough drafts and proofs, and actually took the cover photo as well as the picture of me. Without her, I would not be writing this today.

Finally, thank you. There are many options for your time and entertainment, and your choice of my effort is appreciated more than I can convey. I sincerely hope your investment proves worthwhile.

Jack Jenkins
October 2022

# PART I
# TROUBLED
# BEGINNINGS

# Chapter 1

The child arrived shortly after midnight on the first day of 1922. There was no joy. The farmer needed another son, desperately. Mama dreaded another mouth to feed. Named after her grandmothers, Maddie Pearl Prine was little more than a distracting nuisance to her four brothers. Luke, the meanest and indisputable alpha, enjoyed tormenting her whenever Mama wasn't looking. Jamming peas into her nostrils was fun, as was quietly removing her blanket on particularly cold nights in the unheated shanty. Hog, the paterfamilias, found such antics amusing; Mama fretted impotently; life lurched forward with each suffered day.

The Prine farm, a hardscrabble patch eight miles from asphalt, was part of a crazy-quilt mix of eastern North Carolina properties owned by Boss Lee. He provided no amenities, dealt strictly in cash, and relied on beatings—or the occasional eviction by fire—to enforce his one-sided leases.

It was not Mayberry. Maddie Pearl grew up fast.

Her fifth birthday featured a dry chocolate cake Mama fashioned from old cocoa and weevil-infested flour. There were no presents, except a green snake Luke hid in a box to the little girl's shock upon opening. Even Mama laughed, until Maddie Pearl's tears forced a modicum of mothering. It did not come naturally to the bitter crone, and her child's hysteria only worsened. Hog slapped the birthday girl hard; she "SHUT THE HELL UP!"

The tenth birthday brought Maddie Pearl a "new" dress for church—a hand-me-down Mama bought for ten cents at the general store in Tuck. The ill-fitting, off-white garment had a small, brown stain slightly below the waistline in the back.

"Nobody will notice," Mama promised.

Everybody noticed, especially after Luke spread it around that Maddie Pearl had "crapped herself."

Christmas was no better no matter the year. There were no toys to open or bells to jingle. Hog had no money for such; Mama considered Santa antics blasphemous. So each December 25th they'd gather in the cold, drafty hovel as Mama read from the King James Christian Bible her parents had given upon her marriage years ago.

*        *        *

Their relative isolation and deep poverty hindered interaction between the Prine children and peers. Church, Maddie Pearl's main exposure to the outside world, was a severe all day affair in a tumbledown hut at the end of a gutted cart path. Silly girl chitchat on the back pew was scorned. So each Sunday she sat rigidly, listened to Preacher Roe's damnations, sang the hymns, prayed to remain awake, and accepted the fate because she knew no better.

School likewise provided no social opportunities. Public education, widespread across most of North Carolina, had not found this part of Webster County. So Mama taught the three R's and young Maddie Pearl learned her lessons, alone.

The lack of socialization and formal education was of no concern, however, as only farming and working mattered. Men toiled in the fields. Women cooked, cleaned, chored, and bore male children to raise in the wasteland to work on the tenant farm growing the same tobacco or cotton year after year to the total degradation of the soil they didn't own anyway.

Like every girl in that hopeless world, Maddie Pearl was condemned to a life of work, struggle, church, hunger, children, work, quiet desperation, church, old age, and merciful death with attendant church funeral. Travel, adventure, accomplishment, happiness, and self-actualization were as foreign as Venus and Mars.

But things could have been worse.

Roughly a mile away down the path was "*Darkieland*," a barren, rock-strewn, strictly-off-limits awfulness where the African Americans were relegated.

*        *        *

In this America the beautiful with spacious skies and amber waves of evil inequities, Maddie Pearl matured quickly.

She grew up tall for a preteen, and very pretty, with natural, Irish Setter red hair, creamy white blemish-free skin, and the stirrings of an attractive womanly figure under her worn jeans and ragged tops (and brown-stained dress on Sunday). She needed no makeup—there was none anyway. But perhaps more important than beauty and brains, the girl had spunk.

Her attributes notwithstanding, Maddie Pearl was a liability to her bloated, alcoholic father. Females were silly daydreamers incapable of working like men. Had Hog been semi-intuitive, he would have realized her potential as bait to hook boys with strong backs to work the farmland. But even if Maddie Pearl had been dangled from a line in the dating pool, the fishing would have been poor, at best, with so much inbreeding, destitution, and sheer ignorance.

Mama likewise was a female millstone to Hog, but for a different reason. Long before becoming "Mama," she had been a fifteen-year-old from a good family with a bright future. Hog, meanwhile, was a brute from nothing with an animal allure that attracted all the young girls. At a church homecoming, he enticed the child behind a tobacco barn, a scandalous pregnancy ensued, and "either do the right thing or die" was proposed. They did the right thing, of course. Tate arrived a few months later, breech.

From an early age, Tate seemed... *strange*. Peculiarities manifested in everyday activities. As a teething baby, he gnawed on wood like a rat. As he grew, the boy ate dirt, was a bed *defecator*, walked late and spewed uncommunicative gibberish.

"You gave me a God damn retard, you slut!" became Hog's familiar refrain, usually shouted between slugs from a bottle and smacks to Mama's face. The subsequent production of Luke, Levi, Ethan, and Maddie Pearl, all healthy bouncing babies, never remedied Mama's original sin with Tate, and never would.

*       *       *

Most of 1930's eastern Carolina was a contrast of white have nots and desperately destitute blacks. Webster County was no

exception. Maddie Pearl's people—WASPs all—had no education, manners, cultivation, sophistication, awareness of history, or interest in crop rotation. Nevertheless, they were considered superior to the negroes who were little more than glorified slaves.

Maddie Pearl had seen but not known black people throughout her short life. If nothing else, the lay of this backward land dictated happenstance contacts between the races. Although close interaction was rare and off limits, she'd see them in the fields or along the shared path. They'd nod or she'd eek a timid "hello" and each would go their own way.

That changed one nondescript summer day in Maddie Pearl's twelfth year, thanks to a very special, four-legged friend.

*          *          *

She loved all animals, and had a special place in her soul for Daisy, the family's old, half-blind mule. She particularly enjoyed feeding her mulberries and blackberries that grew randomly about the woods. Maddie Pearl loved playing with the chickens and the feral barn cat that kept the rats away, but petting Daisy's thick mane while hand feeding the beast brought the most joy.

Hog, on the other hand, saw Daisy as an implement to be used and then discarded. The creature rarely if ever had a day off, even in bad weather. After being overworked to near death, the mule no longer had any value, so Hog "offered" Daisy to the blacks in exchange for "some" free labor. With no leverage and a field to be plowed, the blacks accepted. Untold man-hours later in the blistering southern sun revealed the deal's unfairness. Hog came away seriously self-satisfied but, as noted shortly, the last laugh was on him.

The day Hog suddenly yanked Daisy away and half dragged her to Darkieland, Maddie Pearl was crestfallen. Her spirits buoyed, however, many Sundays later when walking to church.

The common path connecting the various farms scattered about Boss Lee's land was roughly the width of a cart with a mound of weeds bisecting two worn tracks. On one end was the Indian's place, Farmer Hunt, who dealt in crops and livestock. On

the other end was the church—whites only. In between, the path meandered by the Prines', Darkieland, a smattering of other properties farmed by desperately poor tenants, and rotting-stump-laden wasteland devastated by Weyerhaeuser years before. Scattered between the tracts was unproductive lowland with boggy cypress trees and snakes, insects, and assorted waterborne flora and fauna.

Perpendicular to the common path near the black families' spread was a track leading north toward paved State Road 1043 and civilization. A right turn at SR 1043 headed east to Tuck a few miles away; a left turn led west toward the far more developed Piedmont of Raleigh, Durham, and Chapel Hill. Maddie Pearl had never been to the intersection with SR 1043, much less Tuck or Raleigh or anywhere else.

On this particular Sunday, Maddie Pearl had struck out for church alone rather than waiting for her brothers and risking tardiness. As she neared the negroes' land along the common path, the preteen noticed something vaguely familiar roughly fifty yards up. With each cautious step closer, making sure her eyes weren't deceiving, she soon confirmed: *DAISY!*

*Or was it?*

The creature stood beside the path nibbling on weedy undergrowth scattered among rocks and dirt clods. She definitely was a mule, more or less Daisy's size, and female. However, only when Maddie Pearl actually touched the mane did the young girl know for sure that this truly was her long-gone friend.

The transformation in such short time was phenomenal. This new and improved version seemed younger somehow, with a shinier coat and brighter eyes. All the sores from neglected bug bites and the resultant infections were long-gone. Most telling, however, was her demeanor. She was alert—almost spry—and expressed happy recognition of her human buddy with vigorous prancing and a loud proclamation sounding like a cross between a donkey's *hee-haw* and a horse's *whinny.*

Maddie Pearl hugged the gentle equine mix and kissed her soft muzzle when, as if from nowhere:

"Whatchoo doin' with my Daisy?"

Mule and tween stopped dead in their reunion. Maddie Pearl frantically looked about but saw nothing. Had she imagined it, she wondered, but then, "Well! Whatchoo doin'?"

She honed in on the unmistakable voice this go-round and spotted a girl, roughly her age but a little shorter, standing slightly behind a tall pine tree just up ahead along the path. She had an expressive face, athletic body, and beautiful black skin.

Maddie Pearl eased away from Daisy, took a couple of steps, and replied, "I ain't doin' nothin'."

Trying to speak in the black girl's vernacular, the words came out awkwardly, almost insincere. Despite her many flaws, Mama had taught the three R's well, especially Readin', and Maddie Pearl used incorrect English as poorly as a politician feigns integrity.

"Look like you doin' sumtin' to me," said the stranger.

Maddie Pearl looked at Daisy and then back at the girl. "I's jes pettin' her, that be all. I's do swear it."

The black girl stepped forward from the tree with a cocked head. "Why are you speaking in that manner?" she asked in proper English.

Now fully perplexed, Maddie Pearl didn't know what to say or, more specifically, *how* to say it.

The black girl persisted, "Were you making fun of me because I'm a negro?"

Shocked at the suggestion and more than a little intimidated by a black person aggressively saying such a thing, Maddie Pearl took a few steps back toward home and considered hightailing it. But then she thought, "*I haven't done anything wrong, and if she doesn't like me petting Daisy then that's her problem.*"

She stood her ground and asserted, "I've known Daisy since I was a little girl, and the last thing I would ever do is hurt her."

The girl got within five feet and stopped. "You're a Prine, right? Hog's youngin'?"

Maddie Pearl was startled that this stranger she'd never seen knew her name and family. Unable to think clearly through a good response, she just stammered, "Yeah... so?"

As soon as "so" came out, she frantically wanted to grab the word and stuff it back in her stupid mouth. If for no other reason, she desperately wanted to come across as friendly to de-escalate the situation. Instead, she had sputtered "so" in a manner that seemed to say, "So...*what are you going to do about it, bitch?*" It was the last message she intended to send.

The girl gave Maddie Pearl a confused, almost hurt look, and responded, "*So...* nothing. I was just asking. You are, aren't you?"

Still muddleheaded from the "so" inanity, Maddie Pearl had no idea what the girl was asking and thus replied, "I am what?"

Once again, it came out wrong, almost like an accusation, and, just as "what" wafted into the girl's ears, Maddie Pearl realized the question's true innocence. It was too late.

"Look, I don't care who you are," said the stranger somewhat harshly. "I was trying to be polite, you know, like normal folk. But I guess you're just as crazy as the rest of your people."

"But wait, I--"

"HEY... SIS."

Maddie Pearl looked around and there, maybe a stone's throw down the path, were brothers Luke, Levi, and Ethan. In the confusion with Daisy and the stranger, she'd completely lost touch with why she was walking this way in the first place.

"What... you waitin' on us?" Luke said as they ambled up.

"No. I was just talking to this girl."

"What girl?" asked Luke, with a hint of skepticism.

Maddie Pearl pivoted and pointed... to a lone pine tree with no girl in sight.

Perplexed, she said, "Well... she was just here a second ago."

Luke noticed Daisy, shook his head in derision, and then said to Levi and Ethan, "Dumbass thinks this old piece-of-shit mule is a girl just like her." He turned back to his sister, "You and Daisy having a good talk, are ya?"

As his audience of two snickered, Luke slapped Daisy hard across the snout. The gentle beast clogged away as fast as possible in fear and pain.

"I guess that's about right," Luke said to his brothers as they continued on to church. "They're both big ol' asses... dumb asses!"

Maddie Pearl suppressed the tears as well as she could and waited for distance between them. Once they were out of sight, she investigated the pine tree closely. There was no black girl. She considered calling out, but figured the girl was long gone. Besides, she didn't want her brothers to hear. She did call to Daisy, but the creature was now across the field and definitely not coming back, at least no time soon. After weighing her options, regaining her composure, and straightening her Sunday dress with the brown stain, Maddie Pearl resumed her trek to Preacher Roe and the white church at the opposite end of the common path.

*"I don't know who she was,"* thought Maddie Pearl, *"but I don't care what she says. I'm coming back to see Daisy again, and next time I'm bringing some treats!"*

"Next time" proved to be the following Sunday. Maddie Pearl had obsessed all week on Daisy's metamorphosis and couldn't wait to bring her fresh berries and greens and maybe even a stray wild peach if she could find one in the woods. But that was secondary: her real mission was the girl. Or, more specifically, setting things straight with this stranger who seemed to materialize from nothing beside a tree and then disappear just as mysteriously moments later.

She'd played and replayed their impromptu conversation over and over, and shuddered at herself with each remembrance of *"so"* and *"I am what."* As the mental reel played each time, she'd wince at Luke's brutality that, no doubt, the invisible girl had seen and catalogued for future reference.

Fortune appeared to be on Maddie Pearl's side that next Sunday when she found a small stand of sweet grass and some muscadine grapes. She knew that Daisy liked the greens better than anything, although she'd likely not turn up her muzzle at the fruit. With delicacies in hand and far better prepared for whatever may come, she marched forward with determination and confidence. It evaporated in an instant as she rounded a bend in the path and saw... *them.*

In the same spot as before, Daisy stood solidly, looking even better than last week. Beside her were the girl... and a second

person! The girl's body language and facial expression conveyed "*stay away, or else.*"

Maddie Pearl got the signal, and almost heeded the unspoken warning, but then her blood pressure began to rise, and adrenalin pumped, and her breathing quickened, and she thought, "*All I want to do is pet Daisy and give her a treat or two, and I'm not about to let these... these... people stop me!*"

She shook the beautiful red hair from her face, straightened the brown-stained dress, flexed her body taut, and marched straight to the mule without so much as saying "*boo.*"

The girl's accomplice, a tall, very fit, deeply handsome African American boy maybe four or five years older, didn't flinch as the young white girl arrived. Maddie Pearl was determined not to make eye contact with either, but from the corner of her eye she could swear that the boy had a slight grin on his angular, black face. The girl, meanwhile, stood rigidly beside Daisy as if guarding the beast from a predator.

Soon enough, however, Maddie Pearl's true purpose revealed as she pulled the grapes and sweet grass from a burlap satchel and offered them to Daisy. Just like the week before, the mule danced, whinnied, and preened not so much at the treats but, clearly, at Maddie Pearl. As the black pair stood mutely, Daisy and her white buddy interacted like lost friends reconnecting.

The palpable mutual affection made an immediate impression on the young man, and he took the initiative. "I'm Sal, and this here is my sister, Nomita. We live over there in the community," he pointed. "She tells me you're Hog's daughter. Is that right?"

Maddie Pearl had never heard such a deep, melodious, roundly-comforting voice in all her twelve (almost thirteen) years. It was so wonderfully pleasant she almost trembled, as her mind blankly malfunctioned eliminating any possibility of reasoned response.

"See, I told you," said Nomita. "Just like her brother said, *dumbass* through and through."

Nomita's sharp observation snapped Maddie Pearl back to planet earth. "What'd you say?"

"I said you're a dumbass, just like that dumbass brother of yours said."

Maddie Pearl's teeth clenched as her fists balled, and just as she jerked forward toward the adversary, the god-like boy/man intervened, "Now hold on, both of you. There's no need to fight."

His muscular hand on her shoulder sent electric shocks throughout Maddie Pearl's young body. Whatever anger she harbored vanished in a poof like some taut balloon popping into a flaccid crumble of rubber and string. There would be no fight, not here and now, not with this... *presence* in control.

Maddie Pearl backed off, turned in the direction of the white church, and began walking. Sal said solemnly, "Don't go. Not yet. Let's talk for a minute, okay?"

Nomita tried to lurch away but was stopped by her brother before two steps could be taken.

Both young girls, caught in Sal's psychological if not physical grip, eyeballed each other, shrugged, and relaxed—slightly.

"Your people will be coming along any minute." said Sal, "So let's make this quick. You *are* Hog's girl, right?"

Still enamored by his being, it took her a second to fully grasp the question before responding, "Yes. I'm Maddie Pearl... Maddie Pearl Prine."

"Okay good," Sal said. "Now the way I see it, you both think the world of Daisy here, and I can see why. She's pretty much saved our farm, and she sure is easy to be around, huh?"

Neither girl answered.

"So anyway," he continued while looking down the road toward the Prine property to make sure the coast was still clear. "You two need to figure out a way to share Daisy, not fight over her. I mean... I'm not sayin' you should overfeed her or what not, but since both of you care for her so much, doesn't it make sense?"

Neither girl wanted to be the first to concede. Sal recognized the impasse borne solely of stubbornness, and took action. He gently grabbed Nomita's hand and held it out to Maddie Pearl. "Here, shake this."

Maddie Pearl looked at the hand, then at Nomita. Nomita looked away at first, then reluctantly nodded. With neither saying a word nor making further eye contact, the hands shook together.

"There! Now that wasn't so hard, was it?"

Again, neither chose to answer, but it didn't matter. Deep down, both knew Sal was right and now, with the handshake, the ice had been broken, the connection made.

It wasn't much, but such was the beginning of a friendship that would last the rest of their lives.

# Chapter 2

As Maddie Pearl grew from awkwardly tall child to teen burgeoning on womanhood, she hung out with Nomita regularly and became acquainted, at least superficially, with many from the "nobody wants this rocky wasteland" part of Webster. They all had proper names, but most used handles, like Stump, Sow Belly, Pickles, Jawbone, and Nomita's brother Sal, which incidentally was short for Sallerhead.

"Sallerhead?" a friendly stranger once asked. "What kind of awful insultin' name is that?"

"Well, when I was little," he responded, "my hair was kinda crazy, sticking out all over, and my pa one day just said, '*Boy, you look like a Sallerhead.*' And I don't know, it just kinda stuck."

"So he didn't mean nothing by it, I guess."

"Oh no, sir, not at all, and I've never taken it that way either."

Insulting or not, the name became "Sal" over time and stuck like gum under a school desk. In body, mind and soul, he was vastly superior to any of the area whites. It was of no consequence. That part of North Carolina in those days neither recognized nor rewarded talented blacks with what they considered "white man characteristics." He could have discovered cancer's cure and they would have beaten Sal mercilessly for blasphemously destroying the cancer cells that GOD himself had created.

Maddie Pearl liked Sal, a lot, probably because he was everything no other male in her life had been. From Hog and Luke and her three other brothers, Maddie Pearl had learned that men were impatient, uncaring, small-minded, and cruelly selfish. But Sal seemed stronger than any of them, and smarter, and had none of those traits. She'd heard her whole lifetime "dem niggers are soulless savages" that "stink" and "ain't got the sense God gave

'em." But like Nomita, Sal was humane, didn't smell bad, and had more sense than Hog and her siblings altogether.

It was more than just that, however. He was late teens, a bit more mature, and had a confidence that she'd never witnessed. He reminded her of Preacher Roe, although the reverend was much older and far less attractive. But each had a certain something that made them stand apart, as if somehow they were above all the pettiness that poisons the day with infectious inanity.

Sal's man-among-men persona was innate, going back to childhood. His physical prowess in the fields as a youngster was the stuff of legend. And when he got a little older, Sal figured out what crops to grow, how best to rotate them, and which tilling techniques maximized yield. Then there was the time that a large, black bear appeared in the sweet corn as if from nowhere and began growling menacingly. The grown men scattered in every direction, but not Sal. The boy stood his ground, stealthily paced toward the monster, and within five feet began growling back with that deep, dark, man-among-men voice. The bear's eyes widened, its ears perked straight up, its large mouth opened agape in stupefied awe, and off it galloped away as fast as its mighty legs could scramble.

Such exploits ensured Sal's position of leadership within the black community, including among the elders. But it was something altogether different that shot Sal from mere mortal to Zeus-like status among his contemporaries and the younger Darkieland denizens.

In the woods off the common path, not far from the spoke heading to SR 1043, was a circular clearing some forty feet in diameter. Secluded amidst deep vegetation, the hard packed ground evidenced no sign of life. Local lore suggested the Devil himself danced maniacally around the perimeter on quiet, moonless nights celebrating his purchase of yet another hopeless soul. Preacher Roe called such talk "silly superstition."

"This isn't the Devil's tramping ground," he reassured the faithful. "Why... this dead zone is nothing more than an Indian graveyard imbued with life-sucking Godless spirits."

No matter the cause, the circle's mysterious lifelessness kept white and black away for years, until Sal turned thirteen and everything changed.

The anniversary of his thirteenth orbit was much like every other day: rise early, work late, get to bed shortly after sundown. The precocious boy, however, had other plans. Once the last fire was doused and the snores began snorting, a dark figure crept away from the shanties scattered in a semi-circle around an old stump in the heart of Darkieland. He quietly meandered down the pathway into the darkness beyond until reaching... "it."

First looking back to make sure no one had followed, Sal stealthily penetrated the dense brush and disappeared. Some sixty feet into the thicket, the clearing emerged. It was deathly quiet, and moonless—perfect for Devil tramping or spirit life sucking.

Sallerhead ventured to the center, sat cross-legged on the ground, and waited. His nerves were electric as every sense tuned sharply to whatever may come. An eternity in ten minutes passed, and then another. He had no clock, but instinctively knew as the seconds piled into minutes that much time had elapsed, and yet— nothing.

At some indistinct moment when drowse had overtaken, something perked him back in an instant!

As the adrenalin pumped and every sense ached for input, the rigidly tense new teen dared not budge. And then, from the corner of his eye, movement!

His first thought was to bolt for the path and home and bed and safety, but his intellect held sway, and he stayed, motionless, waiting, and watching.

And there it was! Twenty feet away, just at the woods' edge, cautiously creeping between brush and barrenness, watching Sal's every breath and eye blink... was a small rabbit with a bushy white tail, soft fur, and wriggling little nose sniffing for sustenance.

Sal couldn't help but let out a relieved laugh. The rabbit noticed, stopped still, waited, blinked, and then continued its foraging foray. Suddenly emboldened, Sal stood defiantly and bellowed, "DEVIL TAKE ME NOW, OR FOREVER LEAVE ME BE!"

Breathing heavily, sweating from fear now released into relief, Sal stood, waited and, again... nothing. So he upped the ante by peering down at the ground and gutturally asserting in his preternatural voice, "Show yourselves now, spirits, or show yourselves never."

More relaxed, but still on full alert, the young man waited. But no Devil swooped in from the perimeter dancing about in evil glee; and no lost spirits from some netherworld below emerged to taunt hauntingly. Instead, within seconds, a second rabbit came scurrying beside his sibling, and they looked at Sal, and he looked at them, and they went back to feeding, and he laughed out loud.

Convincing his contemporaries had proved difficult, at first, but in due course Stump, Pickles, Jawbone, and even his sister Nomita bought into the idea that maybe... just *maybe*... the circle wasn't demon-infested after all. Although no one could explain the dearth of living things, they had to admit that nobody actually had ever seen the Devil there, or Indian spirits flying around in wispy smoke curls.

Only by day initially, then some during early evening hours, Sal and one or two others would go to the circle and—just to be extra sure—tempt fate. But fate never came, tensions eased, and before long the circle had become *the* place to be—and be seen—at least among the young blacks from down the path.

Sal built the first fire there, against the wishes of several who feared it'd be seen by the whites and lead to trouble. But Sal countered with, "They won't see it, and even if they do they'll assume it's the Devil and stay even farther away." The logic made sense, the fire was set, the cool fall night became quite toasty around the circle, and the whites were none the wiser.

Maddie Pearl didn't know Sal and Nomita when the "Fire Pit"—as it came to be known—was founded. Even after she'd befriended them, her first visit didn't come for some time.

Despite her burgeoning relationship with the black siblings, the others weren't comfortable having one of "them" around. In particular, mixing with whites socially always led to problems, like when Lil' Tom Washington was seen picking wildflowers near the ridge where a white girl happened by. His bloated body was found floating in the bottom of a well.

But aside from the obvious racial overtones, many Fire Pitters simply didn't want the whites to figure out that the circle wasn't haunted. "They'll chase us out and take the whole thing over" was the familiar refrain. In all likelihood, the sentiment was deadly accurate.

So Maddie Pearl remained persona non grata, at least as far as the Fire Pit was concerned, as she grew into her teens. Like most walls, however, the Fire Pit separation of white and black eventually, reluctantly, slowly began crumbling as that "white girl" proved her trustworthiness over and over again.

The night of integration was particularly cold, drawing everyone in ever closer to the flame. Sal and Nomita were late, but most of the regulars already were engaged in silly teenage chitchat, gossip sharing, and the like. One of the stronger boys kept trying to impress one of the prettier girls by retrieving particularly large log sections and tossing them on the heap with one hand. She'd smile, and then turn to her friends and giggle.

As the fire settled into shimmering hot coals and a general quiet overtook the gathering, the familiar twitch of dry vegetation sounded from the path's direction. Everyone sat up and took notice. Each "knew" it was Sal and/or Nomita, but black youngsters in 1930's white North Carolina knew better than to ever let down their guard. To their collective relief, Sal and Nomita appeared. But then Maddie Pearl emerged, and the disquiet returned.

Before anyone could complain, question, or march off in militant protest, Sal assumed control. "You all know Maddie Pearl here, and you know her people and everything, and you know me and Nomita too." He stopped for effect. The coals crackled in the cold, clear night as not a breath was taken. "So you know I speak the truth when I say there ain't no reason in the world why she shouldn't be here." Several heads exchanged glances gauging each other's unspoken reaction. "Now I can't make you accept her," he continued with strength borne of being the well-deserved leader, "but I'll be deeply disappointed in you... if you don't."

Like a beloved coach or inspirational teacher, Sal held psychic sway by mere presence alone. To a person, no Fire Pitter desired Sal's disapproval. They were peers and friends and desperately poor blacks together in the Carolina swampland, but Sal stood above all nevertheless. He was the strongest; He was the hardest worker; He was the smartest; He was the protector; and He was the best of them all, bar none. And if He said Maddie Pearl was all right, then it was all right with them, and that was that!

None could foresee, not even Sal, where that fateful decision would lead.

*        *        *

The Fire Pit became Maddie Pearl's home away from home. Being different and white and exotic and full of fresh stories and ideas and perspectives, Maddie Pearl added a dimension to the regular get togethers that proved spellbinding to Stump, Jawbone, Pickles and the rest. From being unwelcome, she had become the most popular Pitter of all, even surpassing Sal on some levels. He didn't mind; the more he knew, the more he liked.

Maddie Pearl's kin, meanwhile, had no knowledge of these regular liaisons. The girl was as discreet as a nun in a condom shop, for good reason. Hog could be vicious for heinous offenses, and consorting with *them* was about as heinous as it could get.

Nevertheless, hang out Maddie Pearl did, for months that grew with her budding teenage body and mind. Despite her upbringing, she never allowed the white supremacist culture to alter her walk along the path from the Boss Lee ramshackle her family called "home" to the only real friends she'd ever known. Having actually read the Bible, Maddie Pearl knew Jesus said, "*Do unto others as you would have them do unto you.*" And that was enough for her to justify, if not admit, socializing with *them*. Unfortunately, neither Hog nor any of the area's other white, God-fearing, Christian soldiers for Jesus considered the Golden Rule applicable to integration, miscegenation, or even fraternization.

Maddie Pearl worried that, sooner or later, her forays over "there" would be exposed. Webster County, like all small communities, was a place of secrets known by all. Despite her best efforts, therefore, her liaisons became manifest in due course.

Maddie Pearl first knew for sure the secret was out early one fall morning three months before her sixteenth birthday. After feeding and watering the chickens, she was intercepted by Luke just inside the barn door.

"Nigger lover," he whispered under his breath.

Not completely sure what he'd said, Maddie Pearl asked, "Huh?"

"You heard me, you God damn nigger lover," he said slightly louder but still low enough to keep the message solely between them.

Maddie Pearl stood stunned, speechless, and wholly terrified. She'd imagined this moment many times for months, but not with Luke. In her mind's eye, it'd always been Hog. He'd come to her just as she'd seen him approach Mama dozens of times. He'd bellow, she'd crouch, he'd swing a switch or fist, she'd feel the instant pain, he'd continue, she'd endure, and then it'd be over. She could handle it; she'd *have* to handle it, just as Mama had handled it so many times before.

And then in the aftermath...what?

The unknown thereafter was far more frightening than the first beating's inevitable pain and suffering. *"Would he cast me out, to fend for myself, with no roof over my head or food or clothes? Would he chain me to a stake in the yard like some wild animal and hold me hostage? Would he just keep beating me every night like he does Mama or—Jesus—instead of Mama? Or would he do something even... worse?"*

In these mental meanderings, however, the image of Luke never appeared. But now here he was, in her face, delivering the one message she'd prayed against over and over. And she had no answer, not for *him*, and Luke knew he had his sister right where he wanted her.

"I ain't told Pa, yet," he said with unequivocal danger.

She just stood and stared, witless with fear and loathing.

"But I will... when I'm good and ready, and there ain't a God damn thing you can do about it, *missy.*"

He flashed a malignant grin, stared her in the eye, spit tobacco juice on the ground inches from her feet, and then strolled toward the day's labor ahead.

# Chapter 3

"What are you gonna do?" asked Sallerhead with sincere concern.

It was another night at the Devil's Tramping Ground full of no Indian Spirits, and the mood was as somber as a child's funeral. Maddie Pearl had taken a serious risk just coming, but she loved these times too much to forgo. Her usual lie to Hog about "taking a short walk" fell flat on his flabby fat ears but prompted a glare from Luke. She left nevertheless. As usual, she visited Daisy along the way, met up with Nomita, and the two girls came to the Fire Pit together.

There's something magical about fire. The dancing, flickering, liquid light opens the soul and deep wonders hidden within. As she sat before the flame with her true friends, Maddie Pearl couldn't help but worry about her predicament. Here she was doing the one thing she liked most, with the people she loved, and yet this same activity now presented a clear and present danger she didn't know how to evade, and probably couldn't.

" *What am I going to do?* " kept rolling over and over in her pretty head. She also wondered how Luke had found out, and why would he hold off telling Hog? "S *urely he's got some plan,* " she figured, " *but what?* " Luke's retribution, however, would be small beans compared to her father's response.

Hog was a large, ignorant lout fully capable of abject despicability, especially when tanked up on mash. The Webster County powers-that-be would not tolerate murder, at least not by a white father against his teenage daughter. Even then and there, *that* would be a bridge too far. But anything short of death was fair game, and they'd never bring Hog to justice for a mere beating or neglect. "The bitch had it coming," they'd say. The sheriff would never investigate, the DA would never bring charges, the judge would never hear any case, and the jail would never house Hog.

Sal knew it, as did Maddie Pearl and the other Fire Pitters. And the thought that she had no rights, no protection, and no options consumed the young redhead as her beautiful face glowed in the fire's yellow light.

"I don't know, Sal, I just don't know," said Maddie Pearl. "I guess I could run away."

Several heads around the fire reacted to this preposterous idea.

"Run away?" replied Sal. "To where, and how? You have no money, no car, no place to go, nothing!"

He was right, of course. Maddie Pearl was as stuck as a truck in the mud. Money basically didn't exist, at least not eight miles from asphalt. Barter and sweat were the currency. The few dimes and dollars stashed away were far more precious than gold for they covered the rent and bought access to *out there*, the world, the place from which Bibles and metal tools and guns came. Such jewels as coinage were not entrusted to kids, especially of the worthless female variety.

Maddie Pearl had seen money before, at home, when Hog would make one of his rare, special trips to "Town." She never fully understood exactly what was happening, just like a little kid doesn't fully *get* what's going on with Christmas. But, she knew that somehow these über special coins and bills magically transformed at "Town" into wonderful things like cloth, feed, food, and the magic carpet on which Hog would ride, a Hoover Cart—a rusty, old, Ford Model T with a two-mulepower "engine." (That is... the motorless relic had two mules attached for propulsion.)

Her ignorance of currency totally was of no consequence, because the "Town"/money/cloth transformation mattered only for those with the aforesaid coins, bills and Hoover Carts. Being coinless, bill-less, and Hooverless presented only one of several impediments to Maddie Pearl's great escape. Aside from not really comprehending what is "Town," she had no idea of its location. In her few years, she never had ventured more than a handful of miles from home. What she had seen was not promising.

*There* looked the same as *here*—a lot of woods with a few cleared fields and sporadically spaced white people with gaunt faces, hollow eyes and—apparently—not many coins or bills. If she ran away to there, they too would disfavor her choice of

acquaintances. In fact, they'd disfavor it more, because she wasn't their kin.

No. Running away was off the table. And lying wouldn't work since everyone knew her secret. Maybe she could explain. *"They'd understand, wouldn't they? They're family; they know me; they respect my choices; they love me; they'll accept me for what I am. But what am I? Let's see... I'm a female, which is no good unless I can spit out a few male offspring some day. I'm a hard worker, which is useless because even on my best day the boys can outdo me two to one. I'm really smart, which has no value because brawn rules while brains rank with canker sores and head lice. I'm pretty, but who cares when my only womanly role is fornicating for Jesus and XY chromosomians."*

As Maddie Pearl and the ten or so black kids lingered about lost in thoughts and the fire quietly crackled, melancholy feelings brought the gathering to séance-like somberness. She wasn't the only one trapped for life in this earthly perdition. Each was condemned as surely as Lil' Tom Washington at the bottom of a deep, dark, abandoned well. There was no escaping, never had been for generations, and never would be, and they knew it each and every—

"What was that?" Sal's ears pricked like a Rottweiler on watch. Breaths held around the ring; eyes stared wide open; butterflies fluttered in every young belly.

*"There,* hear it?"

Just beyond the perimeter, in the thicket, came another... *twitch?* Was it a jackrabbit wandering by, or maybe a possum clumsily navigating the dry, fall undergrowth?

"It" sounded, again... a little louder, and closer. The first could have been fire echoes, but not this. *"Please Jesus don't let it be that bear, or...God forbid...the Devil himself!"*

But what could be worse than—

INSTANTANEOUSLY FROM EVERWHERE RUSHED white hooded apparitions with clubs and energized hatred! "GOD DAMN NIGGERS" and such accompanied blow after savage whack upon the now-bleeding heads and cracking arms, backs, and legs of the once-sweet young faces of Nomita, Sallerhead, Stump, Sow Belly, Jawbone, Pickles and everyone else—except Maddie Pearl.

"STOP! STOP!" pleaded Maddie Pearl to unhearing ears.

One brutal blow caught a little girl perfectly in her eye socket ensuring that for the remainder of Blossom's fifty-odd years she never would see sunlight, birds, and flowers therefrom again. The white hood laughed hysterically. Another smack, in the knee of the second hardest farmworker after Sal, rendered him a helpless cripple and worthless worker, his eventual suicide ensured. Three smallish hooders, perhaps apprentices just learning the ropes, slung a line over a tree limb, secured its bitter end to a stump, and commenced after—Nomita!

Maddie Pearl sprung toward her best friend screaming maniacally, "STOP! DON'T! NO! NO! DON'T DO IT!"

Outside Maddie Pearl's eyesight, one of the co-conspirators shiftily slid near her path and jut out his leg. She flailed to the ground, catching mud in her mouth. She looked up. The tripper looked vaguely familiar, in the eyes at least, which was all she could see, but his size, demeanor, and body shape were not alien either. Her quick mind synthesized the input and nausea overwhelmed.

"*Luke?*"

Before Luke could respond, Sal swooped in as if from nowhere and began pummeling Maddie Pearl's older brother near senselessness until some white cracker conked Sal sideways with a tree limb. Sallerhead was stunned, and prostrate, but still aware— even if temporarily incapacitated.

Meanwhile, the littler punks had Nomita and were wrestling her toward the makeshift gallows! Some victims had scattered, screaming in the night with broken lives and battered futures, leaving Sal, Maddie Pearl, and a couple of others. She was cringing on one side of the fire while, on the woods' edge, she saw through miasmatic flames the specter of Nomita with a rope around her neck, hands tied, and several little hoodsmen flinging about disjointedly in a half-ass attempt to string her up!

With a voice resonating from every orifice, organ and organic tissue, Maddie Pearl howled, "STOP IT RIGHT NOW! I KNOW EVERY ONE OF YOU, <u>LUKE</u> INCLUDED!"

Slightly dazed from the Sal beating, Luke called out, "Hold on, boys. *HOLD ON!*"

Almost as if choreographed, the evildoers stopped instantaneously. Luke motioned, and two of the bigger brutes

aggressively grabbed Maddie Pearl on either arm. Sal's attempt to stop them was thwarted by a particularly nasty thwack in the back. He fell, his face inches from the hot coals at the Fire Pit's base.

With the situation fully under his control, Luke surveyed the gathering with a self-satisfied smirk. "Well well well, nigger lover," he said to his sister. "Look what we got *here.*"

Maddie Pearl struggled to free herself, but the bigger boys' grips were lock-tight. As Sal tried to get back up, Luke pressed his farmhand boot directly on the black man's face, with heavy pressure. Nomita, standing by the makeshift gallows with feet and hands tied, could only watch in horror. She tried to speak, to plead, to scream for help, but the filthy rag in her mouth was choking the girl silent.

Horrified at the predicament and not fully understanding exactly what her malevolent brother had in mind, Maddie Pearl frantically thought of what to do. Neither she nor Sal could fight back, and there really wasn't any question who would win whatever battle could be waged.

Did Luke really intend to lynch Nomita, right here, right in front of his own sister? Was he really that stupid? Did he not realize that there'd be all these witnesses, including her? He was as bad as bad can get, but surely Luke wasn't that hatefully idiotic.

After she considered her brother's options and sensing he had none—other than perhaps scaring the bejesus out of her so that she'd never go back to her black friends—Maddie Pearl threw caution to the wind and took the offensive.

"What do you think you're going to do, big man? Kill Nomita? Sal? And even me?"

Luke glanced away momentarily, subtly, as if his bluff had been called.

"Is that it, *big man...* kill us all, right here and now?"

Steam trapped in a fairly large log reached the breaking point prompting a loud POP! Everyone jumped involuntarily. In the instant, Maddie Pearl saw Luke's reaction, like a scared little boy, and she *knew* he had nothing.

"You don't have the *guts,*" she said with raw emotion, as if threatening him to follow through.

Nomita's eyes widened in full terror. Even Sal flinched at the challenge, knowing full well from experience not to

underestimate silly little hooded bigots in large groups. But Maddie Pearl stood confidently, despite being restrained, outnumbered, and without leverage but with wholesale lack of faith in brother Luke.

Luke walked over to his sister, temporarily freeing Sal until another back thwack kept the black man down. Luke's face inches away from hers, he said, "You best watch yourself, bitch." He slapped her hard across the cheek leaving a brutally red mark. "One of these days, it'll be your fucking neck in that noose, YA HEAR?" He slapped her on the other cheek, even harder, sending spittle out of her pretty mouth and onto the coals below causing a singeing sound as they flash boiled in the extreme heat.

Luke motioned and the hoodsmen obeyed, pushing and knocking their black adversaries aggressively while exiting the dead circle for their hike through the woods toward the common path and their shanty tenant homes scattered about Boss Lee's quilt-work land holdings.

They'd probably be back, someday, to get even for the fight they'd already won, but not tonight, and so they left.

With the last twitch of the last twig of the last straggling pointy-hatted punk, the only sound in the cooling night was the reddening fire—the source of so much soul searching just minutes before, the moaning of a little girl with a permanently blinded eye, the wail of a once strong man now crippled for life, and the heavy breathing of them all. And beneath a stout tree limb with a rope dangling in her face, Nomita stared in wonder at her redheaded friend who'd just done the unthinkable, and gotten away with it.

# Chapter 4

Sal's formal name was Walter Carver Jefferson, but no one called him that. The sort of person that others wish to be but cannot emulate—even with exercise, study, diligence, and dedication, he was the personification of Nietzsche's *Übermensch*. Although still a teen, Sal had left boyhood long ago, and never looked back.

It wasn't a routine thing, but he'd been beaten before. The Fire Pit Incident, as it came to be known, was the worst, but he knew the sting of a switch across his back or the thudding pain of knuckles to the face. Bucks like Sallerhead were targeted specifically to set examples for the rest. Like recalcitrant mules or unbroken horses, the darkies had to be tamed, and the preferred domestication included fists and whips, or even the occasional noose and lynching.

The little girl had been tamed with a destroyed eye socket. She never saw a doctor because there were none in Webster County for bantamweight, blind, black girls. Thus, Blossom spent the rest of her days with no depth perception and a disfigured face that guaranteed she'd never wed and ensured scorn and ridicule whenever she was around healthy people with two functioning eyeballs.

The second strongest farmhand after Sal limped home after his taming, collapsed in the dirt in front of his parents' lean-to, and moaned through the night like a coyote baying at the moon. No one came to help, except his mother, but she had no medicines, no pain killers, and no bandages to stop the blood flowing from the six inch gash above his torn meniscus, ruptured anterior cruciate ligament, fractured femur, and cracked kneecap. The wounds would never heal properly ensuring permanent incapacitation until the day "Gimp" died by his own hand. It was preferable to a handicapped life of poverty, hunger, and wholesale dependency on others.

Even though this wasn't the first time the Klan—or Klans in training like Luke and his posse—had hassled the community, the Fire Pit Incident stood out. Sal noticed it, as did sister Nomita, and it was seriously disconcerting for them both.

Aside from its unusual viciousness, never before had any white defended any black. It just didn't happen. But there was Maddie Pearl one-upping her brother in defense of Nomita and the other blacks—in front of everyone. There would be repercussions.

Even more troubling, it was readily apparent that Luke had not yet told Hog of Maddie Pearl's activities. If Luke was a storm, Hog was a Cat Five hurricane, but the fat man's unimaginable havoc had not been wreaked.

Most disconcerting, however, was Luke's warning: "*One of these days, it'll be your fucking neck in that noose.*" Sometimes such things are spewed in insincere anger. A child spills milk in the new car and dad yells, "I'm going to kill you for that!" Luke's admonition, however, seemed far less abstract. He said it like he *meant* it, like he'd thought about it—a *lot.*

Certainly Luke couldn't get away with murdering his own sister. Even Hog couldn't do that—no matter if she *did* consort with coloreds. It wasn't that the white supremacists who ran every corner of the county from the courthouse to the outhouse drew some line at homicide. They didn't. Dumping Lil' Tom Washington to his watery grave, castrating the rare homosexual, or the occasional hanging of some negro was accepted, and somewhat expected—like hunting deer in the fall. But stringing up a pretty, white, teenage girl—from a Klan family no less—was a noose too far, even in this backwater haven of ignorant intolerance.

So what *was* Luke up to? Why'd he come out to the Fire Pit in the first place? It seemed too organized to be happenstantial rabble rousing, but insufficiently thought through to be some strategic move or mission.

Sal would discover the truth, soon enough, and it would shake his world to its very foundation.

\*          \*          \*

A few days after the Fire Pit Incident, Sal was working the small, rocky field near his home helping Daisy drag an ancient, rusty plow. In actuality, Walter Carver was doing more pulling than Maddie Pearl's special friend, but Daisy had been a Jefferson a while now and, despite her shortcomings, was doing the best she could with what she had... bless her heart.

Mules are too dense for such things, supposedly, but Daisy and Walter Jefferson had a bond much like a well-trained hunting dog with her master. And there wasn't an ounce of stubborn in that creature when working with Sal. On some level no scientist could explain or instrument measure, they shared a wavelength—an understanding really—that made their sum far stronger than the constituent parts. Perhaps it was just their mutual affection that prompted each to work harder for the other, but whatever the reason they managed to get more done in a day than most accomplish in a week or more.

It was a cool day, and recent rain muddied the field making the work ever more strenuous. "Come on, Daisy, you can do it," Sallerhead encouraged, and Daisy did "come on" a little more, and "do it." There was no whip, no kick in the side, and no slap on the muzzle. There was no need. Daisy had pulled this old plow many a time through this rocky field and mud and everything else that the good Lord above had thrown at her.

Sal noticed a deep, impassable divot just ahead that would take some manual dexterity to clear. "Okay girl, break time... for you at least." He reached into his pocket, pulled out a peach, and gently brought it to Daisy's mouth. She couldn't see it at first through her near blind eyes, but with Sal's help she managed to grip it in her mouth and began jawing her jowls sideways back and forth. Sal moved ahead to the divot and, just as he began the arduous task, heard something at the field's edge. He squinted, as did Daisy, and detected a handful of men coming their way.

"Now what?" he said out loud. He stood upright and grabbed a large stick he had come across when they had first begun with the sunrise.

It was Luke. A small gang of troublemakers followed closely in a cluster just behind. They walked as if on a mission, and they too carried what looked like weapons of some sort, probably homemade bats. Walter Carver Jefferson stood his ground, but

there was nowhere he could run anyway. He would fight, if that's what it took, and he might lose, just as he had a few nights before around the fire.

Luke and gang arrived and surrounded Sal. From behind, before even a word was said, one of the bigger accomplices swung a bat thwacking Walter Carver squarely in the back. WC crumpled to the ground in grotesque pain. Luke inched closer and kicked the fallen teen in the face, then ribs, and then in the back of Sal's head.

"That was for the other night, nigger," said Luke. "Don't ever hit me again, ya got it?" On the word "it," Luke whirled his bat wildly knocking Sal viciously yet once more. The pain emanated from everywhere, but Walter remained aware, awake, and alive, his body crumpled at the feet of these white goons. He frantically thought of how to cope, how to fight back, how to survive, but his synapses fired up no suggestions. There were none, at least none that would work in this here and now in the field with the rocks and mud near his shanty home that neither he nor his people ever would truly own.

Luke sauntered over to Daisy and petted her reassuringly. Sal could only watch. "Had this beast a long time now, huh?" Luke asked, knowing the answer. "I remember when my dad gave it to you people. She weren't no good to us. Too stupid and weak, just like you." To Sallerhead's horror, Luke held the bat high in the sky and swung it down on the poor, dumb, loving, sad creature whose whole world was living with the gentle black folk and helping them and doing what she's supposed to and looking forward to Maddie Pearl's treats and being the barn cat's best friend and just being good.

Daisy reared up at first, stunned but defiant, ready to fight just like her brother, but the yoke yanked her back. Luke motioned and the others commenced to beat the animal from all sides. They smacked Daisy's old legs, her fat belly, her long snout, her slumping back, her ears, head, and especially her face. She stood as long as she could, unable to rear or run with the plow firmly attached, and suffered the slaughter with no ability to fight back or even understand what was happening.

Ultimately, defiantly, she cowered a bit, and then fell slowly, like a great prizefighter unwilling to quit, going one more

round, struggling to the very end without ever giving up. And Daisy did not give up, but her body had no choice, as no beast could withstand this carnage, and she fell, lifeless, in the dirt and mud.

Splayed on the ground with blood gushing everywhere, she died. Her eyes were wide open, staring at Sal with an expression, " *Why?*"

All people, no matter constitutions, have breaking points. Sal wept.

The big beater who hit Sal first, cowardly from behind where Sal couldn't see what was coming, laughed out loud proclaiming, "Hey, look! I beat the shit out of her."

He was pointing to Daisy's blood-soaked rear end. In the pool was the mule's colon, expelled from the body by one of the blows, still full of fecal matter. Among other ingredients were the oats she had that morning. Breakfast was her favorite; she loved eating beside the cat with its milk in a small bowl and the chickens with their grain.

The big guy hit Daisy again, just for fun.

"Listen up, shitty head—or whatever your damn fool name is," said Luke to the prostrate Übermensch. "If you even look at my sister again, if you're even in the same place as her, she's deader than that goddam mule."

Sallerhead tried to rise up, but Luke kicked him back face-first-mudward. In a calm, wicked voice that would resonate in WC's ears, Luke continued, "And everybody gonna know _you_ people did it."

There was no fight to be had, at least not here and now. Walter Carver Jefferson stayed down, didn't respond, and no longer tried to get up. He just lay there, waiting, praying for them to leave. They did, but in no hurry.

One looked about the plow as if seeking something to steal. The implement was too old, rusty and ruined for pilfering, even by a poor, malnourished, ignorant redneck. Besides, with Daisy dead there was no way to transport it. So he let the thing be, but not before breaking three of the tiller wheels thus rendering the tool wholly worthless.

As they exited, one boy, a little runt not much older than Maddie Pearl but far less developed physically or mentally, pulled out his Johnson and urinated on Daisy. A couple of others noticed

and followed suit, with one taking aim and successfully shooting the stream into Daisy's open mouth where she had been enjoying the sweet peach just seconds before. They laughed maniacally, especially when one started pulling down his pants to defecate.

Luke cut it off, casually saying, "That's enough boys, *for now.* Let's git." He was the leader; they followed.

As they entered the woods at the edge of the muddy, rock-strewn field now littered with the carcass of one of nature's gentler creatures and the wrecked remains of one of man's great inventions, Luke turned back and yelled ominously, stupidly, "YOUR DAYS ARE NUMBERED, SHITHEAD, AND YOUR PEOPLE TOO!"

Walter Carver Jefferson lowered his head in pain, tears, and anger.

*        *        *

Nomita awoke the next day and wandered over the dirt floor to the shanty's main room. It was chilly, as the fireplace—such as it was—had gone cold hours ago in the plank-walled "house" with no insulation. The sun was just rising, which meant the workers long ago had gotten up and started tending the fields. But as she headed toward the communal outhouse, Nomita noticed something strange: the others were in the well-trod, hard-packed dirt patch, just milling about.

"What's going on?" Nomita asked no one in particular. Hearing no response, she walked out among them. She intended to ask her brother, but he wasn't around.

"Where's Sal?" she asked, again to no answer. The nervous looks generated a seed of doubt in Nomita's athletically taut belly. She looked about one last time, and then demanded, "Someone tell me what's going on, now!"

Pickles spoke up. "Sal ain't here."

Nomita eyed Pickles closely. "What do you mean, 'ain't here'?"

"He ain't here. We came out to see what we're 'sposed to be doing today, and he just didn't come out."

Red flags flew throughout Nomita's suddenly troubled mind. Her big brother always came out first and gave everyone

instructions for the day's labor. The adult men, what few there were, had learned long ago to defer to the best among them. And Sal merited the authority. He was as reliable as the sun in the morning and moonshine at cross burnings. But he wasn't here this day; and Nomita knew well that something must be wrong, terribly wrong, but what?

Nomita took charge in her brother's absence. "He might have already taken Daisy and the plow out to the field with the big rocks. Pickles, you and a couple of others head out that way to see if you can find him." She then directed two to check a different field, and gave further instructions to investigate other unlikely places her brother possibly could be.

As the men and boys left, Nomita considered the situation with grave concern. She had seen Sal hit that white boy—Maddie Pearl's brother—more than once the other night, hard. She knew that was many lines crossed, even in the heat of battle. Black people just don't hit white people like that, especially people like Luke. Nomita feared the worst—that Luke had come back and gotten her brother—but when, and how? He couldn't have done it last night, because everyone would have heard and gotten up.

"*Did Sal come home last night... from the field?*"

She didn't remember seeing him, but that would not have been unusual. He worked harder and longer than anyone else, and oftentimes got up before Nomita and went to bed after she and the others long had been asleep. And he always was good about being quiet when he came in late, and never woke anyone with his stirring about while settling in for the night.

Nomita thought about his routine this time of year and remembered that, usually, he worked the field where Pickles was headed. "*If he's there,*" she thought, "*we'll know in a few minutes.*" While she waited, Nomita headed over to the barn. As she suspected, both the plow and Daisy were gone. "*That's gotta be it,*" she thought. "*He's at that rock field.*"

The sense of relief was short-lived, however, when Pickles and his small crew returned.

Pickles walked up, tears flowing, and said, "Daisy's dead. Beaten... bad. In the field."

Nomita was stunned. "What about Sal?"

He was reluctant to answer. A strong man in his own right, Pickles nevertheless had his limits too, and they had been reached.

"WHAT ABOUT SAL?" Nomita frantically pleaded.

Pickles regained his composure just enough to respond, "He wasn't there, but there was blood, a lot of blood. Everywhere."

An ICBM could not have hit Nomita harder. She lost her footing a bit, and stumbled a couple of paces to an old tree stump that served as their community's hub and meeting point. The teen felt weak with fear and horror. "Oh my God," she whispered, more to herself than anyone else.

"Oh my God."

# Chapter 5

It wasn't written in bold, underlined, italicized letters. Hog and Mama didn't sit the child down and explain. Preacher Roe at the drafty shack that passed for a "church" didn't sermonize it.

But she'd crossed a bright white/black line, repeatedly. And now, after the Fire Pit Incident, Maddie Pearl learned for the final time:

*DO NOT FRATERNIZE WITH THEM!*

What she didn't know, however, was just how dangerous crossing that invisible line had become.

With no televisions, telephones, tweets, texts, emails, newspapers, magazines, or smoke signals, communication with the outside world didn't exist—at least for Maddie Pearl. Even church provided nothing, as the strict strictures dictated devoted dedication to the biblical Word of God, not the gossipy word of fellow congregants. Aside from the filtered input from Mama, Hog, and her brothers, Maddie Pearl knew precious little of what was going on out there. And now with the unsaid but unequivocal prohibition against Fire Pitting, "out there" included whatever info her best friends had to share as well.

Living in the Prine farm bubble, Maddie Pearl had no idea of Luke's little visit to Darkieland. She knew not of Daisy's demise, Sal's beating or disappearance. Most significantly, she was oblivious to the death threat against her by Luke, a boy with whom she ate every day, slept under the same roof every night, and prayed every Sunday in Preacher Roe's little church.

She was not ignorant, however, of the significant change in Luke's behavior.

He'd always been a bully, especially to her, but much of his shenanigans could be attributed to childish pranks, sibling rivalry and, as he grew older, male testosterone. After all, Levi and Ethan had their moments too, and even gentle Tate could be difficult, occasionally.

After the Fire Pit Incident, however, Luke's mischief morphed from putting a harmless green snake in a birthday box to hiding a water moccasin among her meager clothes. Thank goodness the thing was sleeping when she discovered it. Being a country girl, Maddie Pearl managed to grab the venomous viper and return it to the swamp, but not without a fair degree of drama.

Luke didn't hit Maddie Pearl, at least not since the Fire Pit Incident, but did other things letting little sis know exactly where life stood. And these "things" bordered on bizarre.

One Sunday morning, Maddie Pearl slipped on her church clothes—the brown-stained dress now long outgrown and ripped to rags. The "new" dress, her only, was a hand-me-down from an uppity white woman in "Town" whose spoiled debutante daughter refused to be seen in anything so ugly. To Maddie Pearl, it was the most beautiful thing she'd ever known. Plain and white with no special adornments, the dress still somehow transformed Maddie Pearl into a fairy book princess. And every Sunday, young Princess Prine managed to catch the wandering eyes of men and boys alike while Preacher Roe droned and flies buzzed and congregants suffered.

On this Sunday as always, the family trekked along the weedy common path to church at the other end of Boss Lee's holdings. Because Maddie Pearl happened to lag last, nobody noticed. It became clear as soon as they arrived.

"Oh my God... what's *that?*" croaked a particularly busy body. Heads turned to see Maddie Pearl, standing alone, with a "*why are you looking at me*" expression. To her horror, the fifteen year old found out.

The white, unadorned princess dress she adored had a hideous bloodstain covering much of the rear end, as if she'd been menstruating without protection. "Oh, you've finally become a woman," exclaimed Mama with pride and joy for everyone to hear. Actually, Maddie Pearl would not experience the bloody curse's prideful joy for another three months. It didn't matter. Luke's humiliating damage had been done.

Like many country kids, Maddie Pearl befriended various wild animals around the property, at least to the extent a wild animal can be a human's friend. One squirrel in particular had taken a shine to Maddie Pearl because of the odd goodies offered

daily. The feeling was mutual, and one of the girl's joys was hand feeding "Nutty." The squirrel was wild and never a pet, but in some ways this made the relationship all the more special.

Six weeks or so after the Fire Pit Incident, Maddie Pearl skipped out of the house one morning toward Nutty's usual hangout near the well and along the woods' edge. He didn't come tiptoeing out. Maddie Pearl looked around, and even called, "Nutty... Nutty!" She was about to give up, and then noticed something along the tree line.

It was Nutty, or at least his body. The head was gone. The tame squirrel with a taste for treats and a sweet disposition had been decapitated with its limp little body folded over a thin limb. Later that day, after the crying and wondering, she found Nutty's head, nestled in her things beside the bed.

There were other incidents, some even more grotesque. Maddie Pearl mentally convicted the culprit of each without jury and judge. She recognized that Luke was paying her back, getting even, and letting her know just where she stood in this family, and with him, all because of her social preferences.

Of some consolation, however, was that Hog's day-to-day had not changed one iota. Surely if Luke had spilled the beans, Hog would be on Maddie Pearl like cockroaches on cake. But he wasn't, which made the situation all the more confusing. Why was Luke still holding off? A tidbit this rich was too tasty to not share. From all appearances, however, a secret it remained, at least so far.

Hog's apparent obliviousness notwithstanding, Maddie Pearl's predicament remained untenable and, with each passing week, only worsened. Having no friends or even siblings on whom to fall back, she considered seeking Mama's help. Her mother, however—like most long-suffering rural women, had no affinity for some whining youngin'. She'd probably take Luke's side anyway since, after all, he was a boy. Maddie Pearl, having so deeply disgraced the family with her XX chromosomes, had no standing to complain about anything.

So Maddie Pearl endured, and maintained, and the dirty tricks escalated, and weeks passed, and she wondered whatever happened to her true friends now gone from her world... *forever?*

\*    \*    \*

Nomita wondered, as well, but less about Maddie Pearl and more about Walter. At first, she knew her brother would be home any minute. He was strong, as healthy as a blue-eyed Scandinavian, and more than capable of handling some silly little whities. This denial of reality shifted to anger when Nomita considered the possibility that he was out there, somewhere, maybe suffering, without her ability to help. The bargaining with herself—which went nowhere, and the depression—to which she long ago learned by hard experience not to submit, led Nomita to acceptance: she was sure Sallerhead was dead, probably beaten, and now hanging from some tree, like a stuck pig, as a warning to "*STAY AWAY FROM MADDIE PEARL.*"

But his body never turned up, and surely even boys this unenlightened knew enough to string the remains in broad daylight to be seen by all. Hiding their kills was not the KKK way, especially when the homicide was justified by the recklessness of some uppity nigra thinking he can socialize with a pretty white girl. How dare he! The son-of-a-bitch was asking to be strung up by his nuts, and the Klan was more than obliged to rope his scrotum!

With each passing day, however, a disturbing possibility began germinating in Nomita's fertile mind, and it was a weedy thought indeed. "*Could it be that he ran away?*" The mere idea was repugnant: Walter Carver Jefferson runs from no man, especially the cowardly Klan prancing about in their Halloween costumes. But he wasn't hanging around, either here at home or from a tree, and nobody had found his body, so what did that leave but...

"*Maybe Maddie Pearl knows something?*" Nomita thought hopefully to herself one afternoon while walking near the Fire Pit. To Nomita and the rest of her friends, Maddie Pearl no longer existed. She had neither been seen nor heard from since...

A new thought entered Nomita's brain and swirled about like a tiny tornado trapped in a snow globe. "*Could Walter and Maddie Pearl have run off... together?*" Nomita knew it was one plus one equals a storm of trouble, but the windy, rainy components meshed perfectly. He obviously had reason to run, she had nowhere to turn, and she sure didn't seem so popular with those boys that night either, especially with brother Luke. Could

they have gone off? Are they hiding in the woods? Or worse, have they left... *forever?*

# Chapter 6

Forever to country teens is a summer working tobacco. The forever feared by Nomita in self-torment proved even less than three months. It ended one night while she lay awake in bed worrying about... forever.

She slept closest to the window, and even on cool nights the outside may as well have been the inside with the thin walls and broken glass windows. She sleeplessly was looking through a crack at the bright full moon and noticed some slight movement near the community stump. "*Probably a fox,*" she thought, "*or maybe a possum.*" Then suddenly the movement was closer, and the creature was bigger, much bigger. She sat up in bed carefully so as not to wake her cousin, and perked her attention fully through the crack into out there.

At first, nothing. Then suddenly there was a quiet but sharp tap on the fragile window itself! Nomita jumped a bit in surprise, then her brother's smiling face reared up from the window's bottom into Nomita's full view!

A great smile spread while Nomita hustled as quietly as she could from the bed and through the small shanty out to the yard and her brother. She raced up to him arms extended; he caught her mid-flight; they hugged for what seemed like minutes.

It really was *HIM!*

Both knew the importance of cloaking, and each desperately tried to stay as calm and quiet as nature would allow, but the moment was too grand and each was too happy to stay too quiet too long. Nomita was first to break, with tears streaming down her beaming, beautiful face. Walter too was touched to extreme but, without giving in, ushered his sister away from the stump and toward the common path. Nomita practically danced as they headed for the Fire Pit far beyond any hearing ears, black or white, and out of sight of the semi-circular cluster of dilapidated

shanties surrounding the large old stump that served as the African American community.

When they reached the Pit, both gave in to the situation's enormity. The reunion was ecstasy for Nomita. Until this moment, she had idea not of whether her beloved brother was hanging from a tree, hiding in the woods, committing suicide by intentionally consorting with an underage white girl, or any number of other outcomes the imaginative teen's mind could conceive. Walter Carver Jefferson showed his feelings in a manner reserved only for real men—he sobbed.

Upon regaining at least some composure, Nomita asked, "Where've you been? We've been so worried about you. What's going on? Why—"

Sallerhead put his strong hand gently to Nomita's mouth. "I'll tell ya, but we don't have much time. I can't stay, and you can't tell anyone you saw me."

Nomita looked perplexed. Her tear soaked smile withered to a worried, questioning frown. " *What?* Why not?"

"It's Luke and the rest. The Klan, or at least the Klan's Junior Legion. They paid me a little visit, few weeks ago."

"I knew it. I just knew it! Those damn—"

Sal cut her off again. "We don't have time. I've gotta go. I never should have come here to start with. But I've got to tell ya. Whatever you do, no matter what, stay away from Maddie Pearl. I mean it... *stay away from Maddie Pearl!*"

Nomita received his input quietly, pensively, and then asked, "Why?"

Sal pulled back a tad from his little sister, and held her at the shoulders, arms length. He looked directly into her eyes glowing in the brilliant fall moonlight. He was as serious as the barrel of a gun crammed full bore into a nostril. "It's her brother, Luke. He's hatched this crazy plan—or somebody has—and he's carrying it out."

Sal's voice suddenly stopped; he turned his head and pricked his ears. "What was that?" he whispered.

Nomita detected nothing, and shook her head as if to say, " *What? I didn't hear anything.*"

Walter stayed paranoid alert for several seconds, relaxed some, and then turned back to Nomita. "Luke plans to kill Maddie Pearl and blame it on me."

Nomita was aghast. Her mouth opened but nothing came out. She was too shocked even to respond.

"So I can't be here," Sal continued. "Anywhere near here. And I can't be seen, by you or Maddie Pearl or anyone else, especially not Luke or his buddies."

Nomita processed the information. It didn't compute. Her face a question mark, she said, "But this makes no sense. He's not going to kill his sister. No way. It just isn't going to—"

Yet again, Sal interrupted. "We don't have time for any of that. Trust me. It IS the plan, I know it, and you've got to believe me."

Unconvinced, her independent and highly intelligent mind unaccepting the premise, she continued, "Well why *you*, then? Why not Pickles or Jawbone or any others? Why not me? I'm closer to her than any of us."

Sal looked around cautiously then turned back to Nomita. "I don't know. That part makes no sense to me either, but I've got an idea, a guess really. You know, I got him pretty good, when we were here, you know... before. I guess he's gettin' even, or maybe more. But it doesn't really matter. We just—"

Now it was Nomita's turn to knife into the conversation. "This is crazy! You can't just run off be—"

"He told me."

"*What?*"

"Luke told me, to my face, that day he and the others killed Daisy," said Sallerhead. "He told me exactly what they were gonna do." A long, serious pause passed between siblings. "And I believed him."

Nomita shook her head in disbelief, still not fully appreciating the situation's reality but nevertheless trusting her brother over her own instincts. "I still don't believe it, but I believe you. I'll let Maddie Pearl know—"

"NO! You can't do that!" Sal's outburst startled Nomita and she physically reacted involuntarily. In the distance, a dog roused. "You can't go to Maddie Pearl! Ever again."

A farm animal—a mule, ironically—sounded loudly on a nearby, equally dirt poor farm. It was an omen. The time had come. Brother and sister hugged one last time, closely. Her head over Sal's shoulder, Nomita asked, "Where will you be?"

Sal pulled away, straightened his clothes, and put his hand on Nomita's shoulder reassuringly. "I can't tell you. I can't risk it. Just trust me, okay? I'm fine, and you'll be all right too, long as you don't... you know."

"But what if..." her voice trailed off.

Sal anticipated her question, reached into his pocket, pulled out a folded paper, and handed it to Nomita.

"That Indian guy, over on the other side of where Maddie Pearl lives... Farmer Hunt, he's a friend," said Sallerhead.

This was news to Nomita. Everyone knew there was a Native American over there, somewhere, but nobody *knew* him, at least that's what Nomita thought. He always kept to himself. The Klan no doubt didn't like the man, but he was off the beaten track, literally, and posed no real threat, so they ignored him. The blacks likewise never had any reason to go toward his property, had no interactions with him, and pretty much didn't worry one way or the other about the man.

"A *friend?*" asked Nomita.

"He can be trusted, and he's got a truck, a real truck, that works."

This too was news to Nomita. Virtually no one around here had enough bills and coins to own anything like that. Except when tractors with trailers hauled produce to market in "Town" after harvests, only Boss Lee ever came around in any sort of vehicle, and that was just to collect rent.

"Yeah... okay," said Nomita questioningly. "And...?"

"If you need me, and I only mean if you *really* need me... like an emergency or something, this has a number on it, a phone number. I can be reached at that number," said Sallerhead.

Phone numbers were mystical to most denizens of these parts, especially among the blacks. No one had phones, and the few places with them relied on operators for connections, not numbers.

"I don't understand," said Nomita.

"Just listen, okay? If there's trouble, go to Farmer Hunt. He'll drive you into Tuck. It only takes a few minutes by truck. And he'll get you to the store... there's this store there. Well, it's kind of a store and diner both, but mostly a store, and he knows the people, real well. Anyway... he'll get you to the store, and they'll let you use their phone."

Nomita's head was swimming with questions about this fantastical manner in which to contact her brother in times of need and desperation. Sal sensed her utter confusion.

"Look, just go to Farmer Hunt, and make sure you have this piece of paper. He'll help you, and so will the people at the store. But don't do it unless it's a real emergency. You'll be taking a huge chance just going there, and they'll be taking an even bigger chance helping."

Nomita's tense body language relaxed, slightly.

"Quit worrying so much," big brother reassured. "I'll be around. You'll never see me. Nobody will. But if you or anybody needs me, you do what I said, and I'll be here. Like I said, trust me... just trust me."

She gave her big brother a look that said, *"I trust you, but..."*

Sensing her lingering uncertainty, he hugged Nomita one last time, then said softy, reassuringly, "Everything is going to be okay. I promise."

Each knew it was a promise that couldn't be assured.

Walter Carver Jefferson then turned and quickly, athletically, silently ran away from the Fire Pit, away from Nomita, and perhaps away from this place—*forever?*

# Chapter 7

True to his word, Walter Carver "WC" Jefferson, a.k.a. Sallerhead, was gone, and stayed gone. For the first few days and then weeks after their midnight rendezvous by the Fire Pit, Nomita routinely would awaken at odd hours to look out into the community area hoping to glimpse his clandestine return. But he didn't appear, and she went on with the business of growing from a precocious teenager to a talented woman.

Because she knew nothing, Maddie Pearl's situation was far more precarious. The greatest source of fear is the unknown, and the southern girl remained totally in the dark. She knew nothing of Luke's plan, was not privy to Sal and Nomita's cloak and dagger meeting, and now—after many moons—didn't even know if Nomita was alive or dead.

Although Maddie Pearl saw neither Nomita nor her ebony friends anymore, she still overheard rumors—very sporadically—mostly from her brothers but, occasionally, at church. Specifics and facts, unfortunately, were as rare as equatorial ice. Maddie Pearl's true friends, the people who no doubt knew the real story, were a mere mile distant, but they might as well have been on another planet in a different galaxy far... far... away.

From the snippets here and there, Maddie Pearl surmised that Sal was missing, or gone, or at least no longer in the black community. *Sallerhead had died* was one of the many rumors, but she didn't believe it. Some even said he'd been killed and his body had been cut up and fed to the hogs. But this didn't make any sense to Maddie Pearl; the whites would have bragged about it. A few thought Sal had run off to "Town," changed his name, and somehow disguised himself as a white man to get a job. Most thought Sal was living in the woods, alone, like a hermit.

There were tales of strange fires a few miles away, in the part of Webster County so awful with marshes, insects, snakes, and

related bogginess. Wild yarns of Sal sightings at night enlivened the day from time-to-time with accounts of this Yeti-like Wildman seven feet tall with a long, scraggly afro, prickly coal-black beard, and piercing eyes that glowed in the darkness.

Maddie Pearl considered all such fables hogwash, but the lack of facts about Sallerhead's situation never escaped her mind.

What really bothered Maddie Pearl the most was the rationale for Sal's absence in the first place. If he in fact really were gone, then why would he leave? Surely he wasn't *that* frightened by what happened at the Fire Pit Incident. He'd been beaten before, much worse—hadn't he? He could take it—couldn't he? Luke was crazy, no doubt, but he was a mere child compared to Walter Carver Jefferson. Surely Luke hadn't done anything, not to Sal, not just because she and Sal were friends. What about Levi or Ethan, or even... God forbid... *Tate*. Certainly Tate hasn't done anything—has he?

Tate probably would be diagnosed intellectually disabled today, or perhaps mentally deficient, but his oddness never expressed with cruelty or meanness. In fact, he was the gentlest person in the family. He was bigger than either Luke or Sal, strong as a bear and even looked bear-like with scraggly hair and an animal vacancy in his eyes. But despite the wild look and strangeness, "No Mind"—the nickname his thoughtless parents bestowed—was naturally gentle and kind, and a follower. Pretty much everyone, except Maddie Pearl, took gross advantage. If given an awful job, like cleaning Daisy's pen, get Tate to do it. Tree trunk needs clearing, where's No Mind? A rotting deer is blocking the cart path... "No Mind, gotta job for ya."

Among his many limitations, Tate couldn't recognize right from wrong. In fact, Maddie Pearl suspected that No Mind had carried out some of the outlandish things she'd experienced, at Luke's command. After all, no sane person with even a nugget of *normal* would ever put a hive of angry, displaced bees in the enclosed bin his sister—and *only* his sister—opens each morning to feed the chickens. If nothing else, whoever did it would get destroyed by... I don't know... hundreds of stings. But *somebody* did it, and Luke never seemed to be suffering from any welts. And even when Tate was swollen up the day it happened, Hog and Mama were convinced that their no minded No Mind had nothing

to do with it. He had placed his inflamed catcher's mitt hand on the treasured family Bible and sorely sworn to God and Jesus that "it weren't me" and that was good enough for them, bless their stupid hearts.

Deep down, Maddie Pearl didn't fault No Mind, for he knew not what he did—if he did anything. To some extent, she didn't fault her family either—except Luke...maybe, and Hog. Pretty much all she knew, about everything, had filtered through them, one way or another. Among those lessons was the manly ritual of putting on white sheets and destroying lives in the name of "God." She didn't know for sure whether Hog was part of that, but she suspected; and Luke prancing around in one of those silly costumes at the Fire Pit Incident sure suggested some Klan participation by him, on some level—or at least some desire to be a part of it, someday.

But this God to whom they prayed didn't sanction such things—did he? Surely he could not have approved Luke's many misdeeds. Yet everyone she'd ever met seemed to believe in this God, and seemed to find justifications for such acts somewhere in the Bible they sanctified so fully. The many contradictions confused and befuddled the young girl, beyond distraction.

This is not to say that Maddie Pearl lost her religion; she didn't. But in time, she came to accept that religion is a slippery eel incapable of grabbing with one or even two hands. She didn't like this resolution but, aside from outright disbelieving, it was the best she could derive. And disbelief simply wasn't an option, not in this place and time, and definitely not among these people.

Nevertheless, just when she thought the message was clear, some new truth would slide the certainty needle slightly southward on the scale of devoutness and clean living. Thou shalt not kill, for instance, was a hard and fast rule; but then Maddie Pearl learned that there were some special exceptions. For instance, it was okay for God to send the Angel of Death to kill the firstborn sons of the Egyptians; and stoning was perfectly acceptable biblical punishment for adulteresses; and thou shalt not kill somehow didn't apply to David with his slingshot.

Killing, however, wasn't the only eel-like, *"but"* law.

Maddie Pearl knew biblical passages by heart, not only from the easy New Testament but also the older, more troubling

books, like Exodus and Leviticus. And it was apparent to her that everyone was playing by the "*buts.*"

Leviticus 19:27 strictly forbade shaving; *but* Hog and all the boys (except No Mind) were beardless.

Exodus 35:2 mandated death for working on the Sabbath; *but* everyone worked Sundays, especially during cultivation, planting, maintaining, and harvesting.

Leviticus 11:10 deemed shellfish consumption an abomination; *but* it was fishy how Mama cooked crayfish every chance she got.

And then there was Leviticus Chapter 25, Verses 44-46, a passage that troubled even Mama. As Hog summed up regularly: "I ain't got nothin' 'gainst dem God damn nigras... I think everybody oughtta own a few."

He meant it, too, because the Bible said slavery was just fine and dandy. In fact, it had been the American way since America's genesis. But then those snowflakes had to come in and ruin it for everybody with their emancipations and their proclamations and what not! If only John Wilkes Booth had shown up a little sooner.

So maybe, in some wildly befuddling way, God's plan included obliteration of little Blossom's eye during the Fire Pit Incident. Possibly it was His way of testing the innocent black child who had never harmed anyone. And perhaps the assailant was merely carrying out God's will, an innocent tool, like the Angel of Death with the Egyptians. Maddie Pearl wasn't so sure, but Mama and Hog and even Preacher Roe himself had taught, "God works in mysterious ways." Blinding Blossom seemed pretty mysterious indeed, but such was Maddie Pearl's religious education.

Her other schooling consisted of reading, writing, and arithmetic drills repeated regularly under Mama's strict tutelage. There was no book, very little paper, and nothing beyond the R's. Blessed with an exceptional intellect capable of absorbing information with sponge-like proficiency, Maddie Pearl mastered all that Mama could convey and ached for more. She found a new source, of sorts, at church.

A rich woman from "Town" with shiny jewelry and beauty shop hair had donated several boxes of books to Preacher Roe. "These are for your church people," the snob oozed through fat,

Header: Jack Jenkins 49

ruby red lips, "if any of 'em can read. But not for dem nigras, ya hear? They'd just tear out the pages to wipe their nasty asses."

Almost all were water damaged from a hurricane that had blown through eastern Carolina the year before. Had they been in decent condition, the society lady never would have given the books away. Nevertheless and despite the mildew, pages permanently stuck together, washed out words and warped covers, Maddie Pearl savored them like a fine smorgasbord. Every Sunday she'd borrow several, race home, then return the following Sabbath eager for more.

The books were no substitute for actual school with teachers and desks and students and tests, but they exposed something otherwise closed to the young girl's open mind. Unfortunately, that "something" was limited severely by the books' condition and, even more problematic, subject matter.

Almost exclusively, the boxes contained children's books full of blackbirds cooked in pies, pigs building houses, horses piecing together cracked eggs, little teapots, and incy wincy spiders. It wasn't much, but it was all Maddie Pearl had, and she took full advantage every week until finally, inevitably, inexorably even this became flavorless and stale—except for one, very special book.

Buried within the water-tainted trove was a black and white picture tome about Italy. Most of the pages were destroyed, but Maddie Pearl was able to view a few, and they were magnificent. She saw the Colosseum, or at least part of it, the Pantheon, and even half a page of Michelangelo's Sistine Chapel. Although she learned precious little, the glorious pictures revealed a world heretofore wholly unknown. It was beyond magical to the impressionable youngster as she studied the pictures for hours on end, and developed stirrings in her soul for something... *more*.

\*       \*       \*

From an early age, Maddie Pearl innately knew that there simply had to be more than this, and the spirited girl was determined to find it! But *this* was all her parents, grandparents, great-grandparents and so on ever had known. For millennia, it had been all right for them, and it likewise had been all right for everyone else down to Luke and his mentally deficient brothers.

And eventually, it would be just fine with their inbred offspring and so on some more. Such too was Maddie Pearl's fate... or was it?

Sensing that this was neither all there was nor all that could be, Maddie Pearl's youthful longings yearned less toward carnal knowledge and more toward getting the hell out of hades. But how? The limitations somberly examined around the Fire Pit on the night Luke and the boys came a-beating remained as true as mosquitoes in summer.

As time immemorial proved generationally, no one here got out alive, at least not the women folk who couldn't soldier up. (And even the local Doughboys sufficiently fortunate to leave here for "over there" never made it back in one piece.) There had been rumors of war, and problems in Europe, but such people and places didn't really exist in these parts, and—aside from the occasional reference to Italy—meant nothing to Maddie Pearl. And they definitely didn't offer any hope for a southern girl focused on escapism.

She'd heard stories of women escaping, but such was the stuff of fairy tales she'd come to know too well, and Maddie Pearl didn't have Rapunzel's hair or fantastical mysticism. The reality was planting in spring, scratching parasitic bites all summer, harvesting in fall, and freezing in winter. Some girl supposedly had left for "Town" and gotten a job cleaning cesspools. Maddie Pearl didn't know what was a "cesspool" but, if it were a cool place to swim in August, she definitely was for that. Then there was the story, or myth, about that teenager with the yellow hair who married that guy with the Ford and how they left and never came back. Maddie Pearl knew that story was true, at least about them leaving, but had no idea where they went or what they did or whether they even survived—out there.

And how was Maddie Pearl supposed to get wherever she was going—*out there?* Unlike the yellow-haired teen, she didn't know anyone with an automobile. In the time since the Fire Pit Incident, nothing had improved regarding Maddie Pearl's sense of directions, absence of outside acquaintances, AWOL job skills or, most critically, coin and bill deficiencies. And besides, she still really was no more than a kid.

Her spunky spirit, however, stirred like a spewing volcano threatening to erupt. And so what if she'd only experienced some

sixteen solar revolutions? Most folks in that time didn't live past fifty or so—sixty, tops. As far as Maddie Pearl was concerned, her life already was a quarter done. If not now, then when?

But culture is a wide chasm that Maddie Pearl seemed destined not to cross.

Mama hinted routinely that Maddie Pearl some day "soon" should find a nice boy and settle down. Maddie Pearl knew exactly what that *really* meant: Marry. Fornicate. Spit out boy from uterus. Wash. Repeat. Somewhere in this, supposedly, was fulfillment and self-actualization, the American dream, success! To Maddie Pearl, it was so much cock-a-doodle-do. But if not that, and if leaving was no option, then what remained beyond toil, misery and, eventually, sweet death at which she can be memorialized by some preacher who knows nothing of her real life?

Although her faith had been shaken with her uneasy resolution of the myriad biblical contradictions, Maddie Pearl remained a Christian and continued to pray to the aether for salvation from this place. Having never seen a miracle, the young girl was skeptical, but with such limited options there was nothing else upon which to tie her thin strand of despairing hope. With the mantra, "*Our father who art in heaven, thank you for... well... thank you, and please God help me find a way out,*" Maddie Pearl prayed with circadian rhythm in quiet despondency. There was no answer, no voice from above, no secret sign in the leaves, lake, or clouds. There was only silence and inaction and the steady drum of time beating toward deliverance from evil, life everlasting, some preacher spewing eulogy nonsense, and that would be it.

\*        \*        \*

As regularly as Hog getting drunk, beating Mama, sleeping it off, and starting another day just like the one before, Luke's vileness continued. Maddie Pearl had grown used to her brother's routine, numb really. Which is not to say she enjoyed it—she tolerated it, like an old nag tolerates the incessant biting flies on a hot, windless day.

If nothing else, Hog never took out his misplaced vengeance on Maddie Pearl, which suggested that Luke had kept quiet their little secret. She didn't understand why, but assumed he

had his reasons. As time passed, however, she began to think that maybe the storm had passed, at least the most dangerous part of it. Maybe Luke was satisfied that the little rampage with the boys had sufficiently persuaded his sister to back away from the negroes.

From all appearances, the message had been received. For all intents and purposes, Maddie Pearl no longer left the Prine property, except for church. And even on Sundays, she never left early anymore. Ever since the Fire Pit Incident, she'd waited for the boys and walked with them. It ensured she'd be late for God, to Preacher Roe's chagrin, and no longer commune with Daisy, but it eliminated any question of whether she secretly was still seeing *them* each Sabbath.

She'd also stopped going out each night for a "walk," as Luke surely knew what *that* really meant. She'd get up each morning, do her chores, handle whatever Mama or Hog or even Luke ordered during the day, help with supper, then dutifully go to bed. Scattered throughout would be Luke's dirty little tricks, of course, to which she'd become accustomed. Aside from precious few stolen minutes gazing at water-ruined fairy tale books and rippled pictures of Roman relics, nowhere in the schedule was time for joy, happiness, reflection, or even human companionship.

And throughout every waking hour, for weeks that became months, her ample mind shot one troubling bullet after another into her uncertain cerebrum. *"What's Luke's end game? Why is he doing all this? Is he really this mean? Does he truly just hate me this much? Has he told Pa? If not, why not? If so, why hasn't Pa done anything? What is Hog going to do? What am I going to do? Why won't God answer my prayers? Why can't I escape? Will I be here forever, just like Mama and everybody else? Oh Jesus, what's to come of me?"*

And ultimately, in the summer of her seventeenth year, one of these stray bullets hit home.

*     *     *

No Mind Tate had the daily duty of feeding the two mules the family used for farming and pulling the Hoover Cart. On this warm day, Hog planned to go to "Town" with his coins and bills to buy what people buy there to bring back to the farm and use, eat,

feed, or spread accordingly. As Hog approached the barn, he noticed something odd. The door was partially open.

"*Uh oh*" thought Hog while cautiously peering inside. As feared, one of the mules was bleeding profusely having been attacked by... something. The predator was gone, but the damage was done. Not desiring to waste a precious bullet, Hog grabbed an axe and brutally put the beast into severe misery to put it out of misery. Then he went looking for the miserable person responsible.

He found Tate toiling in the sun with Luke and others. Judging by the sweat and exhaustion, they clearly had been at work for some time or, at least, long enough for a wild animal to enter the barn, attack a valuable farm asset, and then skulk away unnoticed. Hog stalked up to No Mind and demanded in his typically slurred speech, "WHY DIDN'T YOU CLOSE THE BARN DOOR?"

Tate responded, "Huh?" His cloudy brain incapable of computing the clear message.

"The barn door! You left it open and something got Skeet!"

Luke wandered over and inquired, "Something got Skeet? You sure about that, Pa?"

"Damn sure did! Had to put her down! And I wanna know what Tate here plans to do about it!"

Luke considered the situation, looked at Tate, scratched his head a bit, and then smiled ever so slightly that no one could have noticed the naked hatefulness.

"Well Pa," Luke began, "it's like this. I was with Tate when he fed Corncake and Skeet, and I remember him closing that door."

Tate looked at Luke as if to say, "*What?*" He then opened his dumb mouth and began to contradict his brother with, "But Luke, you weren't—"

"Remember, Tate? You and me... remember? It was us, together, *remember?*" Luke asked in a way that any normal person would sniff the drift, especially after three hints, but Tate was no drift sniffer.

"But Luke, you were over by—"

"That's right, I was over by the barn... with you. That's the truth, Pa. It was me and him, and I saw him close that door. In fact, I double checked it just to make sure cause we've been seeing those coyotes lately, ya know?"

Tate stood dumbfounded, his mouth ajar, and just stared at his brother, pondering how this possibly could be true when he knew better. Or did he? Pa meanwhile processed this information and, in fact, already had considered the probability that a coyote had committed the natural crime. His thoughts then drifted from Tate and coyotes to... Maddie Pearl! Goddam Maddie Pearl!

Hog stomped off back toward home, back toward the place in which the sweet seventeen was sitting quietly practicing her letters and thinking of how cute the hungry chickens had been that morning when she fed them and then closed the bin lid carefully, as always, and then gave Skeet and Corncake some sweet grass treats, as always, and then closed the barn door, as always, and then came inside to do the rest of her chores, as always.

Hog burst in on Maddie Pearl's serene reflection, grabbed her soft, young arm viciously, and dragged her outside.

"*What! What did I do?*"

Maddie Pearl's flabbergastion was met with severe lashes from a particularly prickly switch over and over again. The overpowering madman with a bully's whip and a gullibly mistaken mindset beat the poor child mercilessly. It lasted for at least a minute—an hour or more to Maddie Pearl—and then it was over.

As he stormed away, Hog bellowed over his shoulder, "That's for the barn door, NOT THE *OTHER* THING!"

Maddie Pearl cowered on the ground near the semi-wet well and wept profusely. From her suddenly swollen wounds oozed blood copiously. The pain radiated throughout, vibrating harshly with each throbbing heartbeat. And her mind was a storm of confusion. *"What barn door? What other thing? Does he know about... them? Jesus Christ Almighty... does he know about THEM?"*

*              *              *

As Maddie Pearl lay crying, Hog went back to the barn where Luke was loitering.

"Hey boy," he said gruffly. "That thing with your sister...it's time."

# Chapter 8

After dinner, Maddie Pearl left to take a "walk" for the first time in months. She'd planned her exit all afternoon, and was prepared for whatever Hog might say or do. This was survival mode now, and he wasn't going to stop her. Shockingly, he didn't try. To some extent she was disappointed, having readied for battle only to be ignored. *"Maybe he doesn't know after all,"* she thought. At this point, however, it didn't matter, and in due course she found herself on the common path connecting all of Boss Lee-dom—including Darkieland.

As she arrived in the fading glow of the summer sunset, a three-headed dragon could not have been more conspicuous. In the good weather, and after a hard day's labor, pretty much everyone was milling about the community stump shooting the breeze. But all activity stopped with the appearance... of her.

The awkward silence greeting Maddie Pearl was compensated by her confidence as she held high her head and purposefully walked up to Nomita. With everyone trying to listen, Maddie Pearl calmly said to her best friend, "We've got to talk." Nomita grabbed Maddie Pearl's arm, pretty much where Hog had gripped some twelve hours earlier. Maddie Pearl winced openly. Nomita noticed.

"You okay, girl?" asked Nomita.

"No," replied Maddie Pearl. "That's what I've got to talk to you about."

Less forcibly than before, Nomita ushered Maddie Pearl away from the commons and down the same path that Nomita and brother Sal stealthily had trod just a few months before. Beyond the herd's hearing range, they stopped. "What in God's name are *you* doing *here?*"

"It's Luke. He's out to get me, and I need Sal to help me get back at—"

"I guess you figured out his... *plan?*" Nomita cut in.

There was a long, pregnant pause between the best friends who had not seen each other for months and, until now, didn't know for sure whether either was still among the living.

"Plan? What... *plan?"* Maddie Pearl's question hit Nomita hard, realizing immediately just how out of school her inquiry had been.

"Oh nothing," Nomita desperately tried to cover. "So—"

"What plan?" Maddie Pearl persisted aggressively, undeterred by Nomita's weak attempt to change the subject.

The girls stood staring at each other in the fading light. Various insects had begun their dusk symphony joined by a chorus of croaking frogs, chirping birds settling in for the night, and a couple of dogs back at the common area barking playfully at each other. The beautiful sound was deafening.

"What plan? What are you talking about?"

Nomita thought long and hard before responding. Three things were indisputable. *"First, Maddie Pearl doesn't have a clue that her own brother has been plotting to kill her; second, if I tell her, then everything is going to change, forever; and third, if I'm silent and something happens, then I'll never forgive myself."*

She had no choice; she had to come clean.

"Luke is planning to kill you and blame Sal," said Nomita bluntly, without emotion.

Maddie Pearl immediately laughed out loud. Nomita's expression never changed.

"I'm not joking. That's the plan. Has been... ever since... you know, when we were attacked, at the Fire Pit."

The laughing stopped abruptly. In the near darkness, Maddie Pearl's blood-drained face shone like a small full moon on the moonless night. Her knees buckled and she slumped down to a kneeling position. Nomita tried to catch her but only aggravated Maddie Pearl's sore wounds, making the situation worse. As gently as possible, Nomita comforted her friend by stroking the beautiful red hair.

After an eternity, Maddie Pearl said, "I... I... just don't believe it. Luke? It can't be true. It just can't!"

Nomita let the words slither in the air like curls of filthy smoke slowly ascending from a smudge pot. She tried to hug

Maddie Pearl, but the pain was near unbearable, so Nomita pulled away slightly, and looked Maddie Pearl straight in the eyes.

"It's true, Maddie Pearl. I know it, for a fact."

Having regained at least some composure, Maddie Pearl responded, "But why? It's crazy. Kill... *me?*"

"I said the same thing," Nomita replied, "almost the same words. And I agree, it *is* crazy. But it's true. And I know it."

Maddie Pearl's mind was awhirl with flinging thoughts of why and how and when and whatever else any intelligent person would juggle under such circumstances. She wanted to ask everything, and more, but somehow this didn't seem like the right time or place, so she cut to the chase.

"How do you know—and don't lie to me."

"I have never lied to you, and I'm not going to start now. But you've got to promise to believe me, and not question all I say, okay?"

Maddie Pearl paused in reflection. "Okay," she said, half-heartedly.

"I mean it, Maddie Pearl. You better listen, and listen good, cause your life might depend on it, and even mine!"

The threat's escalation changed the dynamic and all trepidation evaporated into the muggy, buggy, hot air.

"All right, Nomita, I believe you, but you've gotta tell me how you know."

"Luke told my brother, directly, and in no uncertain terms," Nomita explained.

"What? When?"

"A couple of days after the fire pit. Luke, Tate, and some others confronted Sal, out in the field. Made his plans clear."

"Just like that?" Maddie Pearl replied. "They just walked out, made a crazy threat, and left? I'm sorry, and I hate to say this, but that just sounds like baloney to me. What makes you—"

"They beat my brother almost to death, and they killed... Daisy. Beat her and beat her and then... they peed on her, and in her mouth, and then they beat her some more."

Maddie Pearl suppressed a retch, unsuccessfully, spewing her family dinner of weedy greens, semi-sour milk, and stringy venison onto Nomita's bare feet.

"Jesus," exclaimed Maddie Pearl. "Not... *Daisy.*"

Nomita swallowed hard. Her voice took on a much deeper timbre. "Luke *meant* it, Maddie Pearl, he damn sure meant it."

Maddie Pearl slumped back in deep contemplation, still trying to regroup from the news about her beloved Daisy. She couldn't help but recall all the times she had petted the creature, and it had responded by leaning her head closer, nodding up and down as if asking for more. She recalled Daisy's soft muzzle, and how she'd struggle to retrieve some grass or a peach only to "smile" once she'd successfully taken the treat. "*And these bastards beat hell out of her*," she thought, "*and peed in her...*" She couldn't finish the thought, as another wave of nausea forced a dry heave.

When finished, her demeanor turned on a dime from horror and sadness and bewilderment to anger, sheer unadulterated adrenalin-pumped rage and fury and resolute wrath.

"God damn them all," she said gutturally. "God damn each and every one."

Nomita was taken aback by Maddie Pearl's blasphemy. Although they went to separate but unequal churches with different rituals and customs, they prayed to the same God. They both knew well that taking HIS name in vain was a serious sin.

Neither knew what to say, but somehow the birds and dogs and insects recognized an inflection point and, as if on cue, became eerily quiet.

Composure somewhat regained, Maddie Pearl turned to Nomita. "That still doesn't explain what I've got to do with it. Why not Sal? Why... me?"

Nomita chose her words carefully before responding. "Think about it this way." Nomita cleared her throat. "And trust me, I've wondered about this too, for weeks now, and I think I've about got it figured out."

Maddie Pearl listened with a cold, expressionless, Roman stone statue stare.

"No offense, but your brother... Luke... he's a moron. Maybe not as dense as Tate and the others, but he's... pretty, well... stupid. Agree?"

Maddie Pearl just stared.

"So I don't think Luke came up with this. I think it—"

"Pa? You think Pa is in the middle of this?" Maddie Pearl interjected.

"I do," said Nomita.

Maddie Pearl reflected before responding. "I've wondered what Pa would do if, you know, he ever found out about me hanging out with you. I know he'd beat me and all, maybe even cast me out of the house, but murder... He can't just get away with murdering his own flesh and blood... can he?"

"He can if it looks like somebody else did it, like Sal."

"Yeah, okay, I get that part, but it still doesn't make sense. I mean, go to all that trouble, and take that kind of risk, just because I'm friends with you and Sal and the rest? I know being with you folk is a serious offense, but it sure doesn't justify murder... does it?"

"I don't know," replied Nomita, "but here's the deal, I think. That Boss Lee owns all this land. You know, the one we pay rent to."

"I don't know who you're—"

"All right, well take my word on it then. There's this man named Boss Lee, and he owns all of this, and he charges rent for your folks and me and everybody around here—even that Indian down the path—to live here."

"Yeah. So?"

"So he's a big shot in the Klan. Even you ought to know that. But anyway, best way to get in good with him is with the KKK, and I *know* that to be true."

"So Pa's gonna get Luke to kill me to impress this Boss man?"

Nomita gave her friend a "*shut up and quit being sarcastic*" look. Maddie Pearl recognized the hint, but remained indignant.

"Now the way I see it, Hog and you folk are barely hanging on over there. I mean... you're about as poor as us, and for a white person that's a sin."

"How would you know what our money's like?" Maddie Pearl couldn't resist.

"I see that Lee asshole from time to time, since I pay the bills now that mom died from that damn consumption, and he's usually about half lit, and he grumbles sometimes, not even thinking."

"Grumbles? About what?"

"Oh... I don't know. This and that, about the weather or horseflies or whatever, and more than once he's said some things about... well... your pa."

Maddie Pearl looked on unblinking. A nearby hawk in a tree nest squawked, as if telling the girls to hold it down so he could sleep.

Nomita continued, "He ain't happy with how you people don't pay your bills proper like."

The news was a hard slap to Maddie Pearl's face. She knew next to nothing about money or bills, but assumed Mama and Pa handled such things properly, whatever that may be.

"What... uh... what does it mean?" asked Maddie Pearl.

"It means that Boss Lee could kick your ass off the property, all of ya, if rent ain't paid right or whatever. And trust me... he'd do it in a heartbeat."

"Well... why hasn't he then? I mean—"

"I'm guessing he ain't got anybody to replace you people. I mean, it's not like folks are lining up to live *this* shit life, now is it?"

Maddie Pearl thought about the situation for several seconds, and then asked, "But what does any of this have to do with Luke... and me?"

"If you'd give me a second, I'll tell ya."

Maddie Pearl didn't like Nomita's insolence, but chose to hold her tongue, for now.

"So the way I see it," Nomita continued, "Hog's got two options. He can come up with more money, which just ain't likely to happen absent some miracle, or he could get in good with Boss Lee and maybe catch a little slack. And I know for a fact that your well is all but dry and it's keepin' you from proper watering, especially along that land near the cart path, where you used to grow cotton."

"Yeah, and...?"

"And maybe if ol' Hog could get our well, the one that Sal dug and our community uses, well... maybe things could turn around over at your place. Maybe he wouldn't have so much trouble paying his bills like he's s'posed to."

"But if that was the plan, why wouldn't this Boss guy just kick you people off, let us have it, and fix it that way? I mean, don't

think I'm being uppity or whatnot, but we both know that ain't no Klan man going to favor you over me."

Nomita ignored the opportunity to strike back and answered logically. "I thought about that, but there's one problem. We pay our bills, the right way, and you people don't. He ain't about to chase off one of the only good paying tenants he's got, even if they are a bunch of nigras like me."

"Okay, then. So, what does—"

"Luke's gonna kill you, tell everybody Sal did it, and set off a fight like these parts haven't seen in years. And when it's over, and it won't last long, Hog'll be the poor victim who lost his beloved daughter, but he'll also be the hero who got even with the goddamn niggers who did it! I know it's crazy as bat shit, but at the end of it all, my folk'll be chased off into the night clutching whatever we can carry on the way out, and you people will ease on in and take over our place, including the well, and ain't no judge or jury this side of Raleigh gonna convict anybody for that!"

Maddie Pearl contemplated the plan's understated genius. Surely Hog wasn't that smart—or was he? But there still was a flaw: why go after all the blacks? Wouldn't revenge get extracted only on Sal? And, if so, that wouldn't be enough to run off the rest.

As if she could read her best friend's mind, Nomita piped up. "He's not just gonna kill you, Maddie Pearl. Least I don't think so. For this to work, it's gonna take more... than just that."

With trepidation, Maddie Pearl had to ask. "Like... *what?*"

Nomita came closer to Maddie Pearl and lowered her voice. "What if they could make it look like a pretty young white girl was making it with a big black buck? And what if that buck, along with some of his nigra buddies, decided to get together and have, you know, a little party with that white girl?"

"Party? What do you mean?" Maddie Pearl asked naively.

"Party," Nomita answered. "You know, they share you, you know... sexually, like a rape."

Maddie Pearl's mouth opened wide. "Oh my God! Are you serious?" she replied in shock.

"Well, think about it. And I'm not sayin' they actually, you know, rape you. I'm just saying they make it look like that, and then they kill you and spread the story to everybody about Sal and

the other black boys and the rape and murder and everything. Can you imagine—"

"It'd be a bloodbath," Maddie Pearl cut off Nomita with the obvious. "They'd be able to massacre you all—"

"And there's not a sheriff anywhere who'd stop 'em," Nomita continued. "And just like that, they'd get rid of Sal and me and the rest of us, and the landlord—you know, Boss Lee—would have no choice but to let you have it—I mean, your people, not *you*."

"Oh my God," Maddie Pearl said while looking away deep in thought. "They really plan to kill me."

"I told you it's true. But like I said, I'm guessing about a lot of the other stuff."

"But the way you describe it, it makes sense, a lot of sense. I mean... God almighty... they're really going to kill me." Maddie Pearl paused for several seconds. "Is that why Sal... left?"

Nomita's eyes moistened ever so slightly but, even with the sunset complete and the darkness pervading, Maddie Pearl could see the emotion.

"That's why, isn't it?" asked Maddie Pearl. "He left to protect... *me*."

Nomita could only nod her head.

"So where is he?" Maddie Pearl asked the obvious.

Nomita regained control of her emotions and replied, "I don't know. He wouldn't tell me. He just said don't worry, that he'd be around if, you know, I needed 'em."

Maddie Pearl chimed in, "Right about now sure seems like a good time, at least for me."

In the distance they heard a male voice calling, "Nomita... Nomita!"

"That's Pickles," Nomita said. "I gotta go. Everybody saw you come, and I'm sure they're worried sick right about now."

Nomita straightened up herself and turned directly toward Maddie Pearl. "We need to stay in touch. But we can't let anybody, and I mean _anybody_, see us together. So don't be coming up to the stump again. Find me out in the field or something, or sneak up late at night, but don't come up again like you did tonight."

"I won't," promised Maddie Pearl.

"Now you go home," Nomita replied. "Don't say anything to anybody. But watch yourself! Carefully!"

"I will," Maddie Pearl assured. "But what are we going to do? I had planned to get Sal's help with the stuff Luke's been doing to me, but that seems like nothing... now."

"I don't know, Maddie Pearl, I just don't know. But I guarantee that you and I together are twice as smart as any of them. So I know we'll figure out something. For now, just be careful. Damn careful!"

Despite her sore back, arms, legs, and everything else that Hog had beaten earlier for something she hadn't done, Maddie Pearl leaned in and hugged Nomita tightly. The pain was excruciating, but worth every wince. She never had loved anyone as much as Nomita, and the feeling was mutual.

# Chapter 9

Maddie Pearl left Nomita's embrace to commence the mile trek back home. She had been taking a "walk" a little too long and was concerned about the greeting she might receive. It was completely dark now and, although her eyes had adjusted, the journey was difficult without the benefit of moonlight. Her head swirling, she wasn't paying much attention to the surroundings and didn't notice the figure in the path straight ahead until she practically stumbled directly into him.

It was Luke!

"Where you been?" he demanded sternly.

Shocked, Maddie Pearl couldn't muster any response.

"You been at the niggers'?" Luke "asked" in a manner that was no question.

Her mind racing, her heart pounding, all Maddie Pearl could utter was a weak, unconvincing, "No."

"DON'T LIE TO ME, BITCH!" Luke yelled while punching Maddie Pearl hard in the gut! She doubled over and collapsed in a muddy patch along the ditch that paralleled the path.

Standing over his fallen, younger sister, Luke demanded one more time in a lower, meaner voice, "Where the hell have you been?"

In the gloom on the ground along the path that leads from the poverty she had lived her entire life to the abject destitution of her only friends, Maddie Pearl spotted a medium sized rock about the mass of a grapefruit. She stealthily grabbed it as she got on her knees and pounded it hard into Luke's groin.

"AHHH!" he screamed, jack-knifing in agony. Maddie Pearl stood and ran not toward home but away—as away as her long legs would carry—toward Darkieland. Her lead was short-lived. Luke gathered himself, stumbled in chase, and tackled Maddie Pearl some fifty yards closer to *those* people.

Their tussle was brief. Maddie Pearl fought like a wildcat but Luke was much bigger, stronger, and meaner.

After gaining advantage pinning her to the ground, Luke spit in Maddie Pearl's face.

"Fuckin' nigger lover," he gurgled with raw, putrid hatred. "I've been waiting for this a long God damn time."

He pulled from his jean pocket a strand of rope, violently flipped Maddie Pearl over onto her belly, and forced her hands behind. It was a ferocious struggle for both, but with his knee horribly crushing her back and his sheer weight preventing any escape or retaliation, Maddie Pearl's counterattacks were gallant but pathetically futile.

Luke gained full advantage, and knew how to use it. Her hands now were tied firmly, too tightly, behind her back, and her feet were tied securely as well. Maddie Pearl was in no position to defend, and fell back on her only recourse—she screamed and screamed and SCREAMED!

"Shut up!" Luke demanded. She continued. He retorted, "SHUT THE FUCK UP!" She screamed some more.

They were approximately halfway between the black and white worlds, and Luke realized that someone from either planet might hear, so he frantically sought a way to shut her the fuck up!

Within arm's reach was a clump of poison ivy. He desperately grabbed it and, mid-scream, crammed it into his sister's yelping mouth. She coughed severely, retched, and made progress expelling the noxious weed. He grabbed more and shoved it past her beautiful young lips and teeth into the gaping mouth beyond. This batch did the trick, perhaps too well, as she began choking, fiercely struggling for breath. Luke was callously indifferent.

"There," he sputtered while catching his breath. "That oughtta shut you up."

She continued gagging, but found sufficient air passage to survive, albeit tiny and littered such that each inhale carried dirt, flora bits and particles down her windpipe and into her healthy lungs becoming increasingly poisoned with each toxicodendron radicans-infected breath. All was lost with her ultimate fate at the hands of this malicious brother who had planned to kill her for months and had been seeking the opportunity that she inadvertently provided tonight by stupidly taking a "walk" to *there*.

# Chapter 10

The boys awoke before dawn and sat down to eat in the shanty's central room with the fireplace not lit in the summer heat. Usually about this time, Mama and Maddie Pearl would parade in with bowls of whatever was to be eaten. Mythology dictates a large feast of wonderful *country cookin'*. The reality is that poor white trash in rural down east a hundred years ago ate whatever crap their tobacco-stained, grubby little hands could grab.

The boys were starved and ready, but had no expectations of anything beyond a few measly eggs, some watery grits, salt-stored venison that tasted more like leather than food, maybe squirrel meat or opossum flank, or even some cooked, weedy greens plucked from a nutrient-starved farm field. But this morning, not even tripe was forthcoming.

After stupidly looking at each other for a minute or so, Levi, Ethan, and No Mind Tate jointly realized that the rest of the clan wasn't there. Also conspicuously absent: breakfast. With no words spoken, they ventured outside to investigate.

Several hundred yards down the lane in the predawn was Mama. It appeared that she was yelling and looking about somewhat anxiously. As the three brothers approached, Mama turned and said, "Luke and Maddie Pearl never came home last night!"

"What?" Ethan responded.

"They're gone. They never came back!"

Mama asked, "Any of you see Luke last night, or Maddie Pearl?"

Tate had a dumb stare on his face, which came naturally. The dimwitted oldest chimed in, somewhat for the mute group, "Last I see 'em, he headed off to get her, last night, like Pa told 'em. He was headed toward dem nigra houses."

Tate's small input roused Mama's biggest dread: Maddie Pearl had gone... to *them*. And now Luke's gotten into who knows what with those savages!

"Where's Pa?" Levi asked. "Did he come home last night?"

Mama distractedly cast a side-glance to her three sons, but didn't bother to answer.

"Where's Pa, Mama?" Levi persisted.

Annoyed, Mama barked, "He's out looking for 'em. Been out since last night. Now quit bothering me!"

The boys looked at each other, fully confused. Tate, motivated more by practical needs than missing persons, blurted out, "Where's my breakfast?" Levi and Ethan snickered.

Mama whirled on No Mind and slapped him, hard. "Half your family is gone, and all you care about is *FOOD?*"

There would be no more snickering, or breakfast, that morning.

\*       \*       \*

Hog returned roughly an hour later, alone, smelling strongly of grain alcohol. He burst into their derelict abode and bellowed in slurred speech, "I've been every God damn place but one, and I ain't seen hide nor hair of the boy."

Almost afraid to ask, Mama weakly eked, "What about Maddie Pearl?"

Hog spun round to his wife, glared, and slobbered, "Huh? Wha?"

"Maddie Pearl... did you find her?"

Bespeaking his deep fury, Hog clinched his jaw momentarily, then uttered through his teeth, "I weren't lookin' for that nigger lovin' bitch."

Mama raised her hand to her mouth slightly hiding the look of shock she hoped not to reveal.

"GOD DAMMIT!" Hog exasperated in a manner unbecoming a community pillar who went to church weekly and burned crosses every fourth Wednesday in the name of Jesus.

Without another word, he took off down the path toward Darkieland. No Mind Tate, Levi and Ethan followed closely

behind. Mama, scared witless, held back, fearful of what might happen, what she might see, and how this might change everything, forever.

For an obese, short-winded, eventual coronary victim like Hog, the walk was long and difficult, but he managed through sheer anger and hatred-fueled adrenalin spurting in every vein and artery. Obliviously, he lumbered directly over the blood pool from the spurting veins and arteries of the daughter he never wanted and preferred dead. As the mob reached the Fire Pit Incident vicinity, they were greeted by a lone raccoon that, upon their approach, scrambled through a thicket and up a pine tree off the beaten track. Undeterred, they turned toward the blacks' shanties, grabbing old broken limbs and similar instruments of anticipated destruction as they progressed.

At the edge of the ring of small shacks occupied by this African American community since slavery allegedly was abolished, Hog stopped. The small entourage following the Exalted Ass awkwardly stopped as well, slopping into each other in a comic Stooges' stumble. No one was out; no one was stirring. Aside from a dying fire, it was if the entire village had been deserted.

"ANYBODY HERE?" Hog yelled angrily, menacingly. No answer. "WHERE'S MY BOY?" Again, silence. Hog turned to face his meager troops and spoke in a voice sufficiently loud to ensure auditory reception by every nearby ear, if any. "ALL RIGHT GODAMMIT, LET'S BEAT IT OUT OF 'EM!"

They initiated a march toward the closest shack. Along the way, Tate stuck his small branch into the fire until its dead leaves lit. When they reached the house, a young woman emerged a couple of doors down. She was about Maddie Pearl's age, uncommonly pretty, with a healthy body, clear eyes, and beautiful, jet-black skin. To No Mind Tate she looked vaguely familiar, but how, or why?

"She's not here," Nomita said.

Hog stomped over, stood inches away, ignored the reference to his daughter, and thundered into Nomita's face with spittle hitting her cheek. "WHAT THE HELL HAVE YOU SAVAGES DONE TO MY BOY LUKE?"

Nomita didn't move, didn't give ground, didn't flinch, didn't wipe the spit that smelled of booze and sour tobacco juice, and didn't even blink. "I said *SHE's* not here."

Hog studied this exotic creature before him, harrumphed, looked her hard in the eyes, and said ever so slowly yet emphatically, "Where the fuck is my boy Luke?"

Nomita stared him right back, unafraid, strong, and oddly confident with what seemed nothing to be confident about. Several seconds passed surreally. A bull and a mouse, head to head, and neither was budging an inch. Tate stepped forward, half-ass torch in hand, but Hog held him back, never taking his eyes off Nomita.

"I'm gonna ask you one more time, *nigger girl.* Where is Luke?"

"And I'm going to tell you one more time, *cracker man. She's* not here!"

Before Hog could explode, Tate fearfully interjected, "Pa, look."

Hog broke his gaze from Nomita's eyes to see a small army of African descended boys and men armed to the teeth with boards, hoes, rakes, clubs, and even a smattering of ancient blunderbusses. Hog's four-man battalion stood no chance.

"You people think you can do this, TO ME? Do you know who I am?" Hog's entreaties fell on deaf ears. Like Nomita, there were no flinchers in this army. "We'll be ba—"

Nomita cut off Hog before the threats could be formalized. "You want to know what happened?"

Interrupted in a manner experienced routinely outside the Prines' farm where this self-important poo-bah was little more than an ignorant redneck with a small brain and big belly, Hog answered, "You God damn right, jigaboo. What the fuck happened?"

"*She* came here... I said 'she,' not 'he'... *SHE*... by *her*self came by a little after dark. Nobody asked her here. She just showed up."

Nomita paused for effect. It worked. Hog, No Mind and the others stood open jawed in wonderment at whatever this magnificent being was going next to say.

"She was sick. Very sick. And bleeding, a lot. Her skin had no color and felt cold to the touch. She was shaking, and

mumbling nonsense." Nomita continued, looking around at her audience and meeting each person's eyes like a topnotch criminal lawyer making her final argument to the jury.

"We didn't know what, but we knew *something* had to be done." Several of the African Americans nodded in agreement. Nomita scanned her listeners closely as they leaned in for more, "Something... or she was gonna die."

Nomita stopped to let this sink in, fully recognizing that at least one and probably most of her white spectators process information more slowly than non-inbred sapiens.

Hog looked back to Nomita continuing his ominous glare and inquired oh so slowly, "What happened to my boy, Luke?"

Ignoring Hog's continued intentional ignorance of his daughter's situation, Nomita responded sternly, "We helped *HER.*"

The answer seeped like ashes in the lungs. These people, these... these... cannibals... helped *Maddie Pearl?* But what about Luke? What had they done to Luke? Did they "help" him too?

"I want to see my boy, NOW, or I'm gonna burn down everything on this shit hole and kill every animal in sight, including *YOU, MISSY,* if I have to."

The black entourage with their sticks, clubs, blunderbusses, and healthy fists reacted to the direct threat by inching closer to Hog and Nomita—ready for battle, if need be.

Nomita considered this demand for several seconds. She looked around at her kin and friends. Some nodded negatively to silently warn, "*Don't say too much.*" Nomita knew the real danger this situation posed, not only for her. She was wise beyond her less than two decades and recognized that Hog needed more than what she had offered so far. But what else could she say? A few more seconds passed awkwardly. Nomita returned her gaze directly to Hog, cleared her throat, and proceeded ultra cautiously.

"We don't know anything about Luke... or any other boy. We never saw him. He was never here. He's not here now."

She spoke slowly, deliberately, choosing every word cautiously. "But you can find Maddie Pearl, you know... your *daughter* Maddie Pearl... in 'Town,' at the doctor's."

The info hit Hog like a flounder slap to the face. "What? WHAT? The doctor? In TOWN?"

"That's all I'm gonna say. But she's there, right now. And as to your boy, or any boy, I... we... don't have a *fucking* clue!"

The use of such language and the young woman's absolutely severe, fearless demeanor startled Hog. His reaction was palpable. This parvenu beauty dared stand up to him *mano-a-mano.*

"And by the way, *Hog,* Maddie Pearl was very much alive when she left here."

The sarcastic emphasis on "Hog" startled the punch-drunk fighter, but he was much more shaken by the reality that the plan, *his* plan, the plan for Klan influence and personal fortune, had failed! Luke was supposed to find her, make it look like a gangbang rape then murder, and return home unscathed carrying the deceased girl. He'd have a bug-eyed demeanor and wild story of "*catching 'dem niggers in the act, scaring 'em away, and then doing everything possible to save his sweet sister whom he loved so dearly.*" The retribution would be swift, personally led by Hog himself, utterly devastating to "*those goddam spearchuckers that did this to my only girl.*" Those with robes in Klan Clown conclaves, especially Boss Lee, would universally praise him with awe and envy.

His anger seething but with nothing more to do, for now at least, Hog motioned and his family trudged back toward home. There might be a battle, and the retribution Hog so craved, but not here, not today, not without more information, and a bigger, better-prepared army.

As they departed, there were no "*thank yous for saving Maddie Pearl's life*" or "*we're sorry for threatening you*" or "*kiss my ass*" or anything, because such was the way then, as it is now, in this part of the greatest nation in the history of this planet.

And along the long walk back, Hog's feeble mind swam with muddy questions of how, and why, and what, and "*God damn that fucking Luke!*"

# Chapter 11

From the darkness emerges... what? As if materializing from nothing, she is back, but where? She is wandering, but why? Is she still outside on the cart path leading from home to... there, or on the cart path toward the field, or... wait. She sees a shadow, indistinct at first, then emerging in the backlit darkness... a person, a tall person, a man she thinks, but who, and why is he here, and where is she, and where is this leading? And... he gets closer. She can't see his face and doesn't recognize him; everything is black and white, but why; she begins to fall, from weakness, but he catches her, and holds her up, and clutches her close, and carries her... Blackness envelops everything. There is nothing. It is over. And... just like before... it is nothingness.

\*　　　\*　　　\*

It begins again, but differently this time, better somehow, warmer, and in color. She is outside on a nice summer day. She wanders over to sweet tea in a jar beside a blanket by a cool pond with a gentle, comfortable breeze oozing thru so placidly inviting her to lie back, relax, and gaze at the fluffy clouds above. This reverie, as pleasant as anything she'd ever experienced, seems to last for hours and days. She no longer is alone in the dark black and white world with the stranger carrying her... away; she is—

Happy... perhaps for the first time in her life. In fact, "happy" is too quaint, too weak and pedestrian, to describe this rapturous, joyous, better-than-even-heaven-can-be state of pure bliss. She embraces it with her mind's arms, revels in its luxury, nuzzles it like a bitch snuggles her newborn pup. And she feels like a newborn, like a babe released from some wicked womb, with promise and hope and happiness and ecstasy enveloping her very being in a warm, passionate embrace. And she loves the feeling,

*and never wants it to end, and even thinks ever so briefly that—just maybe—it never will.*

*But then some strange sound emerges from outside the über-heavenly cocoon. It is low and indistinct, definitely not of this place, and clearly becoming less muted, more obvious, and deeply invasive. She fights it ferociously, desperately staving it off at every turn, but it is persistent, and pervasive, and not to be denied.*

*"Go away!" she frantically demands. Her words won't come out; she is screaming no shriek, just a soundless, frustrating, "Let me be!" And it hears nothing, and keeps intruding. She tosses and turns, kicks and swings her fists, all to no avail. The intruder is coming, coming, coming... and she has nowhere to run and cannot hide and is losing her grip on... this world, this place, this nirvana from which she never wants exit!*

*And then—*

The obnoxious rasp... rasp... rasp... sound of air flowing in and out, in and out, from the Draeger Pulmotor awakes Maddie Pearl with a lightning bolt of fear, distress, and adrenalin! Her eyes wide, her mind screams again and again, "*STOP! STOP! LUKE, NO! NO! PLEASE GOD NO!*" Her lips, however, merely mumble through the mouthpiece with which her breathing has been manipulated for hours now.

She sees a woman, in white, standing above her... in a strange room with... some man, also in white, with something strange coiled about his neck dangling down to his belly, and... Maddie Pearl panics! "*Klan? It's Klan!*" Her limbs begin working, as if by magic, and she thrashes wildly, frantically, uncontrollably! The nurse desperately holds her down; the doctor approaches with a cloth soaked in some foul appall. He removes the mask from her face and holds the cloth firmly over her mouth; then someone says, "Hold on! You're back."

"*Back. Back? From where?* Where's Luke? Someone stop him! NOW!" Maddie Pearl anxiously tries to fight, but the nurse has leverage. The doctor's smelly cloth over her face makes Maddie Pearl almost retch, and then she falls back into—

*A liquid slumber of dreamscapes and fantasies, but this no longer is the place "back" from which she just came.*

*It's too bright, and the warmth has been replaced with an uncomfortable heat, like middle of the summer, Fire Pit heat. And there's a great light, just ahead, nearly melting her eyes, but she can't look away, and she must go to it, and she ambles then paces and finally runs and—*

*Darkness. A dark unlike anything she's ever seen. Total and complete, blindness really, but she's conscious, and it's not as warm, and from the absolute black emerges white shards of light here and there, but it's different this time, not as brilliant as before, and the warmth is becoming an autumnal coolness, which feels good at first but then seems cold and colder and then shudder unbearable. And she shivers, and it's that hallway... there... that leads, where? She wanders toward the passage, unsteadily but surely, with shooting pains down below where she urinates, and the pain gets worse, then excruciating, and then the light pulls her... away, but to where? And then she sleeps a dreamless, restless, worthless slumber... UNTIL—*

Without remembering waking, Maddie Pearl is being carried out of "The Doctor's Office" which also was known as "The Hospital" but really was no more than an old, two story Victorian with several parlors, studies, closets, and boudoirs all now converted to examination spaces and patient rooms. She is weak, her mouth is raw, she cannot taste and barely can summon any spit, and the pain... *oh my God the pain...* is beyond gruesome, particularly down there. Her neck is sore; her face feels swollen although she neither can see nor touch it with her hands covered under the sheet in which she is mummy wrapped. Her mind, slowed by sleep-inducing ether, struggles to fathom her predicament and begins to speak only to be prevented by a big hand, a big black hand.

SAL's HAND!

He carries her outside. The brilliant sunshine fully blinds Maddie Pearl, even with eyes wide shut. He is running now, with her, and she almost faints from the light and heat and throbbing and soreness. Through her severely swollen lips she spews vomit onto Sal, but it's a liquid green ooze with... is that... leaves, or dirt, or... what *is* that? As it emits, her inner mouth rages with an odd combination of stinging and itchiness, and it's frustratingly

unscratchable. The strong, large man sprints with his human load across the little, blacktop street in front of the Hospital/Doctor's Office and the two melt into a wooded area beside yet another Victorian that could be the "hospital's" twin.

\*　　　\*　　　\*

Maddie Pearl revived in the cool clearing hidden among the forest's trees. Walter Carver Jefferson noticed her rousing and rushed over to comfort his patient. He gently combed her beautiful but fully disheveled hair with his fingers, held his hand to her inflamed mouth—without touching—to signal *"Be Quiet"* and then skittered back to the woods' edge to keep watch. It was still early morning, with few out and about, and it appeared that no one had spotted the large black man hastily carrying the young, redheaded, white girl into the woods to do who knows what to her.

Once assured of their stealth, he came back and cradled the young woman in his arms. "Maddie Pearl... Maddie Pearl, are you okay?" He spoke lightly but with real concern. She opened her eyes slightly, looked up at Sal, and began muttering in a questioning voice. She was alive, and "awake," and that answered his question, for now, so Sal cut her off.

"Not now. I'll explain, later. We need to get out of here, before your pa comes!"

The tone in his voice upset Maddie Pearl, and she reacted by attempting to get up. Sal held her down and intoned, "Stop! I've got you. Just hold on."

Maddie Pearl had no idea what was happening or whether this might be yet another dream. To test, she pinched herself hard on the leg and stoutly shouted, "OUCH!"

"What?" Sal was caught between scoping out their escape and caring for Maddie Pearl. Both could not be done well simultaneously.

Now realizing the genuineness of this very dire situation, she came to her senses somewhat but still couldn't relax fully. "Sal... what can I do... to help?"

The black man kept his watch on the white world outside this woodsy bubble and responded without looking at her,

"Nothing, now. Just stay quiet. We've got to get out of here. He'll be along, any minute now."

"*He'll?* You mean... Pa?"

Sal glanced back at Maddie Pearl, initially confused by the question. "Yeah... I mean no. I mean... yeah, your pa could come along any minute, but I'm talkin' about our ride."

Anticipating her question, Sal cut in, "I can't explain, now. Just hold on. You holding up okay?"

"I've been better," she responded, exhibiting her still intact sense of humor. "But yeah, I'm all right." Maddie Pearl raised herself from the ground enough to check out the area. They were a few feet hidden in a wooded patch with sufficient summer foliage to obscure their presence but not so much to preclude viewing beyond the woodline. She could see the Hospital/Doctor's Office, which sat on the narrow, paved street in what appeared to be a row of similar houses. However, not every lot was cleared, including the one on which they were hiding.

A Chevrolet tooled by slowly, its driver aimlessly paying scant attention, then disappeared as easily as it had approached. A Ford likewise came through, then a Buick, but overall traffic was light, since traffic pretty much always was light in small town eastern Carolina, particularly on the cusp of the second World War.

Maddie Pearl could tell that Sal was looking for a particular car, and it didn't take long to arrive. She noticed his body turn taut when the car first appeared around the curve some three football fields down the road—a Plymouth, new and shiny. Behind the wheel was a young white man about WC's age, with closely cropped hair and a military demeanor. He pulled to the side of the road adjacent the hiding place. Sal picked up Maddie Pearl less gently than before, raced to the waiting auto, crammed her into the back seat, climbed in the front beside the driver, ducked down, and off they went leaving the woods and the Victorians in their dust.

*       *       *

Just as the shiny new Plymouth rounded the bend and proceeded out of sight, a borderline-broken-down Ford truck pulled up to the "Hospital." The cab was full of men, as was the

truck bed, and they were carrying shotguns, iron pipes, and clubs. From the bed, overloaded with some of the South's finest, emerged Hog and Tate. "Wait here," Hog said to no one in particular, and then proceeded on a mission into the large Victorian house with his half-wit son in tow.

# Chapter 12

The jostling of the Plymouth in the town streets gave way to a smoother ride in the country. Sal remained crouched low, out of sight. He was not worried about being identified, but knew the appearance of a black and white man might draw suspicion. Under ordinary circumstances, their being together fairly easily could be explained without incident. There was no explanation for Maddie Pearl, an attractive, teenage, white girl with severe wounds suggesting a recent beating and a bleeding vaginal area that, upon examination by even an incompetent doctor (which, incidentally, was the norm in 1930's eastern Carolina) exhibited obvious signs of at least one rape, if not many. And even if somehow Maddie Pearl's wounds could be explained, neither Sal nor the driver had any believable justification for snatching the severely hurt girl away from a place of healing. Being stopped, therefore, was not an option.

The rumbling drone and nonexistent conversation coupled with the ongoing fogginess from the ether lulled Maddie Pearl back into a fretful sleep that continually was interrupted by her pounding head, stingy/itchy mouth, throbbing wounds, and piercingly sharp pains between her legs. She desperately needed rest, and this wasn't restful, but the journey continued and she fully trusted Sal, so Maddie Pearl gave in, closed her eyes, and hoped for sleep while praying for relief.

Some time later—Maddie Pearl didn't have a clue how long but it now was dark so it must have been hours—she found herself on a cot in a long, narrow, barracks-like room amid a small sea of cots all evenly spaced and arranged with severe precision. Although the outside darkness shown through the windows—all equidistant and exactly two-by-three feet, a smattering of low-wattage light bulbs infused sufficient photons to see about, at least superficially.

She tried to arise and scan her environs but was stymied not by the IV in her arm but by the covers in which she was

wrapped much like a child tightly tucked for bed. By painfully raising her head ever so slightly, she could see that almost every cot was empty with neatly folded sheets and perfectly placed institutional pillows at each cot's foot. Several cots over to the right, there appeared to be someone under the sheets, but not as constrained by white cloth and not being fed who knows what from a hanging bottle. To the left appeared to be a nurses' station, but it was spartan and unoccupied.

"*It must be the middle of the night,*" she thought as she lowered herself painfully back to a supine position in the cot. The military-issue bed would be god-awful to almost anyone but to Maddie Pearl it was by far the nicest in which she'd ever slept, and sleep she did.

When Maddie Pearl next awoke the room was alive with light but remained virtually abandoned. Her pain had subsided slightly, and upon lifting herself this time and scanning left she noticed at least two people at the nurse's station, a man and a woman. Both seemed young and were dressed very similarly in white. The man, no more than early twenties, happened to glance around and catch Maddie Pearl's eye. He alighted at the sight and came hustling over with a quick gait.

"Good afternoon, Maddie Pearl! We've been waiting for you to wake up!"

Although Maddie Pearl was in as vulnerable a position as possible considering she was severely injured in a strange bed in some unknown place unlike anything she ever had seen in her seventeen years, the young man's soothing voice and confident demeanor immediately put her at ease. It didn't hurt that he also happened to be the most handsome person—not just boy or man but *person* of any sex or persuasion—she ever had seen. He was tall, probably six-two or so, with broad shoulders, clear blue eyes, a beautiful smile, and clean cropped hair that... "*wait a second... that hair, or lack of it... I've seen that before... is he... is he the 'He'll be along, any minute now' guy in the car?*"

"I'm David," he said with a creamy, hypnotic voice. "But everybody calls me 'Doc.'"

So mesmerized by this vision above her in white, Maddie Pearl momentarily considered whether this might be heaven. The thought doused with the toilet waft sifting down the hallway from

someone's particularly successful bowel movement—or was that vomit?

"How did you know my name?" Maddie Pearl asked, almost afraid to speak for fear of uttering some idiocy exposing her countrified, farmhand ignorance.

"Oh, we know all about you, from WC."

"WC? Who's WC?" asked Maddie Pearl.

"You know, your friend... the guy that got you from that doctor's office back in Tuck," Doc answered with his patient hanging on every word.

"You mean... Sallerhead?" she inquired.

"Sallerhead? I don't think so. His name is Walter, Walter Jefferson, but we call him 'WC' because of his middle name, you know, Carter."

"You mean *'Carver'* don't you?" Maddie Pearl stupidly corrected the dreamboat, possibly destroying any chance she might have.

"Oh... yeah. Carver... sure. I don't really know him by that, but I knew it was something like that. Anyway, you know, WC, the nice guy with the dark complexion."

Maddie Pearl smiled at the small joke noticing immediate pain from her swollen lips. *"My lips,"* she thought. *"My face! Oh my God! I must look absolutely dreadful."* She tried to cover her face a bit with the sheet, but David a.k.a. Doc stopped her.

"Now don't go about trying to hide. You're okay here. No need to hide from anybody. You're safe." Doc said reassuringly.

*"Thank goodness he didn't realize what I was <u>really</u> doing,"* Maddie Pearl thought, with a tinge of embarrassment at her vainness.

Maddie Pearl looked up at Doc and then around at the vicinity. "Where am I?" she asked.

"You are in what's known in the United States Army as a 'field hospital' except this one is not in a field at all. It's also much more... shall we say... 'finished off' than a true field hospital would normally be... you know... like in a war or something," Doc answered.

"But where is... this *field hospital?*" she asked somewhat hesitantly because she never had heard of such a thing and had no idea such 'hospitals' even existed.

"Oh, I see what you're asking. Sorry about that. You're at Fort Bragg, which is a giant Army base in a town called Fayetteville, North Carolina."

"Fayetteville?" she asked like Dorothy upon first encountering the Munchkins. "Where's that?"

As *where's that* spewed out, Maddie Pearl desperately tried to retrieve the hillbilly words spoken with a thick nasal overtone from overcompensating for her semi-working lips. She felt certain that whatever impression she might be making was south of good, first with her hideous appearance and now with stupidity spewing from once attractive lips—now ugly swollen bulbousness—fully capable of streaming smart sentences evidencing more than a modicum of innate intelligence if less than a complete education. But whatever harm had been done seemed to wash over Doc, unnoticed.

"We're... I don't know... not too far. Maybe a hundred and fifty miles from where we got you."

"*A hundred and fifty miles!*" Maddie Pearl considered the information with more than a taste of incredulity. She never had been more than a stone's throw from home and here she was, all of seventeen. From the cocoon in which she was born, grew, and matured—to the extent a mid-teen is "matured"—she never had ridden in a car, been to "Town," been in a hospital (the Victorian in Tuck notwithstanding), slept in anything even remotely as luxurious as an Army cot, and certainly never had encountered any creature as blissfully perfect as David the Doc boy/man. Maddie Pearl's reflection was interrupted by a familiar voice.

"Maddie Pearl! How're we doing?"

Sal was a sight for eyes that literally were sore.

"SALLERHEAD!" Maddie Pearl's involuntary enthusiasm startled both Sal and Doc. She tried to hug him but the pain and sheet and IV were just too much. "Oh my God, it's great to see you!"

"I'm so glad you're awake! How're ya feeling?"

She winced a bit from her exertion and started to respond but was interrupted.

"I see," interjected WC "Sallerhead" Jefferson. "You don't need to say another word about that. So... I see you met my buddy."

"Yeah, we've met," said Doc. He looked around the empty hospital. The other occupied cot Maddie Pearl spied in the night was vacant now, with perfect sheets, pillow and placement in line with every other unoccupied luxurious bed. "My best patient, by far."

Maddie Pearl noticed her solo status, and inquired, "I thought there was somebody else in here, you know... last night?"

"There were two, actually," said Doc. "WC was here, sleeping in his bunk in the back, and that 'patient' you saw was me. I always stay whenever we have business. Can't leave someone without the medic, in case anything happens."

The other "patient's" identity was only one of perhaps hundreds of questions for which Maddie Pearl desperately wanted answers. From the last day or so, Maddie Pearl was a font of question upon question, beginning with Nomita in the dark near the Fire Pit, followed by the Luke attack, mysterious dreams, her presence in the first "hospital," Sal swooping in from nowhere to save her, the *"He'll be along, any minute now"* guy, waking up here in the middle of the night and... well... with the here and now. No answers were to be forthcoming, at least not here, and not now.

But she was safe, and comfortable, and among good people, and away from Luke and Hog, and divorced from the nightmare back home....

Or was she?

# Chapter 13

On the night Maddie Pearl went for a "walk" and Luke went "to find her," Hog lost his mind. Shortly thereafter, Mama took to the bed in a dervish whirl of worry and dread. She wasn't that old, but the hard years she'd lived had taken their toll. Life at the Prines' had changed forever.

Levi and Ethan were followers by nature, always doing whatever Hog or Luke instructed. Although capable if somewhat dimwitted, neither had any interest in playing leader. Tate, likewise, was a follower deeply disinclined to assume the role. However, he was bigger, stronger, and too stupid to say "No." By default—much like American presidential elections, the least qualified took charge. Likening it to inmates running the asylum would be to insult inmates, and asylums.

Hog had abdicated his responsibilities in favor of prolonged absences to... who knows where? He'd show up occasionally, but only at night to beat Mama and sleep. By early the next morning, he'd be gone again to... who knows where? Soon enough, all knew his activities.

Like almost everyone else, the Prines were tenant farmers. Hog took care of business, which is to say that Hog was the family's contact with the farm's owner, *the* Boss Lee. On the day this owner showed up to collect rent that Hog had not paid, no one expected him.

No Mind didn't know Boss Lee. Assuming the outsider in the cheap suit driving a strange vehicle was not a friend, Tate addressed the man accordingly.

"WATTA *YOU* WANT?"

"Where's your pa?" Boss Lee replied, somewhat reasonably considering No Mind's tenor.

"AIN'T HERE," yelled Tate in a *"get the hell out of here"* warning.

The white man, a short runt with bloodshot eyes and weak shoulders, skinny but not in a healthy way, and thin black greasy hair slick combed stickily to his scaly scalp, took a few paces forward, looked around for anyone else, and then returned his gaze to No Mind Tate.

"Now, boy, I ain't gonna ask you again. Where's your pa?"

Befuddled by this strange person's refusal to heed his admonition, Tate relented to reptilian instincts by striking a *"let's fight, asshole"* pose. The man was neither afraid nor amused. He calmly walked to the vehicle, reached in the backseat, and pulled out a double-barreled shotgun. He mechanically checked to make sure it was fully loaded, clicked it back into position, and aimed it squarely at Tate's mindless melon.

"I'm not fucking around here, boy. I gotta see your pa, right God damn now."

To say the man was emphatic is to say that urine is sour to the taste. Even No Mind Tate understood the significance of this new development, but his nimble-less intellect computed no response, so he stood there, slightly slack-jawed, paralyzed by witless indecision.

Boss Lee cocked the gun; Tate stood firm.

The man incorrectly interpreted Tate's stupidity as stubbornness; Tate didn't move.

Lee elevated the gun ever so slightly, and... FIRED!

No Mind Tate turned and ran as fast as a jackrabbit chased by a squirrel dog. The oaf never looked back as he entered the woods and wasn't seen for hours. Every animal within half a mile barked and brayed and squawked and squealed in a chorus of *"What the hell just happened?"*

Shaken by the concussion and impromptu concert, Mama ambled out of bed, feebly angled to the door, and appeared on the ill-kempt façade that pretended to be their front porch.

She knew the man, well, and eyed him cautiously, without leaving the relative safety of the rotten decking and roof.

"Robert," she said informally, as if greeting the man on the street.

"Vertie," he replied in kind.

"Anything I can help you with?" Vertie "Mama" Prine asked. Her voice was weak, so he walked toward her.

"That's close enough," Mama said.

They *were* close, once, in another time and place when younger and dumber and less solidified in their age and stations. But that was a lifetime ago, faded memories gone, and now only money mattered, to him at least.

"Hog owes me back rent. I aim to get it," Boss Lee said, holding his shotgun at the waist, pointing down.

Mama eyed the gun. "You just shoot that thing?"

"Yeah."

Mama looked around and saw no witnesses. Tate and her two other imbecilic sons were gone. The grounds were barren, except for a few stray chickens clucking about desperately in search of food that no longer was served reliably each morning by Maddie Pearl.

"You know Hog handles the rent. You need to see him."

"I tried. Your boy said he weren't here. I didn't like his attitude."

A wave of nausea swept over Mama. Had this man shot Tate? She looked around a little frantically, focusing the best her eyes would allow, and didn't see any bodies lying about.

"Where's my boy?" she asked firmly, gaining strength from protective maternal instincts instilled by evolution going back thousands of generations.

"Now you know I wouldn't shoot 'em. But I had to let him know I meant business." His callous indifference to her worst fears was disconcerting. "Last I saw, he was skedaddling"–BAM, he fired again–"that way."

The Christian woman jumped involuntarily from the shot, then turned to Boss Lee and breached Commandment Nine. "Hog works during the day, in Tuck. He'll be back tonight, and I'll get the money. You come back tomorrow, or the next day, and I'll have it for you."

Boss Lee apprised Vertie Prine, considering his options. He looked around at the property's ramshackle condition, the filthy barn that clearly hadn't been tended in weeks, the wandering ill-fed chickens, and Mama's frail condition.

He shook his head side-to-side and muttered, "What happened to you, Vertie? You're better than this. Your people ain't worth a cup of hot piss, but you..."

Post Depression southern tenant farming was a hodgepodge of arrangements exclusively fixed in favor of landlords. The Lee/Prine deal was no exception. Boss provided the land, barn, and house; Hog provided equipment, labor, seeds, fertilizer, and everything else necessary to turn fields into harvests into sold produce into rent payments. A hailstorm, cloud of locusts, broken plow or dead mule could bankrupt overnight.

Hog had been lucky, so far, but his many close calls through the years had depleted any reserves for maintenance and upkeep. The barn and house—*Boss Lee*'s barn and house—had once been among the finest of the Klan man's holdings.

The Prines' place as well as Darkieland had been owned by an African American family. A crooked judge's bogus court order transferred the deed to Robert "Boss" Lee. Magnanimously, the new owner "permitted" the blacks to stay, but only on the worst rock-strewn, stump-stubbed forty acres. The Prines had gotten the rest, including all improvements.

As Robert Lee could see, clearly, what had been a first rate property—at least the Prines' portion—was now a run-down disgrace.

This was the first time Lee had paid any attention to the place in months. He was in the area, frequently, collecting from the blacks and Indian, but almost never directly from the Prines since... after all... Hog was a good ol' boy.

He should have visited more often.

Even the land, which ordinarily had value regardless, seemed worn and worthless. The proliferation of wild cacti and the tobacco's withered crustiness suggested inadequate irrigation. But Boss Lee's trained eyes confirmed something far more sinister.

"My God," he said to himself surveying the terrain. "These fucking fools ain't been rotatin'."

This was the final straw. He could tolerate a fair amount from a poor white man just trying to feed his family, but not this. The structures would have to be razed, of course, but he'd just burn them down and profiteer on government-backed farmers insurance. Salvaging anything from the field, however, presented a far more troublesome issue. There wasn't any government handout for that.

It was a problem, a serious problem in fact, but he'd worry about it later. For now, his first chore was ridding his property of this pestilence.

Shaking his head in frustrated anger, Boss Lee turned to Mama and uttered severely, "You know I hate to do this, to you at least, but you best start gathering up whatever you plan to take with ya, 'cause you people are outta here!"

Stunned silent, she could summon no response. Boss Lee walked to his Ford, placed the shotgun in the back seat, and got behind the wheel. "And you can tell that son-of-a-bitch he can forget the goddam Klan."

"My Jesus," she muttered cryptically to herself as he drove away down the path, the dust obscuring him from view. "Haven't you hurt me enough?"

*       *       *

Tate returned in time for dinner covered in cuts, scrapes, bruises, and torn clothes. His forest foray had taken him places no human ever had explored, or perhaps ever would absent proper... *motivation*. Tate had been more than motivated.

"Where's supper?" asked Tate.

Mama ignored him, but kept looking out hoping to see her husband coming up the path on which Maddie Pearl had gone walking and Luke had gone looking and blood had gone spilling and Boss Lee had come calling and life had commenced changing forever more.

Tate looked at his siblings, but from their empty heads came no answer, so the man/child took it upon himself to scrounge for whatever he could find to fill his famished stomach. There was nothing, so he took up vigil with Mama and his brothers.

Several hours later, an old pickup plied down the path, pulled up to the shanty, and stopped. Hog was behind the wheel, alone. From where had the truck come, to whom did it belong, and how did her husband arrive behind the wheel were mysteries Mama pondered but dared not address, at least not yet.

Hog floundered out of the truck, stumbling on the dirt "driveway." To say he was drunk is to say birds have beaks. Mama had seen her savior like this many times, especially lately, and

anticipated the violence to follow, particularly once he heard about Boss Lee's visit to collect the due debt. Despite the darkness, Hog's massive, round, soft shape was unmistakable, as was the singing of some indecipherable gibberish.

As he staggered onto the rotten porch, Hog was surprised by the presence of his three idiot sons and a devoted wife whom he had fully hated for the better part of twenty-five years after "she" had tricked "him" into marriage and then birthed a retarded son. Before anyone could speak, he matter-of-factly struck Mama, hard, with an open hand across the cheek. She turned the other one, and he smacked that too. Tate and the others had more than enough sense from hard earned experiences not to interfere, so spectate they did, but from a distance.

Years of abuse had hardened Mama to this routine. Thank goodness alcoholism slowed his reflexes and impaired the ability to do more than average harm. She was a survivor; he was her only hope for survival; she took it; there was nowhere else to go.

Almost as quickly as it started, the slaps and smacks abated with Hog deeply wheezing and Mama fully swollen. The dumb boys still stood around, gaunt eyed from lack of food, education, stimulation, and pretty much everything that mutates a growing child into a fully productive member of society. They all looked at each other awkwardly, and then Hog ventured into the house for the anticipated dinner that wasn't there.

"WHERE'S MY FUCKIN' SUPPER?" Hog roared, slurring every word loutishly.

No one dared answer. Hog looked in the "kitchen" to no avail and came storming out toward Mama. Before he reached her, an uneven floorboard caught his big toe and stopped that foot. The rest of Hog's girth, however, thrust forward catapulting the gargantuan headfirst into the wall. Dazed and confused, but only temporarily, Hog re-stood unsteadily and glowered at Mama.

"Where the hell is my food?" he slurred less boisterously but still with sincere impunity emanating from every fat pore.

"Boys, how 'bout you go out now. Pa and I need to talk." They were more than eager to split. In the dust from their frantic escape, Mama faced Hog, "We got a problem."

Mama's directness was unusual; Hog noticed; Mama moved in closer to explain. Hog tried to slap her. She ducked prompting a second spill onto the little home's dirty floor.

"I'll get you for that, godammit!" Hog growled, but whatever intimidation he could exert had worn thin long ago.

" *What could he do that he hasn't done already?*"

"Boss Lee was here earlier, looking for you," she said calmly, directly, with just a tinge of spite. "Said you ain't paid the rent."

This certainly wasn't the first occasion they had experienced money problems, routine for every tenant farmer. But this was different: the best worker and leader, Luke, was gone; the farm basically was dysfunctional; and her AWOL husband was doing absolutely nothing to help. In tough times before, they'd work a little harder, cut back on everything that required any bills and coins, and make it through via sheer grit and determination.

But she knew this predicament was different, much different, and far worse than anything they'd confronted before.

"Did Boss say anything... *else?*"

The nature of Hog's question, the inflection in his voice, and the look on his dirty, sweat wet, jowly face sent up red flags throughout the room. For the first time since Hog arrived home drunk driving a strange truck she'd never seen, Mama felt scared. The usual slaps and smacks and hits and yelling and bounding about lunging at her from every angle was child's play compared... to *this*. A wife's intuition rarely is wrong, and Mama knew something seriously was... *off.*

"Well... DID HE?"

Mama jumped from his outburst, forcing her attention away from mere speculation. With great trepidation, she replied, "Honey... well... he did say something about..."

"ABOUT WHAT, WOMAN? OUT WITH IT ALREADY?"

"He said he was going to kick us out."

The direct statement didn't hit as hard as Mama had anticipated. "Kick us out? For WHAT?"

"Cause of the rent. He said you haven't—"

"Aw hell! He ain't doin' no such thing. That's just his way of scarin' ya. Ain't no way in hell he's throwin' *me* out, that's for God damn sure."

Mama backed away slightly, not relieved by Hog's confidence and still deeply concerned about what *else* she needed to tell him.

"There's more, honey."

Hog turned his bulbous head to the wife. A small taste of brownish spittle rested just below the left side of his mouth. "What the fuck you mean... *more?*"

"Well... he shot at Tate, with a shotgun... right out in the yard there."

Hog glanced out the cracked window and spied Tate milling about with Levi, Ethan, and the starving chickens.

"Looks all right to me. Boy probably had it comin', fucking dumbass."

"And he also said something about... the Klan. I think it was something about the Klan."

Hog's face whitened like a dirty sheet. "The Klan? What'd he say?" Hog grabbed Mama and started shaking her violently. WHAT'D HE SAY, WOMAN, WHAT'D HE SAY?"

Mama started crying uncontrollably, prompting the boy she never loved but had to marry nonetheless to hit her with his left fist and right, then left again. Bloodied but still standing, like some punch drunk prizefighter, Mama squeaked out, "He was mad... <u>real</u> mad... about the farm."

Hog shook her more violently, and then pushed her down hard on the dirty floor. Scowling over her, he bawled, "Watta ya mean, 'about the farm'?"

While she struggled to catch her breath and respond, his impatience instructed his left foot to kick her, in the rib cage. She gasped, then continued, "Said something about the crops... about rotating the crops... and—"

Before she could continue, his right foot joined in. While she suffered, he pontificated, "That motherfucker doesn't give a rat's ass about this farm. He just wants money, or..."

Hog straightened from his crouch over Mama and looked out the window, deep in thought. "Or maybe... just fuckin' maybe..."

The big man stepped over Mama unsteadily and rumbled toward their bedroom. Mama struggled to her feet, frantically wondering, " *What in the world is he doing?*"

"Are they coming... to get us?" Mama asked sensibly.

Hog ignored her as he rummaged through every square inch of their pitiful belongings.

"Honey... the Klan... are they, you know—"

"NO! YOU STUPID BITCH! THEY'RE NOT COMING TO GET US! AND HE AIN'T KICKIN' US OUT, EITHER!"

Fully befuddled, Mama stared speechless at her inexplicable husband wondering if the liquor, moonshine no doubt—probably poisonous—had rendered him a slobbering, hallucinating fool. She had seen moon stupor before, but Hog didn't seem to be seeing snakes writhing about or the like. Having exhausted that tack, she sailed in another direction.

"What can I do, you know... to help?"

Again, Hog ignored her entreaty while wildly rooting through their every possession like a honey badger after a rat in a thicket. At the bottom of her hope chest, which really was a crude wooden box with rusty hinges in which whatever dowry she had was now safely secured for the next generation, Hog found... IT!

"HA!" Hog exclaimed, holding up a black book and treasuring it like a child on Christmas ogling an official Red Ryder, carbine action, 200-shot, range model air rifle—with a compass in the stock. Hog plodded purposefully past Mama carrying his newfound gem as cautiously as a physicist toting plutonium to a missile cone.

As he headed for the door, Mama yelled, "HOG! NO!"

"Fuck you, woman," he callously replied over his shoulder as he exited. "This stupid book is my ticket."

Mama followed and, despite her weakened condition, managed to outrace her hooch-infected worse half to the door of the mysterious truck. Hog brutally thrust the mother of his five children onto the ground and, with comical difficulty, flung his massiveness into the driver's seat.

As he fumbled to turn on the Ford, Mama got up, clung by the window, and pleaded, "NO, HOG, NOOOO!"

Hog ignored her continual sobbing while trying to start the stubborn old thing with which he clearly was unfamiliar. It coughed, sputtered, and then quit. Again, it choked, too fuel full, and stopped. The next try, the battery sounded weaker than before, barely turning the flywheel.

Mama continued her pleas, "IT'S ALL I'VE GOT. IT'S ALL _WE'VE_ GOT! NO, HOG, PLEASE GOD _NO!_"

Frustrated with the recalcitrant machine and fed up with Mama's feckless pleas, Hog violently punched her in the face. She dropped like a felled, skinny tree as gore spurted from her broken nose. Through bloody eyes, she spotted Tate and the other sons cowering in the background behind the plow. Feebly, she pleaded to them, "Help me. Please God, help me."

The ignorant boys, overwhelmed by Hog's menace and mentally incapable of appreciating the situation's true danger, stood mutely like zombies. Meanwhile, the woman who had fed them, nursed them, cleaned their soiled diapers, held them when they needing holding, nurtured them, and taught them what she could about letters and numbers and trees and life lay beaten, battered, and pleading. She had been there—for them—each and every day, forever; they were not here for her, now, as her antagonist—_their_ antagonist—proceeded unabated.

And proceed Hog did, as he finally started the Ford, put it in gear, and drove off with the only item of any real value the chronically poverty-stricken, tenant-farming family ever had possessed: a priceless second edition 1686 _Eliot's Indian Bible_ in the Massachusetts native language—with a dedication to Robert Boyle, Governor.

# Chapter 14

Maddie Pearl's recovery in Fort Bragg Field Hospital # 4 had gone swimmingly and she was up and about regularly now. The girl remained sore, especially when going to the bathroom and walking, but a specialist had come and determined that Luke's brutal attack probably had done no permanent damage. Although the specialist would not commit to a definitive answer, he thought her chances of becoming *with child* some day—if she ever wanted kids—were better than fifty-fifty.

She'd never thought much of having children and raising a family. While Mama seemed preoccupied with the subject, Maddie Pearl's day-to-day was consumed far more with surviving until the next day, and then the next after that. This new diagnosis, and the ever-present aura of dreamy Doc David, stirred Maddie Pearl's impulses away from eating, drinking, and breathing to fanciful thoughts of dancing under the moon and holding hands in a meadow and—dare she even think it—skinny dipping in a placid summer lake.

She didn't know, but Maddie Pearl suspected that Doc harbored similar thoughts. Perhaps he wasn't focused specifically on naked lake swims, but he always seemed extra nice to her, hung out with her every chance, and provided whatever she requested lickety-split. One such request in particular morphed into somewhat of a ritual for the pair.

As the time passed, Maddie Pearl's suffering eased in all aspects but one: she was becoming increasingly, mind-numbingly, soul-destroyingly bored. Forbidden from wandering the base and constrained to a field hospital with no radio, newspapers, or even fellow patients with whom to engage, her day consisted of precious little beyond therapeutic walking up and down the hospital hallway, eating, and engaging with Sal and Doc whenever possible.

Somewhat in desperation, she finally begged, "David... do you by any chance have anything I can read, or something I can do?"

Jumping at the request, Doc brought his latest issues of *National Geographic* and a new game that had just come out called *Monopoly*.

In short order, Maddie Pearl, Doc, and Sal began playing the economic board game when possible, often after lunch. *Monopoly* was sufficiently new and no one, at least no one in Field Hospital # 4, had mastered its intricacies. Nevertheless, Maddie Pearl had a real knack, and soon became the Queen of Park Place and Boardwalk almost every time they played.

*National Geographic*, however, is what really brought Maddie Pearl and David Hodge together. At night, after Sal had gone to sleep and Nurse Crocker had left for home, Doc and Maddie Pearl would quietly comb through *Nat Geo's*. She loved seeing all the places and people. Being a well-read college graduate with a fair amount of traveling experience, he loved filling in the gaps.

He'd talk of the African savanna or why earthquakes cause tsunamis or how salmon spawn and her eyes would sparkle with wonder and excitement. An article about the Romans featuring the Colosseum and Pantheon especially piqued her interest, particularly when she discovered that Doc had visited Italy with his parents and seen the ancient ruins.

Her experience in the ways of courtship and love were constricted severely, but innately she recognized flirtation, and she liked it. And like every pretty teenage girl since time immemorial from Carthage to Katmandu, Maddie Pearl *knew* how to push the right buttons. Circumstances didn't permit full exploration of their mutual attraction, but each somehow recognized that this was more, far more, than friendship or mere camaraderie. Love at first sight? Possibly. More than a passing fancy? Definitely.

Courtship aside, neither Dreamboat nor Sallerhead were inclined to answer many questions. Other than knowing her location—sort of, and her condition—sort of, she knew nothing of why she was allowed to stay there, who was paying, how Sal and Doc were acquainted, why her parents hadn't come to get her, and twenty more questions that each answer no doubt would generate.

They'd just say *"don't worry about that"* or *"we'll talk about it later"* or some similar non-response. So, she stopped asking and started sleuthing on her own. Her detective work proved slightly below Sherlockian standards.

The absence of patients seemed particularly suspicious. In the time she had been there, Maddie Pearl had seen only a smattering of customers and each had stayed overnight only. The nature of their visits also was strange. Each came late at night, always after her *National Geo* time with Doc. The patient would sleep and then leave in the morning. If she didn't know better, she would think that they were not true "patients" in the traditional sense but probably more like Doc, perfectly well people staying overnight as if the "hospital" really were some half-assed hotel. They in fact *were* patients, Maddie Pearl felt certain, because the nurse in white who never came to call on Maddie Pearl but always seemed nearby—just in case—tended to each in a motherly fashion. Maddie Pearl also was awakened, more than one night, by the unmistakable sound of moaning emanating from the hospital's lone bathroom, or sometimes from the doctor's office adjacent thereto.

*"Poor guy,"* she'd think. *"He's really got it bad."* But miraculously, each survived the night only to be perfectly well by morning. *"Doc must be some sort of miracle worker indeed,"* she mused. *"Or that nurse."*

Aside from the dearth of patients, the place also seemed overly permanent to be a "temporary field hospital." There was a hard wooden floor, real walls as opposed to tent siding, and a metal roof upon which the rain would fall creating beautiful melodies to soothe Maddie Pearl as she slid into slumber. *"And why is this place so big,"* she'd ponder, *"with so many beds, and yet there appear to be only three people working here?"*

Sal and Doc's relationship likewise provided a fertile field for her plowing mind. Somehow, they seemed equal here, but why, and how? Maddie Pearl's exposure to race relations was limited to the draconian Webster County world of Luke and Hog and Klansmen and pitiful blacks getting the shaft at every turn. She never had seen nor known anything like this, where a black man can walk right in and hang out with a white man and young white

girl with no questions asked, no shotguns loaded, no crosses burned or necks snapped.

"*Maybe it's just a military thing,*" she considered one day while lost in thought after an especially pleasurable bowel movement that, for the first time in weeks, prompted no gruesome pain. "*But Sal's not in the military, is he? How is he able to hang around a military place?*" Her mind wandered to other questions and subjects and then the unusually tasty soup at lunch—vegetable, with real meat. And—

SLAM!

The heavy wooden door's report from the hall's end snapped Maddie Pearl to fearful attention. Marching officiously in her direction were three very authoritative looking, older soldiers in starched uniforms with shiny shoes that "tapped tapped tapped" in unison as they walked together—not unlike some military dance troupe—ever closer to Maddie Pearl's bed. Her empty bowels quivered as the men neared, the butterflies in her stomach flying wildly like a scene from *The Birds.* Upon reaching Maddie Pearl, she practically spewed tears in unknowing dread of what she had no idea she had done, or not done, or done wrong, or...

"*Wait! They walked past! They didn't even stop! They didn't even look at me! Thank GOD! THEY'RE NOT AFTER ME AT ALL!*"

Maddie Pearl's exhilaration was short-lived, however, as a new, more insidious thought infected her healing mind, body, and soul. "*Are they after... Doc? Or even, oh my God no... Sal?*"

She arose on the cot in a manner just a few short weeks prior would have been painfully impossible. The official men in the perfect uniforms and spit-shined shoes with the flat taps on the bottoms facilitating their musical stroll reached the empty nurse's station and stopped—at attention of course. The apparent leader or, at least, the one who walked in front and seemed a little more tight-assed than the other two, called out in a military-grade baritone, "WHO IS MANNING THIS FACILITY?"

A rustling could be heard in the doctor's office behind the nurse's station. Out came the nurse in white who never helped Maddie Pearl but always seemed ready if needed.

"WHO'S IN CHARGE HERE?" The "leader" belted, projecting his voice unnecessarily under the circumstances since only the three of them, Maddie Pearl, and the nurse were present.

"Uh, well... sir... I am, I guess," the young, intimidated, pretty nurse chirped like a small, scared sparrow having just fallen from her safe nest onto the snout of a sleeping crocodile.

"WHAT'S YOUR NAME, SOLDIER?" Again with the yelling, as if neighboring villages had vested interests in the answers to these questions.

"I'm... uh... my name is, um, Crocker, sir. Nurse Crocker. But everyone calls me Betty, sir."

The leader took one long look at this "soldier" in front of him, squinted his eyes *ala* Clint Eastwood in some dumb spaghetti western, and lowered his tone to a far more threatening volume. "Betty. *Fucking*. Crocker? You've *got* to be shitting me."

Before more mocking spewed forth, the hospital back door opened and in walked Doc and Sal in jocular conversation about some movie they had seen the night before—*Citizen Kane*. They stopped mid-sentence at the sight from the nurse's station. Each immediately stiffened, stood at attention, and cast their gazes straight ahead so as to ensure neither made the horribly punishable mistake of eyeballing any of the vastly superior officers before them.

The unnamed, slightly more rigid person in front walked seriously, sternly, officially to the two young men, eyed each in a manner that only a superior officer can do, cleared his throat slightly, and oozed sarcastically, "And just who the fuck do you two clowns *think* you are?"

Sweat poured down their faces. Neither spoke at first. Neither looked at each other, nor at the leader, nor at the other two superior creatures without speaking parts in this little play, nor at the nurse, nor at Maddie Pearl, nor at anything. Their eyes were fully open, but they saw nothing, and totally intended to keep it that way.

"WELL?" the leader ratcheted up the inquiry.

Doc, being white and the presumptive less inferior of the two subhuman army ants, spoke. "Sir," he snapped militaristically. "Officer Kane... err... Hodge, sir. Officer David Hodge, sir."

The leader considered the input suspiciously, and then turned his beady mean eyes to Sal.

"And you? What's your story, *boy?*"

Sal's countenance seemed expressionless, but Doc, the nurse, and even Maddie Pearl down the hall saw WC's face harden. It was slight, almost imperceptible, but very much there, manifested in a tightly clenched jaw, with ever-so-narrower pupils and a marginally more rigid stance.

"WALTER! CARVER! JEFFERSON! *Sir!*"

Slightly struck by the strong, clear, non-intimidated response, in that voice that always sounded so dramatically perfect, the leader edged so much closer to Sal, their noses practically touching.

"I didn't ask for your name, *coon,*" he whispered menacingly. "I asked for your God damn story! Your rank!"

Sallerhead didn't blink. "PRIVATE FIRST CLASS JEFFERSON, WALTER C, sir. *"* The leader flinched in an embarrassing manner noticed by all. He clearly didn't like it, not one damn bit. And he surely didn't appreciate the lack of emphasis on the word "sir" either.

The leader inched so close that WC could smell the breath coming from the leader's nostrils—coffee, with a hint of bologna, and the leader's underarm odor blended pungently stanching the putridity.

"You smart mouthing me, *boy?*"

WC waited just long enough for effect, relaxed his demeanor subserviently, and then replied calmly in a respectful manner to this asshole before him who deserved no respect but would get it nonetheless because of his rank, race, age, and caste.

"Sir. No sir."

The leader was not amused, but sensed victory in his stupid little battle, and backed off. He glared at all before him, turned to one of his cohorts, retrieved therefrom a very official paper, and then read, bellowing even more loudly than before, like a circus barker capturing a crowd:

FORT BRAGG FIELD HOSPITAL NUMBER FOUR HEREBY IS CLOSED PERMANENTLY AND IMMEDIATELY. ALL PATIENTS

SHALL BE DISCHARGED OR
TRANSFERRED, IMMEDIATELY. ALL
PERSONNEL SHALL REPORT TO THEIR
SUPERIOR OFFICERS FOR REASSIGNMENT,
IMMEDIATELY. THIS BY IMMEDIATE
ORDER OF BASE COMMANDER GENERAL
EBENEZER CAHOON, USA!

# Chapter 15

The Field Hospital # 4 closure proved disastrous for Maddie Pearl, at first. Within an hour, she went from luxuriating in the most comfortable bed relishing gourmet vegetable soup with *real* meat and reliving her painless bowel movement while joyfully fantasizing of dreamy Doc David nudely swimming in Placid Lake, to... *this*. And *this* was sitting in David Hodge's Plymouth, alone, in a vast field of mud, ruts, mosquitoes, and stench from the nearby communal latrines, with several hundred other cars, all empty.

Although she was much better, the long walk from the closed hospital had been difficult in her weak condition, and near the end she noticed a small blood trickle from her groin. She had not looked, because to do so would require exposing herself publicly in front of perhaps thousands of male soldiers, although no one was in sight. Even now, safely ensconced in the relative anonymity of this very ordinary vehicle in this very large place filled with other very ordinary vehicles but no people—ordinary or extraordinary—she felt too self-conscious even to unbutton her old hand-me-down jeans, pull down her hoary underclothing, and look at her young budding womanhood. *"After all, what would Jesus think if he saw me do that?"*

So she sat there, with nothing to do, no food, no water, no explanation, no plan, and no Sallerhead or Doc or nurse. The time? How many hours had passed? She had no clue. The only timepiece she ever had seen was the preacher's pocket watch that he kept close by to make sure his three hour services didn't run short. Regardless of specifics, the day's morning promise had drifted slowly into the afternoon's weary conclusion, and she knew it had been a long, long time since Doc and Sal had deposited her here.

"Don't let anybody see you," Doc admonished in no uncertain terms.

"Don't go anywhere," Sal added most seriously.

"We'll be back, or one of us will. Don't worry, but be *sure* to stay out of sight," Doc had rejoined.

An obedient soul from years of observing Commandments and enduring Hog switchings, Maddie Pearl did as she was told. And she waited, and tried unsuccessfully to sleep, and held herself below the window line uncomfortably, and peeked up only to be disappointed with each sound of a passing pedestrian or the wheeling of tires leaving or entering the filthy mud field. The bleeding below had stopped long ago, but a new pain had begun shortly after Sal and Doc left. She wasn't too worried, because it was far less than anything she had been experiencing over the last few weeks, but it reinforced that she was not truly, fully well.

Wellness was not Maddie Pearl's primary worry, however. Of far greater concern was her current predicament. With nightfall, those worries intensified. *"What if they don't come back? What if they got in trouble, real trouble, locked up in jail trouble, and they can't return to get me? What if I starve out here, waiting, unable to go anywhere or do anything? Jesus... am I going to die out here, alone, in a car for God's sake?"*

The fitful mental meanderings tossed and turned her for unknowable minutes into hours, but thank goodness sleep finally found Maddie Pearl. It was an erratically disturbed, wholly unrestful snooze, but slumber did she. In the middle of a superiorly frustrating dream where she needed to get somewhere and do something but just couldn't put it together and kept failing at every effort, she was awakened with a sharp jolt when the Plymouth started and began moving abruptly. Sallerhead was behind the wheel!

"Stay down!" Sal ordered strictly. "And don't say anything!"

Maddie Pearl, again, did as she was told, and the vehicle rumbled slowly over the ruts and mud and unevenness and through the foul odor of human feces and urine and within the fog of mosquitoes toward an exit and... where?

Maddie Pearl said nothing from her low perch in the back seat but could see out the window and noticed pine trees, and more pine trees, and then ever green more. They clearly were out of the parking lot now, and driving through what appeared to be a heavily wooded forest, so she felt somewhat safe to talk.

"What's going on?"

"SHHH! Don't say anything. We're not out yet!"

"*Out,*" wondered Maddie Pearl to herself. "*We're in the woods, aren't we? Is it not safe even here?*"

Her questions were answered shortly thereafter when Sal looked frantically in all directions, took a deep breath, slowed the Plymouth to trolling speed, and turned to Maddie Pearl.

"You okay?"

"Can I speak now, or are you, and only *you,* allowed to say anything?"

Maddie Pearl's frustration, bordering on anger, was palpable... and justified. She had been hostage for hours without food, water, or information and now, upon "rescue," she remained a hostage without food, water, or information! She sensed that Sal and Doc sincerely were doing what was best, but that didn't explain the secrecy. She was a young woman with a fully functioning mind more than capable of computing input and rendering reasoned responses thereto. How dare they treat her this way!

Sal recognized her irritation and wisely chose not to respond in kind.

"I'm so sorry, Maddie Pearl. I never should have gotten you into this mess in the first place."

Sal's tone and apology were comforting and appeared heartfelt. Maddie Pearl's resentment relented somewhat.

"I'm sorry too, Sal, but I've been out here all day and night getting eaten alive by every insect in the world, and while they've feasted, I've starved, and I feel like hell... er... I'm sorry... I feel really bad and you've told me nothing and—"

"I know, I know," Sal cut her off. "And I really am so sorry. So is Doc. It couldn't be helped. I think we're in the clear now, but there were some things we had to do to... you know... take care of things."

"No, Sal, I don't know. *That's* the problem. You haven't told me anything, and I'm sick and tired of this!"

He pulled the Plymouth to a little clearing in the woods aside the two-lane blacktop. With some difficulty, he maneuvered in reverse behind a small stand of elaeagnus bushes to render them fully out-of-view from inadvertent snoops passing by on the road from Fayetteville heading east toward, inter alia, Webster County.

He motioned for Maddie Pearl to get out.

"Thank God," she said. "I need to go, now!"

Sal turned away as nature's call was handled frantically. Thereafter, they settled near the car's hood. Moving her legs felt joyously heavenly, especially with the pain and bleeding now fully abated. She stretched in every direction and, despite the hunger pangs, felt as good as she had in a long, long time.

Sal helped her sit on the hood, took a spot beside her, considered what to say, and then proceeded with hopes of bringing an end to Maddie Pearl's magical mystery tour.

"Nomita told you about Luke's plan to make it look like me and a bunch of others raped and then killed you, right?"

Maddie Pearl was stung by Sal's directness. "*So much for easing into this,*" she thought.

"Yeah," she replied haltingly. "She told me, that night it all happen..." Maddie Pearl's voice trailed off and, even with darkness's shroud, she turned her head away so Sal could not see her whimpering.

WC reached out, held her warmly, and whispered over and over, "It's all right, Maddie Pearl. It's all right."

She regained her composure just enough to utter weakly, "Yes, she told me."

Sal waited to allow the atmosphere to clear.

"I don't think it was Luke's plan. This might shock you, but I think it was your pa's."

Maddie Pearl turned to Sal, now much more under control. "Nomita said that, and I've thought about it... a lot... ever since... you know. And I think so too."

Walter Carver breathed in deeply, exhaled, and then began to reply when Maddie Pearl interjected, "You don't know Pa like I do. He's not like, well, he's not like what people around home think."

People around home thought Hog was an obnoxious, race-baiting, fat-assed idiot, but Sal knew not to go there, not here and now. So he listened without comment, giving Maddie Pearl whatever space she needed to get out whatever she needed out, and he sensed a lot needed outing.

"He hates Mama. Always has. Blames her for Tate being so... so... so damn stupid. And he beats her, bad. And he beat me

too, maybe not as much but still... And Luke and Levi and all... they'd just sit there and watch, and laugh. And that smirk on Luke's face... that awful little mean smirk."

Maddie Pearl's demeanor quickly was changing as she spilled the miserable history all over Sal. Her tear-jerked recollection of Luke's brutality had washed away exposing the raw, jangling, pulsating nerves of pure hatred, revulsion, and loathing she had harbored against her father for his meanness and drunkenness, and her mother for not standing up to him, and her brothers for never once stopping the monster, and herself for being so weak and timid and caught up in Jesus and turning the other cheek and only seeing the good in people and all the rest of that bullshit that sounds so good but fully fails in real life. In ways she never had before, Maddie Pearl's eyes saw herself so differently right now, the years wasted, the time spent on nothingness, all the anger pent and the realities ignored and the longings left unfulfilled.

"DAMN THEM!" she concluded out loud for only Sal and the forest denizens to hear. "DAMN THEM ALL STRAIGHT TO HELL!"

Maddie Pearl did not break down in tears. Her fists were clenched; her jaw was as tight as a snapping turtle on a snake head; her eyes were set firmly, straight ahead, at nothing and everything!

"This is going to stop. Right NOW!"

Sal never had heard Maddie Pearl speak so bluntly, so sincerely. He considered the thoughts her mind had created, and he saw that it was good.

"Take me there! Take me back home, now!"

Sal thought first before responding. "I planned to do that. In fact, we're on the road there right now. But there're some things you need to know... *before* we go anywhere."

Maddie Pearl pondered Sal's comment, and replied, "Well tell me, right here and now, cause I don't plan on waiting around much longer." She hopped off the hood, straightened her clothes, ran long delicate fingers through her bright red hair glowing beautifully even in the scarce night light, and said, "Well?"

Sallerhead jumped down too, turned to Maddie Pearl, and said, "Let's get some food in you first. There's a place, about four miles up. *Green Book* says it's ok."

As he pivoted to reenter the Plymouth, Maddie Pearl asked, "What's a *Green Book*?"

"Trust me. There's a place nearby. Let's get something to eat, and I'll fill you in on what's been going on."

Maddie Pearl got back in the rear seat, tucked low yet again so as not to be seen, and rode with her best friend—a black man in a South still clinging desperately to a cause lost so many decades before. Together they made their way to a place, one of the very few, that actually served honest, hungry, paying African Americans in a country known as "America the Great" where all men are created equal, sort of.

# Chapter 16

Maddie Pearl could not recall a better meal, ever. She devoured the fried chicken, gnawing on the bones like a starving dog, and inhaled the beans and potatoes practically without chewing. The water, drawn from a horse trough pump, tasted sweeter than honey. Maddie Pearl gulped every drop like a castaway upon rescue. Sal likewise enjoyed the repast but, having been fully fed each meal all day, was nowhere near as famished and thus gave Maddie Pearl much of his spread.

They had eaten in the Plymouth parked behind an abandoned tobacco barn in a fallow field, another victim of tenant farming diseconomy. Aside from a few croaking tree frogs and twitching crickets, it was silent, and they were alone. Maddie Pearl was stretched out in the back seat, digesting the feast. The time had come for some answers.

After a long pause, Sal spoke, "Do you remember Daisy?"

Maddie Pearl perked up slightly from her reverie and replied, "You mean my best friend ever, that my daddy gave your family?"

Sal chuckled to himself. "Well, he didn't exactly 'give' us anything. Pickles and Stump had to work your fields all summer, with no pay, and had to lug their own food and water."

Maddie Pearl shook her head in disgust. "That's what I'm sayin'. My pa is a real piece of—"

"I know, I know," Sal interrupted. "I'm getting to that. But Daisy, well, she was about the only thing that kept us alive a couple of years there."

Maddie Pearl smiled warmly. "I always loved her. So sweet. Ever since I was a little girl, I gave her treats, like some wild grapes or whatever I could find. Sometimes I'd even slip her an egg or a carrot from home, if no one was watching."

Sal pivoted in the front bench seat to face Maddie Pearl head on. With a slight pause before speaking, he said solemnly, "Maddie Pearl... Luke... well, he beat Daisy to death right in front of me. I—"

"Nomita told me... about Daisy," Maddie Pearl cut in. "The night I got..." She couldn't finish the sentence with the tears welling. Sal handed her a napkin from the dinner, she dabbed her eyes and blew her nose in a manner a lady cannot unless with her close friend between whom there are no secrets, or will be no secrets shortly.

"Well that day, with Luke and all... your brother... well, he was stupid enough to tell me what the hell they were gonna do. And the way they beat Daisy, over and over, like nothing I'd ever seen... *mean*... like possessed demons or something. Well... there was no doubt he meant every damn word."

Maddie Pearl had heard this part too, but rather than acknowledging her awareness she got to the heart of the matter.

"So why didn't you come to me? And tell me?"

Sal bowed his head somberly, in shame. "It's the biggest mistake I have ever made."

He turned away, but Maddie Pearl could see his eyes in the rearview mirror moistening ever so slightly. He took a deep breath, rubbed his face with both hands, and looked into the back seat at Maddie Pearl.

"I will never forgive myself for how I handled... things. I didn't know what to do. I knew Luke was going to follow through. I *knew*... but I figured he'd get that idiot Tate to do it for him... er... sorry..."

"No need to apologize. I know Tate is... well, Tate."

"Thinking back, I know I was wrong, but at the time all I knew to do was get away and make damn sure Luke and Tate and none of the rest ever saw me and you anywhere close together, and I mean not even in the same field. So..."

"So you ran away."

Sal lowered his head yet again and nodded dolefully.

"What in the world good was *that* going to do?" demanded Maddie Pearl sternly, in a manner revealing the true extent to which she had considered this possibility over and over at night when going to sleep and during the day when doing mindless tasks

and when in the doctor's "hospital" in Tuck and when in the Army cot alone for those weeks in Field Hospital # 4 and throughout pretty much every waking moment for days and weeks now.

"Like I said, Maddie Pearl, I was wrong," he mumbled his feeble, indefensible response to this strong young woman who by the minute was becoming increasingly fed up with stupid, weak men who steered her life where she had no interest traveling.

"Yeah. You were wrong all right. Just like it appears you were wrong back at the Army hospital or whatever it was."

Sal looked up and furrowed his brow as if to say, "*What do you mean?*"

"I don't know what was going on back there, but I know it wasn't right! I saw those men coming in at night. I heard the moaning. I haven't seen much in this world, but I've got an idea of what it was." Every ounce of Maddie Pearl's biblical training spewed forth in her righteous indignation straight out of Leviticus. "And I don't blame them for shutting down that... that... den of sin!"

Sal's somber demeanor turned on a dime as he burst into wild laughter.

"What? *WHAT?* What in the world are you... good Lord," he stammered between hoots of hilarity. "That's got to be the damnedest thing I've ever heard!"

Maddie Pearl sat slack jawed, incapable of interpreting what this jabbering idiot in the front seat was trying to say. She waited for him to calm down, which took much longer then it should. "*Good Lord*," she thought, "*Whatever he thinks is funny, well, it's not THAT funny.*"

"Stop laughing at me!" she finally snapped. He continued. "I mean it. STOP!"

Realizing her sincerity, and recognizing the dire need for clarification, he struggled but finally succeeded in regaining some power over his heretofore-uncontrolled emotions.

"Maddie Pearl, it wasn't what you think," he stammered, still catching his breath and reliving the humor on a smaller scale. "I've read Leviticus too, all of it. Nobody was, you know, well, let's just say... Nobody was violating any of those laws. Okay?"

Dumbfounded, Maddie Pearl demanded, "Well then, what *was* going on in there?"

Sal couldn't help himself as he broke out in laughter again, albeit more subdued. "I'm sorry, I'm sorry. I didn't mean to..." He struggled yet again to catch his breath. "Listen, it's like this."

Standing firm with her consternation like a schoolmarm confronting a pupil who didn't do his homework, Maddie Pearl insisted without even a hint of humor, "Are you going to tell me, or *WHAT?*"

Again wheezing from the laughter, he finally uttered, "Those guys... and they weren't all men by the way... but those people were sick."

"Yeah, *I bet.*"

"No, seriously. Sick as a dog. Every one of 'em."

"From what?"

"You remember that food you were getting, how good it usually was?"

Maddie Pearl reflected back to that magical vegetable soup, with real meat. "Yeah. Sure. So?"

"Well that was outside food. Stuff we brought in, from off the base. Sometimes I'd get it, sometimes Doc. Even Betty brought in every now and then, but not as often, and sometimes she'd cook at home and bring it."

"Why did you do that? Didn't they have food at... what's it called... Fort something or other?"

"Bragg. Fort Bragg. But yeah, they have food there, or at least they call it 'food.' But it was more like horse squeezings with ladles of sour latrine water."

"What do you mean?" asked Maddie Pearl, still dubious.

"Those patients coming in, every one of 'em, they all were suffering from food poisoning. Each and every one."

Maddie Pearl was skeptical.

"I'm serious. That's the only real reason they kept the hospital open, to care for troops sickened by the sickening food. I mean... I guess we would have taken whatever came in the door, but the only thing that seemed to ever come were soldiers with sour stomachs full of rancid food... or sometimes too much whiskey."

Maddie Pearl analyzed the information like a detective solving a crime. "Well why would they go into that office, and not the bathroom?"

"Didn't you notice how that latrine... we call bathrooms latrines... but didn't you notice the smell?"

Thinking back to the wafts of foul odor that seemed to permeate the hospital on certain days depending on atmospherics, Maddie Pearl answered, "Yeah. It reminded me a little of the barnyard, back home."

"If you've ever had food poisoning, and I hope you never do, but if you've ever had it you'd know that the last thing you need if you want to get better is to be sticking your head down into a half-ass toilet in a field and sniffing human crap while you vomit over and over."

"So why the office? You didn't have any toilets or anything in there, did you?"

Sal responded, "No. Of course not. But we figured out over time that the best way to handle cases was to put 'em in there, with the door closed cutting off as much of the latrine stench as we could, and let them throw up in a bucket. When they got through, we'd put 'em to bed and dump the bucket."

Maddie Pearl thought through the explanation, starting to buy in. "So... what was that nurse doing? She never helped me, but she sure seemed awfully friendly, late at night, when those *guys*... er... people were in bed."

Sal looked at Maddie Pearl somewhat incredulously. "Are you not familiar with what nurses do?"

Hoping not to expose her ignorance, even to this most trusted of friends, she held off responding. Truth be told, Maddie Pearl never had seen a nurse until that night Luke attacked her and she mysteriously ended up in a large Victorian hospital house.

"Let me just say," Sal toned in, "that's what nurses do. They kind of mother people, help them feel comfortable, you know... make 'em feel better. They do a lot more, too, but that's all she was doing with the food poisoned people."

"Well why didn't she tend to me?"

"She did, when you were sleeping and such, but to be honest... and I probably shouldn't say this... but she knew Doc was kinda, I don't know... he was kinda sweet on you, if you know what I mean."

Maddie Pearl had suspected as much, and hoped it to be true, but never knew for sure until now. The thought brought

warmth to her core, and she liked it. And it all made sense. With Doc's extra attentiveness, and Sal on top of that, Betty Crocker really didn't *need* to help anyway.

A long, pregnant pause passed between them, with each pondering what next to say, where next to send this increasingly long conversation sitting in a Plymouth behind an abandoned tobacco barn in a field no longer worked because tenant farming doesn't succeed for anyone but the landowner.

They both spoke at once, stopped in sync, then laughed at the mutual faux pas. Obeying "ladies first," Sal motioned for Maddie Pearl to proceed.

"So what's the deal with that hospital? Why was it even there, and why was it closed? It didn't have anything to do with me, did it?"

Sal chuckled warmly at her concern. "Lord no, Maddie Pearl. You had nothing to do with anything. Since you weren't a soldier or whatever, you weren't supposed to be there of course, but that base is so big and nobody knows what anybody is doing on any given day. So, as far as anybody knew, you were a WAC in need of care."

"WAC? What's a WAC?"

"Well technically, it's the Women's Army Corps. Around the base and all, there are a few women here and there doing jobs that, well, to be honest... only women usually do, like that nurse. We call them the WAC's for short."

"So the hospital?" she persisted.

"I asked Doc the same question when I first joined and got assigned there. I'll tell you about all that in a minute. But anyway... I asked Doc, and he said that the base... you know... Fort Bragg... that it was built right at the end of the Great War, you know with Germany and everything."

Maddie Pearl had less than a vague idea of the "Great War" and Germany and history in general having been raised mostly on Jesus and chores, but she nodded along as if she were aware.

"So anyway, the US got into the war late, and had to ramp up everything real fast, so places like there got built, kinda overnight. As it turns out, that was pretty much the exact same time that the Spanish Flu hit, and it hit hard, especially the military."

"The Spanish Flu?" Maddie Pearl asked, further exposing her wholesale ignorance of history, among other things.

"Yeah... about twenty years ago, there was this Spanish Flu that went through. Around the world, it killed millions, according to Doc at least. Since the soldiers were going everywhere—usually together on ships overseas—to fight, they started giving it to each other and, before anyone knew what was happening, tens of thousands of Army men were dying left and right, so this hospital, along with others all over the country just like it, were built to handle the sick. Doc says even though it seems huge, that he read it wasn't even close to being big enough to handle everybody."

"Well, so, when did the flu end?"

"Oh I don't know for sure. Doc and I didn't talk about that, except he did say he'd been there going on two years and he had never had more than a handful of patients and, almost always, they were these people sick from the shit food on base... oh... and sometimes we'd get somebody too drunk to stand up, but we always treated them the same, since what they had kind of was like food poisoning too."

The conversation lagged momentarily, giving a screech owl the opening to announce her presence. Sal and Maddie Pearl reacted involuntarily at the unexpected SCREECH, smiled, and then Maddie Pearl rejoined.

"Sal. Tell me about... you. How did you end up, you know, there?"

Sal had a fairly large gulp of horse water, set the container down on the Plymouth's dashboard, and continued filling in Maddie Pearl on all the questions she'd been fretting over for weeks.

"Wasn't much to it, really. When I... you know... when I left, I hung out in the woods, for a short while. You go a mile or so, I don't know... maybe two, beyond your church, and you get to that swampy area, the one everybody's scared of. Well I sorta camped out there, for a while, but I'd come in kinda close like, at night, to the community... just to check on things. I let Nomita know that I was around, but didn't tell her much cause I didn't want her or anybody trying to find me. Wouldn't be good, for you or anybody else, if I was seen around."

"No... I'm talking about the Army and Doc and all that."

"I'm gettin' to it. So once it seemed like things had started to quiet down, I went into 'Town'—had to walk, but that was okay— and stayed behind this place that serves us... that is, serves colored people. That's where I found out about that *Green Book*, from the folks there. And they were real nice to me, and helped me get food—leftovers from the day usually, but that was all right with me, and there was a little shed that kept the rain off and so on. So it wasn't too bad, really."

"You never did tell me about this *'Green Book'* thing?"

"Oh, it's just this book somebody puts out that lets people know—negro people, I mean, where they can get food or stay overnight or whatever."

Maddie Pearl considered the concept, noticed the book on the front seat, retrieved it, and squinted in the darkness at the cover.

"Where'd you get it?"

"From a guy on base, an orderly. Said he never went anywhere, didn't need it. Sold it for fifty cents."

"Where'd he get it?"

"Now you'll have to ask him that, I 'spose, but if you look at the cover..." He stretched over the front bench and pointed at the book in Maddie Pearl's hands "There, you'll see it says 'Esso.' That's a gas station, so I guess you can get these there, at those stations."

Maddie Pearl eyed the *"Proudly Distributed by your friends at Esso"* label at the top of the book, then tossed it back to the front seat and looked up at Sal.

"Okay... so... getting back to the story. Were you still coming back home... at night at least?"

"Yeah, but it wasn't as easy, since I was not as close, but the store—it was a diner too, sort of... but the people there who were letting me stay in the shed, they got a lot of their vegetables and some meat from Farmer Hunt. He's that Indian fellow just down from your place, on the other side. You probably know him."

"No. I'd heard of him, a few times, from Pa and sometimes even Luke, but they said never go near there, said he was an evil spirit or what not and the land was cursed. I always thought they were full of beans, but I didn't head that way. Didn't need to

anyway, since nothing's down there except him. Everything I care about, like the church and you folk, is in the opposite direction."

"Well this Farmer Hunt, that's what everybody calls him... or at least, what those store people and I call him. Turns out he's a real nice man, and has no problem dealing with us negroes... I guess those injuns get treated just like we do, maybe worse. But so he said to the store people, who weren't white either by the way—"

"Wait. What color were they?"

"I don't know, for sure, but they looked Chinese to me... you know, with the slanted eyes and kinda yellowish skin. That'd be my guess, anyway."

Maddie Pearl never had seen anyone other than Caucasians and African Americans. From her experience, the world was white and black. Indians, Chinese, nurses, doctors, Plymouths... this was all novel to her, and both scary and exhilarating, as this brave new world was beginning to expose itself, *finally!*

"But anyway, getting back to Farmer Hunt, he told those restaurant people, or store people—the Chinese, that he could sure use some help getting stuff from the farm to places like theirs. They introduced me to him, and for a little while there I was going back and forth almost every day, and some days I'd just stay overnight in my hideout around the swamp, just to keep an eye on things... to keep an eye on Luke and Tate, since I knew what they were up to."

"So were you the one who helped me that night, you know... *the* night?" Maddie Pearl asked.

"Oh no, I was long gone by then, to Fort Bragg."

"So... who got me to that doctor's place, in 'Town'?"

"Well let me tell you about the Army and Doc and all that first," Sal said.

"I don't care about that right now. Tell me about who got me to that place... and by the way, was it in 'Town' or Tuck?"

"They're the same thing."

"What are?"

"Tuck and 'Town.' They're the same place. Everybody back home usually calls it 'Town' but officially, like on maps and such, it's really Tuck. That's where you were."

"So if 'Town' and Tuck are the same thing, why does everybody call it 'Town'?"

"I've never understood that either. I guess it's the only place anybody ever goes for anything, at least if you're from our neck of the woods. The place always seemed so mysterious to me, but now that I've been there some... trust me... it's not much. Just a crossroads really, with a few houses, that doctor's place, a general store, and this place I was just talking about that's sort of a store but also a diner. There's not a whole lot else to it."

Maddie Pearl synthesized this input about the magical place she'd wondered about her whole life and often longed to visit. In her mind, she'd built it up into Shangri La, Oz, and Heaven Almighty all in one.

"Well... that's disappointing," she mumbled under her breath.

"Huh?" said Sal.

"Oh... nothing. So... getting back... if it wasn't you, who helped me get to that doctor's office in Tuck?"

"Well... that was Nomita, or really Nomita and Farmer Hunt," Sal replied.

"Nomita... how in heaven?"

"I'm getting to it," Sal replied, "just hold your horses."

Maddie Pearl crossed her arms and plopped against the Plymouth's backbench to communicate, "*Okay, I'm ready for the long haul here, but get on with it!*"

"So that night, like I said, I was gone, to Fort Bragg. But Nomita, after she talked to you, started heading back home. About halfway there, for some reason she can't explain, she just felt like she had to go back and check on you. She said the feeling was so strong that she couldn't resist."

"Jesus," uttered Maddie Pearl inadvertently.

"That's what Nomita thinks too, Jesus," said Sallerhead.

Maddie Pearl snapped back to attention. "No, I wasn't saying Jesus like 'Jesus did it' or anything. I was just saying Jesus, you know, like an expression. And I apologize for swearing like that."

"Well swearing or Jesus or whatever, Nomita somehow knew, and as she got closer she started hearing you. She said it sounded real muzzled, like you had an apple stuck in your mouth

or something. And even though it was really dark she could see somebody on the path and somebody else jabbing and jabbing over and over again at the person. She didn't know what was happening, but she just knew someway that it was you and Luke."

"Oh my gracious! So what'd she do?"

"It sounds to me like instincts took over or whatever, so she grabbed a big rock, you know they were right beside that rocky field that we farm, the awful one, so there were plenty of rocks around. So anyway... she grabs a big rock, runs up, and conks Luke right on the head. He raised up a bit, and started to lunge, but Nomita got him a second time, right in the face, and that was all it took."

"So she... *killed* him?"

"Be patient! I'm getting to that. But *NO*, Nomita did NOT kill your brother."

Maddie Pearl deliberated momentarily, and then said, "I was right there, and I don't remember any of this!"

"She said you were out of it by then, just moaning and squirming on the ground and so on, and even in the dark she could tell blood was everywhere, cause she stepped in it, like a puddle, and she didn't know what to do."

Maddie Pearl blanched at the bloody reference.

"I'm sorry," said Sal, realizing he was perhaps being too graphic. "I shouldn't have said anything about all that."

Maddie Pearl got past the appalling visual, and continued, "So what did she do?"

"She carried you some, then dragged you, to the Fire Pit, and then ran like hell to get help. Pickles, Stump, Sow Belly... almost everybody came. You remember my cousin who lost her eye?"

"Yeah... Blossom, right?" replied Maddie Pearl.

"Yeah, Blossom... well she was the one who held you in her arms and got all those leaves—poison ivy—out of your mouth. She's awful allergic, stayed broken out over a month or so."

Maddie Pearl couldn't speak, overwhelmed with the communal kindness for her, a white girl, from a white family with at least one and maybe more Klansmen right there at the dinner table each and every night.

Sal continued, "I told Nomita about Farmer Hunt helping me and all, so she told Fleet to go get him. I hear it wasn't more than ten minutes before that Indian came driving up in his Ford truck ready to help in any way he could."

"So he took me to that doctor?"

"Yep. Put you right in the back, in the bed, with Nomita right by your side. When they got there, you were completely out, and still bleeding a lot, and Nomita said you looked whiter than a dead ghost. So Farmer Hunt parked his truck around the corner, out of sight. They brought you to the door, knocked, and then ran like hell, but they waited to make sure you got in. When you did, they hightailed it back home. Whole trip probably took 'em no more than thirty minutes or so, since Tuck is pretty close really, if you have a truck."

Maddie Pearl thought long and deep about this unreal story. Among other things, she thought of how "Town" always had seemed so far away, so exotic, so impossible to reach, and now she knew that, with a truck, you could get there and back in less than an hour. It angered her that she never had been, that she never had seen the stores or learned about "out there" or even been allowed to see it from the road.

Nomita, Farmer Hunt, what Luke did, the little girl who lost an eye... it was almost too much to take in, especially considering how fresh the wounds remained. But even with all of this, the story wasn't complete; it wasn't even close to complete.

"What happened to Luke?"

WC "Sal" Jefferson stiffened noticeably, and did not answer.

"Sal... what happened to my brother?"

"I think we might need some air," he said while exiting the driver seat. Maddie Pearl got out as well and leaned up beside him on the Plymouth's hood.

He waited a long time to answer, too long, and Maddie Pearl was becoming more concerned as the seconds ticked by. Almost as if they knew the importance of this moment, neither the screech owl nor any of the other night creatures made a sound. The stillness of the darkness and the silence of the air were deafening.

"Sal. *Please* tell me. My brother... Luke... what happened?"

Sal finally resolved internally that silence was no option. He looked Maddie Pearl directly in the eyes, grabbed her by the shoulders and, as calmly, cooly, and candidly as this great human with the mental and physical gifts envied by all men regardless of color, answered, "Your brother is no more."

The words hit Maddie Pearl like a rifle shot to the temple. She stumbled, sliding against the car, and would have fallen to the ground had Sal not caught her. She resisted his assistance initially, but relented in a heap of emotion.

"There was no choice, Maddie Pearl," Sal whispered into her ear. "There just wasn't any other choice."

"I need to sit," said the girl who had just learned brother had been killed because of her.

Sal helped Maddie Pearl into the front passenger seat. She sat back, took several deep breaths, retched but did not vomit, and then slowly, surely started inhaling and exhaling at close to a normal rhythm. As at least some portion of her resolve returned, she stared straight ahead out the windshield toward the barren field and asked, "Tell me what happened to him. I need to know."

"You don't want to know the—"

"TELL ME!"

Sal flinched, stood straight out from the car's doorframe, surveyed the dark horizon and sky above, and then continued.

"I guess you should know, so I'll tell you, but you can never, and I mean _**never**_, say anything of this again, to _**anybody**_. Do you understand me?"

Maddie Pearl's gaze turned away from the nothingness straight ahead and directly toward Sal, her eyes like two laser beams in the night. "I understand."

Sal took a moment for emphasis and to compose his thoughts, not wanting to say too much but recognizing that too little was not an option.

"I'm not going to tell you who. You don't need to know who, and even if you thought you did I still wouldn't tell you. I'm not going to put anybody else's life at risk. Enough bad has happened to enough people already."

Maddie Pearl stared noncommittally at Sal, expecting more... much more.

"Somebody... let's just say 'somebody,' went back and found Luke on the path. He was still knocked out, from Nomita's rock, but very much alive. Well... this somebody—how do I say this? He... ugh... I mean this somebody, well... this *person* finished the job."

Maddie Pearl's tears streamed down her face, but she was determined to know, so she piped in, "What do you mean, 'finished the job'?"

"Sure you want to know?"

"I'm getting tired of begging, Sallerhead, tell me! NOW!"

"Hacked him into little pieces with an axe, and fed him to the livestock down on Farmer Hunt's land."

Maddie Pearl fainted hitting her head slightly on the dashboard! Sal rushed to the doorway, pulled her back upright in the seat, and lightly slapped Maddie Pearl on the face, to no avail. He frantically looked around, and noticed the Mason jar that held the horse water from the "*Green Book* approved" restaurant down the road. He grabbed it, unscrewed the lid, and gently poured what little was left onto Maddie Pearl's face. She roused, but not enough, so he began again with gentle slaps, saying continuously, "Maddie Pearl! Maddie Pearl! Wake up, Maddie Pearl! It's me, Sal. Come on, wake up!"

She turned, groaned, opened her eyes, and vomited all over the formerly pristine clean, almost brand new Plymouth. Sal took hold and gently urged her out of the vehicle and onto the ground. He took off his shirt and wrapped it around her, then lay beside and held Maddie Pearl's full body to generate warmth and provide comfort in the only way he could think to do. For a few minutes that seemed like lifetimes, Maddie Pearl slowly revived. Sal didn't let go, but kept holding her while singing "Amazing Grace" softly, gently, beautifully, because it was the only thing that came to mind and seemed to make sense under the circumstances.

Maddie Pearl finally regained sufficiently to pull away from him slightly, and sit upright.

"Tell me this isn't true. Tell me it's just a long, bad dream."

"Shhh," Sal cooed. "Just relax. It's okay. Everything's okay."

Several seconds passed. Again—as if on cue—the forest symphony began anew. First the screech owl, then some wild birds

no doubt awakened by the excitement, and finally most everybody else. In a strange, rough way, the cantata made the world less awful somehow.

Nothing was *better*, per se; perhaps nothing ever would be better. But life now seemed likely to go on, and the sun likely would rise again tomorrow, and Maddie Pearl and Sal were going to survive this night, and thank God—or goodness or Mother Nature or whatever—that we have these singing creatures and this beautiful earth and these wonderful, barren, dying farms to hide from bigots and share our secrets and figure out what happened and how we're going to keep going from here.

# Chapter 17

Hog had played the ace of spades, and lost, but his trouble began long before Maddie Pearl survived and Luke went missing. He'd been dealt a good hand years before, or so it seemed at the time. More than sufficient acres with a well, barn, house, and arable fields, and all he had to do was pay rent to keep it going. What could go wrong? He could always use more help, but at least Hog had four strong boys. Mama and Maddie Pearl were hungry mouths to feed and provided precious little in return, but could cook and take care of the basics. And with cash crops like tobacco and cotton, the sky was the limit.

Then came the Depression.

America's economic calamity didn't impact lowly farmers in rural states... initially. Hogs were not Wall Street investors. And so long as local farm supplies extended credit and landlords forgave occasional late payments, banks were as relevant as English cricket scores. But the butterfly effect is real. The little tycoon arms flapping as the financially ruined jumped out Wall Street windows stirred the atmospherics. The reverberations reached eastern North Carolina in due course.

With less money to spend, fewer shirts and cigarettes were purchased. The resultant glut of cotton and tobacco drove down commodity prices, narrowing profit margins. This was a survivable tide, just a normal supply and demand ebb and flow. But it persisted into 1931, then 1932, and the profits got squeezed ever more. Fortunately, an election rolled around, and thank goodness Franklin Delano Roosevelt had a New Deal, and the future looked bright, for some.

But FDR's safety net only captured the unemployed penniless. The typical farmer was neither. So while many among the masses began building roads and bridges (WPA), national and state parks (CCC), or widgets in factories (CWA), farmers languished. It wasn't until 1937 that the Farm Security

Administration was created, a too little too late afterthought famous today for its pictures chronicling the pitiful plight of farmers left behind. There were other programs, of course—there always are with government—but the Depression cut a muddy rut through agricultural America, including Webster County.

Hog's plight may have been avoidable but for three problems: his well was unreliable, foreman Luke was gone, and his fields were depleted. This third thorn was the prickliest. King Cotton and the golden leaf provided top profits, but each eats richly from the soil, too richly. With neither proper crop rotation (why grow anything else when these are so profitable) nor sufficient fertilization (who can afford fertilizer—there's a Depression on), his once bountiful fields had become unsustainable, barren hardscrabble.

The neighboring African Americans were sustenance farmers, growing mostly corn, sweet potatoes, squash, cucumbers, cabbage, and occasionally cantaloupe and watermelon. With young Walter Jefferson's awareness of nutrient depletion, no predominate cash crop inhibiting rotation, and produce far less soil taxing, sustainability was maintained. Through their deep well to fresh water and daily dedication removing rocks, stumps, gullies and the like, *Darkie*-land was aptly named with its prime fields of rich, arable, black soil.

And Hog wanted it all, for himself.

Had the plan played out, he'd be raping that land already. But in some mysterious way Hog would never discover, Luke had screwed the pooch and, evidently, run away in shame. His master plan in shambles, Hog had been desperate for weeks, and not just about the money and farm.

His slow pay had damaged relations with Boss Lee, but not irreparably. The common knowledge of Maddie Pearl's relations with the "nigras" had done far more harm. Unless Hog did something about it, and fast, he'd lose his standing among the good ol' boys. That was imminently more dangerous than missing a payment or so.

And so he came up with the plan, and it was perfect. In one fell swoop, he'd rid himself of the daughter he never wanted, chase off the darkies down the path, take over their property—and deep well, get his finances back in order, and maybe even climb the

Klan chain of command to Wizard or even Warlock. And all it required was for Luke—his best and least stupid—to strike the match; and the insipid son-of-a-whore couldn't even do that right!

In the aftermath of his son's failure, Hog's nightly meanderings started as a search for answers. He wanted to know where was Luke? And what happened to Maddie Pearl? And where was that goddamn nigger boy she liked so much? His unsuccessful investigation became an outlet for drunken tirades, first about the unfairness of it all but then, after a time, about the Klan itself.

Somehow in his twisted, booze-soaked noggin, Hog had become convinced that his problems were the Klan's fault, that "Boss Lee wasn't controlling dem nigras like he should," that if only Lee would "run off those Darkieland jigs" Hog would be back in business. And more than once he swore, "Just you wait. I'm a-gonna take over this here Klavern some day, and when I do you won't be seein' no fuckin' nigger farms around here, that's for God damn sure!"

In his sloshed stupidity, he'd never imagined his big words filtering back in small whispers to the one person on whom his whole world depended. But when Boss Lee said something to Mama about the Klan, that possibility raced through Hog's slow mind like lightning. Being past due with nutrient dead fields and unkempt structures was survivable; having a "nigger loving" daughter he couldn't control was unforgiveable; threatening to take down Boss Lee himself... *that* was a death sentence, literally.

With such thoughts polluting his mind amid smacks to Mama's face, a wild inspiration flit through his thick skull like squeaked static on a shortwave radio late at night: "the injun Bible!" Within seconds he had found it, and hope was returned!

It was so simple, so easy. Why hadn't he thought of it sooner? The damn book was nothing, to him; but *out there*, among people with too much money, it was worth a fortune. He'd present the treasure to the great man directly, on bended knee if necessary, and even beg forgiveness for his sins. He'd pledge allegiance to the man, and blame his big-mouthed rumblings on liquor and desperation. He'd even volunteer to quit the Klan, if that's what Boss Lee wanted.

And in return he'd simply ask for the farm. Surely the Bible was worth more than the property and everything on it, much much more. He'd be a landowner, a "made man," a person of substance. He'd be gentrified, and that surely would trump the foolish daughter too ignorant to know right from wrong, and all would be forgiven, and his place would be secured, if not in the Klan at least in the community, and life would be better than ever.

And to think that all along he had this magic ticket right there under his bed—every night—just sitting there in his wretched wife's old wooden box!

*          *          *

While Maddie Pearl was learning why brother Luke had been murdered after stabbing her repeatedly in the vagina with a stubby stick, her drunken father with a small book and big dreams was pulling up to a closed gas station in a Ford truck that he had browbeaten from Farmer Hunt.

The dirty, small, wooden interior was polluted with a cloud of smoggy tobacco smoke through which Hog could see the regulars: all white, all men, all snakelike in their cheap dirty clothes with their dry craggy faces fronting cold reptilian minds. On the shelves were cans of oil and hair grease, cigarette packs arranged in no particular order, a smattering of tins of this and that, and nondescript parts to repair old cars built long ago on the great Highland Park assembly lines some 769 miles away.

In the only comfortable seat in the far corner, next to a potbelly stove that was glowing with old coals, sat Boss Lee.

Hog didn't see him at first, but could sense his presence. He tread cautiously across the room to avoid doing anything particularly stupid, like the night he tripped on a board thereby plunking both hands into the pickle barrel trying to catch himself. Thank goodness Boss Lee was away, up to mischief no doubt with some underage girl or recalcitrant nigra.

No one said anything as Hog approached the exalted one. They knew the basics: Hog wasn't paying; the property wasn't being tended; Hog's girl was a nigger-loving slut; and Hog had threatened Boss Lee himself—repeatedly. At issue wasn't whether

Hog was in deep shit; at issue was what Boss Lee would do about it.

The answer came soon enough.

Hog reached the corner, stopped, and assumed incorrectly that Boss Lee would speak first. But the burden wasn't on the great man, so he sat, and scowled, and waited, and the acid in Hog's gut kept pumping and burning and gurgling.

Somewhat in exasperation, Hog finally initiated, "Evening, sir."

Boss Lee just sat, impassively, and glared at this huge human piece of shit now so little before him.

"Got your money, sir," sputtered Hog ultra nervously. "I mean, your payment, right here, just like you asked."

Boss Lee continued to sit, without blinking, and glared. The cold, dark eyes pierced Hog's soul. The fat man felt his bowels loosen ever so slightly, and the shine from earlier started eating the inner lining of his stomach like palmetto bugs chewing a rotten pumpkin's guts.

Hog pulled out the second edition 1686 *Eliot's Indian Bible* with a dedication to Governor Boyle, the very Bible his wife had brought to the marriage as her dowry, the one and only non-living thing in this world Mama ever truly cherished, or ever would cherish.

"Here, I brought this, for you," Hog said meekly as he handed up the rare treasure.

Boss Lee didn't extend his hand; he didn't even look at the Bible initially. Instead, the king upon the corner throne kept his regal gaze squarely on Hog.

Finally, the exalted spoke. "What the fuck is this?"

"It's a Bible, sir, an old Bible. It goes back to the sixteen hundreds or something, I think."

Boss Lee glanced superficially at the first few pages. "What *is* this piece of crap? Ain't even in English."

Hog had never even glanced at the thing. He'd never really glanced much at their King James Bible either. Typical of so many then and today, he was a staunch Christian, attended church every Sunday, and was quick to play the Jesus card whenever some verse or Commandment served his purpose. But had he ever read the

source material, the tome setting forth all that is right and mighty and just and holy? Hell no.

Boss Lee likewise had fuzzy ideas on morality borne from a lifetime of scant reading and incuriosity. He believed firmly, but really had no idea what he actually "believed." He also knew nothing of collectibles, biblical or not, and thus had no appreciation just how valuable was this thing before him. He cared about cash, or perhaps a night with a redheaded daughter. Neither was being offered, but it didn't matter anyway.

Lee had reached the end of his rope with Hog. The fat man was always late, drunk, and a pain in the ass. And his family was no better, especially that coon-loving daughter of his. And then there was the property—Lee property—with the dilapidated structures Hog had done nothing to maintain and the once richly fertile acres Hog had done everything to ruin. But most importantly, there was the Klan thing, the rumor that Hog had become... *ambitious*. That would not be tolerated—could not be tolerated—no matter what.

The great man casually tossed the collectible into the coals immediately prompting a small fire as the priceless pages burned to nothingness.

With small rivulets of smoke signaling the fat man's fate, Boss Lee peered directly into Hog's soul with eyes redder than the burning Bible. "I'm not gonna kill you, cause I feel sorry for that pitiful woman of yours, but if I ever catch you in these parts again, I'll string your fat ass up from the tallest fuckin' tree in Webster County."

The man in charge turned away from the loser before him, casually surveyed his minions, and unemotionally said, "Get your torches, boys. We got some burnin' to do... tonight."

# Chapter 18

While Hog's dreams of financial salvation were burning in a potbelly stove, Maddie Pearl and Sal were heading toward Webster County in a Plymouth with vomit stains on the front seat. In the twenty minutes or so since leaving the back of an abandoned tobacco barn on a once flourishing farm now dead, no words had been spoken. Maddie Pearl remained in the back, cowering from fear of being seen with a black man in a new car that would be super suspicious indeed. But there was virtually no traffic and the area was heavily rural, so she cheated some by peeking her head up enough to watch the world travel by. Sal noticed and frowned; Maddie Pearl caught the look in the rearview mirror.

"You know what," she said aggressively. "I've just about had it with all this hiding in the back seat business!"

"But—"

"But nothing! I had to squat back here in this tiny space all day, and you never came or even told me what was going on. And I'm pretty tired of it, *Sallerhead.*"

His name oozed from her lips with an intentional tinge of sarcastic denigration. Ordinarily, she preferred "Sal," partly because it was easier but more so since "Sallerhead" sounded somewhat racist. She never saw him as black, any more than she considered Nomita to be any different from herself. Nevertheless, if he acted like an ass, black or white, she'd treat him accordingly.

"Look," he said with some exasperation. "You don't know what's going on—"

"Oh I know plenty," she cut in.

"No, Maddie Pearl. You don't. And before you interrupt me again, let me explain the facts of life to you."

She harrumphed while defiantly stretching up to be fully visible to any passing vehicle, fore or aft.

"It's like this, Maddie Pearl. Negroes and pretty young white girls just don't go driving around the countryside at night, especially in a shiny new car. They just don't."

"Well why the—"

"Let me finish, dammit! You don't seem to understand, but you've got the kind of looks people notice. Now I'm not trying to pump any sunshine up your skirt, but you're a tall, beautiful young woman—that's right, *woman*—and with that red hair and all, well, people just naturally notice you... especially since you're white. Now if you were some dumpy old hag or whatever, or black, nobody'd give a rat's ass, but when somebody like you goes out and about, with a black man no less, well... it attracts attention."

"Yeah yeah yeah... so...?"

"So, somebody sees us out and about, in a new car, at night? They're going to get suspicious. Like... real God damn suspicious. And they're gonna ask questions, or they're gonna call the cops and say something like, '*I just saw some nigger with a pretty white girl*,' and trust me... that would make anybody around these parts wonder why in the world. And they ain't gonna give me the benefit of the doubt. They're going to assume you were kidnapped or I was takin' you out somewhere to rape you or even worse, and before we know it I'm in jail and I haven't done a damn thing, not one damn thing!"

"You are so full of it. All we gotta do is tell 'em the truth."

"Oh *really*... and exactly what is the truth?"

She ducked slightly, more by habit than intention, at an oncoming car. Once it passed, she answered. "The truth is I was hurt and you helped me and now you're taking me back home. Simple."

"And you think *that* bullshit's gonna flush... here... in Crackerland? Like I said. You don't have a clue."

"Yes I—"

"So why am I helping? Where are your parents? Why did I take you almost two hundred miles away? Why aren't you at that place in Tuck with the doctor there? Whose car is this? Why are we driving some white guy's car? How do we explain that? I could go on and on, but trust me... they'd take one look at you, and they'd put one and one together and get... I don't know... fifteen. '*I stole the car*' they'd say, and '*kidnapped you*,' and now I'm takin'

you off to some shack somewhere, or behind some barn just like where we were a little while ago, where I'm gonna have my way until the cows come home. That's what they'd say, and I'd be lucky as hell if they didn't just lynch me right then and there! Just like they lynched my father, in case you don't believe me!"

The last sentence struck Maddie Pearl, hard. For the first time in their adventure since leaving the Victorian house with the doctor and nurse and foul smelling ether, reality hit the budding young woman. Up until now, it'd been mostly a painful inconvenience mixed with the best food she'd ever eaten, the most comfortable "bed," and blue-eyed David "Doctor Dreamy" Hodge. Now it was real, too real, and down right scary. She ducked back down to avoid detection.

"Okay. I hear ya. I do... but what *do* we do?"

"Whatta ya mean?"

"I mean... what do we do if, you know, somebody sees us?"

"I've been worried about that ever since we took you out of the field hospital and put you in the back of this car. Truth is, we'd have to lie, but I haven't come up with a good story... at least not yet."

Maddie Pearl stretched out on the bench seat and stared at the cloth covered Plymouth ceiling above. "Well... if I were one of them, and I saw us, I'd wonder why you were driving instead of me, why I'm in the back seat, and how we came to be in possession of this brand new car. I guess the night part—that we're out at night—would be a good question too, to me at least."

"Yeah I've been thinkin' along the same lines."

"Couldn't we tell 'em we're just friends takin' a trip somewhere, just like anybody else?"

"Black men and white women aren't 'friends,' not after sundown, and trip... where are we going on some trip together? Doesn't make sense."

Somewhat frustrated with his summary dismissal of her idea, Maddie Pearl demanded, "Okay then. So what have *you* come up with?"

He noticed headlights far behind them, but getting closer. He wasn't overly worried, yet, but it's mere presence brought home the seriousness of their discussion.

"How about this," he began. "What if we say that I'm your driver, like I'm being paid to drive you, by your daddy, and that this is his car?"

"But my daddy's poorer than a field rat. He could never afford a car like—"

"They wouldn't know that. For all they know, he's the almighty governor of the entire state."

"So why're you driving me? Where are we going in the middle of the night?"

The approaching car reached Sal's rear bumper, honked, and then passed them by. It was a nonevent, a routine pass, but Sal's heart skipped a beat nevertheless.

"All right then... we could tell 'em... *truthfully*, that it's Doc's car, and that *Doc*'s the one paying me, not your pa."

"And why would Doc do that?"

"Because... well... I know! Because he's your doctor, and he needs to get you to... to... Raleigh, the state capital, for special treatments, and we could say it's like an emergency or something, and you need to get there ASAP!"

"ASAP? What does that mean?"

"It's just an Army thing. Means as soon as possible."

Maddie Pearl thought through the elaborate lie. A sour expression came across her face involuntarily. "I still can't believe this. I mean... you haven't done one thing wrong, and neither have I. Here we are, in a car that our friend loaned us, driving down the road just like we're supposed to do, at the right speed and all, and minding our own business. And just because it's nighttime, and you're a negro and I'm a white girl, we have to come up with all this... this stuff. It just isn't right!"

"Welcome to my world," replied Sal, with a degree of resignation. "It's all I can do sometimes to keep from just screaming at the top of my lungs, but what good'll it do? So I just keep on keeping on... just like everybody else... right here in the land of the free and home of the brave."

"Land of the what?" said Maddie Pearl, exposing the sad fact that she'd never heard the national anthem.

Sal ignored the question and Maddie Pearl let it slide. She was too lost in anger and frustration to care about the details. Within a minute, road noise reemerged in their silence as each

repaired to their upset thoughts. Sal had learned to live with the inequities long ago. He *had* to, just as his people before had been forced to do since leaving Africa in cages on dysentery infected rat ships. But Maddie Pearl was new to this game, this grotesque abomination wrought by ignorant men in an unwritten but strictly enforced caste system of *haves, have nots*, and *subhumans*. And the more she thought, the more she fumed; and the more she realized there wasn't a thing she could do to fix it, at least not yet, it infuriated her even more.

*         *         *

Maddie Pearl roused from a restless sleep in which she dreamed Sal was imprisoned. She kept pleading to let him out. With one hand, the cop kept lashing Sal with a whip. His other kept handing Maddie Pearl candy bars and cake against her wishes. "BUT I DON'T WANT THAT," she'd scream, to which the policeman kept answering, "But you deserve it, sweets for the sweet. You deserve it!"

"Fucking police," she said aloud, still halfway asleep, using a taboo word she'd never knowingly uttered in her short life.

"Huh?" replied Sal to the unsolicited, out-of-context statement. "What police?"

Not even realizing she'd said anything, Maddie Pearl demurred. "Huh? Wha... Oh nothing. Just some stupid dream."

While Sal gave her a look in the rearview mirror, they passed an old billboard barely visible in the headlights with a sexy girl pointing: *The Army Needs You!*

"You never did tell me about the Army," Maddie Pearl said. She remained ultra wary of any possible onlookers, but couldn't resist perching her sweet face slightly above the top of the front bench seat like a little kid.

"Oh yeah, I forgot. So... what do you want to know?"

"Just tell me about it... how you joined, what you do, Doc... you know."

"Like I was about to say before, there really isn't much to it. Let's see... where did I leave off?"

"You were telling me about being in that shed, in that town—Tuck, and helping that Indian man."

"Oh yeah, okay. So anyway... Farmer Hunt turned out was a good man... still is... But he's the one who gave me the idea."

"How?"

"We were heading back to the diner one day... I keep calling it a diner, but it was really more like a store, but anyway. We had a pretty big load of corn, and we passed this sign, this billboard, and it had this girl on it kinda pointing at us."

"Did she have on a little Army suit, saying something like 'The Army Needs You'?"

"Yeah. It did. How'd you know?"

"We just passed a sign like that, maybe a minute ago."

"For real? I never saw it. Huh... I guess I'm tired-er than I thought. But anyhow, so we—Farmer Hunt and me—we passed this sign, and he said something like, 'Not a bad life, if you can get it.' I really wasn't thinking much about the sign, even though I had seen it too, so I asked him, and he started in with the military and how it's a good job and you can see the world and so on."

"How did he know?" Maddie Pearl asked. "Was he in the military or something?"

"I asked the same thing, and it turns out he had been in the Army infantry long ago, in the Great War, and he knew all about it and how it works and everything."

"You mentioned that war before," Maddie Pearl responded, "when we were talking about the field hospital."

"That's it," Sal said. "The one and the same. But anyway, so he was in that war and then when it was over he stayed in... you know... stayed in the military, for a few years, and he said it was pretty good, even though they gave the bad jobs to people like him, being an Indian and all. But he said even with that it still was better than most other jobs around, and at least it had steady pay."

"So he talked you into it?" asked Maddie Pearl.

"Well like I said before, there wasn't a whole lot to the story. My options seemed about down to nothing, since I couldn't go back to the farm anymore, and nobody was going to hire me to do anything else, at least not anything worth doing, so I figured 'why not?'"

"So like I just said, you joined just like that?"

"Pretty much. I went to Belton, and—"

"Belton? Where's that?" asked Maddie Pearl, further exposing her total ignorance of much beyond her family, farm, immediate friends, and church.

"Oh that's a town about twenty, maybe twenty-five miles from Tuck. It's bigger and, since it has a college there with guys our age that might be interested in the military, they've got what they call a recruiting station. Farmer Hunt told me about it, and he even drove me there, to enlist."

"All right, I'm listening. What about Doc and Fort Bragg and that field hospital and all?"

"You might be the most impatient person I've ever known," Sal retorted affectionately. "If you weren't so damn smart, maybe you'd quit getting ahead of me and let me tell my story!"

Maddie Pearl laughed, and then ducked down low as a car—a Buick—passed by from the opposite direction. Both Sal and Maddie Pearl looked back nervously to make sure it wasn't turning around. It wasn't, so Sal continued.

"What they do when you join up is send you off to what they call 'boot camp.' It's where they teach you all about being a soldier, except the boot camp for negroes ain't the same as white man boot camp. The whites have their own place, and I hear it's okay, although the work is hard, and they learn all about guns and marching and rules and what they like to call 'esprit de corps.'"

"Spray the what?"

"Esprit de corps. It just means teaching everybody to work together without any of that 'each man for himself' stuff."

Maddie Pearl thought about the concept, and then observed. "It sounds like on the farm, when like we have to get something done because the sun's going down or storm's comin' and everybody's got to get going, even Mama and me. Is it like that?"

"Yes. Exactly. It's like everybody working together for everybody's benefit. And in the Army, that's like the law, and you got to work together, or they'll call you out for it, big time."

"So why didn't you have to do that... what did you call it?"

"Boot camp?"

"Yeah, boot camp. What did you do instead?"

"Well that's where Captain David Hodge comes in, or 'Doc' to you."

"Finally," Maddie Pearl said, in mock exasperation.

"The negroes don't get any formal training or anything. They figure none of us are smart enough to hold a gun and march at the same time. So they assign us to anybody who will take us, and then we learn how to do something, on the job. In fact, that's what they call it."

"What?"

"OJT, or on the job training. And so that's what ended up happening to me. Doc needed somebody at the hospital to help with carrying out the vomit buckets and cleaning up and so forth, so he put in for a trainee and I got assigned."

"So... *that*'s what you do? Clean out vomit?"

"That's why I got put there, and that was all Doc expected, at first at least. But somehow, we just hit it off, right from the first day. And I guess he started to figure out that I was... you know... smart enough to do some things beyond the bucket brigade. One thing led to another and, well, for all intents and purposes we both were running that little hospital."

"But he's a doctor and everything. You don't know anything about doctoring, do you?"

"Funny you should say that. Turns out, he's not a doctor at all. He went to college. In fact, he went to that little college in Belton I was tellin' you about. But he learned how to be a teacher there. English. He didn't learn squat about cuts and bruises and food poisoning and the like. Not one damn thing."

Maddie Pearl was perplexed. "But he's called 'Doc,' and he treats patients and everything?"

"He's a medic, which in the Army just means that he's a guy that's had a tiny bit of medical training and then is sent out to deal with minor things, like people throwing up from bad food." Sal clarified, "Now don't get me wrong, he's smart as a whip, and he cares for people too, a lot, but he doesn't know much of anything about medicine once he gets beyond putting in a few stitches or wrapping a splint around an arm."

"So what happens when somebody comes in, like me, with real sickness or injuries?"

"There's a real doctor on base, several of 'em, but they don't work the field hospital, not unless they have no choice, and they usually find ways to choose to stay away. But you remember

that specialist that came in and checked on you, on about the second day or so you were here?"

Maddie Pearl had been in such a fog that she'd forgotten, but Sal's question jogged her memory. "Oh yeah. I remember, sorta. He said I probably still could have babies, some day."

"Well, he was a real doctor, and there are others who come around if a special case comes up, like with you. And he had looked at you, and so had another doctor, just a regular doctor, but that was on the first day you arrived and you were so tired and ill and all that I'm sure you don't remember him."

Maddie Pearl had a vague memory of somebody poking around, but at the time thought it was all part of her ongoing dream and hadn't given it any mind, until now.

"So what did he do?"

"He didn't really *do* anything. He just looked at ya, pretty close like, especially down there, and said you needed to see a specialist, which is what led to that other guy coming by the next day. Oh yeah... he also said that—except for down there which he didn't really know how to deal with—he thought you were going to be fine. Just needed a lot of rest and healthy food, not that Army rot."

"So that's why I kept getting the outside fancy food, huh?"

"Yep. And because Doc, the nurse and I didn't want to eat the base crap either."

Another car approached from behind. Sal admonished Maddie Pearl to "get down," which she did. The car followed them for a couple of miles.

"Now Maddie Pearl, I don't know who this is or what he wants. But if he stops us, like if he's a cop or something, you're going to need to do all the talking, not me. Got it?"

"Me? Really?" asked Maddie Pearl nervously.

"And listen now, let's just stick to the story, you know, like we were talking about."

Maddie Pearl had been thinking about that story, both consciously and—apparently—while asleep. The details still seemed mushy, borderline unbelievable really, but the mere thought of even having to concoct such nonsense still infuriated the temperamental redhead. It didn't help, either, that she'd been cooped up all day and into the night because somebody,

somewhere, might be too damn ignorant to understand that yes, in fact, this *was* a friend's car and yes, in fact, they *had* borrowed it with his permission and yes, truthfully, the large black man driving *was* doing the young white girl a favor. Every time she considered their totally idiotic plight necessitated by such evil ignorance, her blood pressure rose ever so slightly more.

But all of that had been a low boil until this car had come up and the raw nerves were tweaked anew. Now her angry blood was near spurting from her ears.

"What are you going to say?" she demanded, to make sure they coordinated this ridiculous ruse.

"I'm not saying anything other than 'yes sir' and 'no sir' and 'thank you, sir.'"

"That's it? Why?"

"Because that's just how it is, Maddie Pearl... The..."

She noticed a flashing red light envelope the Plymouth.

"Goddammit!" Sal growled.

She felt the car suddenly slow upon Sal's braking. "Damn red light. We're being stopped."

Maddie Pearl popped up in her seat, straightened her hair and clothes as well as she could, cleared her throat, and prepared for battle. Her eyes were practically red with rage, matching her strikingly beautiful hair.

As he pulled the new Plymouth over, Sal said sternly, "Don't mess around here, Maddie Pearl. This is serious. Stick to the story, ya hear?"

"Oh... don't you worry... don't you worry one bit. I'll stick to the story all right, I'll stick it right up this guy's rear end!"

Sal was more than a little shocked by her demeanor accented by this new predisposition to talk like a drunken sailor on Shanghai shore leave. But what could he do now, other than pray the cop had at least an ounce of sense—highly unlikely in the here and now.

The trooper, a big white man with a fat gut sticking out, belt stretched tight below, and an imposing gun strapped thereto like Sheriff Dillon in *Gunsmoke*, walked slowly, menacingly up to the Plymouth and approached Sal's window. He looked long and hard at Sal, surveyed the brand new car, then stuck his bulbous head into the window and glared at Maddie Pearl in the back seat.

"What do you think you're doing here, *boy?*" the trooper asked with total disdain dripping from his fat lips.

Before Sal could answer, Maddie Pearl from the back seat piped in directly, "Why are you stopping us?"

The trooper was taken aback slightly by her aggressive tone. ""Ma'am, I'm gonna need to see some—"

"You didn't answer my question! We have just as much a right to be on this here road as anybody, including you!"

"Well ma'am, I—"

"That driver there, <u>my</u> driver, he's my personal driver, and my daddy pays him good money to get me back and forth to that there base in Fort Driggs—to see my boyfriend!"

"Fort... *Driggs?* Don't you mean Fort—"

"DON'T YOU TELL ME WHAT I MEAN! YOU HEARD ME!"

The trooper looked at Sal as if to ask, "*Is she for real?*" Before anyone could get in a word edgewise, however, Maddie Pearl continued yelling.

"AND MY BOYFRIEND IS THE DOCTOR AT THAT BASE. YA HEAR? THE DOCTOR HIMSELF! AND HE'S OUT CURING PEOPLE OF ALL SORT OF DISEASES AND ALL, WHILE YOU'RE STOPPING US FOR JUST DRIVING DOWN THE ROAD MINDING OUR OWN BUSINESS?"

"Ma'am, I didn't mean to—"

"AND HERE I AM, SICK AS A DOG, AND THIS BOY HERE IS TAKIN' ME ALL THE WAY TO RAW TOWN, TO SEE A SPECIALIST—AND THAT'S THE CAPITAL OF THIS WHOLE STATE!

The trooper tried to interject, but Maddie Pearl wouldn't listen, and continued screaming uncontrollably about the law and the "HOME OF THE FREEZERS" and her daddy the "GOVERNOR HIMSELF" and "THE LAND OF THE CAVES" and so on.

Meanwhile, Sal cringed horribly with every ludicrous defense, knowing full well it'd be a night in jail, at a minimum, dishonorable discharge from the Army, and who knows what else.

The trooper finally had to back away from the window and catch his breath in the cool night air. He let her continue ranting on about one nonsensical thing after another, like how her

boyfriend was a "FAMOUS DOCTOR" and how her parents "OWNED HALF OF THE STATE–THE GOOD HALF" and "MY DRIVER HE'S A GOOD MAN AND A SOLDIER AND DEFENDING OUR COUNTRY, GOD BLESS IT!"

After a good minute—plus—of nonstop Maddie Pearlisms in a holy rage at the top of her lungs, the trooper leaned in the car, took a long hard look at poor Sal sitting there fully expecting to be put away for life or perhaps given the electric chair. Finally, the trooper took one last long look at Maddie Pearl, turned back to Sal, patted him on the shoulder, and said,

"Son, I'm not going to run you in." He took another look at ranting Maddie Pearl. "Lord knows... you've got enough trouble as it is."

He walked back to his vehicle, turned off the red light, hit the ignition, and drove on past the Plymouth giving one last, sad look of sincere concern to Sal as he sped away from the redheaded psycho as fast as he could.

# Chapter 19

After another hour or so, Sal and Maddie Pearl crossed the Webster County line and made way for the rural area in which both had been raised and from which both had escaped, at least temporarily. It had been only a few weeks since Maddie Pearl's departure, but no local knew her fate. Her sudden appearance surely would be a shock to one and all. As it turned out, Maddie Pearl was the shocked one.

"Can't get too close," said Sal as he maneuvered David "Doc" Hodge's Plymouth down the unpaved track leading from SR 1043 to the common path connecting all of Boss Lee's lands. Roughly two miles equidistant both from his home and hers, Sal stopped and said, "I'm gonna hide the car here, and then let's walk the rest of the way."

They exited the car, now parked behind a small grove of scraggly bushes, and proceeded on foot toward their respective destinies. At the tract Weyerhaeuser had timbered and close to the scene of the Fire Pit Incident from so long ago, the path forked, with Sal going left and Maddie Pearl right.

She turned back to Sal and asked, "When are we going to meet back up?"

It was a question Sal had hoped to avoid altogether. From the moment he'd "saved" Maddie Pearl from the large Victorian house in Tuck that the local doctor used as his "hospital" and home, Sal had considered many times but not resolved the core question of this entire exercise: what happens... after?

There were no good options.

He could ensure she never returned to this childhood home that Maddie Pearl quickly was realizing had no redeeming factors whatsoever. But that would not be fair to her. She had no ability to survive on the outside, and he neither had the resources nor the skin color to house, feed, and care for her. Besides, their relationship never had been like *that*. Each was extraordinarily

attractive and, at least until Luke's brutal beating, perfectly healthy with solid, open minds and clear thoughts of right, and wrong. But 1939 Webster County was not situate in a nation where people are judged by the content of their character instead of the color of their skin. Furthermore, any thought of any "relationship" between any white girl and any black man was reckless and stupid, particularly where Jim Crow still ruled firmly—without exceptions.

He had hoped that Maddie Pearl and Doc might hit it off. Doc was a winner, no doubt, and had a future. Furthermore, he could do a lot worse than Maddie Pearl. That option might have remained possible, until Field Hospital # 4 suddenly closed and Doc had been redeployed to California. At that very moment, in fact, Uncle Sam was transporting David "Doc" Hodge west. It had not been a joyous bon voyage.

"Once you take care of Maddie Pearl," Doc had said hurriedly while haphazardly throwing his every belonging into an oversized duffle bag, "sell the car and send me the money."

"Where do I—"

"It's a place called Mojave Anti-Aircraft Range, I think. Just send it to me care of there. I'll get it."

"How much should—"

"Get whatever you can. I dunno... five hundred, maybe six."

HONK HONK! The impatient sergeant driving the Army truck outside Field Hospital # 4 was growing angrier by the second.

"Look, just do what you can," said Doc as he slung the heavyweight bag over his shoulder and began running outside. "I gotta go."

And just like that, the man was gone; and just like that, any chance of Maddie Pearl and Doc evaporated like some mirage on a hot Mojave day.

With even the Doc option now vanished, Sal settled on the only logical course left: take Maddie Pearl home and let her sort it out.

She was extremely bright, if uneducated and unexposed to the real world, and had gotten by pretty well for seventeen years. With Luke now... *gone*, she was much safer than before. Hog was still around, of course, and No Mind Tate, but so was Mama. Furthermore, Maddie Pearl was now armed with the knowledge of

Hog's true intentions, and would be better prepared to deal with any problems he might spawn. It was imperfect, and risky, but better than the other impossibilities. As a precaution, Sal figured he could return from time to time to check on things, to ensure Maddie Pearl was getting along all right, just like he'd been doing with Nomita and his family.

Private Jefferson hadn't been reassigned to any new duty station, yet. Based on his limited military experience, Sal knew his Army future depended much on whether another officer retained him. If no one so opted, he'd be unpaid but technically still in the Army and fully beholden to Uncle Sam. Legally, therefore, he'd be unable to simply leave for home and take up where he left off in Darkieland. He wasn't too concerned, however, because the European hostilities—getting more serious by the day—practically guaranteed that a lot of soldiers would be shipped out just like Doc. If so, there'd be work to do. After all, they'd never abandon a base as big as Fort Bragg, and *somebody* had to stay behind and take care of the day-to-day.

So right or wrong, his plan was to take Maddie Pearl back to Webster County, hide the car, split up at the fork, circle back and make sure that Maddie Pearl got home okay, quickly check on Nomita, and then hustle to the Plymouth, head back to the alternative universe of Fayetteville, and leave Maddie Pearl behind without explanation. It was tough, but in the best interests of Maddie Pearl, and necessary.

But now she'd asked, and he'd never lie to her, and so he'd have to confront Maddie Pearl. And just as there were no good options, there were no good ways to explain what he had chosen, so Sal opted to hit the nail head on.

"Maddie Pearl, we're not meeting back up."

"What?"

"I'm leaving you here, and I'm going back to Fayetteville. Tonight."

The child called Maddie Pearl had expired on this same path a few weeks before when a sibling jabbed a stick into her body over and over again. The woman reborn no longer could be told what to do, how to do it, and when... especially by men who always think they know what's best for her when they don't have a clue! It was that same new woman who emerged just an hour or so ago

when some hick cop tried to tell her what was what, and it was that same new woman who stood now before this strong, wonderfully gifted but misguided man on a path that leads... nowhere.

"If you think I'm going to live in that shack one more minute, you are deeply mistaken," Maddie Pearl stated in no uncertain terms.

"Maddie Pearl, it's best for—"

"NO! It's not best for me, or anyone else. I will NOT be staying there! You WILL be taking me back, tonight! And THAT's THAT!"

Once again, Maddie Pearl's newfound assertiveness startled the man. He admired her spunk but despised her insistence on a plan that could not—would not—work.

"Maddie Pearl, I can't. I just... well... I just can't."

"You CAN, and you WILL!"

Sal was becoming self-conscious of the volume that kept increasing with each new Maddie Pearlian demand. He looked around checking to see whether anyone might have noticed and be on the way to investigate. He motioned Maddie Pearl back off the path near some bushes, and continued.

"I've got nowhere to keep you, now that the hospital is closed. I don't even know where *I'm* supposed to be staying, since I usually spent the night there."

"I'll stay with Doc. He'll take me in. He'll take both of us in."

Maddie Pearl didn't know, yet, that Doc was gone and never to be seen again. But even if Doc were still around, Maddie Pearl's suggestion was impossible. Doc had a room in a boarding house occupied by as many as a dozen other soldiers... white soldiers... white male soldiers. Successfully sneaking in a large negro man and a tall Caucasian girl with vibrant red hair was like sneaking a rhinoceros and giraffe into ballet class.

"Doc's gone, Maddie Pearl. He got assigned, to a place called California."

The revelation more than stunned Maddie Pearl, but on this night of stunning news she had become more than a little hardened. After all, Doc's redeployment was child's play compared to learning that her brother had been axed, dismembered, and fed to pigs, mules, cows, and probably coyotes.

If she could handle that morsel, and she had, then almost nothing could pierce her fierce determination to get past the past and move on to what must become of her life.

"So Doc's gone. So what? I can work. I can do things. I'll make my own way. You don't have to take care of me, Mister Jefferson. I'm perfectly capable of taking care of myself!"

Sal's smirk inflamed Maddie Pearl.

"NOW LISTEN HERE! YOU'RE TAKING ME BACK, AND THAT'S FINAL!"

He knew the game was lost. His prodigious mind immediately moved on from failed Plan A to their next course. He remained highly dubious, but she clearly was giving him no choice, and he relented.

"All right... I'll tell ya what. Let's do this. How about if we go, *together*, to your place first. I'll hide, but watch you walk up. You go in, see everybody, and all that. It's late and you'll be waking them up, for sure, but they'll be shocked to see you and I suspect you'll need an hour or two... you know... to explain and all, what's been going on. And don't dare tell them too much. They don't need to know about me and Doc and Fayetteville and everything else. Just make up something about all that. Some stranger in Tuck helped you, or something like that. At some point, you'll go to bed, just like you used to do. When everybody's settled back down, sneak out and catch back up with me. How does that sound?"

Maddie Pearl thought about the proposal. It made sense, more or less, but she was worried about being able to sneak out when everybody slept so closely together. And she wasn't sure whether it would take an "hour or two" like Sal thought, or much longer. If nothing else, Mama would want to talk and rehash and discuss for who knows how long?

Maddie Pearl went over her concerns with Sal. He thought about it, and replied, "Yeah, you might be right. Tell you what... let's do this instead. I'll go with you, and just make sure you get in okay. Then I'll head over to see Nomita. I've done that a few times now, and it never takes more than an hour or so. When I'm done, I'll go back to the Plymouth and just wait for you."

Maddie Pearl considered the proposal, then said reluctantly, "I don't like it, cause I doubt I can get out that fast, but I guess it's the best we can do."

Maddie Pearl turned right down the path toward home. She pivoted, "You coming?" Sal noticed this new, assertive, confident Maddie Pearl, and he liked it, very much, even though it had ruined his plans and probably changed his life for the worse.

They walked the short distance in silence. Along the path, Maddie Pearl noticed that things looked... *different.* For this time of year, the fields didn't appear quite right. It was dark, and she wasn't certain, but the glimpses were disquieting. Sal noticed it too, but didn't say anything. Nomita had hinted that Maddie Pearl's kin hadn't been doing too well since she and Luke had gone, but this looked worse than he expected. "*What have Hog and No Mind been doing? They know better than this,*" thought Sal as they proceeded.

Upon reaching the clearing at the family shanty home, Maddie Pearl and Sal both were aghast. It looked totally abandoned. Nothing had been tended for... what... maybe weeks. Instead of safely sleeping in their pen, the chickens were gone. The barn door was open, and Corncake, the one surviving mule after No Mind's inattention to barn door etiquette ensured the death of Skeet, was nowhere to be seen. The porch, which Mama kept swept religiously, was unkempt.

Maddie Pearl turned to Sal and said, "What the hell?"

He shrugged in response as if to say, "*I don't know.*"

Sal held back, behind the barn, and watched as Maddie Pearl approached the house. She opened the door, and called out, "Hello? Hello? It's Maddie Pearl. I'm back."

There was no response. Sal could make out Maddie Pearl wandering further into the structure. He heard her again, louder, "MAMA? PA? ANYBODY HOME?"

Again, nothing was heard, just the muffled sounds of night creatures that talk in darkness to no one in particular.

She came back out and walked up to Sal emerging from his hiding place. "What in the world? Where did they go?"

Before Sal could answer, the unmistakable sound of a vehicle could be heard. They turned to see the headlights of at least two trucks careening down the path directly toward the house... and them! They also could hear what sounded like drunken hoots from male voices.

"Come on!" Sal grabbed Maddie Pearl and they ran as fast as they could in the opposite direction. They entered the woods in full gallop and hid behind an old tree that had fallen during a hurricane some three years ago and never been cleared even though Hog had told Tate to do so maybe ten times. They watched in horrified silence as the two old pickups screeched to a halt in front and several men in white sheets and hoods sprung forth with torches in hand and raced to the house! Screaming and hollering for all to hear, they broke every window and flung their torches therein. One bold soul kicked down the front door and poured gasoline inside, igniting a blast of flames and conflagration. A couple headed, more like staggered, to the barn and within seconds it too was fully engulfed.

The glow lit the sky bringing near daylight to the dark night scene. Suddenly, Maddie Pearl and Sal were ensconced in brightness and visibly vulnerable. With not a word spoken, they jolted from behind the hurricane tree and raced away into the woods uncertain of where they were heading but certainly getting away from there.

In time they reached a safe stopping point and paused to catch their breath and regroup. Without thinking, they hugged each other, tightly, and didn't let go for what seemed like minutes. Maddie Pearl was too shocked to cry; Sal was too concerned to let go; and they stood there, together, and commiserated without uttering a syllable. It was not a romantic embrace, but there was love, and each knew it, instinctively, innately, deeply.

Maddie Pearl finally, reluctantly broke away, and asked, "Where are we?"

"We're about a half mile or so away from your place... er... I guess what used to be your place, and the same distance from Nomita."

"So you know how to get there, you know, from here?"

"Oh yeah. This isn't the first time I've been in these woods. Let's go, in case that liquor starts telling those rednecks to burn up some negroes too!"

Sal trudged knowingly through the thicket and trees and weeds and wet areas like a bloodhound on the scent. It seemed to her like they were going in circles, but Maddie Pearl had faith in Sal and chose not to say anything. Her thoughts were elsewhere

anyway, back home, back to the only place she ever had known. *"What is going on? Why? What did Pa do this time? Or Tate?"* It would be a long time before she got any answers.

# Chapter 20

Maddie Pearl awoke with a start to Sallerhead, crouched beside her, gently shaking her from slumber in a cot in abandoned Field Hospital # 4 on the Fort Bragg Base of the United States Army situate in Fayetteville, North Carolina. Except for the blaze at her former homestead, she remembered precious little of the night before. The whirlwind began with a race through thick woodland to Darkieland to the Plymouth to the highway to here. They had not seen Nomita, but Sal had managed to warn Pickles of what had transpired. Maddie Pearl slept most of the drive, and only roused when Sal snuck them both into the hospital using the key on the lock that the Army had neglected to change. It was a lucky break, because they had nowhere else to go, and the heavy rain during the muggy drive back would have rendered the car an insufferable steam bath. But it was only temporary, and hide they must, because any discovery would jeopardize everything.

But what was "everything?" What *did* they have to lose?

Maddie Pearl was now abandoned by her own family, or so it clearly seemed. She had no idea where they had gone, or why the only home she ever had known was burned to the ground by two truckloads of rabble-rousing hoodheads. She had no job, no skills, no prospects, and a brain full of Bible verses and Jesus quotes which perhaps were nice to know but utterly worthless in pre-WWII USA. In God we may trust, but American stores, businesses, banks, and restaurants trade in hard cash—only—and Maddie Pearl had none.

Sal's situation, his "everything," was equally precarious. He was considered a "private" in the Army, but for all intents and purposes was little more than a day-to-day laborer. Without David "Doc" Hodge, Walter Carver Jefferson was a jobless soldier. Unless someone else took him on, unemployment would remain his unpaid military occupation. His strength, intellect, and many

superiorities notwithstanding, few wanted a black onboard. As Sal knew from his limited time in service, Doc's willingness to "employ" an African American was the exception, and exceptional people like David were hard to find on the base named after Confederate General Braxton Bragg—a cruelly incompetent man widely despised by troops and fellow officers alike, generally considered the worst general of the Civil War and principally responsible for the South's defeat.

"You hungry?" Sal asked.

"Yes," Maddie Pearl replied eagerly. "What have you got?"

Sallerhead lifted a brown paper bag, set it on the cot beside Maddie Pearl's, and proceeded to take out hard-boiled eggs, cold toast, a small jar of what appeared to be congealed grits—or possibly glue paste, and assorted virtually-inedibles including... old spaghetti?

Maddie Pearl blanched slightly, bowed her head and mumbled, "Thank you Lord for this food we are about to receive," and immediately tore into an egg like a great white jawing a baby seal. Sal followed suit, and the fifty-noodle freestyle began with no words exchanged for a solid five minutes.

Now sated, Maddie Pearl asked, "What's for lunch?"

Sal chuckled lightly, then turned serious and replied, "We've got to figure some things out, pretty damn fast."

"I can't go back there, Sal. You know I can't."

Sal shook his head disapprovingly, thought deeply for several seconds, and then replied, "You got any ideas?"

"What about Doc? Maybe he can help?"

"Doc's gone, Maddie Pearl. I told you last—"

"I know, I know. He's gone overseas or something... to California."

Sal couldn't help but smile at her geographical ignorance. "Well... it's not overseas, exactly... but yeah, California is a long, long way from here."

"Well, you've still got your job, right?"

Sal looked out a window to make sure no one was snooping about.

"I don't know if I have a job," he replied.

"But you're in the Army, and they didn't fire you or anything when this place closed."

"They didn't 'fire' me, Maddie Pearl, at least not officially, but without Doc I'm jobless, and if I ain't workin', they ain't payin'."

This was alien to the hick who never had worked for pay and never held a real job of any sort even on the farm and never had transacted business with coins and bills and never been exposed to anywhere outside of home in her seventeen years on the third rock from the Sun. But the conversation nevertheless was very familiar, as Maddie Pearl thought back a lifetime ago to a night at a fire pit with her only true friends. She played the victim then; she was playing the victim now; she determined not to be the victim anymore.

"Let's go to California!" Maddie Pearl exclaimed with naïve, teenage exuberance.

After pondering Maddie Pearl's utterance with more than an ounce of incredulity, Sal replied, "*What?*"

"Let's go to California! You and me!"

"Maddie Pearl... you have no idea what you're talking about," Sal said in a fatherly voice oozing with "*you're such a silly little girl*" attitude.

"We can go in Doc's car. You said yourself it wasn't overseas or anything. We can go to Doc, take him his car. He'll know what to do!"

Sallerhead ambled closer to Maddie Pearl, patted her back gently, and gave her a slight hug.

"Maddie Pearl, you know I respect you. Always have. But there ain't no way we can just get up and drive to California. Ain't happening. First of all, I can't leave the Army like that. It's against the law."

Maddie Pearl walked over to a window, stared out for several seconds, then turned. "We can say you've been ordered to take the car out there... to Doc!"

"And just who would issue a fool order like that?"

"You can say Doc ordered you. He *is* your boss, right?"

Sal shook his head in derision. "Maddie Pearl, I can't jus—"

"Well?" She cut him off rebelliously. "You got any better ideas?"

Sal thought long and hard before responding.

"Yeah. I've got one, but you're not gonna like it."

Maddie Pearl turned abruptly away from her friend, marched to the latrine, and used it accordingly. Sal meanwhile gathered up their breakfast debris, crammed it back into the brown paper bag, and balled it up as tightly as possible.

"MADDIE PEARL," he called out loudly into the latrine, "WE GOTTA GET A MOVE ON."

Maddie Pearl emerged, her hair now straightened and clothes in which she had slept now less disheveled, and stood defiantly face-to-face with so-called "Private" Jefferson.

"I'm going to California in Doc's car, with or without you."

"But how will we pay for—"

Maddie Pearl cut him off starkly. "This isn't a debate. And you cannot stop me!"

Walter Carver "Sallerhead" Jefferson backed away, scratched his head, and resignedly knew he'd lost the game yet again. He grinned ever so slightly—like a proud father smiling contentedly at his kid who just did a nice deed for some stranger without having to be asked. He took a deep if uncertain breath and reached out to Maddie Pearl. She reached back, and they shook hands as Sal said,

"We're going to California!"

# PART II
# A TRIP WEST

# Chapter 21

Fort Bragg, North Carolina to Fort Irwin, California is 2,478 miles. Before Interstates, six-lane highways, city bypasses, rest stops, and fast food oasis every ten miles, it was like Amundsen's 1903-1906 Northwest Passage Expedition. For a black man and white girl, with virtually no money, driving through the most-segregated region in the most discriminatory country in the world, it was Amundsen on steroids.

\*　　　\*　　　\*

On September 1, 1939, a pasty-faced little man in a fancy-pants little suit and tie uttered a few little words to a general in Berlin. A few hours later, thousands of troops with heavy armor, aeroplanes, guns, and bombs barged into a place they had no place being and started a war that would leave some 73,000,000 dead, millions more forever wounded, and a reformed world ravaged with destruction, devastation, and desolation.

Although America chose not to fight for over two years, its supreme leader foresaw the inevitable and thus began ramping up defenses from sea to shining sea. Near the shining sea to the left was a forsaken nothingness in a barren oblivion originally occupied by Native Americans over fifteen thousand years ago. They wisely left for greener environs only to be followed by a parade of explorers and misfits from Spanish missionary Padre Francisco Garcés to Captain John C. Fremont and even the legendary Kit Carson. They all left too, wisely. Fur trapper Jedediah Smith frequented the barrenness, and left as well.

Located roughly between modern day Los Angeles and Salt Lake City, the territory became somewhat of a crossroads, especially during the California Gold Rush that brought the region trade and trouble. Of particular concern was horse stealing, which became so rampant that the United States Army commissioned the

Mormon Battalion to patrol and control the thievery. They too, left, never to return, but the location was favorable and some semblance of civilization remained for decades despite the dearth of water and fertile soil. The environment, characterized under the Köppen Climate Classification system as a "cold desert," was no picnic, with summertime temps routinely exceeding 100°.

By the mid-1880's, freight wagons aplenty prompted the construction of Camp Bitter Springs, a small stone fort encampment from which patrols policed the vicinity. [*And yes, for graphic novel and video game fans, this is the Bitter Springs at which the Great Massacre took place in 2278.*]

The discovery of Death Valley borax engendered a mining boom prompting railroads and leading people to another nearby barrenness now called Barstow. So off and on, since at least fifteen millennia heretofore, this bleak infertile piece of planet had been home to one vagabond after another, each with more than sufficient gray matter to leave.

What a perfect place for a military installation.

While Luke (or was it Tate) tormented his sister with bloodlettings and Nutty beheadings, America's Commander-in-Chief in Washington handpicked the same bleak infertile piece of planet for the creation of an anti-aircraft range. Less-than-creatively named the "Mojave Anti-Aircraft Range," the place would not become known as Fort Irwin for two years. With FDR's order dictated from his wheel chair in the West Wing of the Oval Office, the MAAR magically became real. Certain generals began ramping up, some officer from who-knows-where determined that the presence of troops would necessitate medical personnel, and a penny-pinching bureaucrat at Fort Bragg frugaled Field Hospital # 4 into non-existence thereby freeing-up Captain David "Doc" Hodge. The young non-doctor accordingly received a formal communiqué "inviting" him to report immediately to the wasteland long ago abandoned by Native Americans, Spanish conquistadors, Padre Francisco Garcés, Captain John C. Fremont, Kit Carson, forty-niners, Jedediah Smith, the Mormon Battalion, and even low-life scum horse thieves.

\*          \*          \*

The trip west to this land of abandonment would require extensive preparations, but Maddie Pearl and Sal had no time. Because they could not be seen together and since she had no official business even being on base, Maddie Pearl stayed in Army Field Hospital # 4 while Sal hurriedly gathered whatever they thought necessary. By living in the hospital for several months now, sleeping in a cot set aside for patients who never presented, Sal had managed to save a few pennies and was prepared to spend it all if necessary to ensure safe passage. Several times, he returned with bundles of this or that. Maddie Pearl would gather the items and organize accordingly.

Of particular concern was her clothes or, rather, lack thereof. She couldn't shop at the Post Exchange, so he had to estimate size, fit and fashion. Her tastes certainly weren't refined, and she was ultra easy to please, but nevertheless some of his choices proved almost comical.

"You expect me to wear *that?* Around *people?* It's a burlap sack, with armholes!"

Eventually, however, through more than a degree of trial and serious error, a very modest wardrobe was assembled for the blossoming young woman.

Among other things, Sal procured a map of the United States. Maddie Pearl never had seen anything like it, and studied it like a dog studies a fresh, meaty bone. Gifted in English despite her lack of formal education, Maddie Pearl easily could read the various places thereon and, with some effort, figured out Fayetteville's location, and Webster County's, and then California's. She knew the distance from home to Fayetteville, more or less, having now ridden it three times. She didn't know where was Webster County in relation to Belton, but she knew it was pretty close. From that limited data, Maddie Pearl extrapolated the distance from Fayetteville to California.

She was more than shocked.

Upon returning from his latest provisioning, Sal noticed that Maddie Pearl had become somewhat less enthusiastic. When he arrived, she didn't greet him with open expectations as before. Instead, she stared aimlessly out a window toward the sky.

"You okay?" Sal asked pensively. She didn't respond. Sal inched over and noticed she had the map in hand by her side.

"Get a chance to study up on where we're going?" he inquired in an uplifting manner.

Again, no response, at least not initially. Sal was about to begin another tact when she finally opened up.

"There's no way we can do this."

Sal retrieved the map from her hand and spread it out on a cot. Talking more to himself than to her, he said, "Let's see. Oh, okay... here we are, right here." He reached down and touched his right forefinger to Fayetteville, holding it there to mark the spot. Sal then looked to his left, spotted the west coast, reached his left hand down touching the map yet again, and said, "And *here's* California." He then lifted both hands off the map keeping the distance between fingers unchanged. He pivoted to Maddie Pearl, hands spread wide *ala* Frankenstein, and said, "What's your problem? It's only this far."

She smiled and began to turn away but Sal grabbed her with his open arms, drew her in close, and hugged her tightly, warmly, sincerely.

"As long as we work together, Maddie Pearl, nothing can stop us," he said in cliché speak.

She pulled back slightly, still within his embrace, their faces inches apart and lips practically touching. He was strong, and she was safe, and his skin was dark and clear and healthy, and his breath was warm and moist, and she could see through his perfect eyes into the soul of this most complete man, and a warmth came over her unlike anything she had ever experienced, and it was good, but scary, and she felt... *something*, but what, and why?

And then he pulled away, and it was over... and she *knew*.

*     *     *

When instructing Private WC Jefferson about disposition of one new Plymouth, Captain Hodge provided said Jefferson with an address: "It's a place called Mojave Anti-Aircraft Range, I think. Just send it to me care of there. I'll get it."

Sal was less than optimistic. With this change of plans about which Doc knew nothing, Sal figured he could deliver the car in person and let Doc decide what next to do with his parents' present. *"Besides,"* he thought, *"he said I could drive it, but he*

*didn't say where.*" But delivering the car in person was not going to be a ride in the park munching candy and nuts.

They would leave at night to avoid detection, much as they had left a few days earlier before the torching of Maddie Pearl's home. They had done the math; it was more than daunting. Sal determined that Doc's Plymouth averaged fifteen miles to the gallon; they estimated the trip to be some three thousand miles; they would need at least two hundred gallons. At roughly twenty cents a gallon, they needed forty dollars just for gas.

Neither Sal nor Maddie Pearl ever had traveled farther than home to here and back. They had no clue, therefore, how long it would take to reach—"what was it called again"—oh yeah, the "Mojave Anti-Aircraft Range" near the town of Barstow in the state called California. Sal figured on six days, traveling strictly at night and averaging five hundred miles daily. He had not calculated on breakdowns, getting lost, flat tires, cop stops, white supremacists, and the absence of roads and even trails.

Sal's food calculations likewise proved inaccurate. Using his *Green Book* as a guide, he judged two meals a day for two people for six days to total another forty dollars, not including the provisions they were bringing. Had the voyage actually only taken six, the cost would have been almost double, and as it turned out they needed far more than six days.

Having never owned a vehicle, neither Maddie Pearl nor WC had any idea whatsoever of routine maintenance costs. They learned quickly, the hard way. Having never spent night after night cloistered across a bench seat, neither Maddie Pearl nor WC had any conception of restricted movement causing constricted arteries causing great pain and suffering for hours on end. They learned quickly, the hard way. And having never navigated city streets and county roadways, neither Maddie Pearl nor WC had any notion of being lost and alone hopelessly in civilization and wilderness. They learned quickly, the hard way.

*        *        *

The adventure's first night, however, proved uneventful. Webster County happened to be along the route, or so they thought. No one stopped them, and they continued for another

hundred miles beyond until they reached the outskirts of Raleigh, the state capital. Near dawn, Sal pulled the Plymouth behind a billboard surrounded by overgrowth, cut the engine, and heaved a sigh of liberation.

"So far, so good," he said in an exhausted but excited voice.

"How much longer do you think we need to go?" asked Maddie Pearl like a child perched forward from the back seat eagerly hoping for good news.

Sal took out the map, spread it for Maddie Pearl to see, and drew a line from Fayetteville to Raleigh. It was almost an inch, no more.

He reached to Barstow and replied, "Oh, I don't know. Maybe another twenty inches or so."

Maddie Pearl plopped back in the rear seat, defeated. Sal, meanwhile, studied the map in greater detail, his brow furrowing more fully by the second. He looked up at the odometer and fuel gauge, then back at the map. After several thoughtful seconds, he turned to face Maddie Pearl.

"We've got a problem."

"I know," replied Maddie Pearl in a frustrated tone. "Got another twenty inches to go!"

"Yeah, well, that's just part of it. Check this out."

He spread the map again for Maddie Pearl.

"First of all," he continued, "I messed up. We could have gone to Raleigh this way," he said, pointing at a path on the map. "Unfortunately, we went this way." His pointing clearly revealed the error.

Instead of driving straight, which would have entailed roughly eighty miles, they had taken a huge, triangular deviation through Webster County and around Belton more than tripling their distance. They had traveled a fraction of the planned five hundred daily miles. Furthermore, the anticipated half tank of gas to reach Raleigh wasn't even close, as the needle unequivocally pointed at "E."

"Good grief," Maddie Pearl said in astonishment. "It took us all night to go... what... a hundred miles?"

"No. It took us all night, and a full tank of gas, to go eighty."

Seeds of doubt wedged into each bright mind and dire thoughts began germinating in the fertility therein. Forty for gas, forty for food, and a hundred for incidentals crafted a budget of $180. Sal had brought every dime he had, which totaled $259.87. With more than a $75 cushion, which to each was a fortune, surely they had enough to make the entire trip.

Now they were highly skeptical.

"Here's something else," said Sal. "This car was empty right after we got back the other night. I filled it up the next day, and it took just under twenty gallons. I remember because I had to pay for it and it was kinda frustrating since Doc didn't leave me any money for that. But anyway... it looks to me like we just used twenty gallons of gasoline to travel a little over two hundred miles."

"That's not fifteen miles to the gallon," Maddie Pearl said in exasperation.

A silence fell within the gas-guzzling behemoth. This was going to take at least twice as long as expected, and cost at least twice as much, and they had a full twenty inches to go.

Their troubles had only just begun.

# Chapter 22

The next few days out of Raleigh continued uneventful, more or less. To avoid trouble—to the extent trouble could be avoided—Sal wore his Private Jefferson uniform, always drove slightly below the speed limit, used almost exclusively back roads, and demanded Maddie Pearl stay out of sight around cars or pedestrians. So far, so good. At a country store near Winston-Salem, Sal managed to "borrow" a better map from a sympathetic owner who happened to be a World War I veteran respectful of his comrade-in-arms. The *Green Book* proved invaluable, providing guidance on everything from where blacks could eat to where an African American's public presence strictly was forbidden after sundown. The sweet land of liberty proved somewhat sour for some, especially in the Confederacy through which fully half the journey would traverse.

Five hundred miles a day proved to be a goal manifestly unattainable, like so many NBA dreams of little white boys shooting baskets all day on their backyard hoops. Sal had worked on tractors and similar farm equipment since he was a boy, solely for white farmers since any machinery which happened to fall into black hands summarily would be stolen without penalty or punishment by white hands belonging to someone like Luke or Hog. Sal's skills enabled progress despite the Plymouth's propensity to overheat in the steamy climate. Sleeping, however, continued problematic, for several reasons.

The accommodations, with Sal stretched across the front bench seat and Maddie Pearl across the back, wholly were inadequate, for each. Even feather beds with silk sheets would have failed them, however, because neither could sleep well in the broad daylight hidden behind some barn, billboard, or thicket with southern mosquitoes, horseflies, and no-see-ums incessantly partying on their skin in the 90°+ temps and 100% humidity. The fear of being discovered likewise wreaked havoc with each passing

car or muffled sound of some distant farmworker or screech of a startled bird rousing both Sal and Maddie Pearl from their fretful slumber into stuporous wakefulness. Something had to give, especially for Sal.

Walter Carver was a strong, smart, super capable man, but the toll of everything was beginning to crack his ordinarily impenetrable façade. He was fully responsible for the planning, car maintenance, meals, gas, "lodgings," security, and financing; Maddie Pearl was responsible for... nothing. Although she provided lively conversation, which Sal relished, the 17-year-old did little else. It was not her fault; she was more than capable. But Maddie Pearl never had learned to do much of anything back home, and Sal determined it was time for that to change.

To avoid the Appalachian Mountains as much as possible and because the roads seemed slightly less traveled and thus safer, Sal had chosen a southern route which would take them through a small part of South Carolina and then Georgia, Alabama, Mississippi, Louisiana, Texas, New Mexico, Arizona, and then the promised land of milk and honey, Golden Bears, and the Mojave Anti-Aircraft Range. It was the Deep South land of cotton and lynching for sure, but he sensed that a more northerly path through the likes of Tennessee and Oklahoma would be no better.

Furthermore, he determined—again from the indispensible *Green Book*—that several of those states where old times there are not forgotten were too backward to require driver's licenses. Let freedom reign, their leaders believed deeply, and those freedoms entailed permitting anyone to drive anything on any road without so much as a minute's worth of training or experience.

So the absurdity of freedom turned on its head in the form of license-free states opened the door wide to Sal's own plan for his freedom from, if nothing else, having to do all the driving. With the Palmetto red freedom-state beckoning, Maddie Pearl's worthlessness was about to change.

The fourth day found our duo inside a dilapidated tobacco barn in Godforsaken County, South Carolina. Like so many Carolina farm fields then, there was no farming. Several factors contributed to the collapse, with most traceable directly to greed and ignorance. Some blamed the Dust Bowl or Depression or impending conflict in Europe or weather or the *Farmer's Almanac.*

The truth, however, was far starker and inherently unpalatable. More often than not, the diseconomies of tenant farming coupled with the unwillingness or incapacity of tenants to adapt wrought the easily predictable downfalls. This farm, for instance, died because tobacco requires a very specific climate and soil that simply does not exist here. Now, if the genius had done any research before investing and planting and failing and depriving his family of food and shelter, he would have known that the region is unsuitable for the golden leaf. But he didn't, and he nosedove, and he's gone, and our couple is here, and they are safe—albeit temporarily.

Late in the afternoon, shortly before their customary time of venturing out, Sal turned to Maddie Pearl and said, "So, you ready to drive tonight?"

Sal had not even hinted of Maddie Pearl's driving. The opportunity just never seemed to present. He had put it off for dread of her response. His fear was unfounded, to say the least.

"It's about time!" she belted in no uncertain terms.

"*Thank goodness*," Sal thought to himself, and then said, "Great! Let me show you how."

"You don't need to show me a thing," she resolutely shot back. "You think I've been sitting here all this time with my eyes closed?"

Maddie Pearl got out of the Plymouth with the iffy radiator and faint smell of vomit on the front passenger seat. She came around to the driver's door and said, "All right, big shot. It's my turn!"

Sal slid over onto the puke stain but kept the keys firmly in hand. Maddie Pearl got in, adjusted herself in the seat as well as possible, and said, "Okay, how do I start this thing?"

"Before we begin, there's a few things I want to go over," said Sal paternally.

"Come on, come on! I'm ready to GO!"

Maddie Pearl's enthusiasm failed to thrill the doubtful Walter. He took a deep breath, smiled, and continued, "Now Maddie Pearl, it takes a little practice to do this... you know... right. I'm not saying you can't learn. You can, and will. But nobody can do it, well, safely... you know... the first time."

"Oh piddle-de-spit," she retorted nonsensically. "If you can do it, so can I!"

On the word "I," she snatched the key from Sal's hand, thrust it in the ignition, turned it, and stomped on the gas. The Plymouth menacingly ROARED to life. As Sal tried desperately to turn it off, Maddie Pearl slapped away his arm, yanked down the transmission lever situate on the side of the steering column, and flung back in the seat soundly as the car spun wildly forward directly into the west wall of the abandoned tobacco barn. The Plymouth stopped with a start, the engine cut off abruptly, smoke and dust arose around, and Sal looked at Maddie Pearl with a bug-eyed "*WHAT THE HELL*" gawk.

Some lessons definitely were in order.

The Plymouth was scraped but not seriously damaged. Still, the dead field's loam turned out to be too sandy soft to negotiate for any further lessons, so Sallerhead took back control and drove, for now.

For the next hour or so, neither spoke. He remained in a zone between shock and awe; she descended from her high as the endorphins burbled back to wherever they hide when not agitated. In each cranial cortex, the wheels were spinning. He thought of abandoning the mission altogether, heading back to Fayetteville, finding another officer for whom to work, and taking Maddie Pearl back to where she belonged, wherever that may be now that her family had... left. Maddie Pearl's mental wheels sharply stayed focused on getting back behind the steering wheel.

Near the South Carolina/Georgia border in a particularly remote part of nowhere, Sal noticed ahead on the right what appeared to be a large, open field covered in low vegetation. It certainly wasn't grass, at least not the sort found in yards on clean streets in perfect little neighborhoods adorned with mailboxes and driveways and pretty white children selling lemonade. But it was low enough to suggest that perhaps the field was drivable, so Sal pulled off the lonely two-lane blacktop on which he had been traveling his customary forty-five miles per hour and along which they had not seen another car for at least an hour. He walked over to check it out, determined the field was suitable, and returned to the sitting Plymouth to find... no Maddie Pearl.

"*Lord,*" thought Sal. "*What now?*"

Within a few seconds, she returned, having snuck away to relieve herself. While walking up to the car, she straightened her

rumpled dress she'd been wearing pretty much nonstop for days and fluttered her vibrant hair. She cared what Sal thought of her, and he smiled.

"It's time for your next lesson, if you're ready, and <u>only</u> if you'll do what I say!"

Maddie Pearl gave Sal a "*don't talk to me like that*" look but reluctantly conceded with a sarcastic yet flirtatious, "I promise."

Sal nudged the Plymouth to the field's edge, changed seats with Maddie Pearl, and calmly said, "Okay first, let's talk about how this all works."

He showed her the three pedals on the floor: the gas, brake, and clutch. As he tried to explain each, Maddie Pearl jumped the gun.

"What does that 'clutch' thing do?"

"That? Well, it's hard to explain, but I'll put it this way."

"Don't waste time telling this and that way, just tell me what it does!"

He didn't like the demanding attitude, especially considering the teen's absolute ignorance of everything before her.

Ignoring her and despite his displeasure, Sal continued, "The clutch takes the engine out of gear."

The conversation disintegrated from there, with the inevitable "what's a gear" and "why do we need gears" and "why won't the motor just go" and "do you even know what you're talking about" and "you're about the worst teacher I've ever seen" and "quit treating me like a child" and on and on.

Not without Herculean effort, the most patient man east of Mississippi finally managed to orient his most impatient pupil sufficiently for actual motion.

It did not go well.

"Now *slowly* ease your left foot off the clutch and, at the same time, *slowly* touch on the gas."

Somehow, the young, healthy, athletic, beautiful seventeen year old girl with bright red hair and silky white, unblemished skin either functionally failed to hear "*slowly*" said twice or mentally declined to compute its meaning. She yanked up her left foot and slammed down her right. The brutal lurch practically dislocated Sal's spinal column from his cranium.

Anyone who ever has learned to drive a manual transmission knows the routine from here. There were many more lurches, much gnashing of teeth, and even a few "GOD DAMMITS" here and there coming solely from the young woman who had spent her life nose deep in the Bible reading fully and daily about not taking her Lord's name in vain.

Sometime around midnight, it finally clicked!

That first real drive under control with the Plymouth mostly in first gear was, to Maddie Pearl, the greatest achievement of her life! To say she was thrilled is to say puppies love playing. The field proved a perfect classroom, and for at least two hours she drove and turned and shifted gears and sped up and slowed down and even backed in reverse.

She remained super aggressive, consistently driving much faster than Sal preferred as evidenced by his repeated "WATCH OUTs" and "STOP! STOP! STOP!" Only when absolutely necessary did she heed his admonitions, as Maddie Pearl "knew" what she was doing and no man, not even one as great as Walter Carver Jefferson, was going to tell her otherwise.

By sun-up, she was ready for the road; by night's end, Sal was ready for sleep.

"So what direction from here?" asked Maddie Pearl eagerly.

Sal gave her a pensive look and replied, "Sleepville."

"Sleepville? Where's that?" Maddie Pearl inquired naively.

"Sleepville... you know... off to sleep. Can't go now, it's daytime, and I'm exhausted."

"The heck we can't go now," she said sharply. "I'm better than you at this, we have a long way to go, and I'm ready."

Sal reached over, turned off the Plymouth, and removed the key.

"No way, Maddie Pearl. Can't go now. I'm beat and, besides, can't drive in the daylight. You know that."

" *You* can't drive in the daylight, but *I* can," she said wearing a coy, shit-eating grin.

Sal, who had put his head back on the seat and closed his eyes, sat up. This strategy fully had bypassed his planning.

"Huh?" he mused out loud.

"Think about it," she persisted. "I agree that a black man driving a shiny new car that Lord knows he must have stolen cause no darkies can afford it would draw all kinds of suspicion."

She looked at him; he looked back knowingly; their wavelengths synced.

"But what about me?" he wondered. "If you get stopped, how do we explain... well... the presence of this large dark man?"

"Oh don't be silly," replied Maddie Pearl, obviously having given the issue significant thought. "First of all, I'm not going to be stopped. Second, even if I am, I'll tell 'em you work for me."

"I work for you?" he said doubtfully.

"Yeah, you know, like you're my assistant or something or... I know... you're my yardman but you're too dumb and untrustworthy to let drive. Yeah, that's it! You're my yardman!"

So I do yard work... for *you?*"

"Of course you do. I can't be expected to do it myself."

"So I do yard work for you?" he repeated incredulously. "Now tell me, where's this yard of yours?"

Maddie Pearl had not worked out all the kinks just yet, but she never was one to back down from a challenge.

"Like I said, I'm not going to get stopped, so it doesn't really matter."

"Look, we just can't drive in the daytime. It's too dangerous. If we get stopped or have a wreck or whatever, we'll never get to Doc. And... I hate to even mention this... but I'm not sure you understand about... you know... me."

"What on earth do you mean?" said Maddie Pearl, exposing yet again her obliviousness of Sal's acute vision about his prospects in the Deep South driving around in somebody else's brand new car with a young, white, attractive, teenage girl by his side whom he cannot explain other than by saying, "I do her yard."

He could hear the law now: "*We don't need no stinkin' trial. String 'em up, boys, high and tight!*"

"What I mean, Maddie Pearl, is the same thing I meant when we went back home and the trooper stopped us. You know full well I'm takin' the chance of a lifetime just being on this trip with you. You talk about being your yardman or whatever. That's crazy talk. You ain't from these parts, you have no yard here, and it just doesn't make sense that you'd be driving me around hundreds

of miles from that yard you don't have in a car you don't own that belongs to some stranger in California, a stranger who is in the military for God's sakes. Hell, I'll be a yardman all right. My ass will be grass and some hillbilly and his bubba buddies will be taking turns mowing it!"

"Well... okay... so you're not my yardman," she replied, "you're my butler."

"YOU JUST DON'T GET IT, DO YOU?" Sal yelled in exasperation.

The vehemence stunned Maddie Pearl momentarily, nipping her childish energy in the bud. With the sun and heat rising rapidly, and the night's dark camouflage now gone for another half rotation, reality visited harshly the interior of a new Plymouth bought in Belton by proud parents and now on its way somewhere... either west or... perhaps... back east from whence it came.

# Chapter 23

While they didn't sleep for the rest of the day beside the classroom on which Maddie Pearl had sort of learned to drive the night before, not a word was spoken. Private Walter Carver Jefferson spun his options over and over, and with each revolution returned to the same spot: they *had* to go back home. But he just couldn't, not now, not after all this, and not with Maddie Pearl having nowhere to go, nothing to do, and no prospects for survival.

In four days, they were just past Starr near the Georgia border. So much for that anticipated daily average, as Sal had learned quickly that making good time was impossible on unpaved back roads, driving forty-five or less, and getting lost routinely while suffering repeated overheating and two patched flat tires. Last night's lesson, which ensured zero progress for the entirety of day four, didn't help either.

But their problems were bigger and more myriad than mere timing. The Plymouth brand was founded with fanfare on July 7, 1928. It lasted barely four generations, dying ignominiously June 29, 2001. If Doc's Plymouth was an example, the company far exceeded its life expectancy. To call the vehicle bat-crap-awful would be an affront to guano. Overheating was the tip of the iceberg, paradoxically speaking. It sucked gas like a drunk sucks wine. Its rubber tires were thin, like deli slices, capable of absorbing no bounces on the gully-laden pothole trails their secret mission necessitated. The seats were unbearably uncomfortable, especially for sleeping, which mirrored the ride, which was not unlike sliding down a rock pile bare-assed.

Even if the car could make it three thousand miles, intact, with both occupants still present and accounted for, the budget was a problem. Of the $257.89 in Sal's possession upon leaving, only $178.03 remained. The rest was scattered in gas stations, food stops, and black-operated country stores from here to Fort Bragg.

Having covered no more than one-fourth of the way, Sal calculated they would need roughly six hundred dollars. Even the Plymouth wasn't worth that much.

And then there was the Maddie Pearl issue, or rather issues. Superficially, she doubled the food cost without providing assistance. Furthermore, her mere presence was, as they had determined, unexplainable. So far, they had been lucky. But each knew the issue would present at some point, and neither had a plan to overcome.

And there was one other issue, one bigger problem, and it was deeper than mere money and inexplicable circumstances. Each knew but neither dared broach it, because it surely would turn this cross-country adventure into sad tragedy, and worse.

*          *          *

On the fifth night they entered Georgia, Coca Cola's home and the land of nuts and crackers. Maddie Pearl and Sal would encounter each in the Goober State.

After rolling along for an hour or so, and with the sun securely absent, Sal pulled over, stopped, and said playfully, "All right, Miss Prine, you're on." She didn't need to be asked twice.

Ordinarily, Maddie Pearl had stayed hidden in the back seat while Sal drove. With roles reversed, Sal changed the routine and stayed up front, close to the wheel... just in case. Maddie Pearl started the Plymouth, wiggled in the seat to get comfortable, and then *slowly* lifted her left foot while *slowly* descending her right. Miraculously, the car smoothly edged forward, just like it's supposed to do! A broad grin spread across the girl's face as she turned to Sal for praise.

He stayed focused ahead. "WATCH OUT!"

Too soon for reaction, they smacked a signpost— "ROSWELL 26 MILES." Maddie Pearl slammed on brakes; the car pitched sharply to a stop; Sal flew forward and knocked his head on the windshield, causing a small crack therein (the windshield, not Sal's head).

"Oh no! Oh no! On NO! I'm so sorry... are you okay?" Maddie Pearl stammered.

Sal regained his composure and replied surprisingly calmly under the circumstances, "Yeah. I'm fine. How 'bout you?"

"Oh I'm fine, but I am so so so sorry. I never saw it."

"That's all right, Maddie Pearl, it's okay. Stuff like that happens... all the time. And like I said, I'm fine, really."

Maddie Pearl patted his shoulder motherly just to make sure, then opened the door and began exiting.

"What are you doing?" asked Sal.

"I'm getting out, to let you drive."

"Why in hell would you do *that?*" asked Sal.

Maddie Pearl stopped in the doorframe, her body half in half out. With an incredulous look and trembling voice she said, "Well surely you don't want me driving, not now."

Sal leaned over, gently grabbed Maddie Pearl by the arm, and tugged her back into the car. He slid over closer to the driver's area on the bench seat, pulled Maddie Pearl close, and hugged her tightly. Her eyes filled with tears. She drew away slightly to face him head-on and, mesmerized by the moment, leaned forward and kissed Sal hard on the lips.

It was her first real kiss, ever. Instinctively, naturally it was perfect in a soft yet hard, womanly way. He tried to turn, but couldn't, and kissed her back passionately, manly, viscerally, with emotions pent since he first saw her walking up to Daisy while he and Nomita waited so long ago. They jointly pulled apart, gazed into each other's eyes, and re-engaged for seconds that seemed like hours and days and lifetimes.

And just as she *knew* five days before in abandoned Field Hospital # 4 right before they embarked, *he* now knew as well.

\*　　\*　　\*

More out of routine than necessity, Sal drove that night as they crossed central Georgia north of Atlanta heading west toward Alabama and Doc far beyond. There was no conversation. Maddie Pearl pretended to sleep in the back; Sal pretended to focus on driving; both pretended the kissing never happened; each appreciated the significance of what had transpired.

It scared the hell out of them both.

Early the next morning, just as the first photons began hitting the Georgia hill country after their eight minute, 93,000,000-mile journey from the sun, Maddie Pearl really was asleep while Sallerhead began scouting a place to stop for the day. The effects of the trip were hitting him hard; the activities from the night before were hitting even harder. His mind was awhirl with visions of trees and nooses and white hooded men with torches and shotguns when, from the corner of his eye, he spotted in the rearview mirror an emerging vehicle with two bright headlights and a familiar, red light atop.

"JESUS!" he squealed, waking Maddie Pearl from a fantastic dream about being in a rowboat on a pristine lake eating grapes and reveling in the comfortably warm breeze.

"What?" she said spontaneously.

"We've got trouble, and I mean real trouble. Get down, and damn well don't play that governor's daughter thing again. Not here. Not now."

Maddie Pearl slid to the floor and positioned her body over the hump in the middle and under the Army issue blanket they had been using as a cushion on the hard-vinyl seats. Despite the day's first light peeking down, the blanket was deep green, the back was in shadow, and her concealment was marginally adequate, for now.

Private WC Jefferson, in his military uniform, stopped and waited. From the mirror, he spotted a skinny Barney Fife energetically pop from the cop car and strut up to the window.

Looking down at his ticket book, the khaki-clad cop asked, "May I see your license, sir?"

"Yes sir," said Sal ultra politely, "but I didn't think Georgia required driver's licenses."

Upon Sal's inquiry, the small man with the thin tin badge glanced up for the first time and realized the driver was African American.

"Are you back-sassing me, boy?" the cop snapped, reverting from the polite law enforcement officer of seconds ago into the redneck Georgia goober Sal had fully expected.

"No sir. Not at all, sir. And yes, sir, I do have a license, from North Carolina."

Sal handed over his license. The Fife-look-alike studied it closely.

"Where's your registration for this here Plymouth?"

Sal reached into the glove compartment, rifled through the loose papers therein, came across the registration, and handed it over.

As he had done with the license, the cop studied the registration, hard. Sal began to consider the very real possibility that this policeman, or whatever he was, did not know how to read.

His thoughts were confirmed when the cop barked, "What's your name?"

"Jefferson, sir. Walter Carver Jefferson. I'm a private in the Army... the United States Army."

"So... who owns this here automobile?" cracker-boy asked in a nasally, southern, ignorant tone that was a far cry from the official voice he had used ab initio.

"Hodge, sir. David Hodge. I work for him, in the Army."

The cop strolled back to the rear and compared the North Carolina license plate number with the number on the registration. Watching the cop's every move through the mirror, Sal again sensed that this law enforcement official was "reading" nothing but rather comparing shapes and signs.

He came back to the window and said, "So where's this Hodge boy?

"Captain Hodge, sir, is in California, at the—"

"Cali-what?"

"California, sir," Sal replied cautiously. "You know, out west."

"Out west? Watta you mean, 'out west'?"

"I'm taking his car to him, sir. He's out in California, at the Mojave Anti-Aircraft Range. I work for him, and I'm taking his car to—"

"I don't know what in hell you think yer talkin' 'bout boy," the cop uttered in full-throated K-K-Klan-ese, "but I've had all of yer back sassin' I'm a-gonna take, ya hear?"

"I'm sorry, sir, if I—"

"GET OUT," Barney yelled. Maddie Pearl flinched in the back, undetected. As Sal began to emerge, the cop dropped the

registration and license on the road, pulled out his revolver, and aimed it straight at the large black man's head.

"I'm runnin' you in, boy. Git in the back dere," he said, gesticulating his gun to the police cruiser. Shocked Sal hesitated.

"GIT," the cop yelled again and fired his gun over Sal's head! Maddie Pearl popped up to see what was happening. Miraculously, she remained unnoticed as Sal was focused firmly on hustling to the cop car. The Fifian badge-wearer frantically motioned vigorously without so much as looking back at the Plymouth, Maddie Pearl, or anything other than his prize catch.

With Sal secured, the cop hopped in his driver's seat and squealed tires in his old Ford as if chasing Bonnie and Clyde following a bank haul.

Maddie Pearl jumped out of the Plymouth, scooped up the license and registration, pounced in the driver's seat, turned the key, raised her left foot and lowered her right a little less slowly than before, and took off herky-jerky in pursuit!

She had no idea where she was, where she was going, what she was to do when she got there, what was happening to the love of her life—excluding Doc, perhaps—or even what she was doing behind the wheel. So far, she'd run through the gears and now was cruising fairly easily a few hundred yards behind Sal and Jack-Be-Little the Gun-Toting Fool. Heaven help her if she had to begin stopping and starting and maneuvering around traffic or making turns or doing anything beyond steering straight and cruising at fifty.

Meanwhile, in the cop car, no pleasantries were being exchanged. Although the sun was rising, it remained sufficiently dark to necessitate lights. Maddie Pearl had neglected in her haste and inexperience to turn them on, which was fortuitous. Without headlights and since she had stayed a safe distance behind, Deputy Eagle-Eye had not noticed that the same Plymouth, whose sole occupant now was firmly ensconced in his backseat, mysteriously had been following him, ghostlike and evidently driverless, for miles now.

Georgia's finest... indeed.

The old Ford stopped at a gas station that was just opening for the day. Maddie Pearl stopped, with some horrendous gear grinding and awkward brake pounding, about a hundred yards

back. The cop didn't notice as he exited his Ford, walked into the store, chatted briefly with the owner, and then emerged with a key to the padlock on the outhouse a healthy fishing cast towards the woods.

Maddie Pearl leapt from the Plymouth, ran up to the cop car, and jutted her head in Sal's window. He casually turned his head and shit-pant-SQUEALED at the shocking sight!

"MADDIE PEARL! What the—"

Before he could say another word, she already had his door open and was dragging him out! He realized what was happening, reached over grabbing the Ford key from the ignition, and sprinted with Maddie Pearl back to the Plymouth. Sal snatched Doc's car in gear, spun tires, and raced down the road faster than he had driven the entire trip.

Within seconds, they screamed past the gas station just as Wyatt Earp was emerging from the shithole. Pulling up his skinny khakis clumsily, he raced to the cruiser, burst therein, and wildly searched for his key that Sal now was tossing into a swampy bog in which it rusts to this very day.

# Chapter 24

Some twenty miles down the road, Sal was driving west with the sun fully shining through the Plymouth's east-facing rear window. Oncoming drivers, no doubt blinded by the light, could not see the black man behind the wheel. But this fortuitous effect would be fleeting, and Sal knew they remained too close to that uniformed, pissed-off pissant to stop for the day. So he drove, and thought, and worried, and kept looking through the rearview mirror as morning faded away.

Maddie Pearl had stayed low, out of sight, once the dawn's early light blossomed into daytime. Like Sal's, her mind was a maelstrom, but not of cops, lock-ups, and ad hoc hangings in the Georgia red clay countryside. Ever since... *then*, she had not been able to reconcile her feelings for this magnificent man not two feet away. She had known love, or so she thought, but even her feelings for Doc had not felt like... *this*. It was a strange sensation fully alien and somewhat frightening but pleasurable nonetheless. Each time she glanced at him, or heard him utter whatever, she felt warm, in her core, and perhaps it's a cliché but her heart *did* flutter a fraction.

Soon, however, the chemical reactions from the right side of her brain gave way to demons lurking on the left, and the tornado thus created rendered rational thought insufferable. She loves a man she cannot have; she needs a man from whom she must hide; she wants a man who cannot survive with her by his side.

As was her wont, Maddie Pearl sought solace from Jesus. He didn't succor. She kept coming back to First Corinthians, where her Lord said, "So now faith, hope, and love abide, these three; but the greatest of these is love." She understood the verse's greater message, to the extent any Bible verse is comprehensible, but why would Jesus say this to her now, again, and again?

Lost in stormy thoughts of Jesus and Sal and Doc and sex and love, Maddie Pearl didn't initially hear Sal. So he repeated, more loudly.

"We gotta do something. I can't be driving in broad daylight."

Snapped from her musing, Maddie Pearl responded, "Oh, sorry... why don't we stop and get some sleep, like we've been doing?"

"Can't. Still too close to that damn cop, and as long as we're in Georgia, he's still a problem."

"What's Georgia got to do with it?" asked Maddie Pearl, once more revealing her recurring lack of exposure to the real world.

"It's the way the law works," he replied patiently. "Once we get into another state... like Alabama, he can't do anything to us."

"So how far is... what did you say?"

"Alabama. I don't know for sure, but I saw a sign a few minutes ago that said something about a place called 'Fort Payne' being a hundred miles away. Check out the map, because I think that's in Alabama."

Maddie Pearl reached up front, found the map above the vomit stain, and retrieved it for study.

"You're right. That's just across the border."

"Great," said Sal. "But we'll need to get gas before then. Check the *Green Book*."

Maddie Pearl grabbed the *Green Book*, flipped through some pages, and said, "There's a place near Douglasville. Are we close to there?"

Sal had seen a Douglasville sign a while back too but paid no attention to the distance. The answer came soon enough, however, when they started seeing the beginnings of a town emerge. Sal pulled off to figure out the location, then resumed. Within a quarter mile, he turned onto a small, unpaved side street filled with run down shacks. Maddie Pearl peeked to witness the abject poverty, filth, and awfulness. Throughout the trip, she had seen many bad places, but nothing like this. It made her home, and even Sallerhead's,

look over-the-top, wealthy ostentatious. She was more than transfixed, in a stunned sort of way.

Sal crept along slowly, and found the place near the street's end. There was only one gas line, ancient, with a hand crank pump. A decrepit old black man wobbled out of the ramshackle "store" and meandered over.

"I need to fill up," said Sal.

The man looked at the car, brand new, and then at Sal, in uniform.

"You military or sumtin'?" asked the old man.

"Yes sir. Army. On my way out west."

The old man looked inside and spotted Maddie Pearl.

"What about the girl?"

Sal was taken aback. The *Green Book* had been very reliable about locations "safe" for African Americans and, so far, he had not been hassled by anyone. Now, all of a sudden, *this*, from *this* guy, a fellow African American?

"Oh, this is her car," Sal said uncertainly. "I'm actually driving her out west."

"I thought you said you were in the Army?" questioned the old man.

"Well... I am... but, well, you know," replied Sal less confidently as he struggled to explain Maddie Pearl.

"Well... what is it? You in the Army or you work for her?"

Just then the back passenger window rolled down and Maddie Pearl stuck out her head.

"Boy, come on now. What's the delay? My daddy is expecting us." Maddie Pearl's tone was surly and cold, in a superior manner.

Sal gave Maddie Pearl a weird, hurt look, paused, and then .continued in a thickly subservient, antebellum voice, "Yes-um, ma'am, can't keep the general waiting ma'am, sorry ma'am."

The old man paused to compute, thought better of questioning a white woman, surveyed Sal yet again from head to toe, and then continued in a disgusted voice.

"All right, then... but need the money upfront, *boy*," he said caustically.

Sal leaned in and said to Maddie Pearl for the old man to hear, "It'll be three whole dollars, ma'am. Dat okay?"

"You're doing just fine, boy, and run along now and pay it with those bills I let you hold onto for me." Maddie Pearl was truly hamming up the performance. Sal gave her a double take as if to say, " *What the hell is this?*"

The old man shook his head again and said, "Pump it you-self, boy." He pocketed the cash and turned to walk away. "And not one goddam drop above fifteen, *got it?*"

Sal finished the task and off they drove.

"What in heaven's name was all that?" asked Maddie Pearl.

Sal didn't respond until they were back on the highway headed toward the Alabama state line.

"Well?" Maddie Pearl followed-up.

Sal still didn't respond for a good minute. Maddie Pearl could see his face in the rearview mirror. It was stern, serious, agitated.

Finally, he replied, "Ever hear of *Uncle Tom's Cabin?*"

"*Uncle Tom's Cabin?* No, what's that?"

"It's an old book, from long ago... 'bout slaves."

"Yeah, and..." said Maddie Pearl, fishing for more.

"Uncle Tom was this old slave, and he gave in to... well, everything from the *man*. In the end, he got beat to death... *by* the man."

"Oh yeah, Mama told me about that book, a long time ago. But... what's that got to do with anything?"

Sal held off for several seconds. "Let's just say I ain't no Uncle Tom, to *anybody*."

The way he said "anybody" struck a chord with Maddie Pearl. She recognized his real message: "*Don't you ever treat me like a nigger again!*"

They continued traveling in silence for many miles. Despite the sunny day, the Plymouth spent much of the trip secluded in the shadows of various mountains and tall trees. Sal had hoped to avoid such terrain, as much as possible. The first map, which proved somewhat inadequate, had appeared to show the Appalachian range dissipating long before now.

When he got the second, better map, Sal realized that these mountains were going to be a larger part of the expedition. Nevertheless, the car had held up better than expected—this day, with only some overheated brakes every now and then from the changes in elevations. Of more concern was permitting Maddie Pearl to drive in these conditions.

It was one thing for a rookie to drive across a flat field with no cars in sight; it was another animal altogether in hill country. Nevertheless, he knew the time was coming, and he had prepared himself for the inevitable.

He had not planned for what lie ahead just short of the Alabama state line.

Sallerhead had not kept track of mileage, but he knew the border must be close. Although he was beginning to feel a slight sense of relief, the man remained obsessed with the rearview mirror. During one of these peeks, Sal failed for slightly too long to look ahead. When his gaze returned forward, he was upset to see what appeared to be a conglomeration of cars about a mile ahead, blocking the road. The sight prompted him to slam on brakes, jerking Maddie Pearl to full attention in the back seat.

"What the—" Maddie Pearl stopped mid-sentence at the sight and studied the scene ahead. "Are they... blocking the road?" she asked more to herself than Sal.

He didn't answer, but Sal pulled up on the gearshift lever placing the Plymouth in reverse and gently backed into a small, out of sight opening just off the road. It appeared the law had been too preoccupied with the line of stopped cars to notice the distant Plymouth and its suspicious movements.

"Do we have to backtrack?" Maddie Pearl asked, in a panicky voice.

"No way," replied Sal. "This is the only road for miles. That's how they knew where to put up that stop. That goddamn cop knew we were headed west, and this is the only westward road for probably a hundred miles north or south of us. God fucking dammit!"

Maddie Pearl was struck by Sal's unusually vociferous reaction. She suspected he was still upset with what had

transpired in Douglasville. She had seen him upset several times, but not like this, and it scared her.

"Well... what then?"

Sal didn't know, but he was thinking of a plan. Without consulting Maddie Pearl, he put it into action. The Plymouth roared to life, and Sal headed back east.

About ten minutes down the road, they came back to a dead gas station killed long ago by the Depression. Sal got out and headed behind the store to a collection of maybe ten to fifteen junk vehicles. Maddie Pearl had no idea what he was doing, but snuck out to the store's opposite side, pulled up her dress, and as demurely as possible relieved herself.

As she was walking back briskly to the Plymouth, Sal exclaimed, "GOT IT!"

He came running back to the car holding two pieces of flat, rectangular metal: old Georgia license plates. Maddie Pearl watched as Sal fiddled first in the rear and then the front. When finished, he took the Plymouth's former, still-shiny-new North Carolina plates and hid them in the trunk under the spare tire. He then came around to Maddie Pearl and pulled her out of the car.

"You've got to drive."

"What?"

"You've got to drive us up to that border and sweet-talk us through. There's no other way."

Maddie Pearl looked flummoxed at this great man who suddenly seemed loony.

"Are you crazy?" she demanded, totally serious.

"I just might be, but what choice do we have?"

Maddie Pearl considered the possibilities. "How about we stop for the day and hope that, by tonight, they're gone?"

"Can't chance it. They probably just saw us a few minutes ago. For all we know, they've already sent somebody out looking for us. They might pass by here any second."

"Well if we hide good enough, they won't—"

"Dammit, Maddie Pearl! We can't hide, and we can't outrun 'em. You're the only way."

"But—"

"Ain't no buts about it. You're ON!"

Maddie Pearl paused, deep in thought. "But where're you gonna be?"

"In the trunk. You can wrap me in that Army blanket and I'll hide in there. They won't look. And even if they do, maybe they won't see me."

"Oh come on. They'd see you in—"

Sal grabbed Maddie Pearl hard by the shoulders and glared at her with a face she'd never seen. He was darker than usual, mean, and scary—like a cornered wild animal with nothing to lose. Her fragility in the large, strong, Nietzsche-esque super man's arms was all too clear, and horrifying. At that moment, any last remnants of her quickly fading youth washed away like a frail bridge in a mighty flood. Luke had destroyed her innocence; this would make—or break—her adulthood.

"Give me the damn key," she demanded, "and let's make sure we agree on the plan!"

Sal smiled broadly, and spontaneously hugged her. Whatever love, emotion, joy, and happiness he'd ever derived from his parents or anyone else felt nothing like this, and he knew that this spunky woman from nowhere somehow was going to make this stupidly impossible scheme work!

With Sal hidden away, Maddie Pearl slowly pulled the Plymouth up to the line of stopped cars. There were maybe five or so ahead, so she had five or so stops-and-starts-and-stops to compose whatever faux confidence she could muster. It wasn't enough time, but would have to suffice.

In what seemed like a millisecond, Maddie Pearl's turn arrived. She pulled up, rolled down her window, and faced the High Sheriff himself who happened to be the one to approach *her* car.

"What can I do for you, officer?" she said as sweetly yet provocatively as she could.

The Sheriff ignored Maddie Pearl completely while scanning the car from bow to stern.

"Stay right there," he ordered.

He walked back and checked out the plate, strolled to the front to survey that plate, shook his head, and then returned to Maddie Pearl.

"This your car?" he asked while looking at a clipboard.
"Yes sir, it most surely is," she cooed.

He paid her no attention. Without looking up, he yammered, "Gimme your license and registration."

"Well now, honey, I don't have those things."

"Ma'am I ain't got time to mess around here," he said while staring back at the increasingly long line of cars awaiting seizure and search. "There're at least ten cars behind you. Now give me the damn registration!"

Maddie Pearl pretended to look for the registration that she knew Sal had hidden securely under the spare tire with the North Carolina plates in the trunk over which he now was temporarily residing.

"I'm sorry, officer, but I don't seem to have one of those... what'd you call it... registration thingy things."

"Get out of the car!" the Sheriff barked.

Maddie Pearl followed orders, making sure that a long stretch of her firm, young legs shone in the bright sun and within clear eyesight of four cops ably assisting the boss. She winked at one, a skinny guy dressed differently from the rest, tossed back her auburn hair seductively, and awaited further instruction with her breasts practically busting through her thin dress which—not by happenstance—had a couple of buttons unbuttoned.

The Sheriff ransacked the interior focusing primarily on the glove box, determined in fact that there was no registration, slammed shut the door, and returned his attention to the driver. Before him stood a statuesque, young Maureen O'Hara. Instantly, the asshole became an ass admirer.

"Well, uh, ma'am, uh... you see, ma'am, it's like this." The High Sheriff, temporarily stunned by the beauty he'd not noticed until now, exposed his low abilities in the high ways of charm and seduction.

"Yes... *sir*," she purred, her eyes washing over his body like a judge appraising a prize bull.

"Well ma'am, it's like this. We got this here," he fumbled with his clipboard in an effort to summon the summons he'd been delivered earlier that morning. "This

here summons thing, and it says we need to find a car that sounds a whole lot like this one."

"Oh *this* car," Maddie Pearl responded, leaning full body forward and touching the hood with both hands to ensure complete cleavage for all to see. "Well my daddy bought me this car, today."

The Sheriff and her audience practically didn't hear a word she said because their ears were wrapped around her ample breasts and breezy, easy disposition.

"Your daddy did what, ma'am?" mumbled the Sheriff, not really understanding anything he'd just uttered.

"That's right, back in Douglasville."

The word "Douglasville" roused the Sheriff back to semi-consciousness. "Douglasville, ya say?"

"Yes sir. Bought it off'n some black guy this morning. Big one. Seemed nice, but he was real scared acting, like he was in trouble or something. Daddy had two hundred, and woulda paid it too, but he figured the man was desperate and offered only a hundred, and the guy said 'okay.' Daddy let me keep the rest!" She reached down into her bra, ensuring another fine showing, and pulled out a hundred dollars in cash, the money Sal had determined would be enough if a bribe became necessary. "See," she held the cash strategically for the best view.

The Sheriff, his deputies, and the odd, skinny, khaki guy all looked past the money at the hint of a loose nipple protruding beside a flimsy bra stretched thin and inelastic from too much mammarian pressure.

"You say he bought it off a nigger?" the Sheriff asked, his eyes fixed firmly on the scenery behind the bills.

"Well Mister Sheriff, *sir*," she said flirtatiously, "I don't like to use that word, but yes sir, and that young black man... like I said... he sure looked scared, to me at least, like he was in a hurry or somethin'."

"Tell *me* what he looked like?" asked the skinny guy from leftfield.

Slightly startled by the unexpected entry into the conversation, Maddie Pearl stepped a couple of feet closer to

the scrawny one and answered breathily ensuring her moist warmth fully bathed the man from head to heart.

"Oh he was big and strong," she breathed heavily, "like an animal, and he was dressed funny, like... I don't know... a Army guy or what not."

The Sheriff intoned, "An Army guy?"

She turned her head back to the Sheriff, but kept her place practically nudging Jack Sprat with her hips and rear. "Yes, sir! Just like a real soldier."

The Sheriff faced the skinny man. "That's got to be the guy."

"No doubt," said the man who didn't fit in with the rest. "So what about her?"

Perhaps it was the money or maybe he'd just regained his temporarily lost swagger, but the Sheriff reverted to the redneck jerk he'd been initially. He pulled Maddie Pearl over, close, too close for officialdom, and said, "Oh I don't know. Ma'am, what do *you* think I *oughtta* do with you?"

Maddie Pearl smiled sweetly at the gathering and then peered directly into the Sheriff's bloodshot eyes. "Well sir, you know I'm here to help... in *whatever way* I can."

Her emphasis on "whatever way" sent precisely the message intended. Sal, able to hear through the fuel cap, cringed. "*Dammit, what the fuck is she doing?*"

Slightly startled by her unmistakable directness, the Sheriff flinched a bit but, before he could summon any sensible response, a loud HONK squawked from a waiting vehicle. Like a treeful of quiet cicadas sounding spontaneously after the first brave insect, all the cars started BLARING in unison.

It was fish-or-cut-bait time, and the Sheriff didn't even have a working pole—or did he?

"God dammit," he said absently while glaring at the impatient motorists spoiling his fun.

"All right, all right, I HEAR YOU! SHUT THE HELL UP!" His instructions fell on drivers too deafened by horns to hear, and their honking continued, unabated.

The Sheriff motioned to his deputies. "Go tell those sons-a-bitches to shut the hell up. We'll be with 'em shortly."

The deputies did as they were told, but the lean bean held back.

"You too, ace. Go deal with those assholes, while I handle missy here."

The khaki-clothed, skinny lawman reluctantly did as he was told, slowly, while continually looking back at the Sheriff, the teenage loveliness, and the car that he _knew_ was the one.

"All right, sweetie, come over here," the Sheriff cooed while forcing her behind the Plymouth just out of sight but still abutting the gas cap and Sal so close yet so far away.

The Sheriff looked up to ensure no one was within earshot. Then he grabbed Maddie Pearl hard by the arm and moved within an inch of her face.

"Listen up, girly. If I wanted to screw ya, I'd screw ya, got it?"

Maddie Pearl was too frightened to respond or even motion with her head.

"GOT IT?"

Maddie Pearl slowly nodded.

"Good. Now here's the deal. There's an old place few miles back, been closed for years. Gotta a lot of junk cars and trucks. You know where I'm talkin' 'bout, dontcha?"

Maddie Pearl stood frozen in fear. He was not asking; he knew she knew; and her nonresponse was a clear reply.

"Yeah... thought so. I saw you turn around, awhile back, but it sure as shit didn't look like _you_ drivin'."

Maddie Pearl continued her statue pose, rigid, terrified, wanting to scream for Sal's help but knowing it was not to be.

"And you... or that GODDAM NIGGER BOYFRIEND OF YOURS," he yelled directly toward the Plymouth's trunk, "ought to know better than to put expired truck plates on a brand new Plymouth sedan, tryin' to fool the High Sheriff no less."

Maddie Pearl never had been in a posture quite like this, and knew not whether to talk or stand or run or scream or what. So she did what most of us would do: nothing.

"Now the way I figure it," he continued while looking back again to check on his colleagues who still were fanning out among the now fifteen cars and trucks waiting their turns to pass. "Since I don't care to fuck ya, you've got one option."

Maddie Pearl finally stammered a weak, " *What?* "

"You can pull that cash out from your pretty tits there, and hand it to me real quiet like, and I'll choose not to open that trunk and snoop around a bit."

A couple of the deputies began making their way back to the scene.

"What's it gonna be, missy," the Sheriff whispered without once taking his eyes off Maddie Pearl. "Want me to open that trunk?"

The footsteps were getting closer; the Sheriff took a step toward the trunk; Maddie Pearl looked back to see the skinny man whom she now recognized from earlier that morning. She did what had to be done, knowing full well it doomed their westward odyssey.

"Here," she said, frantically snatching the bills from between her breasts. "Take it, take it!"

As slickly as a Vegas dealer retrieving spent cards on the Black Jack table, the Sheriff cuffed the money into his pants pocket. This was not his first shakedown.

"I thought you'd see it my way, missy," he said like an Army drill instructor feigning concern for a weary recruit.

The men arrived back as the Sheriff slid a pace away for all to see that in fact he had not touched the buxom girl.

"I'm sorry for holding you up, ma'am," he oozed polite proper protocol. "You can go your own way now."

"But wait a sec—" the skinny man cut in slightly out of breath after hustling back from the furthest car in line.

"Fuck you, Lester. Your man's in Douglasville. Find 'em yourself!"

The Sheriff waltzed beside the Plymouth and swung his arms like a bullfighter directing the car's path westward with the beauty upfront and fugitive in the trunk.

"All right, boys," the Sheriff instructed, "let's close this shit down."

As she crossed the Alabama line, Maddie Pearl saw in the rearview mirror three cars with little red lights atop driving away in the opposite direction. And there, in the mountain dust, stood a skinny little, tinny-badged, khaki-clad, sourpussed cop watching his quarry careen forever away.

# *Chapter 25*

Safely in Alabama, Maddie Pearl pulled down a rut-strewn path and stopped. She opened the trunk and helped Sal out. Having been crouched in a fetal position, he was sore but, after stretching, was ready to tackle their next big issue: money. After the border fiasco, they now were down to $93.77, and California remained several inches away. Nevertheless, Sal was proud of the manner in which Maddie Pearl had pulled them through, and realized that there was a whole other side to her that he had not seen before.

He liked how she shunned the "N" word and portrayed him as positively as possible, under the awkwardly horrible circumstances. And he liked her amorous portrayal of some wanton young vixen—a lot.

Maddie Pearl had surprised herself as well. With the possible exception of David "Doc" Hodge, she'd never had a real boyfriend and Sal was the only person she ever had kissed *that way*. Experienced in the ancient art of seduction she was not, but instinctively Maddie Pearl knew what to do, and excelled. It was all new and strange... and terrifying.

She liked it a lot—too.

The screaming *KEE-EEEEE-ARR* from a large hawk above snapped Maddie Pearl back to the here and now. Uncertain how Sal felt about her "performance," she said, "I'm really sorry about, you know... what happened back there."

Still stretching his long, strong arms skyward while looking at the big bird, Sal replied, "What do you mean?"

"You know... back there. What I said and all and... what I did?"

Sal moved to Maddie Pearl and gently hugged her while softly stroking her hair. "You did what you had to, and it was great... beyond great even."

She pulled back. "But you know. It was... sinful and all."

"Survivin's no sin, Maddie Pearl. Like I said, you did what you had to... to survive... for *us* to survive."

"But the money? I gave it all away. All of it!"

"I know, I know. We'll figure something out. We will. Trust me... one way or another, we'll make this work."

"But how?" asked Maddie Pearl, desperately.

"I don't know," said Sal. "But we will, and as far as I'm concerned, there's no turning back!"

"But Sal," said Maddie Pearl, "you've seen the map. We've got a lot longer to go than if we just turned back. If we don't eat or anything, and with me driving some, we can get back home in... what... three or four days, and there's enough gas money for that, isn't there?"

Sal walked the ten paces or so from the Plymouth to the edge of the road. He looked east, toward Georgia, South Carolina, North Carolina and... *home*. But was there any "home" after all that had transpired, especially with Maddie Pearl's family? Then he gazed west, toward the bulk of Alabama and then Mississippi and the great unknown... out *there*. He put both hands to his handsome face and rubbed, then returned to Maddie Pearl.

"Gotta keep movin'. I'll drive."

Sal got in, as did Maddie Pearl. He made a multi-point turn to reorient the Plymouth forward on the old path, and then pulled up to the road. There was no traffic in either direction, but he paused for a long time nevertheless. He looked at Maddie Pearl, kissed her on the cheek warmly, and said, "Let's go *home*."

Sal then turned *left,* away from NC, SC, GA and everything either had ever known.

*     *     *

An hour into Bama, Sal found a safe spot to stop. They had not eaten, and planned to cut back to one "meal" a day consisting of as little as possible to subsist. Like castaways on a raft at sea, they would be rationing. Sal had done the math and, while not promising, there was reason for hope. He estimated they had been a little less than a thousand miles, with roughly two thousand to go. Even though two-thirds of their budget had been used to get one-third of the way, he determined that gas alone should cost no more than forty dollars. With Maddie Pearl driving too, even in the daytime, they could double their daily average. With a lot of luck, they could make it in a week, or probably less. If the Plymouth held up, and if there were no more surprises, they still could make it to the Mojave Anti-Aircraft Range and their new home in a strange place called California.

If only...

Although their spot was shady with a gentle breeze to keep things cool, both struggled for sweet sleep. The past few days' adventures and tomorrow's daunting realities were hitting each like sledgehammers pounding nails. Whenever she found herself in times of trouble, God came to Maddie Pearl through prayer. So she quietly prayed to herself:

> *Our Father, who art in Heaven, please forgive me for my sins, for I have been sinful. I have lied, and used your name in vain, and consorted with a man, a good man but still a man not my husband. Oh Lord, I am sorry. And I have sinned in the flesh, or at least pretended to be a sinner in the flesh, to gain advantage over a man, and I was wrong, and I knew I was wicked but I did it anyway, and I am sorry, and I ask forgiveness, Oh Lord.*

> *I have run from home, and I am lonely, and I did not tell my mother, and I know she loves me, even if she doesn't always show it, and is worried about me, and I promise Oh Lord to tell her of what I've done as soon as I can, and*

*I pray to you, Oh Lord, to keep her safe, and help her mind be at ease and show her that I'm safe and will be back... someday.*

*And Lord I pray that you help Tate 'cause he needs help, and help Levi and Ethan and keep them safe, and I pray for Nomita too and her people and, Oh Lord, I pray for them all and ask that you be with them and look over them just as you've always looked over me.*

*And Lord, heavenly father, I don't like to ask anything for me, especially since I'm a sinner and have done bad and am sorry and I'm not worthy, but Lord, dear Lord, I ask that you help us—me and Walter—on our journey. I've never known about much in my life, Oh Lord, but I know in my heart that he is a good and decent man, a great man, and I love him as I have never loved anyone, and I ask for your help, Oh Lord, in getting us safely on in our travels.*

*Thank you Lord, for all you have done for me, and for all you have done for us, and in Jesus' name I pray, Amen.*

When she concluded, Sal quietly whispered to himself just loudly enough for Maddie Pearl to hear, "Amen."

# Chapter 26

They awoke late in the afternoon, famished. Each conducted his/her daily constitutional, discretely, and readied for travel with hopes of finding at least some morsels soon. They were in luck—for once—as the *Green Book* described a place not more than twenty miles away. So on they went, west toward the rest of Alabama and then Mississippi, Louisiana, Texas, New Mexico, Arizona, and the Golden State of anti-aircraft ranges and dreamy medics.

The eatery, *Roscoes* without an apostrophe, was off the beaten track near Scottsboro. Per their custom, Maddie Pearl stayed behind while Sal went into the all-black establishment. He returned shortly with a bag of food for one that would have to be shared by two healthy adults with appetites for four.

"Damn crook," said Sal.

"What?" asked Maddie Pearl.

"Charged me six damn dollars."

"SIX DOLLARS? For what?"

"For one damn chicken dinner, that's what," said Sal in disgust. "Nothing but a damn crook."

Maddie Pearl could smell the chicken, and with hunger trumping anger she tore into the bag, as did Sal. It was cold, greasy, stringy, and awful, but they ate like wild beasts devouring a fresh kill. After gorging accordingly, and expensively, Sal turned the Plymouth's key and... nothing. He turned again, and... nothing.

Sal got out, popped the hood, and peered into darkness without a flashlight. He assumed it was merely a dead battery that could be rectified fairly easily with a jump, if only they had someone to play jumper. They didn't, but Sal figured that maybe somebody from within could lend a hand—

or a car with jumper cables—and help them on their way. So he retreated back to the scene of the chicken dinner crime.

Within minutes, he returned to the Plymouth along with two large African American men who made Sal look rather small, if that's possible. They weren't smiling. The one without a hat got in the driver's seat, noticing Maddie Pearl in the process. The other, wearing an old, dirty, white cowboy Stetson, looked at the motor while thrusting a lit candle into the oily, gassy enclosure.

Again, nothing happened when the key was turned. The man fiddled with the motor, his large Stetson rubbing somewhat against this and that, then closed the hood and turned to Sal.

"It's shot," said Stetson.

"I know that," said Sal. "Can't we jump it?"

"Nope, won't help. Alternator's shot."

Sal knew what this meant, and realized the new seriousness of their already precarious situation.

"Anywhere around here to get it fixed?" asked Sal.

The hatless man got out and joined Sal and Stetson, responding, "Yeah. Roscoe. He can fix it, but it'll cost ya."

Already wary from the meal that cost three times what they'd been paying thus far, Sal was skeptical.

"How much?"

"Oh... I don't know... how much ya got?" asked Stetson, who appeared to be the leader.

"I've got thirty dollars," Sal lied. "That's it."

Hatless motioned Stetson away for a quick caucus, then turned back to Sal.

"Tell ya what, Georgia," Stetson said in reference to the Georgia plates on the Plymouth. "We'll give ya a break. How does fifty sound?"

"But I've only got—"

"Yeah, we heard ya," Hatless cut in, "but it's still fifty... unless you want to..." the man looked in on Maddie Pearl and then back to Sal. "You know... make a *deal*."

Sal's suspicions piqued past dubious into outright repugnance.

"No... *deal*," he said firmly, sufficiently emphasizing "deal" to convey that he knew <u>exactly</u> what they were suggesting and it was <u>off</u> the table.

Stetson wandered over to the Plymouth, leaned in, and eyed Maddie Pearl closely.

"Hey darlin'... wanna have some fun?"

Sal raced over and pushed Stetson away. "I said, no deal!"

Hatless came to his cohort's aid but Sal managed to shrug him off. He positioned himself between the car and the large antagonists and balled up his fists in prep for whatever they wanted to bring. They moved in threateningly, ready, anticipating battle, and then—

"I've got fifty... fifty dollars," Maddie Pearl exclaimed frantically. "I got it, right here," she continued, holding up five tens.

Stetson and Hatless paused and looked at each other. Their little ploy had worked. Whether they really intended to follow through was immaterial, as Maddie Pearl had ensured the Plymouth would live another day, Sal would escape a certainly severe beating, and she'd avoid "fun" with Stetson and Hatless.

Their ten-dollar alternator in which they invested fifty now in working order, Sal and Maddie Pearl sped away from Roscoes. Although neither said a word, each knew their California dreamin' wasn't becoming a reality.

*     *     *

On the outskirts of town aside a large, lush field full of well-fed cattle at which they'd spent the night, the couple awoke with the fresh sun to reevaluate their sour situation.

Sal stood by the pasture fence and gazed across the large expanse. There appeared to be hundreds of cows, all scattered about in clusters eating the rich green grasses. At the far end stood what appeared to be a complex of barns, corrals, processing stations, and a large plantation-style house. He never had seen any farm quite this impressive. Maddie Pearl likewise couldn't help but admire the scenery. Despite

their predicament, at least somebody seemed to be doing well in life.

The eight-hundred-pound gorilla stood dominantly by their side, but neither could broach the inevitable. Each knew it was over, and in fact Sal's thoughts already had evolved from getting west to returning east, and home. With insufficient funds to reach either, he was flummoxed.

Maddie Pearl too was confused, about everything... but especially about Sal. Her feelings for him only had grown in the last few days, first with his decision against all odds to keep heading west and then with his willingness to stand and fight and possibly even die to protect her. She never had known any man willing to do anything like that, not even her own father or brothers, but the warmth for being loved so completely was cooled by the reality of their situation.

They could never date, be lovers, get married, or have children. And now here they were, standing by some field in some far off place she'd never heard of until a few days ago with no money, plan, or chance... for anything. It was over, yet life would go on. But where? And how?

"Maybe we can sell the car," said Sal, breaking Maddie Pearl from her ruminations. "That's what Doc wanted me to do in the first place. Wish I'd listened to him when I could."

"What good would that do, selling the car?"

"We could take the money, and use it to get back home somehow, on a train or whatever."

"But what about Doc? Wouldn't that be *his* money?" said Maddie Pearl, exposing yet again her strong moral compass wrought from a lifetime of Jesus and Mama.

"Yeah, but once we got back I could work and save up the money and pay him, somehow," answered Sal.

"I could work too, I suppose," said Maddie Pearl, trying to be helpful.

Sal was reluctant to go there, to Maddie Pearl, and to her situation and what she would do upon return to a home she no longer had, and a family that appeared to be no more. He had no answers for that.

She could not live with him, and she had neither the money nor contacts to secure a place on her own. Even if she

did, it would be temporary at best since Maddie Pearl had no marketable skills or prospects.

Sallerhead would be fine. He had the Army and, with luck, would hook up with another officer in need of a good man. If the Army just didn't work out and he was let go, he could move back to his home community now that Luke, Tate and Hog were out of the picture. Nomita, Pickles, Stump, Sow Belly and the rest would welcome him back, for sure. Or he could work with Farmer Hunt and help out with the Chinese couple in "Town."

But Maddie Pearl... poor Maddie Pearl had nothing on which to fall back in a world where women are second-class citizens unworthy of real work or fair pay despite whatever brains, beauty, and physical prowess they may possess. It wasn't fair but it was reality, and they both knew it, and this absence of any safety net or even remote possibilities stymied whatever plans they could derive.

Sal went back to the Plymouth and retrieved the map. After a quick scan, he piped up, "Huntsville's not too far up the road. Let's head that way and try to figure out how to go about selling the car."

Maddie Pearl came over, looked at the map, and replied, "But Scottsboro looks a lot closer, and it's heading... you know... east, toward home."

Sal looked at Maddie Pearl with a defeated demeanor. "So... you agree we need to head back?"

She took a deep breath, looked absently away momentarily, and replied, "What choice do we have?"

Although no fat ladies were singing, the game was over, and they had lost, badly. Sal folded up the map, tossed it into the open window, and said, "All right, then. Let's get the hell outta here."

Just as they got in and Sal cranked the motor—now working perfectly with their fancy, high-class, rip-off, used alternator—an older white man came ambling up from the pasture.

"HEY, YOU, HOLD ON THERE NOW," he yelled in a twangy, thick southern, genuine Alabama voice.

Sal's first instinct was to yank the Plymouth into gear and speed away, but there was something odd about the man keeping Sal's inclinations at bay. For one thing, he could barely walk. His pace was more of an upright crawl, as if only one leg worked for them both. He also was dressed in clothes too nice for a rowdy redneck farmhand. And his thick voice, while deeply son-of-the-South, seemed tame somehow or—at least—non-threatening. So Sal "held on" as he had been asked, and waited.

The man reached the fence and clearly was having trouble negotiating passage to the other side. Maddie Pearl noticed and quickly rushed over to help. She held one hand as he used his other to foist his lame leg around the barrier. The hand was soft, not roughhewn like Sal's, Hog's, Luke's, and every other worker she had known. And she noticed his eyes, his blue eyes, and what appeared to be... *something* therein, maybe kindness, or possibly wisdom, but whatever... there was *something*... deep, and soulful.

Once safely away from cows and now with humans, the man spoke up.

"Thanks, ma'am, for your help there. Always have trouble with those fences, for some reason."

The "reason" was obvious, he had a bad leg, but his unwillingness to admit the disadvantage somehow seemed endearing to Maddie Pearl, and she replied kindly, "No problem, mister. Glad to be able to help."

"What brings you folks this way?" he asked them both.

The friendliness struck Sal and Maddie Pearl alike as odd. He had not called Sal "boy" or Maddie Pearl "missy;" he had not demanded an explanation for their presence in no uncertain terms; he had made no threats. The man simply had treated them, both Sal and Maddie Pearl, like fellow human beings. It was unprecedented, on this trip anyway, and neither quite knew what to make of it.

"Just passing through, sir," said Sal in his military proper, subservient voice.

"Sir? I ain't no 'sir.' Name's John, John Claxton, but everybody calls me Johnny Bama."

Maddie Pearl slightly snickered at the funny sounding name. Johnny Bama noticed.

"Ya like that, ma'am... *Johnny Bama?*"

Maddie Pearl blushed, and then replied, "I like it. It's kinda different sounding."

"Yeah, nicknames can be like that sometimes. Like I knew this old boy up the road a ways called Bernie Urine. He's dead now, been dead awhile, but that's what everybody called him... Bernie Urine. Imagine riding through this here life with *that* name."

"So, sir...err I mean, Mister Bama... like I said, we're just passing through." Sal desperately was trying to be as diplomatic as possible, hoping to get away unscathed from this nice man who certainly could not be trusted because, after all, he's white and in Alabama... and called "Johnny Bama" for god sakes.

"What's your rush?" asked Johnny Bama. "Can't you just hang around a bit? I know... don't you want something to eat? Got some good fixin's up at the house there," he said pointing across the field toward the large plantation across the way.

Maddie Pearl gazed again at the distant mansion. "You live... *there?*"

John Claxton pensively held off responding for a few seconds, and then said in a more serious tone, "Not any more." He looked away, at nothing in particular. "Not any more, ma'am."

Maddie Pearl and Sal exchanged side-glances. What the hell is going on here? Then the white man with the gimpy leg and soulful blue eyes and long gray-blond hair crawled upright toward the Plymouth.

"Come on. You take me. Let's get something to eat."

So with literally nothing left to lose, Sal and Maddie Pearl threw caution to the wind, helped this strange Johnny Bama character into the front seat of Doc's Plymouth that they must sell to get back home, and headed toward a large estate with the non-owner to get food that, for all they knew, this non-owner didn't own.

What a long, strange trip indeed.

# Chapter 27

Upon arrival, Sal and Maddie Pearl realized the plantation house was even more impressive up close. It was large, well maintained, and attractive from its mammoth front porch replete with several wicker tables and rocking chairs. Johnny Bama led them into the foyer with its twenty-five foot ceiling and chandeliers hanging therefrom. Strangely, the interior reeked of mothballs, and all the furniture was covered in white sheets. As they progressed toward the kitchen in the back, each noticed the house appeared to be unoccupied. Johnny Bama had said he did not reside there, but who did? And if nobody lived there, then why can he just limp in and have the "crawl" of the place? Something was fishy.

In the kitchen, Johnny Bama reached into the fancy, modern icebox and pulled out several bowls. He then started dishing up plates full of potato salad, chicken salad, coleslaw, cold beans, smoked ham, and black-eyed peas. As he was handing a plateful of sumptuous fixin's to Maddie Pearl, the back screen door opened and in walked a tall, youngish man with close-cropped hair, a big nose, and glasses.

"What are you doing, Mister Claxton?" the tall man said.

"*Uh oh,*" thought Maddie Pearl and Sal pretty much identically. "*It's the owner, and he's not going to be too happy about this!*"

"Here... let *me* do that," he said to our couple's surprise.

The tall man took the plate from Johnny Bama and handed it over to Sal.

"Here, sir. Have a seat," the tall man said politely, unexpectedly.

Sal took the plate graciously, said "thank you sir," and sat down in total bewilderment. He and Maddie Pearl sat side-by-side slack jawed at what was transpiring before them. Sensing their confusion, Johnny Bama piped up.

"Friends, this here is Thomas Colton. He's what you call a business manager, I guess," he said, looking at Colton with a quizzical expression. "Ain't that what you are, Tom?"

"Yes, sir, Mister Claxton, that's as good a title as any. I work for Mister Claxton. I run his farms and so forth."

"Nice to meet you," said Maddie Pearl courteously. "My name is Maddie Pearl, and this is Sa— uh... I mean... this is Walter... Walter Jefferson."

"Glad to know your names," said Johnny Bama. He turned to Thomas Colton and continued, "They're just passing through. I ran into... what'd you say... Maddie Pearl and, who?"

"Walter," said Sal.

"Yeah, Walter here. I just ran into them out on the north fence. Said they were headin'... where again did you say?"

Maddie Pearl and Sal looked at each other awkwardly, unsure how best to respond. Then Sal spoke up for the pair, "I don't recall saying, but we were on our way to Scottsboro."

"Scottsboro? Why in God's green earth would anybody *ever* want to go to Scottsboro?" asked Johnny Bama.

"Well, sir...uh... I mean, Johnny... uh, ya see—"

"We were going to sell the car," Maddie Pearl came to Sal's rescue. "In Scottsboro."

"Sell the car? Why?" said Johnny Bama.

"Well, sir... Mister Bama... we need the money... to get back home," said Sal.

Johnny Bama said, "Thomas, I'll catch up with you in a bit, after lunch. Thanks." Thomas Colton understood the implied instruction to exit, and left.

"So what's all this about selling that car? It's a little worn, could probably be cleaned up a bit, but otherwise it looks almost new."

Again, neither Maddie Pearl nor Sal felt comfortable responding, since neither had much of a sensible answer to

the sensible question. The pregnant pause prompted Johnny Bama to persist.

"Seriously... So why? You folks in trouble or something, with the law or whatever?"

Sal finally took the reigns. "No, Mister Bama."

"God dammit, Walter," Johnny Bama said in a friendly but serious manner. "It's Johnny Bama, or JB, or even Johnny for that matter, but I ain't no 'sir' and I ain't no 'mister,' at least not to friends, and you two seem a lot closer to being friends than enemies."

"I'm sorry, Mist— *Johnny*. I'm not used to referring to people... well, like you... without saying 'sir' and 'mister' a lot."

"Look, Walter, I understand, I really do. Ain't easy being black in Ala-fuckin-Bama—excuse my French, Maddie Pearl. Never has been. But we're friends here, at least as far as I'm concerned, and you don't need to be treatin' me any differently than anybody else, ya hear?"

"I do, I do. I guess part of it ties back to my military background too, sir—oops—I mean Johnny."

Johnny Bama looked over Sal's clothes and realized for the first time that he was wearing the worn-remnants of an Army uniform.

"You Army, Walter?"

"Yes I am. Fort Bragg, down in—"

"Hell I know all about Fort Bragg! Used to be stationed there, awhile back and before... well... awhile back. What'd you do there, Walter?"

"I worked in a field hospital."

"Number two?"

"No, sir... excuse me... no, number four, out near that large parking area and the latrines."

"Oh hell yeah, I remember that shithole. Never seemed to get much business. I think they kinda gave up on it after the flu went through, but that was long before my time. So... it's still up and running?"

"Well... actually... no. And that's kinda why we're here... I mean, out this way."

Johnny Bama glanced at Maddie Pearl and noticed her plate had been fully cleaned with nary a crumb in sight. "Need anything, Maddie Pearl? You still look hungry."

"Well, Johnny, now that you mention it... I could go for more."

"Help yourself, please! I could do it for ya, but I suspect you'd do it much faster and better than me."

Maddie Pearl didn't need to be asked twice, and in the process ladled up Sal's plate as well.

"So go on, Walter, tell me about, you know, why you folks are all this way from Carolina."

Sal paused, "By the way, John, almost nobody calls me 'Walter.'"

"So what's your name, I mean... what do they call you?"

"Well... it's Sallerhead, but most folks just call me Sal."

Johnny Bama leaned far back and pondered.

"*Sallerhead?* Sounds like an insult more than a name."

"Yeah, I've heard that before. When I joined the Army, I stuck with Walter, or WC... that's short for Walter Carver. That's my middle name... Carver."

"Well I like that name a lot better. Walter, or even WC. Sounds a whole hell of a lot better than... what'd you say... *Salty-head?*"

"Sallerhead. But it doesn't matter. I'm used to it... and most people...at least the ones I know well... shorten it to just Sal."

"Well fair enough," Johnny Bama said judiciously. "So continue... why are you here, and I mean why are you *really* here, and thinking about selling that fine automobile out there?"

Sal looked at Maddie Pearl as if to ask, " *What should I tell him?*" She nodded affirmatively, which he took to mean it would be okay to open up to Mister John "Johnny Bama" Claxton from Some Giant Farm, Alabama.

Sal proceeded to fill in Johnny Bama on their odyssey's details. At first, he was somewhat reserved, just hitting the highlights, but Maddie Pearl chimed in and,

ultimately, like an old married couple telling timeworn tales, they jointly described the situation in some detail. Neither fully explained exactly what happened with the attack on Maddie Pearl or Luke's punishment therefor. This stranger didn't need to know all of that. But the rest was fair game.

When they were through, Johnny Bama got up with some difficulty from the kitchen table and ambled over to the screen door. He looked out at the rolling hills, farmland, cows, and beauty in the distance for a long, long time.

Sal stood and said, "Maddie Pearl, I suspect it's time we got movin' on." He jerked his head sideways to signal *"let's get the hell out of here, now!"* She took the hint.

"You're right, Walter. It's time we got back on the road. Thank you, Mister... uh... thanks, Johnny, for that wonderful meal and all."

He kept peering out, as if unhearing. They neatly placed their plates on the countertop near the sink that clearly had running water, a luxury neither Maddie Pearl nor Sal ever had experienced. As they began to retrace their steps through JB's ornate, cloth-ensconced non-home, he carped from the kitchen.

"Now just wait a doggone minute there."

The duo stopped, Sal's hand on the ornate door latch, uncertain of whether to wait or run like hell away from this inexplicable place and person. They waited.

Johnny Bama slowly came to them. "I got an idea."

# Chapter 28

We just can't," said Sal emphatically while pacing across the ornate living room with the sheet shrouds over everything but the sofa and chair on which Maddie Pearl, Johnny Bama, and he had been sitting for the better part of an hour.

"Just listen, will ya?" replied Johnny Bama.

"No! I've been listening, and we just can't. I'm really sorry, but—"

"You can, and you should," said JB. "It's really the only option ya got."

Maddie Pearl sat listening, fully engaged without saying anything. Sal was doing the talking, and she trusted his instincts, but a small bird within her abundant brain kept chirping: "*Why not?*"

"We've got options," retorted the recalcitrant Sal. "Plenty of options."

"Like what? Selling that man's car and spending *his* money to go back home? You call that an option?"

Sal didn't respond, having already mowed this yard more than once.

"Or what... getting part time jobs here and there to scrape together enough money to drive back home? You think *that's* gonna work?" persisted the owner of the majestic house in which he didn't live.

Sal again opted not to engage, but turned to Maddie Pearl for backing. She looked away, which surprised Walter Carver Jefferson, U.S.A. To ensure her unquestioning support, he said, "Maddie Pearl... tell 'em."

Maddie Pearl got up and looked out the massive front door to the Plymouth parked in the large circular driveway that fed a long, private, tree-lined drive meandering several

hundred yards before reaching the road and the inevitable decision point: left to California... or right.

"I don't know, Sal. He's got some good points," she said unconfidently.

"Good points? GOOD POINTS? Watta ya mean, 'good points'?" Sal said too ardently. "You think we—you and me—should jump in that car with this guy... this man that we've known, what, two hours... and drive all the way to California? You think quarters have been tight so far, imagine if we add... *him.*"

The manner in which Sal referred to "this guy" and "him" would be insulting to anyone else, and Sal meant it that way, one hundred percent. But Johnny Bama was not anyone else, and he let it slide like water off a cormorant.

"I understand, Walter, I really do, and you're right, you don't know the first thing about me, but I offered to let you both stay here—as long as you want, to get to know me, and you won't do that either." Johnny Bama was patient, but persistent. "Now you ask anybody 'round here, and I mean *anybody*, and they'll tell ya the same. They'll say '*that Johnny Bama is a good ol' boy, he is... drinks a little too much, but he ain't no drunk—and he ain't no mean drunk either.*' That's what they'll say, you ask 'em."

Sal considered the input that he'd already heard at least three times now. He had no intention of scouring the Alabama countryside in search of references for "some guy" with whom he had no inclination of sharing a ride all the way to California. He'd confronted JB earlier with the proposition that if Bama really wanted to help he could buy the car from them and set them up on a train back to NC. Johnny Bama had countered with "*Hell friend, I'd give ya the money, but you don't want to go back to that southern shitland.*" When Sal protested, JB cut him off sternly, like a father admonishing a son, with "*Walter, now hear me. I actually kinda like it back in the land of Tar Heels and the like. Got a lot of good memories there. Might even move back there someday... who knows? So I see why you might long for there, but hear me out—ya got no life there. None! And neither does she.*"

The man was right, but they had no life here either, and they certainly had nothing in California except a soldier Sal barely knew, a job that probably didn't exist, no place to live, no money, and... well... yadda yadda yadda.

"Sal, can we talk... privately?" Maddie Pearl asked, winking at Bama.

"Good idea," the white man took the hint. "I'll just head back into the kitchen."

"No, you stay," said Maddie Pearl. "We'll just step out on the porch."

"All right," said JB dubiously, "but don't you get no crazy idea to jump in that car and drive off. That's the last thing you should do right now, ya hear?"

"We won't," said Maddie Pearl, who had not even considered the thought.

"*We might,*" thought Sal, who had considered the idea repeatedly for the last hour or more.

Once out of JB's earshot, Maddie Pearl whispered, "I want to go to California, with him."

Sal was surprised. From her utterance about his "good points," Sal knew Maddie Pearl's resolve was shaky, but he assumed reason and good sense would prevail. Although Maddie Pearl was uneducated except in the "Readin/Riten/Rithmatic/Religion" basics, the young woman was blessed with a solid, reasonable mind not subject to flighty whims and irrational wanderings. How could she possibly think running off with this gimpy-legged stranger with the weird home situation was a good idea?

"Look, Maddie Pearl, it's crazy. We don't know the first thing about him."

"He seems like a good man, to me, and he obviously has the money... and we don't."

"But it makes no sense. His life is here, with his fancy house and... what'd he say... 'farms'? And he supposedly owns this giant house but doesn't live in it? Why not? What's going on with that? And that manager guy, what's his name?"

"Tom, I think."

"Yeah, Tom or whatever... what's up with him? He supposedly runs the farms, but did you get a look at 'em?

Had that big nose of his in a book his whole life, I 'spect. Bet he doesn't even know the difference between a plow and a hog."

"Well if you're so worried, let's stick around a day or two, get to know him better, maybe check him out like he said."

"Get to know him better? Is that what you said, 'get to know him... *better'?*"

Sal's facial expression spoke volumes, and Maddie Pearl *heard* the silent message clearly.

"Just what's *that* supposed to mean?" said Maddie Pearl, without backing down an inch.

"I think you know exactly what it means," replied Sal, equally entrenched.

"So *that's* why you won't go along. I get it now... you son of a bitch!"

Sal felt the sting like a sharp rap from a spiny switch to the back. She'd never spoken to him like that, ever, but then... he'd never given her reason. And why had he given her reason here, and now? They had no commitment together, no deals or understandings, certainly no wedding plans or the like. They didn't have any chance... *together.*

In 1939 America, and not just the awful, backward, ignorant South but really throughout the country—from closed hospitals in Fort Bragg to open anti-aircraft ranges near Barstow—blacks and whites simply did not socialize, did not date, did not cohabitate, and damn sure did not marry. And Christians all, these Americans, so proud of their God and so believing in the Good Book that preaches tolerance and love and understanding and yet, these holy people, these disciples of God no less, didn't even permit the blacks to set foot in white churches, unless they were cleaning the nasty-ass toilets.

And Sal knew this, knew it well from his short lifetime of long experience, and recognized that there could be no future, no real future, with Maddie Pearl. And he knew it from the outset, when he first saw her walking up to Daisy and Nomita, and when they decided to head west so Maddie Pearl could reunite with Doc, and when they left Fort Bragg under the cloak of darkness and accidentally detoured to

Webster County costing them precious miles and gas, and when they shared a moment in a field gazing eye-to-eye far too long, and just a couple of days ago when they kissed passionately rapturously. Such knowledge didn't allay the pain, however, and didn't ease his decision to let yet another competitor for Maddie Pearl's affections into a trial that, until this moment, he had controlled. But it was a case he couldn't win, a verdict no judge could overturn, and Sal judiciously rendered accordingly.

"Okay Maddie Pearl... you win," Sal said.

His reluctant acquiescence reverberated for the rest of their lives.

# Chapter 29

The plan was simple. Johnny Bama bought the Plymouth, for a thousand dollars. This was twice what Sal expected, but Johnny insisted. Five hundred would go to Doc. The rest was doled out between Maddie Pearl and Sal, but only after WC was made whole from the near two hundred that already had been spent.

On the trip, Maddie Pearl and Johnny Bama would pose as a married couple, the Claxtons. Sal cringed at this, but hid his sentiments and agreed to "serve" as their "helping hand/chauffeur." Bama brought a chauffeur's hat that Sal would wear, which was more than degrading, but Bama promised it was a necessity—like an ID to prove identity or authenticity. They would travel whenever they wanted, in broad daylight preferably, unafraid of being stopped or questioned. They were heading to California to visit relatives that lived near Barstow.

Even though Maddie Pearl and Sal now were flush with more cash than either had ever seen, Johnny Bama would pay all bills. They would get rooms to let at night, separate rooms for the couple, with *Green Book* accommodations for Sal. They'd eat at legitimate restaurants, with food brought out to Sal in the Plymouth befitting the second-class citizen that the fat southern whites with the skinny thin intellects in places like Tallulah and Tyler considered this great, intelligent man.

Neither Maddie Pearl nor Sallerhead had any idea of precisely how much cash Johnny Bama had brought, but they had every reason to believe it was enough... much more than enough in fact. Sal worried about carrying so much money, but JB reassured him. The manner of reassurance was one of many things that troubled Sal, deeply.

"Don't fret none, Walter, about all this money. Nobody gonna mess with us, not with these persuaders."

The "persuaders" were four weapons: a small Derringer, a large Colt revolver, a Smith & Wesson .22 rifle, and a Sturm Ruger shotgun. The guns terrified Maddie Pearl at first but, after a long session on JB's farm, she took a liking to them, especially the "cute little Derringer" which Bama insisted she carry at all times.

For further protection, some of the money was divided into small bundles and distributed about the Plymouth wherever hiding places presented. Johnny Bama made sure that both Maddie Pearl and Sal knew full well each nook and cranny used, just in case "anything happened." His implication that something might "happen" was disconcerting, as were the guns and everything else, but Maddie Pearl and Sal were in it for the long haul now, and fully committed to the plan, warts and worries notwithstanding.

They left early on the third morning. The trio pulled up to the north fence of the Claxton property beside the road, and turned left. The first day was uneventful. Sal drove in front; Maddie Pearl and Johnny Bama rode in the rear. For the most part, Bama did all the talking, but his commentary primarily concerned local folklore and rambling tales of this person and that—people of no concern to the others, either now or evermore.

Despite the drive's humdrum nature, Maddie Pearl was exhilarated. She had come a long way in a short time and, like cotton absorbing blood, was soaking in everything. For the first time—except for the few minutes here and there that she had driven—Maddie Pearl was able to sit upright, watch the countryside, and even put her head out the window to feel the breeze. Now that they could drive on main roads, which were far better, and no longer fearing law enforcement hassles, the relative wind came whizzing by at close to sixty, not forty-five. Maddie Pearl was euphoric.

Sal noticed Maddie Pearl's sunny deportment in the bright daylight drive, and was conflicted. He was pleased that she was happy, and his doubts about Bama had been salved somewhat by the generous Plymouth transaction. "*If worse*

comes to worst," thought Sal, "we at least have enough money now to get back, no matter what happens." The feeling was comforting, but he still harbored doubts. Was he suspicious of Johnny Bama's motivations, or was he jealous? Neither answer was settling, and either scenario was problematic, at least for "Walter," as Bama insisted on calling him.

Lunch had arrived in a horrible little town called Tuscaloosa, just outside Birmingham. Johnny knew the place well, of course, and was greeted graciously by the cook, who evidently was the owner. While "the Claxtons" dined sumptuously on catfish stew, collards, beans, and assorted fine foods, Sal was forced to park the Plymouth in the rear, beside the outhouse that smelled of feces, decaying meat, and skunk. In this appalling locale he ate what appeared to be leftover fish and trimmings from white patrons inside. Even the worst *Green Book* repast, from Roscoes without an apostrophe in Scottsboro, was a feast befitting royalty compared to this crappie.

When finished, Sal got out to relieve himself in the outhouse. He opened the door and nearly fainted. Inside, stuck halfway in the potty hole, was the remnant of a dead fawn, its flesh ripped by some predator revealing split intestines, blood, gore, and slimy shit aplenty. Sal stumbled out and headed for the security of a wooded patch.

Back on the road, Sal drove while Maddie Pearl and Bama slept in the back. He looked at them with disgust. In barely a day, he had gone from leader to slave... to *nigger*... to worst of all, Uncle Tom. His affection for Maddie Pearl subsiding with each bump in the road tossing her pretty-little head ever closer to Johnny, Sal's temperament burned from warm to boiling. But he could say nothing, and do even less, except drive for the man and say "yes ma'am" to the girl and play the role properly and wipe their smelly asses if told so to do!

They crossed into Mississippi before sundown. Even with everything interpersonal percolating, Sal knew this was a far better way of traveling. No longer did he worry about those things that only a black man driving a white woman across the Klan South in somebody else's new Plymouth

considered threatening. They didn't get stopped but, if they did, Sal knew to shut up and defer to *Mister Claxton Sir* in the backseat.

Maddie Pearl had awoken from her nap long ago, but had said precious little since. Her eagerness had faded, like a runner's high after the endorphins subside, and she mostly looked out the window assessing the rapidly changing scenery that somehow had no personality. Just like South Carolina, Georgia, and Alabama, there were magnolias, mountains, and farmland, but there also were shanties, filth, and ugliness. Even though her life in eastern North Carolina had been super sheltered, she had missed nothing, at least not in the Confederacy. The thought made her sad, like the big, bright, beautiful world maybe wasn't all that she had thought and hoped.

After a particularly long conversation drought, Johnny Bama said, "Walter, how ya doing up there?"

It was the only thing Bama had said to Sal in hours, having focused solely on napping with or talking to Maddie Pearl since lunch.

"You talkin' to me, *sir?*" replied Sal with contempt.

Maddie Pearl and Johnny Bama picked up the scent instantly.

"You doing okay, Sal?" Maddie Pearl followed up.

Private Walter Carver "WC" Jefferson, a.k.a. "Sallerhead," ignored her.

"Tell ya what, son, let's pull over next chance ya get, and Maddie Pearl here can drive some."

Sal glowered at Bama through the mirror. "Let's get one damn thing straight," Sal said to the crippled white man who was no more than ten years older, at most. "I'm not your son."

Sal's unmistakably serious tone did nothing to hide the seething cauldron of anger burning deeply in the black man's heart.

"Come on, Sal—"

"Shut up, Maddie Pearl! I'm tired of your shit too," said Sal in a manner not unlike Maddie Pearl's "son of a

bitch" rock thrown earlier. It scored a direct hit, and now they were tied: one to one.

"All right, all right," said Johnny Bama. "Everybody just calm down now. Tell you what... we've been in this damn car all day. Let's stop, get something good to eat, and find a place to stay for the night. Watta ya say?"

Neither Maddie Pearl nor Sal responded, but just ahead was a gas station and Sal pulled in. Adhering to the routine that already had been established, Johnny reached forward with a few bills.

"I'll pay," said Sal coarsely as he got out to take care of business.

"Well.. okay..." said Bama, hesitantly.

Sal filled the Plymouth, which only was half empty and not seriously in need of refueling. He went behind the building to use whatever dead-deer-shit-house or tree he could find.

"Might as well," said Maddie Pearl, more or less to herself. As she leaned forward to escape and find a potty, she glanced nonchalantly at Johnny and did a double take. Although his head was turned away, she noticed the unmistakable trace of a tear rolling down his cheek.

"Johnny? You okay?" she asked in a motherly manner. He didn't reply.

Maddie Pearl remained in place, uncertain of what to do. "*If he's in pain or suffering somehow from his... condition, or whatever it is,*" she thought, "*maybe I can help.*"

"What is it, John... what's wrong?"

He turned to her, his eyes full of tears, and replied, "I just want to help you folks, that's all I want to do." He lurched forward. She quickly moved in for support. She hugged him warmly, like a mother with child, and kept reassuring him.

"It's okay, John, it's good," she whispered in his ear. "We know you're just trying to help, we know, and we can't thank you enough."

Just then, Sal returned, saw them "snuggling" in the back seat, and exploded!

"I KNEW IT! I GOD DAMN KNEW IT," he yelled
to no one in particular and then stormed into the store with
the "WHITES ONLY" sign above the door.

"That's not good," said Johnny Bama with more than a
timbre of fear.

He and Maddie Pearl scrambled to get out of the
Plymouth, but he was very slow and it took much longer than
either would have preferred. Meanwhile, they could hear Sal
inside throwing a tantrum. Then came the *other* voices...
men's voices, loud and menacing men's voices, and they were
yelling things that sounded a lot like "get him" and "fucking
nigger" and "me first" and the like.

With some difficulty, Johnny Bama entered the whites
only zone with Maddie Pearl alongside. Sal was in the back,
cornered, with three large white men holding him in place. In
front of Sal was a squirrelly-looking, young, pimply-pussed
punk with a flyswatter in hand. He was popping Sal over and
over on the face, wicked swats cracking welts with every
whack. A couple of hangers-on hung on, watching and
laughing, with the intellectual "fucking nigger" commentary
heard from outside.

BAM!

Everything stopped! Everyone whipsawed toward the
front door! There, standing firmly with a large, Colt revolver
pointed squarely at fly-swatter-boy, was Johnny Bama, and his
gun was still smoking.

"Any one of you ignorant, racist, corn holing
Mississippi cocksuckers lay one more finger on my friend,"
said Johnny, "and squirrel there is the first pimple to pop."

Nobody said a word; nobody breathed; nobody did
anything... except Johnny Bama, who did his talking with
bullets.

BAM! BAM!

Each shot was close to—but intentionally above—
squirrel's head. The rednecks scrambled like cockroaches
scattering when lights flash on. If not for the situation's
seriousness, it would have been comical. Outside they
sprinted in every direction possible—away!

Now free, Sal hustled toward Maddie Pearl and the front door, partly to exit but also to chase his tormentors. But Johnny Bama held him up with his arm.

"Leave 'em be, Walter... I mean... *Sal.*

Sal reluctantly stopped.

Bama continued, "Do you need anything before we head outta here?"

Johnny scanned the store's shelves and motioned thereto for Sal and Maddie Pearl. They looked at each other, took the hint, and grabbed several items as if in a race.

"No need to hurry," said Bama. "I 'spect dem boys won't be back for awhile... 'specially with all that shit in their drawers."

Sal and Maddie Pearl filled their arms to overflowing with wrapped cakes, cans, assorted candies and so forth. Maddie Pearl found a brush and other womanly necessities along with myriad snack foods and three bottles of pop. Johnny grabbed nothing, but waited patiently aside while they carried out the mission.

Full to overflowing, Maddie Pearl and Sal reached the door.

"Ready?" asked Johnny. They nodded. Then JB pulled out his wallet, placed a fifty dollar bill on the counter, with General Ulysses S. Grant himself staring out in disgust at this obscene little embodiment of Southern heritage not hate he so thoroughly conquered as the Union's Commander.

"That oughtta cover it," said Johnny Bama.

He turned and calmly leg-dragged out the door and toward the Plymouth with Maddie Pearl and Sal crab walking behind to avoid dropping any of their prizes.

A few paces out in the open, Johnny Bama turned back toward the storefront, and said, "Excuse me a sec."

He turned his pistol on the "WHITES ONLY" sign and shot BAM BAM BAM until the termite riddled insult to humanity and all that is good and decent fell harmlessly down in bullet-peppered pieces on the shitty little store's gravel and weed parking lot.

"I always like to leave a tip," Bama said to his co-travelers as they got in the Plymouth and drove away.

# Chapter 30

The rest of Mississippi was no different from the little store that once had a "WHITES ONLY" sign above its door. Whatever wealth, progressiveness, or modernity Ole Miss may boast certainly didn't manifest anywhere near the road from its eastern border to the west. Even the livestock looked impoverished. Johnny Bama couldn't help but recoil at the gaunt faced cows with the sallow look of malnourishment and mistreatment. But the cattle had no monopoly on the pitiful appearance, as unfenced chickens were scraggly, pigs appeared filthy, and even the occasional horse was bloated, uncombed and uncouth. It was an easy drive, so far, but unpleasant, due to the scenery outside *and* the climate inside.

Nary a word was spoken for over an hour as they progressed west. No one quite knew what to say, so no one said anything. Although it had not been discussed in the dearth of conversation, Sal's driving and Maddie Pearl's silence and Johnny Bama's livestock fixation put the plan to stop, eat, and rest on hold, as the daylight faded into night. The goodies "bought" by Bama via his fifty-dollar imbursement sated the appetites and, with the full tank of gas, no need for further replenishment presented, so Sal drove and they rode and the world passed by one mucky mile after another.

While studying the road ahead, Sal could not see past the image of Maddie Pearl and Bama making out in the back seat. *"How could she?"* he obsessed, without considering other possibilities.

Maddie Pearl suspected what Sal was thinking but didn't know how to broach the subject without exposing Johnny's emotional weakness... or upsetting him.

If there are two or more people, there is politics. On a dirty east/west Rebel road in the early evening during the late summer of 1939 inside a new Plymouth once owned by a faux doctor at the Mojave Anti-Aircraft Range still some 1,906 miles away, politics was busting at the seams.

Being worldlier than his political compatriots, and far better versed in winning friends and influencing people, Johnny Bama broke the ice, carefully.

"Thank you, Sal, for driving," he said, out of the blue.

Neither responded, although the Plymouth's wheels weren't the only ones spinning.

"We'd never make it... without you," Bama continued.

Picking up the hint, Maddie Pearl chimed in, "He's right, you know."

Sal looked impassively toward the road ahead.

"I can drive," Bama pushed on, "but with my leg and all, I've got to admit that... well, I'm not very good at it."

"And you've seen me drive," added Maddie Pearl, "and you know where we'd be if I were in charge... of the car, I mean."

A long silence followed. The opening salvo by Johnny Bama reinforced by Maddie Pearl seemed to have missed its target, but then Sal chose to engage.

"I saw what you two were up to back there, and I'm done with... *this.*" He was cold and unemotional, calculated in a manner designed to convey his conviction that the next chance he got was the end of the road for him.

"It wasn't what you thought," said Maddie Pearl defensively.

"I - know - what - I - saw," replied Sal, parsing each word carefully for effect.

"So that's it? You're just going to quit and run back home?" Maddie Pearl questioned less cautiously. "And to what?"

"You two will be just fine without me, and I'll be more than just fine on my own," said Sal obstinately.

The several seconds that passed only escalated the mounting tension. They were at a precipice, and any wrong word would cast them all into the abyss, forever.

"Sal's right," JB suggested to the utter amazement of Maddie Pearl *and* WC. "Maddie Pearl can drive us out there, and I can help, especially when we reach the desert flatlands where there won't be much stopping or the like. That's the hard part, for me. I have to drive using only my good leg, and I have trouble getting it over to the clutch and brake, but once I get going I can steer and all that. And we've got enough money to get out there, and Sal, you should have enough to get back to Carolina... and if you don't, I don't mind helping you out with a loan, and I know you'll pay me back."

Maddie Pearl was stunned. There was no way she would continue without her soul mate. Sal likewise didn't quite know what to make of Bama's... speech. "*Was he serious, or making yet another play for Maddie Pearl... or just trying to bluff me into sticking it out?*"

Before either fully could synthesize JB's amended plan, however, Bama tossed in a nuance.

"You can't leave tonight, anyway, so Sal... why don't we stop somewhere, have a good meal, and celebrate how far you've come and... you know... send you off right?"

Neither Sal nor Maddie Pearl were in a celebratory mood, but it had been a long day and the sugary "nourishment" from the candy, cookies, and pop had given way to near nausea. A meal and a good night's sleep made a lot of sense.

Maddie Pearl leaned up and positioned herself on the top of the front bench like she had done so many times before when Sal and she were traveling clandestinely and she hid in the back except when the coast was clear.

"Whatcha think?" asked Maddie Pearl. "Can't head back tonight. Might as well stop, for now at least."

Sal didn't respond for what seemed like minutes, although actually it was no more than thirty seconds.

"Alright," Sal finally concluded. "Get the *Green Book.*"

"No," JB piped in. "We'll do better than that. There's a place I know... up in Vicksburg, right on the river."

*     *     *

Sal, Maddie Pearl, and Johnny Bama found themselves at a table on an expansive back porch of a nice restaurant in Vicksburg overlooking the banks of the mighty Mississippi River. They were alone. Magically, JB had finagled the blatant Jim Crow violation. Maddie Pearl and Sal asked no questions.

Within eyesight across the water was Louisiana. Maddie Pearl wondered whether she would ever set foot there, or if this would be as far from home as she ever would get. Sal's mind, meanwhile, was set: he was on the next train or bus or whatever it took to retrace his steps. He'd made the wrong decision letting Johnny Bama come along; he wasn't going to make the same mistake twice. He had enough money, and he'd make his own way back—one way or another.

Sal did not expect Maddie Pearl to accompany him, and actually intended to resist her entreaties if the subject arose. He loved her, more than he knew possible, but the black man realized the impossibility of it all, as did she—he assumed. And besides, even if Johnny Bama were no more than a flighty teenage fling, there remained Doc, and Sal had seen a certain "look" about her whenever Doc was around.

Maddie Pearl was right—Sal had nothing back east—but casting his lot west with some cripple and a young woman forbidden to him promised even less, if less than nothing is possible. So he was determined, and nothing tonight was going to change things.

Johnny Bama was on his second drink, a bourbon concoction, but did not appear to be feeling any effects. Maddie Pearl and Sal shied away. Their alcohol experiences were limited to moonshine sips that burned like kerosene and prompted vomit-laden sickness, like eating rotten possum.

"Come on," encouraged Bama, "at least give it a try."

He motioned and a waiter appeared instantly. "Two more please, for my friends." Within seconds, drinks appeared before Maddie Pearl and Sal.

"It's called a Mississippi Haymaker. Try it! This place is famous for 'em, and I promise it won't hurt ya."

Maddie Pearl looked around nervously, as if she was doing something wrong and didn't want to get caught. She cleared her throat, took hold of the glass, reluctantly tilted it toward her lips, and took the tiniest of sips.

"Ugh," she croaked, "what *is* it?"

"You're probably tasting those lemons," he answered knowingly. "They're kinda tart, and it's also got a little vinegar and sugar, some chopped up ginger, and the bourbon of course, Four Roses—the best... at least for a Mississippi Haymaker."

JB motioned to Sal, "Come on, young man, try it... like I said, it's pretty good."

While Sal mulled his decision, Maddie Pearl took another, bigger sip.

"You're right," she said to Johnny. "I can taste something kinda tart, and the vinegar too... I've never had a lemon before, but that vinegar is unmistakable."

Maddie Pearl turned to Sal, "Try it... it's pretty good, really."

Sal finally gave in and took a sip. He didn't like it, but the taste was different from any carburetor juice or peckerhead poison he associated with drinkin', and the warmth slowly enveloping him was pleasing.

Maddie Pearl too liked the comforting sensation, and downed a few more sips fairly quickly.

"Not too fast, Maddie Pearl... gotta pace yourself. As drinks go, this one is pretty tame, really, but ya still gotta watch out, cause these things can sneak up on ya."

Maddie Pearl got the message, as did Sal, but each managed to finish perhaps more quickly than the doctor ordered, so Johnny Bama held off on more drinks and opted for menus instead.

In due course, their meals were served. This was a whole new experience for the Webster Countians, having never eaten in a real restaurant with an authentic waiter and custom dinners cooked specifically per their individual requests. The magic continued with each fresh bite, as the steak and potatoes, green beans, and corn-on-the-cob for Sal and Maddie Pearl's gumbo with rice and okra were beyond

heavenly—not to mention the exquisite hushpuppies, cheese bread, and sweet tea.

About midway through, Johnny Bama arranged another round of Mississippi Haymakers that curiously arrived in larger portions than round one. Face deep in fine cuisine, the two Tar Heels didn't notice, and proceeded to sip and eat and sip again to the glass bottoms.

For dessert, Johnny Bama took the liberty to order for the party.

"What's this?" asked Maddie Pearl enthusiastically.

"This here is called 'Black Bottom Pie,'" replied Johnny Bama. "It's something new from just across the river there." He pointed at the Mississippi River and Louisiana a world away on the other side.

"What's in it?" persisted Maddie Pearl.

"Well... I'm not a hundred percent sure, but you can see the chocolate there, and whipped cream. I haven't had it before, but my friend who runs the place told me it's real good."

"Why's it called... what is it... 'black bottom' or whatever?" Maddie Pearl asked.

"I think it has something to do with the lowlands... along the river. You'll see it tomorrow when the sun comes up. That mud's pretty damn dark along the bank."

Satisfied, Maddie Pearl cut a piece and tasted.

"Oh my goodness. It's... unbelievable!"

She quickly had another bite, then another as if she never had eaten before. Sal, feeling slightly less militant after two drinks and the best meal of his life—bar none—grudgingly pierced a piece with his fork. The effect on him was equally pronounced.

"Damn," he said, his first utterance throughout the meal. "That's really something."

JB then did something that seemed as natural to him as breathing: he smiled warmly.

"Glad you folks like it," he said in a satisfied manner. "Have some more if you want, we got the whole pie to ourselves—and they'll just throw away whatever we don't eat." Maddie Pearl and Sal obediently did their best to waste not.

Their banquet now complete, Johnny Bama motioned, the waiter scrambled, and there appeared three small snifters filled with an amber liquid.

Johnny Bama lifted his small glass and said, "I'd like to make a toast."

His dinner companions looked at JB, bewildered.

"Oh, let me explain. After a nice dinner, it's customary to toast to something... you know... to drink to something."

The others remained in darkness.

"Still muddy? I'll tell ya what, let me give you an example. Let's say you had a great crop and you just got it in and you made a bunch of money. Well, when everything's done and done, you might celebrate... you know... like have a big dinner or whatever, like Thanksgiving."

JB still didn't fully gauge the depths of their poverty and inexperience, having never lived in such deeply neglectful conditions himself. *Thanksgiving?* To them, Thanksgiving was an extra helping of dry cornbread. Sal at least had some inkling of profits from crops, but celebrating with a big dinner—that was crazy talk.

Sensing their continuing confusion, Johnny Bama proceeded with this. "Let's do it this way... I'll do the toast, and you just follow my lead, okay?"

They nodded agreement, and JB proceeded.

"I want to thank you good folks for putting up with me the last couple of days, and I wish you Godspeed as you *both* head back home tomorrow."

Johnny Bama then lifted his snifter and took a sip of brandy.

"All right, now you folks have some brandy too," instructed JB.

For very different reasons, neither complied. Maddie Pearl, visibly stunned by the reference to *both* heading home, sat wide-eyed and confused.

Sal, jaw clenched in anger and consternation, thought, "*Just what the hell does he think he's doing?*"

"Come now... don't be shy, it's sorta like the haymaker, but nowhere near as strong."

It wasn't the alcoholic drink that inhibited their consumption. The *real* moment of truth had come. Twice now, Sal and Maddie Pearl had been confronted with the same issue; twice they had opted to continue west. But the third time was no charm. This was different, and far scarier. Before, it had been a question of whether they *could* make it; now, it was whether they *should* go at all.

Maddie Pearl was dead set on California, since home was no more. But she had no interest in leaving Sal, and deeply feared having to make a choice between Johnny and California or Sal and... whatever awaited a thousand miles east and a lifetime ago.

Until this second, Sal's mind was made—he'd go back, alone. Now, somehow, after all of... *this*, he wasn't so sure... of *anything*. He always had been extremely self-assured and confident in his choices, but his decision to press on as a threesome—and how things had been turning out up to now—struck at his core filling him with self-doubt. The concerns were exacerbated by having to be rescued at the "WHITES ONLY" dump by this... this... lothario with the bum leg, fat wallet, and trigger finger.

Like Maddie Pearl, Sal didn't want to split up, but he no longer could continue the charade, particularly if she planned to flaunt her affections for JB right in his face. Perhaps it was the liquor whispering in his ear but, insecurities notwithstanding, Sal resolved once and for all. *"Before I do anything, I'm going to find out just where the hell we all stand around here, now!"*

"What's your deal, Mister Claxton? Why are you... *here*, with us?" Sal demanded.

"I told ya," he replied easily. "It's something fun to do, for a change."

Sal eyeballed Maddie Pearl and JB together. "I'm not buying it, Mister Claxton. Not for one fucking minute."

Johnny straightened himself up in the chair and looked Sal directly in the eyes. He'd anticipated this moment, and was more than prepared.

"There's something you need to know, Walter, and you need to know it loud and clear."

Sal stiffened as well, ready for whatever challenges this frail, rich, white man might throw at him.

"There is nothing going on between Maddie Pearl and me. **Nothing!** And if you think otherwise just because of what you think you saw back at that God damn rat hole store, then sir, you've got another think coming."

The steady, serious, evocative way in which Bama spoke was more than compelling. And deep down inside, where only unequivocal truths reside, Sal knew Maddie Pearl loved him, and would not abandon him for mere coins and bills. And maybe Johnny was sincere; maybe Maddie Pearl wasn't his quarry. But if not, then what? What else did any of this bring to the table for a wealthy man with a lot of land and a magnificent home where he is known and loved by all? Its nonsensical nature made Sal ever the more suspicious, and demanding.

"So why are you here, then? And don't just say 'for fun,' cause sir, as we soldiers like to say, 'that shit just don't flush.'"

A large paddlewheel boat glided smoothly across the Mississippi River in the background. Its many patrons could be heard partying aboard. They were heading south, with the current, toward Natchez and St. Genevieve and then through Baton Rouge to their ultimate destination: New Orleans.

Johnny Bama studied the boat closely, as if wishing he were aboard headed for Bourbon Street and the French Quarter. There would be less drama, for sure. And if his true quest were mere fun, that's just where he'd be right now. But fun—always front and center for drink-happy, always-smiling Bama—somehow didn't dovetail here, not with these two people, and not on this one strange trip. No... there was something more going on here, but what?

Even Johnny didn't know, and maybe never would.

He redirected his attention to this couple he'd "known" less than a week but somehow realized his fate would be intertwined. Pointing at his leg, he said, "Do you want to know how I got... you know... this way?"

The couple sat, waiting.

"It happened on May fourth, last year... 1938." Johnny Bama cast his stare back to the river and another world, another life, and continued absently, like a robot telling a story, mechanically, emotionless. "I was driving. It was a new Plymouth, just like ours, but not black. I had it special painted... blue... her favorite color. She was sitting next to me, in the front seat, like she always did, and Annabelle was in the back, behind her mother, with a coloring book."

Johnny Bama paused, gathering his wits, the robot having been replaced with a human, a real live human of flesh and blood and now-withered hip and myriad internal deformities wrought by a ton of gnashing metal thrusting wickedly about through skin, bone, arteries and even into his brain.

"It was an unusually warm day, and the car was hot, and I noticed... over my shoulder... that Annabelle's crayons were melting on the seat, and I just had to... had to..."

He broke away again, gone... somewhere not here. The waiter appeared.

"Mister Claxton, sir, will there be anything else?"

JB Claxton turned to the waiter, exposing his eyes to Maddie Pearl and Sal. They were bloodshot from crying, and streams of salty tears rivered down his face, flowing ever so surely past his neck and into the hidden, mangled man beneath the shirt façade.

"Yes, Gilbert, how about another brandy for me and my friends here?"

Before Maddie Pearl or Sal could protest, the waiter hustled off.

As the drinks arrived, Bama continued, "Now... where was I? Oh yes... so anyway..."

He sipped his brandy and motioned for the others to join him. They followed through with unenthusiastic sips.

"So I had to do something, and Jessie Mae couldn't quite reach them, since Annabelle was right behind and all. So I reached back to grab them, just as we came to this curve in the road, and..."

Reliving the memory proved too much. With effort beyond the capability of most, he willed himself up from the

chair and dragged his way to the railing separating the dining area from the riverbank below. He stood there, staring. The paddleboat was long gone, but the Louisiana lights from across the water glittered through the darkness, dancing in the sauna that is Deep South in summer.

Maddie Pearl got up and stood nearby, not crowding him but letting JB know she was there, if needed. Even Sal got up and came over. He still didn't know why Johnny Bama seemed so intent on accompanying them, but at least he was discovering more of this man about whom they knew precious little, and needed to know more before proceeding.

Maddie Pearl broke the silence this time, using the kind, understanding, gentle voice that nature embeds in women alone.

"It's alright, Johnny. You don't need to tell us all this. We understand."

She reached out and patted him on the back, then rubbed tenderly between his shoulders. JB rotated toward Sal.

"Sal... I'm sorry. I really am, but I'm not sure I can answer your question."

Sal looked on stoically.

"It's just that... I don't think *I* know why I want to tag along. It's just... like I say... I don't really know either. But I can't stay back there... in that house... in that place with those... those... memories."

Sal remained uncertain, but sensed that this man's intentions, while unclear, at least were not insidious. He still didn't like it, but whatever deep resolve he once had to abandon ship and swim home was fading... at least somewhat.

He'd think on it overnight, decide in the morning, and that would be that—once and for all!

# Chapter 31

They agreed to meet at eight the next morning by the Plymouth. Johnny Bama knew of a good place for breakfast. They'd eat and then head to... wherever.

Maddie Pearl got there first, a few minutes early, and waited beside the car. At precisely eight, Johnny Bama came stand-crawling up. He unlocked the Plymouth, but neither got in. They'd wait for Sal.

But Sal wasn't there, and they waited, and ten minutes passed, and Sal remained absent. JB had worked his magic again, enabling Walter Carver Jefferson to stay at the ordinarily segregated hotel. Once again, no questions were asked, by anyone. It was a short walk to the car, having been negotiated easily and quickly even by the crippled man. Always the first up each and every morning in the community to lead the men to the farm to work the rocky fields to eek out livings, Sal was no idler. He should have been here by now; he should have been here first, long before eight. But he wasn't, and a nervous nausea began percolating in Maddie Pearl's empty stomach.

"You think something... I don't know, maybe *happened?*" Maddie Pearl asked JB with serious concern. "It's not like him to be late like this."

Johnny Bama harbored other thoughts, but opted to keep them to himself, for now.

"You stay here," said Maddie Pearl. "I'm going to check on him."

The thought of a beautiful, white, teenage female going alone to the room of a strong, black man in a Jim Crow hotel on a Mississippi morning simply was unacceptable.

"No!" said JB sharply. "I'll go."

To Maddie Pearl's chagrin but reluctant acceptance, Johnny ambled back to the hotel while she waited outside.

After several minutes, he returned, sans Sal. Just as Johnny Bama suspected, WC Jefferson was long gone. The bed was all made up, as if nobody had occupied the room. *"Probably left last night,"* thought JB, *"right after dinner. Hopped a freight train or whatever. 'Spect he's halfway to Alabama by now."*

"Any luck?" asked Maddie Pearl hopefully.

"Nope. Gone," replied Johnny.

Maddie Pearl teared up and turned away to hide her response. It was unnecessary. Johnny Bama did a good job hiding it, but he felt the same. He'd known this couple for such a short while, but felt a kinship, a sense of being a part of... *something,* like family but different and, in some ways, better.

For the first time since *it* happened, he felt alive again, back, and real, like a human, like a person with a reason to live, and now... this. Maddie Pearl never would go it alone, not without Sal, not all the way to California. And like Maddie Pearl but for different reasons, Bama couldn't go back, not now, maybe not ever.

She had nothing at home; Bama had everything. But everything served solely to remind him... of Jessie Mae, and Annabelle, and the funny cows with which they would picnic on easy spring days, and the magnificent magnolia that his great-grandfather planted so long ago that now held the perfect tire swing on which his daughter would ride swishing through the clean, sweet Claxton Farms air with each of his mighty shoves. And the house, the great family estate he had inherited—the magical palace he treasured from childhood with all its nooks, crannies, hiding places, and warmth in the winter and cool cross breezes mid-summer—now was just a cold museum tomb of too many memories, too much of what once was... and would never be again.

Like Thomas Wolfe's new book that he had read the past spring, Johnny Bama knew he couldn't go home again. Not now, especially not after Sal and Maddie Pearl and the promise of a new beginning in a new place with wonderful new people and a new life with new memories to be made and new challenges to enjoy overcoming. But in one fell

swoop, it had all crashed and burned, because of him, just like the pretty blue Plymouth that held life itself until life perished—because of him.

It was almost nine now. They had waited long enough, in silence, for the man who wasn't coming.

"Let's get something to eat," said Johnny Bama. "We can figure out what we're gonna do then."

Maddie Pearl surveyed the terrain one last time, hoping beyond hope, but it wasn't to be, so she acquiesced and said, "Let me drive."

The Plymouth started easily thanks to its overpriced, second-hand alternator.

"Where to?" asked Maddie Pearl as she put the car in gear.

"Head out that way," replied Johnny Bama, pointing down toward the river and a cluster of businesses now opening with the morning sun.

Just as they pulled from the lot onto the Vicksburg city street, Bama noticed what appeared to be a pedestrian running down a side alley in their general direction. As they pulled forward, the large Plantation Bank and Trust building obscured the runner, and JB lost sight of him. "*Oh well,*" he rationalized. "*Guess the poor guy's late for work.*"

They proceeded two blocks west until reaching a T-intersection across from which stood a Confederate Monument to some long lost defender of slavery in a state that, to modern times, constitutionally prohibited African Americans from holding statewide office without at least 55% of the popular vote.

Heritage not hate? Indeed.

After turning right, they paralleled the Mighty Mississippi for several blocks until they came upon "*EARLS*" which appeared to be some sort of restaurant. JB pointed where to go. Maddie Pearl parked the Plymouth awkwardly, owing to her inexperience. As she came around to help Bama, they heard someone yelling from down the street.

"HEY! WAIT UP! WAIT FOR ME!"

It was Sal! In a full sprint, he was dashing down the streets of Vicksburg with his gunnysack in one hand and brown, paper bag in the other!

Maddie Pearl ran in Sal's direction, met him about a block away, and leapt into his waiting arms in joyous reunion. On the main street of what once was—and still very much remained—a bastion of Confederate duncery, this black boy swung this white girl around in circles oblivious to the stunned Caucasians, good citizens all, now armed with a breathtaking story to tell the mortified congregation at their pretty little white (only) church in the country aside the majestically-sturdy hanging tree and segregated Christian cemetery.

Johnny Bama managed to reach the swinging couple just as the reunification subsided. He extended his right hand and said sincerely, and loudly enough for everyone to hear, "It's damn great to see you!"

Dumbfounded bystanders—with emphasis on "dumb"—stood slack jawed at this unprecedented and wholly unacceptable abomination playing out right before their unbelieving eyeballs. Nevertheless, JB kept his hand extended and, after a few awkward seconds, Mister Walter Carver Jefferson completed the gentlemanly custom.

There was no policeman in the vicinity, but even Johnny Bama couldn't get away with this behavior for long in this place with these people of this mentality.

"We probably should be getting along now," he admonished.

Maddie Pearl and Sal wholeheartedly agreed, and the trio maneuvered as briskly as possible back to the Plymouth, with Sal behind the wheel. They sped off north along the river, leaving the hayseeds in their wake to eat dust and tell tall tales.

\*          \*          \*

"After we ate last night, I decided to take a walk," Sal explained, sitting on the grass with Maddie Pearl and Johnny Bama in a scenic clearing overlooking the Mississippi River

several miles outside Vicksburg amidst a small feast of sausage biscuits, ham sandwiches, hushpuppies, and johnnycakes—courtesy of the speaker.

"I had the *Green Book*, just in case, but I didn't really need it, at least not until this morning. Nothing was open, and there wasn't a soul about anywhere. So I walked and... I don't know... just thought about things."

"The whole night?" asked Maddie Pearl.

"Yep," he replied. "All night, but it didn't really seem like all that long, not really."

"So," said Johnny Bama. "I guess that explains why you didn't sleep at the hotel."

"Yeah... I guess, but it didn't feel right anyway... you know... being in a fancy place like that and all."

Bama nodded, as if he understood something that no white man who had never been excluded from hotels, restaurants, bathrooms, and even water fountains possibly could comprehend.

"So I found a spot down by the river, near what looked like a swampy area. There were some places down there, a 'negro neighborhood' according to the book, and so I just hung around, by myself, and watched that muddy water just keep on keeping on."

"Is that why you were late this morning?" Maddie Pearl inquired, giving Sal an *out*—if he needed it.

Sal peered at Maddie Pearl and Johnny Bama with a serious demeanor. "No... no it's not."

The three sat quietly, allowing Sal's cryptic response to float about in a small whirl of dreamlike uncertainty.

"Here's the thing," Sal broke the reverie. "I've decided to keep going... to keep on for California... but there're gonna have to be some changes."

As if a dense smoke cloud miraculously had lifted, Maddie Pearl and Johnny could breathe again, and the air tasted sweeter than that honey Sal brought with the biscuits. Maddie Pearl gripped Sal hard and hugged with all her heart. Bama's ever-present smile beamed even larger than usual, as sincerely as a loving groom saying "I do" at the altar.

"How do you want to do this, then?" asked Johnny Bama in a fervent tone that really conveyed, "*Whatever you want, Walter, is fine with me!*"

"Alright... first of all," said Sal, measuring the audience's receptiveness. "I don't like you being married. The Claxton's or whatever. I don't like it."

JB and Maddie Pearl nodded approvingly at each other, then Bama spoke for them both, "Done!"

"And I don't want to be your butler or chauffeur or farmhand or whatever it is you think I'm supposed to do just because I'm black."

Speaking for the rest of the team again, Bama said, "Done!"

"And if I'm not your driver, then I don't want to do all the driving anymore, and I'm damn sure not wearing that god-awful chauffeur hat one more second. I want to sleep some in the back too, and maybe even do some reading on the way or whatever."

"Done!" said them both enthusiastically.

"And one last thing..." Sal said looking at Johnny Bama. "I don't want you paying my way."

At this, Bama was taken aback, and more than a little hurt. Paying for things was not his way of rendering anyone subservient. He just enjoyed helping others and, since luck had blessed him with money, why not use some of it to bless others?

"Why?" was all he could muster in his wounded confusion.

"It's like this, Johnny," said Sal referring to Bama by first name instead of his usual, impersonal references to *you* or *him* or *this guy* or *sir* or *Mister Claxton*. "This world out here..." Sal gesticulated outward toward the field around them and the river below and heavens above. "This world might think people like me are somehow below you two. But in *this* world," he gesticulated inwardly toward just the three of them, "we're equals."

Johnny Bama worked his way up from his squatted position amidst the picnic that Sal had procured and stood before Walter Carver.

"Equals," he said, extending his arm.

"Equals," said WC, shaking JB's hand for the second time that day.

"Equals," squealed Maddie Pearl excitedly as she jumped to her feet, grabbed them both enthusiastically, and engaged in a full-bodied, power-gripped, three-way embrace!

As they happily made way toward the car and their brave new world, Bama unceremoniously tossed the chauffeur's hat into the Mississippi River.

"I always hated that God damn thing," observed Bama, as it meandered downriver to its mucky oblivion on the black bottom of the muddy Mississippi.

# Chapter 32

"With all this mess going on over in Europe," Johnny Bama was talking from the back seat while Maddie Pearl drove across Louisiana with Sal sitting beside her, "I hear they're gonna need some pilots."

"You mean like that guy who drove us across the river on that barge this morning?" asked Maddie Pearl logically.

"Lord no, child," replied Bama. "Like guys who fly aeroplanes, or I think it's 'airplane' nowadays. They call those guys pilots, too."

Sal had seen planes at Fort Bragg, shiny metal boxes with wings and a big propeller. They didn't look too safe to him but, he had to admit, they sure looked fun.

"Yeah, I heard about this general, back home," JB resumed. "Came around looking for pilots. There were these twins in town, Ed and Ted... 'bout your age Maddie Pearl. So the general asked one of 'em, '*Boy, what can you bring to the Army Air Forces?*' Well that boy—this one was Ed, said, '*I'm a pilot.*' That old general just about wet his pants he got so excited—excuse my French, Maddie Pearl."

Maddie Pearl rolled her eyes playfully to convey, "*don't be so silly.*" This wasn't the first time he'd said "*excuse my French*" after saying something off color, and she'd rolled the eyes every time. It had become almost a ritual, like "*Bless you*" following a sneeze.

"So anyway," Bama continued, "the general tells his aide to get Ed all signed up and everything, and off they go. So the general came up to Ted, and asked him what *he* might bring to the Air Forces. Ted spoke up, '*I chop wood.*' The general looked him over and said, '*Now son, we don't have no call for woodchoppers in the Army Air Forces.*' Ted said, '*Well... you hired my brother.*' With some consternation, that

general said, '*Of course we hired 'em, he's a pilot.*' Ted replied, '*So what... I have to chop it before he can pile it.*'"

Johnny Bama broke out in loud, breath-thieving laughter in the back seat. Up front, his companions smiled politely. Sal pinched his nose to express just how much the joke stunk, but Bama was practically rolling on the Plymouth's floor.

He regained his composure, slightly, and said, "I had you, didn't I? You thought that ol' general and Ed and Ted were real!"

Sal looked back and with mock sarcasm said, "So... jokes and such just aren't your thing, huh?"

The good-natured Alabamian took the comment in stride and broke up uproariously again.

Maddie Pearl had been driving since breakfast. She was much more herky-jerky than Sal, and had a propensity to slowly nudge faster and faster until Sal or even JB from the back would notice and encourage her to back down to non-raceway speeds. She was able to keep the Plymouth on the correct side of the road, but the first hour or so proved nerve-wracking as she occasionally swayed left into oncoming traffic or right into the Cajun bog only to wrench back at the last second. But it had now been about two hundred miles, and she seemed to have the hang of it, more or less.

Their next stop would be Waskom, Texas, just across the border. Johnny knew a place—he always seemed to know a place—where they could get gas and vittles. Maddie Pearl loved the exhilaration of figuring out the finer points of driving and was not weary, but Texas was one of those states that required a license. Bama insisted he could handle it, since much of the route through the Lone Star State was flat, straight, and mostly barren of other vehicles. However, he didn't feel comfortable getting through all the stops and starts that were sure to come in Shreveport, and suggested it might be better if Sal handled that part. Maddie Pearl protested, mildly, but lost out to better judgment. So, in a nothing little forgotten place called Red Chute Bayou in Bossier Parish, the switch was made.

After a wonderful, private meal at the Powellton Restaurant, they decided to spend the night. Walter Carver opted to occupy the hotel room this time since, after all, *he* was paying for it. Like virtually everything in Texas then, the establishment was segregated, except for Mister John Claxton and his guests.

They awoke the next day, had a nice breakfast privately at the Powellton, gassed up and, with Johnny Bama piloting, headed west. Just like that, their routine for the next few days had been set. JB and WC compared notes the night before with Sal's two maps and a well-worn one belonging to Bama. They agreed to head toward Tyler and Dallas and then cut north for Wichita Falls. That would be over three hundred miles and probably take until mid- to late-afternoon, depending on traffic around Big D. Thereafter, they'd make their way to Amarillo and Route 66.

Sal and Maddie Pearl had never heard of these places, and had no real conception of what lie ahead. So, Bama took it upon himself to fill in the many gaps. The more he jabbered, the more his companions realized—and appreciated—just how much traveling their newfound friend had done in his relatively short life, and they were envious.

Mile after mile, with his bright blue eyes on the road but his gesticulating hands not always on the wheel, Bama regaled them with one story after another about this place and that, or what Mr. So-And-So did or how Mrs. Who-Knows-Who got into and out of some jam or whatever. Peppered throughout were jokes, sidebars, and funny observations with clever comments. It was like riding with Will Rogers, Mark Twain, and WC Fields all in one, and his audience was enthralled.

Even Sal, who had played hard-to-get for most of their acquaintance, was warming up to this wizened older man with so much to impart. And Maddie Pearl, with so much to learn, likewise soaked up every word like some sea sponge. They may have been rubes from the wrong side of the woods but, as the miles whizzed by, Sal and Maddie Pearl were getting a cram course in everything from geography to history to

human nature to how the world *really* works beyond the incarcerating confines of Webster County, North Carolina.

During a lull along a particularly boring stretch of Texas roadway while Maddie Pearl was sleeping alone in the backseat, Sal asked Johnny Bama, "Have you ever been up in an airplane?"

"You mean like that *pilot* who stacked the wood?"

Sal laughed easily and replied, "No, but it got me to thinking what it must be like up there."

"Oh, it's great," said Bama energetically.

"What's it... you know, like? Is it scary?"

"Well, it can be, especially if you crash," said Bama, his smile fading slightly.

"You ever crash?"

"Once... when I was training."

"What sort of training were you doing... for the Army I guess?" asked Sal.

"Yeah, it was the Army. They had a few planes, at Fort Bragg as a matter of fact. They were old biplanes... airplanes with two sets of wings. You've probably seen 'em before."

"No. Like I said, I saw a couple of airplanes back at base, but they just had one wing... on each side."

"Well in the old days, the airplanes had two sets of wings, one above the other, because the planes were too heavy and the motor was too slow and weak to get off the ground with just one."

Maddie Pearl made a small snort sound and unconsciously repositioned herself across the bench seat while remaining in a deep slumber. Sal checked to make sure she was okay, then returned his attention to the driver with the bad leg but good stories.

"Did you ever learn how, even with the crash and all?"

"Oh Lord yes. That became my military job, for a year or so. I was a pilot of an old Curtiss JN-4, a 'Jenny,' and boy was she a beaut!"

Sal trained his eyes at a large bird flying over—a hawk hunting for some poor creature in the Lone Star wasteland.

"They sold most of 'em, the Army did, after the Big War, but they kept some around, mainly for training pilots.

They were really good for that, since they're pretty easy to fly, all things considered."

"So you crashed when you were learning to fly?"

"Actually, no. I already knew how when I crashed."

"But I thought you said you were training?" asked Sal.

"I was. I was training somebody else how to fly. I was his trainer, you know, teacher."

"Oh... I get it. So you were good enough to teach... I mean *train*, others?"

"To be honest, you didn't have to be all that good to do anything in the Army in those days. It was after the war, a lot of boys had gotten killed or messed up for life... you know, arms shot off or crippled or even worse, and not too many with any sense wanted to have any parts of that."

"So why did you join?" asked Sallerhead.

Johnny Bama considered the question for several seconds before responding, trying to determine the most honest, accurate means to reply.

"Let me put it this way," he said. "You ever heard of a globe skimmer?"

"A 'globe skimmer'? Can't say I have," said Sal.

"Well a globe skimmer is this tiny bug, a dragonfly actually. They're all over the place, even where you're from. You mighta seen one before and not known what you were seein'. Anyway, these little things wander all over the world, sometimes traveling thousands of miles. I first learned about 'em in Germany—I lived in Germany for a while. But anyways... these little things have been found on islands out in the middle of the ocean, like that Easter Island where all those statues were found."

Sal had exactly zero awareness of "Easter Island" and certainly even less familiarity with its "statues." But rather than break up the story, he decided to check into that later, maybe via a book, instead of further exposing his ignorance by asking.

"Anyhow, I've always thought of myself as being a little like that dragonfly, just wandering about from here and there seeing new things, meeting people and so on."

"Is that how you seem to know everybody when we stop at places?" asked Sal.

"Well, that's part of the reason, I guess. But like that first place we stayed... I had been through there on work a bunch of times, with my dad."

"Work? But I thought your dad owned the farm?"

"He did," explained Bama, "but the kind of farming he did—that I do now—ain't exactly like the farming I suspect you've been around."

"What do you mean?" inquired Sal.

"Am I right that your folks grow crops and then sell them at a market nearby or whatever?"

"Well, that's what Maddie Pearl's people do—tobacco and cotton, mostly. We grow things like corn, beans, squash, you know, food crops."

"So you folks are sustenance farmers... grow crops for sustenance, you know, food. Right?"

"Yeah, well, that's kinda right, but we have to sell some... you know, to pay rent. Except a lot of the time the owner, this white guy named Boss Lee, he just takes what he wants and calls it 'rent' and then collects his money rent too. He was cheating us, but we were able to stay on the property, and so long as we didn't say anything it all just sort of... worked."

"I know all about *those* kinda landowners," Bama said, looking absently ahead at the empty road. "God damn sons of whores, the whole bunch of 'em."

"That pretty well sums it up for me too," said Sal. "But at least he didn't whip us or anything." Sal thought back to the night that he and Maddie Pearl witnessed her family home being burned by a herd of white Klanners. "To be honest, I think he was meaner to the white folk than us."

"That doesn't surprise me," added Bama. "They don't like gettin' one-upped by their own, so they keep 'em down, just like they do with... you know... your people."

"I guess that's true, but anyway... how was *your* kind of farming different?"

"Well first of all, we have a lot of livestock, which I 'spect you didn't have."

"There was a man... Farmer Hunt... down the path at the end that had some cows and things, but yeah... for the most part... none of us, not even Maddie Pearl's folks, had many animals. Maybe some chickens, for the eggs, and mules and such, but not much else."

"That's typical, especially with tenanting. Too damned expensive, unless ya get a whole lot of 'em, then the numbers start working."

"Why's that?"

"It's called 'economy of scale,' and all it means is that if you can get enough cows or chickens or hogs or, well, pretty much anything, the cost of dealing with each one gets cheaper and cheaper. Sooner or later, it gets cheap enough to make sense, from a business standpoint."

"So why did that cause your pa and you to travel around?"

"We have a lot of stuff to sell, and I mean a whole *helluva* lot, and the local market for beef and pork and so on just isn't big enough to handle everything, so we have to go out and find places that want to buy what we have."

"So... are you still having to do that, *now* I mean?" asked Sallerhead.

"Not in the last couple years," answered Johnny Bama, "and particularly not since... you know... what I was talking about the other night, with my..."

Bama's voice trailed off, and a glaze came over his face. Sal chose to sit tight. He'd seen it before, and knew that "*I'm so sorry*" or "*it wasn't your fault*" tripe served no purpose. So he'd wait it out.

"That boy you met," Bama finally resumed, as expected. "Tom Colton—back at the house, he takes care of all that now, and let me tell ya something, I'd trust my life with that man... yes I would."

"So," mused Sal, "what do you do, you know, with all your time and everything?"

Bama didn't answer. This second pause lasted a tad too long. Sal knew Bama heard, but started to ask again just in case. Before Sal followed-up and almost as if sensing the awkwardness, Maddie Pearl roused awake in the back.

"I'm hungry," she said, sleepily.

"Okay," said Bama, almost in a whisper. "I know a place... just up the road in Wichita Falls."

Sal's question would have to go unanswered, for now at least.

# Chapter 33

They had traveled five hundred miles, Sal's original estimate for a full day, and could have stopped. But, it was only late afternoon and the meal in Wichita Falls from the place Bama knew had reinvigorated the trio, so they pressed on. Johnny was fatigued, no longer accustomed to driving since *it* happened, so Sal took over with Bama on the back seat sleeping bench.

Their goal was Amarillo, but the road now wasn't as good as what they had been traveling and they were considering stopping sooner, in Clarendon perhaps, or even Memphis (Texas, not Tennessee). Regardless, they now were making good progress and, with the financial issues resolved, California—for the first time—seemed likely instead of just possible. This reality was dawning on Sal and Maddie Pearl as they sat together up front hurtling down the asphalt while watching the tumbleweeds flinging about the landscape, much like themselves.

"What do you think you'll do there?" asked Sal, somewhat from left field.

Maddie Pearl paused in thought before answering. "I've been asking myself that ever since Johnny Bama came along."

Sal looked at her with a frown. "What's Johnny got to do with it?"

"Oh, nothing really, nothing at all. It's just that, until we met up, I had a feeling like we weren't going to make it, you know, all the way out there."

Sal nodded. He felt the same even though he'd never admit it. It was a guy thing... not that he had any animus toward Johnny—he didn't, not anymore; but he was loathe ever to concede an inability to accomplish anything he set out to do. It was a trait that would serve him well as life unfolded.

"So what are you going to do? Think Doc and you might get together?"

Maddie Pearl looked at Sal uncomfortably, conveying "*what about us*" without saying it aloud for Bama possibly to hear.

Sal glanced back to ensure Bama remained sound asleep. He said as quietly as the hot car with the wind howling in every window would permit, "You *need* somebody like Doc."

Maddie Pearl was troubled by the response, but knew it was true. After all, Doc definitely wasn't second-rate merchandise from the bottom shelf. He'd be more than a great catch, if only not for... Sal.

"Maybe so," answered Maddie Pearl, quietly. "But how do I know if he even likes me?"

"Oh, you don't need to worry about that. He definitely *likes* you."

"But you know what I mean," said Maddie Pearl. "We didn't really get to know each other all that well, and... for all I know he's already started to forget me."

Sal paused to deal with traffic. There was a slowpoke in front that he had to pass. He maneuvered the Plymouth perfectly, and completed the task with ease.

"Trust me... his memory' ain't that bad. Besides," he looked at Maddie Pearl, "you're pretty hard to forget."

Bama snorted, ground his teeth slightly, shifted a few inches, and then returned to sleep.

Maddie Pearl waited a few seconds to ensure Bama's obliviousness, and then quietly responded. "So are you."

It was an exchange that merited no further discussion. In so few words, their dilemma was spoken.

"*If only,*" each thought.

If only, indeed.

As more miles passed, both young minds wandered back to the dreaded "what ifs." Their impossible relationship aside, a world of potential problems still presented at the end of the road. What if civilian personnel aren't permitted on base? What if Doc has been redeployed away? Or doesn't

need Sal? Or doesn't want Maddie Pearl? What if Bama comes to his senses and opts to return home? Or what if...?

Lost in thoughts of issues unresolved, neither noticed that Bama had awakened and was sitting up. When he uttered, "Where are we?" both front seat occupants flinched noticeably.

"Didn't mean to scare ya," the Alabaman said. "We anywhere close to stopping. I need to *rest.*"

"Rest" had become code for going to the bathroom. It was more gentile than saying "I gotta take a leak" or the like, especially coming from a man in a young woman's presence—or from the young woman herself.

The code word given, they pulled into the first gas station that presented. All three took care of business, with Sal having to venture out back behind the small building. Some gas was pumped, to legitimize the stop, and then back on the road west they ventured.

"So what'd I miss," Johnny Bama asked openly, hoping to start a conversation about anything.

Sal and Maddie Pearl exchanged a glance that clearly if inadvertently signaled "something." Bama noticed immediately, and followed up. "Come on... Out with it."

After a pause too long, Maddie Pearl finally broached, "We were just talking about... you know... what's gonna happen when we get... you know... when we get there. To California."

"I know exactly what's going to happen," said Bama cheerfully. "That Doc friend of yours is going to welcome you both with open arms, and everything's gonna work out perfectly. And that's that!"

Maddie Pearl's doubtful look expressed her angst.

"I don't get you, Maddie Pearl," Johnny Bama said. "I mean, don't you go worrying so much. It'll all be great, you just wait and see... for both of ya."

Sal had to enter the discussion. "You need to understand something, Johnny. You don't come from the same place as Maddie Pearl and me. You just haven't seen what we've seen, or what we've been through."

Bama took several seconds considering how best to respond. He wasn't insulted by Sal's condescending observation. After all, to some extent the black man was right. Bama hadn't experienced severe poverty, racial discrimination, Klan brutality, or second-class citizenship. And unlike Maddie Pearl, Bama came from a good family, his parents loved him, they had regular meals with healthy food, and books and magazines, and proper education, and all the rest. But Johnny had experienced pain and suffering, and he had the scars to prove it, and not just the physical ones.

"Tell ya what," he said carefully, like a wise parent reassuring his children. "Trust me. Everything's going to be okay. And if it's not, we'll just get you both back to Carolina. Give you a start over, like when you're playing a card game or something and fall way behind... you just start over."

Neither front seat occupant was convinced, but each took some solace in the "do over" concept. It wasn't a salvation, but at least it was a possible lifeline if their boat began sinking. However, it didn't answer yet another question.

"So you say we'll get back home to Carolina," Sal spoke. "But where does that leave you, Johnny?"

"Well first of all, and I hate to keep sayin' this but it's the truth. Everything's gonna work out, just wait and see, and ain't nobody gonna have to go home to anywhere."

"Yeah... well, maybe... but still. What if it doesn't?" Sal pushed.

"Yeah," added Maddie Pearl. "If we go back home or whatever, would you go back to Alabama?"

Johnny Bama didn't answer right away. It was a question with which he had been wrestling ever since his eyes first set on Maddie Pearl and Walter and he knew instantly that somehow, some way, the fate of all three was destined to be intertwined.

He never intended to force the issue, but JB just knew that nature would take its course. So far, his instinct had been dead on, and he had no reason to think it was going to change. Still, he remained troubled by the prospect of the *what if's* he knew to ignore but couldn't. And most troubling,

he realized—even if his gut feeling bore out and everything turned up roses in California—that each inevitably would go a separate way, eventually.

Maddie Pearl would find someone—Doc perhaps—get married, have kids, and live happily ever after. That was not Bama's destiny, and he didn't view the beautiful, ample young teen with wandering eyes. He saw her more as a daughter, perhaps the embodiment of Annabelle—had she only....

And Bama had no doubts that Sal was destined for something far bigger than toiling away in some Carolina shitfield or schlepping at an Army base underlinging Doc or anyone else. JB had met many, *many* people in his worldly wanderings, but never someone even remotely on Walter's level. And it was more than just innate intelligence and natural physical prowess. There was something... *different* about him, something... *special.* More than a charisma really, it was... well... *it.* Walter Carver Jefferson had *it,* like nobody else, and Bama's faith in Sal's future was rock solid.

But getting back to the backseat of this new—albeit slightly used—Plymouth, his first car since *it* happened, and the question before him, Johnny Bama lacked a good answer. He'd do his best nevertheless.

"I don't know, yet, what I'll do," JB replied. "Probably what I've always done, just more."

"What do you mean by that?" asked Maddie Pearl.

"Ask Sal about the dragonfly," said Bama. "He'll explain."

"Dragonfly? What's he talking about?" Maddie Pearl directed to Sal.

"Johnny was telling me about this dragonfly... what was it—globe skimmer or something?" Sal asked JB.

"Yep," replied Bama.

"Anyway, this thing, this insect travels all over the world, and they're everywhere, and some end up on islands out in the ocean, and some cross thousands of miles. They just, you know, wander around—like our friend here."

"They're actually known by some people as a wandering glider," Johnny piped in.

"So," Maddie Pearl said to Bama after considering the brief entomology lesson. "You consider yourself a little bug that flies around everywhere never setting down roots?"

"Not exactly, but yeah, to an extent that's how I see myself."

"But what about your home back in Alabama?" Maddie Pearl said. "And all that land and that house and everything? You've got roots there, deep roots it looks like to me."

"Yes and no, Maddie Pearl. Yes... and no."

"I still don't get it," continued Maddie Pearl, her naturally inquisitive mind working overtime.

"It's like I was telling Walter... err, I mean Sal. From as early as I can remember, my dad and me traveled all over the place. He'd say real serious stuff like, '*John my son, some day all this will be your responsibility, and you must learn how to manage it, because I won't always be here to help you.*'"

"I've heard *that* speech," chimed Sal.

"I haven't," said Maddie Pearl, with a sincerity borne of being raised a girl in a man-centric home by a weak-willed mother and a beastly father intent on beating his wife, tormenting his daughter, drinking his moonshine, and forcing his boys to do all the real work.

"So we traveled a lot," Bama continued, "to markets in other states mostly, and I got to see a lot of stuff that most kids never see, and I kinda liked it."

"Is that how you know everybody?" asked Maddie Pearl.

"I asked the exact same thing," said Sal. "I think I even used the same words."

They laughed softly, in a friendly manner evoking the group's increasingly close-knit nature.

"Yeah, well I guess that's one reason, but there's a little more to it than just that. As I got older, and could drive and all, I started heading out on my own. I went to college of course, down at Ole Miss, even though Pa demanded I go to UA."

"What's UA?"

"Oh, that's the University of Alabama... where all the Claxton men go, except me. I went to Mississippi just to rattle his cage. I was young and stupid... still am stupid, I guess. But anyway... I had a car and could take side trips and what not, like on weekends. I was pretty much the only guy with wheels, so I'd take a bunch of them boys—and girls sometimes—all over the place. Sometimes we'd just take off with a load of beer and not even know where we were headin'."

Maddie Pearl could see the adventures in her mind's eye. It seemed thrilling, and wonderful, but then a slight sadness overtook her upon realizing that such had escaped her, probably forever.

"And after college, I wasn't really ready to go back to the farms, and that just about made my dad as mad as I ever saw him, even madder than when I wrecked the car driving drunk. Now *that* was a bad night, but anyway... He said something about not paying for some 'raccoon coated *Mississippi* hooch swiller' or whatever, and cut me off."

"What do you mean, 'cut off?'" Maddie Pearl asked.

"You know, he wasn't going to support me anymore, pay the bills and so forth. So I was on my own, unless I agreed to come back home and work on the farm, and I sure didn't want to do that, and I damn sure didn't want to get some real job somewhere, like in a bank or something, so I joined the service... United States Army to be precise."

"After what you said about boys not wanting to have anything to do with the military after that war," said Sal. "I was wondering just why in heaven's name *you* joined. Guess I know now, huh?"

"Yeah, for sure... and it was the best decision I ever made, except for Jessie Mae, of course. Taught me things that Pa, God bless him, just couldn't... like about life and taking responsibility. Made a man out of a spoiled little brat, if you want to know the truth."

Once again, Sal and Maddie Pearl found themselves enraptured with the life and times of John Claxton. They only could dream of the places he had seen and the things he had experienced. As JB rambled on, Maddie Pearl's sadness was replaced with a resolve: She was <u>not</u> going to miss out any

more! Sal similarly considered what he had missed, so far, but knew that somehow, someday, he too would be telling stories just like this, based on *his* life and experiences. He found the thought exhilarating, as if he couldn't wait until tomorrow and the day after that and the rest of a life he promised himself would be full and rich and joyous—no matter what!

"But through the Army I got to do a lot of stuff, like flying and traveling and all."

"Flying," said Maddie Pearl excitedly. "You flew?"

"Yep. I was telling Sal about it. I used to fly what they called a biplane, an airplane with two sets of wings."

"WOW! That sounds, like, I don't know! That's unbelievable!"

"I'll save my flyin' stories for later, but yer right—it was unbelievable. But that was just part of it... the Army I mean. I got to do all kinds of things, but I liked traveling around the best, just sort of wandering—like that dragonfly."

"Where else did you go?" asked Maddie Pearl, mesmerized by the prospect of some day following in his wake.

"Oh well, I'm not going to make a list or anything, but you already know about Fort Bragg. I served a short stint there... that was for training pilots. And they sent me around to some other places. Since I was one of the only ones who knew how to operate a Jenny, that opened some doors."

"A 'jenny'?"

"That's the kind of airplane he was flying," Sal explained.

"So why did you ever return home, to Alabama?" inquired Maddie Pearl.

"Well, not much to it, really. Pa got sick, with the cancer, and they needed me. Besides, my hitch came up anyway, and I had been overseas for a while, in Germany mostly—I think I mentioned that before, but anyway. It was just time to, you know, get back."

"How long ago was that?" Sal wondered.

"Give or take, about ten years. Long enough for Pa to die, me to take over, and Jessie Mae to come along... and Annabelle."

Sal noticed a "CLARENDON 13" sign and suggested, "Wanna stop up here? I'm getting kind of tired."

The sun was low in the sky and it had been a successful but long day on the road to Amarillo.

"I don't have any connections there," advised Johnny Bama, "but I'm sure we can figure something out."

Maddie Pearl consulted the *Green Book* and asked, "What's it mean when it says 'Clarendon, Texas is a Sundown town'?"

"It means we're heading for Memphis," replied Sal matter-of-factly.

*        *        *


Sam Houston famously observed, "*Texas has yet to learn submission to any oppression, come from what source it may.*" Guess Old Sam never experienced Clarendon as a black man on a Saturday night.

Too bad.

# Chapter 34

The next morning, just outside Amarillo and their entrée onto Route 66, the Plymouth and its threesome tooled into an ESSO gas station. Compared with the Texas gas traps they had encountered thus far, this was a breath of fresh air mixed with the pleasing aroma of gasoline fumes and just-cooked sausage biscuits.

As the car pulled up, three young African Americans dressed alike in clean, pressed ESSO uniforms hustled out of the new station and scurried up to Sal's driver's side window.

"How can we help you sir," said the handsome, early-twentyish black man to the handsome, early-twentyish black man behind the wheel.

Sal was perplexed, having never experienced anything even remotely like this.

"Ask 'em to fill 'er up and check under the hood," advised Johnny Bama quietly, so the attendant wouldn't hear.

"How 'bout filling her up," repeated Sal. "And please check under the hood, if you don't mind."

The attendants were a whirlwind of activity. One pumped gas; another lifted the hood and checked therein; the third cleaned every window from bow-to-stern. Like a well-choreographed dance, each man knew his part, did it well, and then as quickly as they had begun were through!

"That will be four dollars and seventeen cents, sir," said the attendant to Sal. "It's slightly more, sir, because she was a little low on oil."

Sal reached in his pocket, withdrew five and three ones, and handed it over. "I want you and the others to keep the difference."

Sal turned to his riders, winked, and said in a confident, playful whisper mocking Bama, "I always like to leave a tip."

The attendant smiled broadly, and said earnestly with an air of surprise, "Why thank you, sir! And by the way, do you need anything... *else*... while you're here?"

Sal replied, "Well, we've already eaten once this morning, back in Memphis, but those biscuits sure smell good. How about three of those, you know, for the road, and some water if you've got it?"

"Sure thing, sir." He motioned to one of the others, who ran inside for the biscuits and aqua. The attendant continued, "But sir, you know... are you sure you don't need anything, you know, *else*, for your, you know, *passengers?*"

The emphasis on "else" and "passengers" plus the general manner of questioning puzzled Sal, so he inquired, "I'm not real sure I know what you mean?"

The black attendant politely peered slightly into the window, at the white occupants, then back at Sal.

"Aren't you the chauffeur, sir?"

Before Sal could respond, Johnny Bama piped in from the back seat. "Sir... if I may... Mister Jefferson here owns this new Plymouth, and we work for him. I'm his accountant, and Maddie Pearl here is his secretary. We're on our way to an important meeting in... where was it again, Mister Jefferson?"

Sal, on cue, continued the ruse, "That would be Tulsa, John... in the Greenwood District." Sal then focused back on the attendant and continued. "I usually don't drive, but I just wanted to test out these new wheels... couldn't resist breaking 'em in."

The paradigm shift surprised the attendant, as did the tap on his shoulder from the biscuit retriever. The attendant handed over the biscuits and a Mason jar of fresh water.

"How much?" asked Mister Jefferson.

"Sir," said the attendant confidently, "for *you*, they're on the house."

"You sure you're allowed to do that," asked Sal, with some concern.

"I don't know why not," the attendant replied with an air of pride and dignity, "I'm the *owner* of this ESSO station!"

\*       \*       \*

Route 66 is perhaps America's most famous highway. Established in 1926, the 2,448-mile pavement once ran from Chicago all the way to Santa Monica on the Pacific Coast, crossing Illinois, Missouri, Kansas, Oklahoma, Texas, New Mexico, Arizona, and California. It was decommissioned in 1985, a victim of the new and improved Interstate System championed by Dwight Eisenhower in the 1950's. Before its demise, this "Main Street of America" was a nomadic pathway west, especially during the 1930's Dust Bowl. It also would serve Johnny, Maddie Pearl, and Sal's migration, as the highway passed directly through Barstow near the new Mojave Anti-Aircraft Range and David "Doc" Hodge who was not expecting visitors from the east.

Johnny Bama had traveled parts of the "Mother Road" and, as always, "knew some places" along the way. He read John Steinbeck's newest—and best so far, *The Grapes of Wrath*, when it first came out the year before. He had packed the book, along with a handful of others. So far, he'd been too busy driving, talking, gesticulating, or sleeping to crack any, but he hoped that would change on the trip's second, more boring half across some of the country's least populated, flattest, and most humdrum states.

In *Travels with Charley: In Search of America*, Steinbeck said, "[W]e do not take a trip, a trip takes us." This trip had taken Sal and Maddie Pearl from Carolina swamplands through the heart of Dixie, the land of cotton where most things there seemed surely rotten, and now to Amarillo and the Will Rogers Highway (Route 66 had many names). Their hope for an easier second half was buoyed by the unexpected: an ESSO station of all things. But Bama warned that all would not necessarily be clear sailing and they had to remain vigilant about "whatever may come their way." The first "whatever" came less than two hours after turning onto the great road west.

*          *          *

Johnny Bama resumed driving once outside Amarillo where he could rely on more cruising with less clutch-gas-foot-stomp-repeat for his bad leg. The scenery was blah, the traffic was light, the sun was hot, and the road just seemed to go on forever. Maddie Pearl was fast asleep in the front seat, her head cushioned

by her thick, red hair against the passenger window. Sal was in the back writing notes to himself on some paper he had gotten from JB. Filled to the brim with fresh gas and having eaten a solid breakfast supplemented soon thereafter with the best sausage biscuits ever, there would be no need to stop for several hours, until...

Bama first noticed the symptoms some twenty miles before Tucumcari, a small town known as the "Heart of the Mother Road" and "Gateway to New Mexico." The queasiness was unpleasant but tolerable, and he figured it was related to overeating—having effectively had two breakfasts that morning. "*Why bother them?*" he thought. "*It'll pass in a few minutes.*"

It didn't.

In short order, the cold sweats came, then outright nausea. "*Is this a GI attack?*" he wondered. "*If so, it's the damnedest one ever, that's for sure.*"

Sal glanced up from his notes and noticed Bama through the mirror. He looked pale and colorless, and his constant smile was now a smear of gray disquiet.

"Hey... Johnny... you okay?"

Instantaneously, Johnny Bama spewed a massive projectile of vomit directly into the windshield! A second eruption immediately followed, completely obliterating the view ahead.

Maddie Pearl awoke with a start and exclaimed, "What in the—"

A third involuntary expulsion cut off her inquiry as the Plymouth veered wildly, first right then left into the oncoming traffic they no longer could see but definitely heard. Sal quickly shot forward, grabbed the wheel, and nudged the car rightward as best he could away from the frantic HONKS pitching louder and louder like a freight train approaching an intersection. Cringing throughout in anticipation of the horrific CRASH that no doubt was imminent, Sal and Maddie Pearl suddenly found themselves stopped, on the side of Route 66, fully intact and impact-free. Johnny Bama, however, was covered in vomit and blood, fully unconscious.

Sal's limited medical training kicked into high gear. He carried Bama from the car, stretched him out on the side of the road, freed up his collar, checked his airway for blockages, found a

heartbeat, and then spread the old Army blanket from the trunk over his body. Maddie Pearl fetched the ESSO water and poured some to clean Bama's face and, she was hopeful, revive him.

It didn't.

"We've got to get him to a doctor, stat!" snapped Sal in military jargon. "See if the *Green Book* lists anything around here!"

Maddie Pearl scrounged frantically for the book. With Bama being a good old boy whitey, the "We Serve Negroes" prerequisite was irrelevant, but the *Green Book* was their only reference of *any* kind to *any*thing whatsoever, white or black. Unfortunately, their only hope for finding *any* doctor, of *any* kind, proved fruitless.

"Come on," Sal motioned to Maddie Pearl. "Let's get him in the back seat."

With Maddie Pearl's help, Sal easily managed to move the unconscious Bama off the roadside and into the vehicle. Tires spinning madly, Sal sped the Plymouth westward toward Tucumcari hoping, for once, to be stopped by police.

It was nothing short of miraculous that, just after speeding into the Tucumcari town limits, Maddie Pearl noticed a Caduceus on a sign attached to a house a block off Main Street.

"THERE!" she yelled. "Doesn't that snake thing mean a doctor?"

Sal slammed on breaks and exclaimed, "WHERE?"

Maddie Pearl pointed; Sal saw it. He wheeled the car around the block, and raced to the house. The front door was locked. She pounded and pounded, and after an eternal thirty seconds a decrepit old man with gray, stringy hair not fully covering a substantially bald head opened the door slightly and weakly asked, "You need something?"

After Maddie Pearl's quick, hysterical explanation, the feeble doctor motioned and Sal alone carried John Claxton inside the house and into the remnants of Doctor Graham's long-fading medical practice.

The good doctor, a well-intentioned but woefully intolerant product of America's Shame, said, "You'll need to wait outside, boy. In the back."

Rather than fight this little battle with this little man in this little place and thereby jeopardize any chance whatsoever for his bigger-than-life friend to get at least a little medical care, Sal acquiesced.

"I don't need you either, young lady," Graham said to Maddie Pearl, insultingly.

There was no waiting room, so Maddie Pearl went with Sal and waited in the weedy yard behind the rundown house a block off Main Street in a town once known as "Six-Shooter Siding" that began as a raucous railroad camp and haven of whiskey bars, street fights, and banditti.

Around lunchtime, Doctor Graham emerged from his unpainted, slightly askew back door and approached.

"Got him stabilized. He never woke up, but his heartbeat's good, and his color's come back, mostly. Don't know what's wrong, but I suspect it's to do with his stomach, or maybe kidneys. He's got a lot of... problems down there, you know, below the waist. Looks like it came from some accident or something. Anyhow, he needs to get to a hospital, a real hospital, and I mean sooner rather than later."

"Is there one around here?" Maddie Pearl asked the obvious.

"Well, yeah, if you head west down 66, you'll come up on Albuquerque, but it's a good three hours from here, if there's no traffic."

\*        \*        \*

Johnny Bama "slept" fitfully in the back seat throughout the crossing. Maddie Pearl kept a cool compress on his forehead and sang hymns softly for reassurance while Sal drove as fast as reasonable without endangering the crew. Like in the *Wizard of Oz* that had come out a few months before, the Emerald City of Albuquerque seemed never to get closer, but the tumbleweed desert was no flower-laden poppy field.

Eventually, Emerald City emerged from the arid bleakness and, following Doctor Graham's surprisingly good directions, they found Old Saint Joseph Hospital. They scurried Johnny Bama therein with the help of two nurse nuns courtesy of the Cincinnati

Sisters of Charity. [*Incidentally, it wasn't called "Old" back then. That became the moniker when its successor facility was built in 1968.*]

"This probably will take awhile," said one. "You might want to get something to eat... and a place to stay the night." She gave Sal a knowing glance. "Try the De Anza, on Central Avenue. You won't find it in the *Green Book*, but I suspect they'll be happy to take you in... if you can afford it."

Albuquerque circa 1939 was known as a multiracial city. Nevertheless, of the one hundred or so local hotels, only six accommodated African Americans. The De Anza Motor Lodge was one of them, and after flashing sufficient cash, Sal was able to let a room for himself. Maddie Pearl went in separately, to avoid any appearance of association with her black friend, and arranged her own room, also with a cash flash. They hoped to stay just the night and be on their way, but were prepared to do everything necessary for Bama. Fate dictated that "everything necessary" entailed three nights.

[*Here's another note just between us: If you're a "Breaking Bad" fan, you will remember the scene when Walter White threw out his spare tire to hide cash from a drug deal while his wife was in a hospital giving birth to their daughter. Well... that was filmed at the De Anza.*]

Perhaps it was the suspicious nature of an older white man traveling with a good-looking female teen and strong black man, or perhaps it was just Catholic hospital protocol, but Maddie Pearl and Sal found it almost impossible to gather any prognosis. The Bama uncertainly, coupled with the complexity of moving without appearing to be together, made the time crawl with slug-like meticulousness.

Sal had come upon a couple of JB's books in the Plymouth, and chose to read. He tried the hotel room, but it was musty with no ventilation and stale air. The De Anza lobby, although bright and clean, was too frantic with people coming and going. There was no need to drive, and the Plymouth remained parked on a side street down from the hotel. Its off-the-beaten-track location in the shade of an adjacent building made it the perfect Goldilocks Zone for Sal to rest, relax, and read.

On their second day in waiting, Sal read *The Grapes of Wrath* while stretched out in the Plymouth's back seat. After turning the last page, he found himself full of emotions heretofore never felt, an odd mixture of joy, anxiety, hope, and fear. Perhaps it was mere wanderlust, or experiencing the genius of classic literature for the first time, but sitting in this shiny symbol of American freedom on the very road that led so many lost souls to happy new lives in a better place thrilled this wise but uneducated black man from the Carolina swampland unlike anything previously. Before, it was survival; now, it was the promise of tomorrow, and of each day thereafter being better than the one before. He didn't know how or when, but Walter Carver Jefferson realized—for the first time—the possibilities of an alternative, better, more complete life.

He resolved to let nothing stand in his way.

Maddie Pearl took short walks along Central Avenue to overcome the tedium, looking in shops and checking out scenery. Having never really explored anything like a city, she found it thrilling. After gut-wrenching analysis that led to three visits before pulling the trigger, Maddie Pearl bought a skirt and top at one particularly popular clothing store.

"Oh, you must have a matching purse and shoes, too," exclaimed the pretty store clerk.

"If you really think so," Maddie Pearl responded, caught up in the moment and trusting the city saleswoman over her country self.

Maddie Pearl knew the shoes were a necessity, but she'd never had a purse in her life. She'd fashioned a satchel from a feed sack to tote her broken comb, cracked mirror, occasional Daisy treat, the brush Bama "bought" her after the flyswatter incident, and various similar essentials, including the Derringer. Typical of Depression era families, the Prines wasted nothing, including sacks. In fact, the practice was so widespread that manufacturers began distributing flour, seeds, sugar, animal feed and the like in cotton bags with decorative patterns. Maddie Pearl's satchel, a colorful array of forget-me-nots, had housed chicken scratch before its transformation. Although rudimentary and certainly unfashionable beyond Webster County woodlands, the teenager

had loved it for years. But now, with the new top, skirt, and shoes, it simply didn't suffice.

She couldn't help but wonder if all of this *plus* the purse was just a little too extravagant. Her feelings of guilt for spending a few of her precious dollars quickly were overcome, however, when she returned to the hotel room, tried on everything, and realized how wonderful they made her feel.

Having never experienced starry-eyed prospects bringing flowers and pitching woo, Maddie Pearl rarely if ever thought of boys, marriage, or settling down. Instead, and much like Sal, she focused on Dr. Maslow's lowest hierarchal needs—physiological and safety. Although her eighteenth birthday was just around the corner, Maddie Pearl harbored no worries about love, belonging, esteem, and self-actualization—until this odyssey and, really, until *now.*

This strange new thing with Sal, their obvious affection for one another and the excitement it engendered deep within her being, and Doc too and the possibilities California promised, opened her mind to another, heretofore foreign world. The young woman's flirtatious foray with the High Georgia Sheriff was a symptom of these new, Freudian stirrings. She liked it, and she loved the new clothes including the purse and shoes, and for the first time she really longed to be a woman.

On the first and second days after Johnny Bama was admitted, Sal and Maddie Pearl visited Old Saint Joseph's Hospital in the morning and afternoon. Each visit, "Nurse Ratched" at the front door shooed them away briskly with a "his condition's unchanged" rebuke. On the third morning, however, there was a different gatekeeper, with a different message and attitude.

"Your friend's doing much better," the new nun said positively. "Want to come visit?"

Maddie Pearl and Sal nearly ran down the hall like new puppies on leashes. They turned a corner and were led to a room on the back of the hospital to find their friend propped up in bed with a pretty, young nurse feeding him pudding from a small bowl.

"Come in! Come in!" Bama sang out to his long lost friends. "Let me introduce you to Lillie. Lillie, say hello to my great friends and traveling companions, Maddie Pearl and Walter."

Maddie Pearl ignored the nurse and anxiously asked, "How are you doing?"

"Great! Great!" said JB. "Never been better."

Although his color was much improved from three days previous, it was hard to believe that this relatively young man who now looked old had not experienced "better" sometime back in his day. But at least he was alive, awake, and aware, so Maddie Pearl and Sal took solace in this small victory.

"When are they gonna let you out, Johnny?" asked Sal.

"With a little luck, today."

"Today? That's great news!" said Maddie Pearl with genuine excitement for Bama but also the trip's resumption.

The doctor walked in, seemed slightly surprised by the presence of visitors, and introduced himself. "Well... hello, I guess. I'm Doctor Graham, and you are..."

"Doc, these here are my best friends in the world," Johnny Bama interjected. "They're Maddie Pearl and Walter, but you call him Sal."

Perhaps because a female and an African American faced him, Doctor Graham didn't extend his hand, and no handshakes were exchanged.

"And guess what?" Bama asked his friends. "Do you know who this is, the doctor I mean?"

Maddie Pearl and Sal expressed "No" with indifferent headshakes.

"You remember that doctor back in... where was it again?"

"Tucumcari," the doctor answered.

"Yeah! That's it, Tucumcari," Bama resumed. "Well that doctor there is *this* doctor's father! Can you believe it? Like father like son!"

Maddie Pearl couldn't see the resemblance between that old relic of intolerance and this attractive, forty-something gentleman. Sal didn't really care, being more concerned with JB's condition than the genealogy of some mediocre medical men.

"Mister Claxton, I need to go over your prognosis," the doctor said. "I assume you prefer we do that... you know... in private?"

"Oh hell no, doc, anything you want to say to me you damn sure can say to these folks as well."

Doctor Graham, the younger, raised his bushy eyebrows and reluctantly proceeded.

"Well, as you wish," he looked at his chart. "Here's the thing. You now only have one functioning kidney. The other one's been working, halfway at least, for some time now. But it's given up the ghost."

"What does that mean, doc?" asked Bama, the smile fading from his face.

"Ordinarily, it wouldn't necessarily mean a whole lot. In your case, however..."

"However" hung in the air like an evil ghoul smiling sinisterly at his soon-to-be-victim below.

"Yeah... well... *however...*" lingered Bama.

"Well, it's like this. You have other... *problems*, besides just the kidney."

"Yeah yeah, I know all about 'em... had 'em since the wreck."

Doctor Graham looked at Sal and Maddie Pearl as if to say, "*Are you sure you want to be in here for this?*" They didn't respond, verbally or bodily.

"Yeah... well? Get on with it," said Bama impatiently, sending the clear signal, yet again, that he preferred for Sal and Maddie Pearl to stay right here.

"Okay... Mister Claxton, as you wish." The doctor focused directly, intently on John Claxton. "I'm not just talking about *those* problems."

# Chapter 35

Route 66 from Albuquerque to Winslow, Arizona is 265 miles of small towns, tribal lands, red rocks, Americana kitsch, and vast, open nothingness. It was exactly what the doctor ordered for John "Johnny Bama" Claxton and his traveling companions. Sal drove, Maddie Pearl rode in the front, and JB stretched out in the back, sleeping much of the way.

There was not much to say, and even less to do. Sal's mind wandered to the Okies driving this same road to salvation. His quest was much like theirs. He had left a life that was no more in search of a life that might never be. Buoyed solely by hope and deep determination, he pressed forward. *"But what am I going to do when I get there"* he kept wondering, and his naturally prodigious mind generated no obvious answers.

He assumed that Doc would help. Surely he hasn't "hired" anyone yet; he's only been there a really short time. *"But what if he has, or what if he's not allowed to take on help, or what if... God forbid... he's not even there?"* These haunting thoughts clouded but did not stop the mind from thinking beyond life as some assistant to some soldier in some half-ass military-medi-unit.

John Steinbeck had opened Sal's eyes wider than any Field Hospital # 4 or rock-strewn, mule-tended, eastern-Carolina-field-life ever could. But it wasn't the book's subject matter, which was dreadfully depressing. And it wasn't the route or the destination or the refugees' unification through hardship. It was something deeper, more meaningful, more primal that ate at Sal's soul as the miles passed away and California grew from possible to probable to certain.

It was the idea, the concept, the hope that maybe, someday, somehow, Sal could do what an obscure man in a little place called Salinas just up the road had done through fluid words flowing slowly, beautifully, perfectly from a book called simply *The Grapes of Wrath*.

Sal certainly had never seen Salinas and knew nothing of John Steinbeck's upbringing. "*Was it like mine*," he wondered in semi-daydream, "*or Bama's?*" Considering that spectrum's polar ends, he knew not which was better for a life of letters. "*Maybe hard times make it easier, somehow, or at least more authentic,*" he mused hopefully. "*Or maybe I'm so far behind already that there simply is no chance.*" He thrust the disturbing idea from his mind, yet couldn't help but consider reality: the fact that he could read and write at all was nothing short of miraculous.

*       *       *

Sal's father, Samuel Jefferson, had the good fortune not only of living in the right place at the right time but also happened to be a laborer for Magnus Jacobsen, a young Norwegian immigrant not too long off the boat and now a blacksmith at "Josephus Stables" in downtown Belton, North Carolina. Magnus, a good-hearted man with a gifted sense of humor, took a liking to Samuel and never failed to help him out in small ways and large. If Samuel needed a dollar, Magnus would "lend" him two, knowing he'd be paid back not with coins or bills but rather with even harder work and genuine loyalty. The most significant assistance ever provided, however, came about shortly after the 1898 election.

Although Samuel never had money, position, or power—almost no African Americans did—his inner strength and quiet, intelligent manner were known well to all with whom he interacted. Every shop on Fifth Street, Belton's main drag downtown, was owned and operated by white men; and every shop on Fifth Street displayed a "WHITES ONLY" sign prominently; but every shop owner on Fifth Street knew, liked, and respected Samuel Jefferson. They may have prevented his entrance into their crappy little stores, but they always greeted him outside with smiles, well wishes, and the occasional freebie from within—when no Caucasian customers were looking, of course.

Being a respected citizen interested in the town's welfare, Samuel always voted. He knew the history well of his ancestors—slaves all, and their struggles even after the Emancipation Proclamation. Voting had not come overnight; it had been a long

trail of fears with one pothole after another. But in the aftermath of Reconstruction and during the first few years of Samuel's adulthood, voting had been an important part of his life, and he had dragged many a man from his shanty village neighborhood along the river to the polls on more than one first Tuesday in November.

But the 1898 vote had changed things, and the 1900 election proved far different than before, impacting Samuel Jefferson's life forever. As he had done some five cycles so far, he showed up first thing at the First Street polling station. Roughly a two-mile walk from home, it was in the middle of the side of Belton off limits to blacks at night and only partially welcoming in daylight hours. It also was the closest poll to the blacks' neighborhood, placed there strategically to discourage African Americans from participating in their most basic of inalienable rights. It worked for most, but not for Samuel.

When Samuel reached the table to cast his ballot, the white man there seated never looked up but handed out a paper full of tiny print.

"Read it out loud," he carped brusquely.

To Samuel, some of the symbols looked vaguely familiar, but reading it aloud was out of the question.

"I can't read," said Samuel, a proud man who had to admit this publicly to the little white man seated before him—and to those many whites standing in line impatiently waiting for this black man to get the hell out of here.

"Then you can't vote. NEXT!"

Samuel returned to Josephus Stables, a shamed and beaten man. Magnus Jacobsen heard the problem and determined, "We're going to figure this out, for you *and* me!"

Had Magnus been handed a paper by that little voter man written in Norwegian with all the crazy little lines through letters and squiggles and odd, backward symbols, he'd be voting in no time. But Magnus shared Samuel's affliction, he too was illiterate, in English at least. And like Samuel, he too would not be voting in America, at least not until that illness was cured. Fortunately, a place of linguistic healing was just around the corner.

Belton State Teachers College began operating in the fall of 1901 as a necessity borne of stupidity. Specifically, the brainless

racists running NC's legislature had imposed Jim Crow literacy tests for voting. It backfired when illiterate blacks *and whites* got turned away, particularly in eastern Carolina. "We gotta fix this boys," bellowed newly elected white supremacist Governor Charles B. Aycock behind closed doors in a smoke filled room, "but not for them nigras." And fix it they did, by founding a college to teach teachers to teach whites how to read and write and, most importantly, vote.

BSTC's mission rendered literacy a prerequisite to admission. After all, a student cannot be taught to teach Basic English if the student doesn't know Basic English to start with. Drawing applicants virtually one hundred percent from eastern Carolina, including Magnus Jacobsen, a new issue quickly presented. Fewer than ten percent of the applicants knew how to read and write. The Raleigh brain trust caucused and appropriations were made for remedial programs. They'd teach illiterate whites how to read and write so they could learn how to teach illiterate whites how to teach reading and writing so formerly illiterate white men could vote while thumbing their noses at those ignorant blacks who were too stupid to know how to read and write. Even in Wonderland, Alice's head was spinning from this curiouser and curiouser blueprint for blatant discrimination.

So Magnus began his training at the college by studying Basic English. Daily, he'd bring his lessons to the stables and learn the ABC's with Samuel. Each being highly intelligent, it didn't take long. They soon reached a point of challenge, where one would endeavor to outdo the other with games involving tricky words or complex sentences. Long before the ensuing election, Magnus was sitting on the front row in actual education courses, far removed from the remedial classroom. Samuel became a voracious reader, with books loaned from Belton State's budding library by his pal and co-worker.

When 1902 rolled around, Samuel was more than excited to rekindle his civic duty with the November election. He got up early on the appointed day, dressed in his Sunday best, walked meaningfully two miles to the First Street station, and found himself the first man in line, standing tall. The same small, obnoxious, white man poll worker sat in the same chair behind the same table from two years afore. Just like before, the white man

never looked up but handed Samuel a paper upon which was tiny print.

"Read it out loud," he said familiarly, rudely.

Samuel was prepared, proud of this newly learned skill, and cleared his throat to ensure that the little white man and all the skinny and fat white men behind heard distinctly. He looked at the paper with an air of confidence, and stopped.

It was written in Chinese!

"But sir," Samuel pleaded. "I can't read this."

"Can't read, can't vote," said the man smugly for all to hear. "NEXT!"

Samuel stood off to the side, shocked and humiliated. The snickering whites in line looked at him with repugnance and disdain as they marched forward to observe *their* patriotic duty. The next voter approached, a fat white redneck in bib overalls with a malodorous aroma of swine and cesspool. The little white man behind the desk handed the redneck a *different* paper.

"Please read this aloud, sir, so I can hear," the little white poll working man said politely.

"Uh," the redneck struggled, "the... ball... is... um, um..."

"Perfect," the white little man said, facilitating the phony literacy prerequisite while handing the redneck a ballot.

He then looked up for the first time, glared at Samuel, and said, "I thought I told you to git, ya ignorant nigra!"

Samuel Jefferson moved from Belton not too long afterwards. He wasn't intimidated away by such bigoted shenanigans; his father desperately needed him back home. So Samuel relocated to the farm his father supposedly owned in the next county over—Webster.

Father and son worked the fields tirelessly and learned about fertilizers, wind blocks, ditching, crop rotation, and pesticides. After several years, they began producing some of the best, and most valuable, flue-cured tobacco in the whole state of North Carolina. Samuel got married, built a small, decent house on the property alongside his parents' place, and had two fine children: Walter Carver and Nomita.

Almost before his children could talk, father Samuel began teaching his offspring about letters and words and sentences and and paragraphs. If nothing else, he knew, this was a pathway,

perhaps small and rough and curvy and dangerous, but a pathway nonetheless to a better tomorrow.

Life continued well until the day a man named Robert Lee showed up alongside the High Sheriff of Webster County with a paper that said something about the farm property. His father couldn't read it, but Samuel sure could, and it sickened him. A Superior Court Judge had signed an order directing that the farm no longer belonged to Jefferson. It now was Lee land. There had never been any hearing to which any Jefferson had been summoned. There had never been any opportunity to be heard or explain the chain of title that, by the way, was solidly in favor of the Jeffersons—not Lee—going back to 1868 and the beginnings of Reconstruction. There had never been any chance to negotiate or even learn about Lee's claims. But being magnanimous, this Lee fellow—known as "Boss"—gratuitously offered the Jeffersons the *privilege* of staying on the property, but only on the worst forty acres. Also, they could continue farming, but only as Lee tenants. The best land would be leased to another family, white people with a good-old-boy patriarch everyone called "Hog."

With no appeal and no alternatives, Samuel's father took the offer.

Not one to take things lying down, Samuel Jefferson decided to contest the order that legally was incontestable. There were no black lawyers, and any white attorneys knew better than to take the case of an African American, especially a case pitting said African American against the likes of Boss Lee. So Samuel represented his family *pro se* by filing a paper challenging the order at the courthouse and requesting a hearing before the same judge.

He was found three days later—by the boy he lovingly nicknamed "Sallerhead"—hanging dead from a tree at the corner of the former Jefferson farm.

Magnus Jacobsen, meanwhile, finished his classes at the college, graduated with high honors, and became a teacher of the teachers-to-be at BSTC. Eventually, Magnus became Belton State's second president, and served there with distinction for the next forty-five years.

\* \* \*

Memories of so many years gone by swirled in Sal's head behind the wheel of this new Plymouth with a rich but sick, slightly older white man and a beautiful but naïve, slightly younger redhead hurtling down the nation's Mother Road toward an ill-defined future of uncertainty at best. But compared to the poor Okies and their Dust Bowl oblivion, or his grandfather and father, or his own life back *there* in the land of Boss Lee tyrants and crooked judges, Sal increasingly appreciated his good fortune with each passing gas station or kitschy rest stop.

"*Things could be a lot worse,*" he thought, "*one hell of a lot worse.*"

# Chapter 36

Sal found himself standing on a corner in Winslow, Arizona, but there were no fine sights to see. There *was* a girl, taking a look at him, but not in a flatbed Ford. She was pretty, in a long black dress (no more than eight inches above the floor), a starched white pinafore, and laced-up boots over opaque black stockings.

The young, single woman of good character, all prerequisites, worked as a waitress under a yearlong contract as a "Harvey Girl." Some six years later, this young woman and her colleagues would be memorialized in MGM's *The Harvey Girls* starring Dorothy herself—Judy Garland, as well as Ray Bolger (remember him... the Scarecrow) and Angela Lansbury. On this early evening, the young woman had finished her shift at the famous La Posada, Fred Harvey's southwest masterpiece and last great railroad hotel, and walked next door where she lived with other Harveys.

Well known then, and now, the La Posada accommodated America's finest through the years, including Albert Einstein, Amelia Earhart, Franklin D. Roosevelt, Betty Grable, and right-wing McCarthy-ite John Wayne. On this day, it accommodated our trio for a quick overnight stop. Although not listed in the *Green Book*, Harvey Hotels were a prosperous chain of establishments along the Santa Fe, Atchison, and Topeka railways that did serve African Americans during the Jim Crow era. Fred Harvey, not sufficiently recognized for his visionary contributions to American culture, started the nation's first hotel chain, implemented the employment of those famous Harvey Girls, regularly hired Native Americans when no one else would, and even created opportunities by promoting their exquisite crafts.

Maddie Pearl and a groggy but awake Johnny Bama checked into separate rooms and already had retired. Sal, wound up from driving all day with his mind still awash of yesterday,

today, and tomorrow, milled about the downtown area restlessly. With a little luck, they hoped to finish the journey tomorrow, passing through Flagstaff, Kingman, Yucca, and Needles along the way. It was a push, over four hundred miles they estimated from their three maps, with a lot of nothingness, including a dearth of gas stations. If need be, they would stop, preferably in Needles. Then they'd make the last long jaunt through the Mojave Desert with its Joshua trees and beautiful flowers, two mountain ranges, and deadly heat.

The 1940 Packard, which had come out a few weeks previously, was the first and only car to offer factory-installed air conditioning. The 1939 Plymouth, with no AC, was a black, metal-encased, torrid torture chamber with passengers buffeted by sixty mile per hour relative winds of furnace air blasting through every window for every second of every mile. On an Interstate today in a sleek AC'ed SUV with Sirius/XM, GPS, cruise control, and rest stops aplenty, four hundred miles across desert is a six hour stroll in the park. On 1939 Route 66 in a balky Plymouth with no amenities, that same trip was an all-day hellish nightmare of sweat, nausea, GI attacks, sunburned arms and screamed conversations.

Johnny Bama was not ready to drive, although he bravely volunteered more than once. Maddie Pearl would share the duties, but Sallerhead knew the bulk would fall on him. Sal was not upset about it; the strongest usually bear the hardest burdens. Besides, his thoughts were far removed from the mundane of getting from A to Barstow. Specifically, he worried, " *What happens when we arrive?*" But there was no answering that tonight; so he walked about, partly to stretch his athletic legs but more just to clear his mind. It was destined not to work, and he wrestled with restiveness the whole night through.

Early the next morning, they set out. Maddie Pearl drove, mainly because the first quarter would be the easiest, with Bama co-piloting. Sal perched in the back with another of JB's books. Johnny, now fully reinvigorated, tried to regale his fellow itinerants with wild tales of western gunslingers, bounties, Wyatt Earp and Bat Masterson. While Maddie Pearl feigned interest, out of social decorum, Sal stayed focused on his book, and so the stories fell on deaf ears, and Johnny Bama eventually gave up, temporarily.

Some forty miles west of Flagstaff, they stopped at an ESSO for gas and refreshment. This experience, with white attendants, was positive but far inferior to their first ESSO encounter. Maddie Pearl and Sal played musical chairs enabling Bama to stay put, and off they continued toward Seligman and Kingman.

In short order, Maddie Pearl was in la-la land from the heat and tension of driving with basically no experience. Bama, having been either unconscious or semi-conscious four days now and having been politely rebuked by Maddie Pearl, was eager to talk with his new captive audience.

"I noticed you read *The Grapes of Wrath*," said Bama to Sal. "What'd you think?"

Ever so slightly, Sal rolled his eyes like someone disinterested in talking, similarly to how Maddie Pearl had been responding. He answered noncommittally. "Oh... I don't know."

"Yeah... I thought it was a little over-the-top too," Bama forced the conversation. "They say it's his best so far, but I don't know. *Of Mice and Men* is pretty good too. You read that yet?"

Having been raised on a farm in eastern Carolina where libraries and bookstores were as common as pyramids and French restaurants, Sal had read basically nothing. Although reluctant to engage Bama about it right now, with his thoughts far away on another planet, the truth was that Steinbeck's book had touched him, deeply, and he couldn't imagine any other work being even remotely as compelling.

"Uh... no, haven't read *that* one," replied Sal tersely.

"It's pretty good. Made it into a movie, came out last year. I don't care much for Lon Chaney, but it wasn't bad, as Lon Chaney movies go."

"*Movies? Lon Chaney? What in hell is this fool blathering about?*"

"Pretty good story, though... *Of Mice and Men* I mean. These two guys travel around, sorta like us right now, in search of something, you know... better."

This struck a chord with Sallerhead, having spent a sleepless night wandering the Winslow deadzone for hours... *in search of something.* His attention meter went from two to nine

with Bama's observation, and he perked up in the driver's seat ever so slightly.

"So... what did they do?"

Bama now knew he had a fish on the line, and was more than ready to play it. "What did *who* do?"

"You know... those guys in that book... the one about mice or whatever."

"Oh... you mean *Of Mice and Men*. Well, they did a lot of stuff, along the way."

Too tired for games, Sal nipped, "Dammit Bama, just tell me the story, okay?"

Chuckling slightly at Sal's sincere, good-natured demand, and thrilled finally to have a talking buddy after so many days in oblivion, Johnny continued. "Well it takes place in California, right where we're goin', but not exactly... I mean, it's not in Barstow or that Mojave place, but it's not too far away."

"Yeah... and?" Sal chimed, impatiently.

"Anyhow... they work on a ranch, you know, a farm, sorta like what you did back home, but I don't think you dealt with animals much, right?"

Having talked about this previously, Sal recognized that Bama knew damn well the Jeffersons farmed crops, not creatures. He was on the verge of a minor paroxysm, when Maddie Pearl surprised them both.

"So what's a 'ranch'?" she asked, her head propped on the front bench seat.

"Hey, I thought you were out like a light?" exclaimed Johnny Bama.

"Who can sleep with all this hot air?" she replied.

"Are you sayin' I'm full of *hot air?*" said Bama with a mocking tone.

"I wasn't... but if you keep it up I just might!"

The trio shared a slight laugh at the playful exchange.

"So a 'ranch,' what is it?" persisted Maddie Pearl.

"Oh," replied Bama, "it's just a farm, really. That's sorta what they call farms out west, ranches, but they usually are really big, and have animals, like cattle, or sometimes sheep."

"Yeah, yeah," said Sal. "So what about these two guys, these ranch people?"

"Oh yeah... George and Lennie." He continued, now with two rapt listeners on Bama Airwaves. "So George is smart, and ambitious. He wants a ranch of his own someday, and strikes out with Lennie to make enough money to buy one."

"What's Lennie like?" asked Maddie Pearl.

"Lennie's what you might call 'slow,' and George has to... you know... take care of 'em."

Maddie Pearl peered out the window taking in the story of George and Lennie and mice and men.

"And ol' Lennie loves animals, especially furry ones, cause he likes to pet them and hug 'em and stuff, and he loves them so much that sometimes he accidentally kills 'em—squeezes them too hard or whatever. But Lennie's really just a gentle giant, and can't control himself."

Maddie Pearl thought of another world twenty-five hundred miles and a lifetime away, and of another "Lennie," a mentally deficient gentle giant of a brother, and of a little squirrel she called Nutty, and of what once was, and never would be again.

With all the excitement of the trip, the challenges and getting closer to Sal, meeting Johnny, and the adventures and problems and troubles and now hope of seeing Doc and California and starting this new life and everything else all rolled into one big ball, the teenager had not thought much of No Mind Tate or the farm back east, and her other dimwitted brothers. And she'd not thought of Luke... the late Luke... the evil Luke who faux raped her, and Mama, vulnerable Bible-thumping Mama, and Maddie Pearl's monstrous pa who caused so much heartache for so long.

She had no longing for that life, for the misery, poverty, and stupidity. She had spent her youth not able to go a few measly miles to this mysterious place called "Town" and now, in this Plymouth with these people, she was traveling the great gulf between home and "Town" every ten minutes on Route 66. And she was seeing the world every day, all day, up close and personally, and she realized how easy it all could have been—if only.

She never wanted to go back, and wouldn't, not now, not ever!

"So they're traveling around California," continued Johnny Bama, "and they meet this stable-hand—a fellow who handles the

horses—and he's named Crooks, and he's... well... he's black, like Walter here, and people are, you know... well, they're kinda mean to Crooks—not George and Lennie, they're nice to him—but other people... around the ranch."

Bama cast a side-glance to Sal, just to gauge. "I'm familiar with discrimination, Mister Claxton," said Sallerhead. "Don't worry none about hurting my little ol' feelings."

Bama smiled gently, and continued. "So they have some setbacks, like everybody in a good story, and some things don't work out."

"Like, what things?" asked Maddie Pearl, not wanting any details to be left out.

"Well, you might want to read it someday, you know, instead of me tellin' ya everything. It's a pretty short story. What they call a 'novella,' which just means a short novel. In fact, I think it mighta started out as a play."

"Have you got it?" said Sal. "I mean... with you?"

"No. Didn't bring that one. Could have, but I didn't mean to pack too much. I've got some other stuff you might be interested in, either one of you."

"Like what?" asked Maddie Pearl.

"Oh... I don't know. Would need to pull out the suitcase from the boot and check. I got *The Grapes of Wrath*. Me and Sal were talkin' 'bout that one before you woke back up. And I got... well... like I said, it'd be easier just to pull out the suitcase. Maybe let's do that at the next stop."

"When will that be," asked Maddie Pearl. "I might need a quick *rest*." Seligman was ten miles away and a logical place to stop, so the conversation lagged in anticipation.

Leaving Seligman fully "rested," nine books were now relocated to the passenger compartment. Maddie Pearl and Bama were studying each, while Sal continued driving. The stop had worked wonders, as so often is the case when traveling, and their energy levels were percolating with Kingman so close and the Mojave Anti-Aircraft Range practically in sight.

Maddie Pearl was like a child on Christmas morning—not like *her* Christmas experiences, but like a normal child from a normal family with normal gifts under a normal tree. Each new book opened a whole world of possibilities, and not one was

moldy or torn or full of big bad wolves. She clamored for Bama to tell her every detail of each and every one. For the most part, he demurred by repeating, " *Well, you really ought to read it instead of me tellin' ya everything.*" But Bama did come across two books that he thought particularly relevant, and worth elucidating.

"Now Maddie Pearl, I think you would like this one." He held up a book entitled *As I Lay Dying* and handed it back to her.

"What's this one?" she asked excitedly, as she had about every other suitcase book.

"This lady, named Addie, she dies... down in Mississippi, you know, where we went through a few days ago, and all these people who knew her and the family and all, well, they tell different stories about her and what was going on when she was alive."

"Huh... was Addie, you know, a good person?"

"Well, you really ought to read it instead of me tellin' ya everything," Bama said for the umpteenth time.

"Now that's not fair! You can't just tease me like that," exclaimed Maddie Pearl in mock anger.

"Okay okay... you asked whether Addie is good. To be honest... I don't know. It's complicated. I guess some liked her, some didn't. I mean, when you think about it... isn't that always the way?"

"I don't think so," stated Sal coldly.

"Sure it is," retorted Bama. "I mean, it seems to me anyway, everybody's got some good in 'em, and some bad, and we just have to do what we can to tamp down that bad side, best we can... dontcha think?"

"It's like what Mama used to tell me, about the Devil and the angel," said Maddie Pearl. "She'd say, '*Now Maddie Pearl, you got that Devil on one shoulder and an angel from heaven on the other, and they're gonna talk to you all the time and try to tell you what to do, and you need to listen to that angel, ya hear?*'"

"That's a bunch of hogwash," Sal disagreed, a little too stridently.

The nature of Sal's comment brought the conversation to a momentary stop. Bama glanced back to Maddie Pearl, who returned the scan with a quizzical look. With expressions alone, each was saying, " *Well Sal... we're waiting!*" Finally, he followed up.

"You haven't seen what I've seen. You just haven't. Some people are bad... just *all* bad, and there isn't any fixing them with some angel or whatever."

"But don't you believe in angels and heaven and everything?" asked Maddie Pearl, somewhat hopefully.

"I don't know what I believe," answered Walter Carver. "But I can tell you this... both of you... there are some people out there that I don't care what you say... or that Bible of yours—they're bad through-and-through, and no angel or prayer or even Jesus himself is ever going to fix 'em!"

"I don't know, Sal," Bama injected. "You might be right, but I can say this... I haven't met any of 'em yet, and I've come across some pretty bad people, you can bank on that, as bad as you can imagine."

Sal turned his head and looked at Johnny Bama with a steely, rigid stare and said coldly, "You haven't seen what I've seen."

The Plymouth fell silent for several minutes as the tropical storm force heat winds buffeted each from every window and the endless horizon provided no distraction and the sugar-drink high from the Seligman Gas Emporium dissipated into a post-pop low of near depression.

In the distance, Sal noticed a young man hitchhiking. Without asking his fellow travelers, he pulled off Route 66 and motioned.

"What are you doing?" asked Maddie Pearl, with a tinge of irritation and fear.

"Boy needs a ride. You see somebody out in the middle of nowhere like this, ya help 'em. Besides," he looked coldly at his fellow travelers, "I could use some fresh air."

The boy, probably aged between Maddie Pearl and Sal, hustled up to the passenger window, stuck in his head, and said, "Heading to Kingman by any chance?"

Johnny Bama gave the lad a disdainful look, reached up from the backseat and tapped Sal on the shoulder. "I think we're a little too... *crowded* back here for another, don't you?"

Sal ignored the white man and invited the white boy in. Bama slid as far away as possible, practically edging out the opposite door. Maddie Pearl, likewise, was deeply uncomfortable

taking on some stranger in the desert. She reached into her new, Albuquerque-purchased purse and checked to make sure Bama's Derringer was handy, just in case.

Kingman was relatively close and, for the most part, the ride was uneventful. With his eyes distracted on the road, Sal didn't notice much about the boy, except his conversational tendencies, which were strange. Maddie Pearl in the front seat likewise didn't see much, but heard more than she wanted. Meanwhile, Bama kept a watchful eye, and remained wary throughout.

The boy was named Willy Hooks, and from his responses appeared to be from and heading to nowhere special. He smelled bad, like rotting carcass and, as Bama would describe later, had a wild look in his eyes—otherworldly, evil even. But most noticeable to all three was his behavior. For the first few minutes, he said nothing; then he burst into jittery conversation about "those damn injuns;" then he was silent again; then "dem Harvey girls are hot beauts, huh;" and so on.

Before they reached Kingman, the boy blurted out in the otherwise quiet if windy car, "THERE! THERE! Let me off THERE!"

The three others perked up to see what appeared to be a broken down vehicle some quarter mile ahead. As they neared, it became clear that the old truck with Oklahoma plates overladen with what appeared to be a small family's every possession was stopped with its radiator spewing steam into the boiling desert air.

Sal pulled up behind as the boy leapt out before the Plymouth had stopped fully. The manner in which the boy ran up to the truck suggested he knew the people, but the father, mother, kid, and dog didn't greet him.

Johnny Bama called out from the backseat. "You folks need some help?"

Before the paterfamilias could answer, Willy blurted in his frenetic manner, "I can help! I can help! I know all about cars and motors and such."

The Okie father looked at the boy with suspicion, then back at the Plymouth. He studied the car's occupants. His eyes widened noticeably upon focusing on the large black man behind the wheel. He shook his head in obvious displeasure at Sal.

"Don't need no help from no niggers," the father said.

Sal energetically started to get out as if he intended to confront the ignorant fool, but Bama grabbed the shoulder and said, "Hold on, Sal. Let me handle this guy." Very reluctantly, Sal relented—temporarily at least.

"Listen here, friend," Bama began, using a thick Alabama twang to let the Okie know they were simpatico. "Ol' Sal here is my driver, that's all. He ain't gonna hurt ya none. He's a good old boy."

Sal glared back at Bama, then started exiting again, but Maddie Pearl reached over this time. "Come on, Sal. Leave it be. You know Bama's just trying to help these people."

"I'm not mad at Bama," said Sal, as he backed down reluctantly a second time.

Willy Hooks spoke up wildly. "You guys can run on. I got this. I know just how to fix it. I'm a whiz with old trucks like this."

Bama, Maddie Pearl, and Sal harbored serious doubts about the whole situation. Bama spoke for the group or, at least, for Maddie Pearl and himself. "Be happy to give ya a ride into Kingman. It's big in here. Probably can git ya all in, if you like."

The Okie's wife grabbed up her child defensively and said to her husband. "We don't have to ride with one of... *them*, do we?"

The father turned to Bama, "We'll be just fine—on our own!"

Sal turned to his compatriots. "So you're sayin' these Okie assholes can be redeemed? *Jesus!*"

Reluctantly, Bama called out one last time, and his Alabama accent was replaced with the diction and propriety of a Philadelphia lawyer. "All right, sir. We understand. But I still intend to inform the first gas station along our journey of your predicament. In the meantime, may God be with you good people."

As they pulled away, Maddie Pearl noticed the hitchhiker seemed far more focused on the young mother than the steaming radiator. Bama noticed it too, but what could they do? The Lord helps those who help themselves, and these Oklahoma bigots had chosen the self-help path rather than a safe ride into town.

Some three days later, the *Kingman Daily Miner* headlined, "FAMILY FOUND SLAUGHTERD" (with the blatant misspelling). The assailant, William Martin Hooks, would not be captured until 1947 after a spree along Route 66 that left at least fifteen other victims in his path. Sal, Maddie Pearl, and Bama never saw the article, of course, and never knew their direct connection to perhaps the most notorious murderer west of the Mississippi, at least up to that time.

With Willy Hooks the hitchhiking serial killer now in their rearview mirror, the three continued their odyssey west. Sal no longer was energized about the incident; he'd been there before, many times. And he was not angry with Bama; the black man understood how the game *had* to be played, at least sometimes. He didn't like it, but the world's awful ways weren't the fault of the handicapped man in the backseat.

After a long, quiet hiatus, Johnny Bama spoke up in the hot, gloomy nothingness, "There's a book that you might like too, Sal... if you're interested."

"What?" replied Sal in a flat, *I don't give a shit* way.

"This one," Bama said, holding up a thin, very old book. "It's called *Poetics*, by Aristotle."

He handed the book to Sal, who glanced at it superficially without fully taking his eyes off the empty Mother Road.

"Yeah... so?" he said, tossing it on the bench seat.

Bama picked it up, rifled through the few pages, and then looked up at Sallerhead.

"I know how you felt after reading *Grapes of Wrath*."

"Huh?" said Sal.

"I know how you felt, how it hit you, how it stirred feelings you've never felt."

"I don't know what you're talking about," said Sal defiantly but unconvincingly.

"What *are* you talking about?" asked Maddie Pearl, butting into the conversation that had nothing to do with her.

"Sal here read one of these books the other day—*The Grapes of Wrath*—and I'm just sayin' that I know it touched him, deeply."

Maddie Pearl sifted through the clutter of books and pulled out Steinbeck's masterpiece.

"This one?"

"Yep. That one."

Maddie Pearl looked through the pages and read a snippet from the middle.

"Sal here never read anything like that before," said Bama. "I could tell... hit him pretty hard."

Sal feigned interest in the road and surroundings in a weak attempt to disengage from the conversation.

"For me," Bama continued, "it was *Around the World in Eighty Days*. Ever heard of it?"

Maddie Pearl didn't answer, being more interested in the other book she never had heard of until this trip in this Plymouth with these two most interesting men. Sal, likewise, was unresponsive.

"Really struck a chord in me, about travel and seeing the world and all the adventures and everything. Greatest thing I've ever read... just like that book you just finished, Sal."

After a few awkward seconds, Sal finally re-engaged. "So what does this other book have to do with anything?"

Bama smiled knowingly. "It's about writing, Sal, about telling stories and how to do it... right."

Sal glanced over. "So what's writing stories got to do with it, or me?"

Bama strategically chose not to answer; he'd let Sal stew over things a bit.

Maddie Pearl piped up from the back to no one in particular, "This book, this *Grapes of Wrath*, looks pretty good. Mind if I read it too?"

Bama never diverted his gaze from Sal. "Sure, Maddie Pearl... that's why I brought these."

"Oh goody," squealed Maddie Pearl as she settled back and turned to page one.

After just the right amount of time had elapsed, Bama resumed, "I've seen you takin' notes, on that paper I gave ya. I haven't read any of it... that's your business, not mine. But I've seen ya, and I got a feelin' about... well... let's just say I got a feelin'."

"You talkin' about angels and devils and that nonsense again?" asked Sal.

Once again, JB quietly let a few seconds drift on by.
"I think you know what I'm talkin' about. I think you know *exactly* what I'm talking about."

Now it was Sal's turn to wait strategically, which he did to perfection. At just the right moment, he volleyed back, "So I'll ask again... and I'm not admitting to anything... but still, what does this little book of yours—about poetry or whatever—have to do... with anything?"

"Almost everything today traces back to the Greeks... the ancient Greeks. Science, government, mathematics, philosophy... you name it, they had something to do with getting it started. And maybe the smartest of them all, of all the Greeks, was Aristotle. And he was this genius philosopher and scientist."

"So he wrote this book?"

"Yep. He wrote this book... *Poetics*, and it explains the basics of story telling better than anything ever written, *ever*... by anybody."

"So what's that got to do with me," Sal tried to continue the ruse.

"Maybe nothing..." answered Bama. "Maybe nothin' at all."

# Chapter 37

By midday, they crossed into California. There was no fanfare. The momentous event was marked with a broken-down "CALIFORNIA STATE LINE" sign amid searing, scorching, dry, unbearable heat. The Plymouth's 84 horsepower, 201.3 cubic inch, L-head straight six with a single 1.5 Carter D6 carburetor and 6.7:1 compression ratio handled poorly the strain of pushing its 2880 pounds and three passengers. Twice it overheated: once before Kingman, and once thereafter.

Although the section of Route 66 entering California was mostly concrete, the thin layer of black asphalt atop held the heat like a Dutch oven. For Sal, Maddie Pearl, and Johnny Bama, the math didn't add up: 100% black asphalt; 0% humidity; 120 degrees; 60 miles per hour; 120 minutes without a stop. Now just ten miles or so from Needles, a third problem had arisen.

The tires had been a persistent issue since leaving Fort Bragg. Sal had become somewhat of a master wheel man, but this was different. The two rears, the ones handling the Plymouth's meek power, had scalloped to the point of irreparable dysfunction. In fact, the front tires weren't far from failing as well.

Needles was too far to walk, in this inferno anyway, so they awaited a Good Samaritan. It didn't take long. Desert denizens on Route 66 were somewhat like seamen on the ocean: you come across someone in distress, you stop and help. That was Sal's mentality with the hitchhiker and Bama's with the Okies, to no avail unfortunately.

Within minutes, a 1940 air-conditioned Packard tooled up, and out dashed a twenty-something military man in a rigidly stiff khaki uniform and very officious demeanor. Sal and Bama knew instantly: a full bird colonel—highly rare for a man this young.

"Do you people need some help?" the colonel inquired, knowing the answer before he asked.

"Yes sir, colonel, we do, sir," said Bama, super deferentially.

"What seems to be the problem?"

"Well sir... it's the tires sir," said Bama.

The colonel, tall, athletic, angular with close-cropped hair and a rigid demeanor, walked around the Plymouth, knelt, and studied the rear tires, massaging the rubber to gauge the problem's severity.

After checking the fronts as well, he said, "Happens all the time, especially out here. Looks like they've been plugged, several times. Probably got out of balance, or maybe alignment. No matter, can't fix them. You need new ones, on all four if you can afford it."

"Yes sir. We were thinking the same thing, sir."

The colonel, having been focused on the Plymouth up to now, looked at Bama and Sal. "You men military?"

Sal and Bama regarded each other, not fully sure how to respond. "Well, sir... yes sir, sort of," Johnny Bama finally uttered.

The colonel just stood, stared, and awaited further information. Before Bama could explain, Private Walter Carver Jefferson cut in. "I am a private, sir, in the Army, or at least I was, until a few weeks ago, sir."

"I'm not sure I understand you, soldier. Clarify." The colonel said military businesslike.

"Well, I was stationed in North Carolina... at Fort Bragg, but my duty officer got reassigned out here, to Mojave."

"Soldier, either you are in the Army or you are not. Now, which is it?"

"Maybe I can explain, sir," said Bama. "I was in the Army too, also at Fort Bragg, for awhile at least. Pilot, mostly. Trainer. But I finished my last hitch and went back home to help my pa take care of the family farm, back in Alabama."

"I still don't understand the status of *this* soldier," the colonel wouldn't let go of the bone.

"Well sir, Private Jefferson here is carrying out an order from a superior officer, sir," Bama lied.

"Yes. Go on."

"You see, sir, Private Jefferson was ordered to transport this vehicle... this Plymouth, from North Carolina to his superior

officer's new duty station, at Mojave Anti-Aircraft Range. That's near Barstow."

The colonel eyed Sal closely. "I know where it is." He got close to Sal and looked him squarely eye-to-eye. "This true, soldier?"

Sal stood at attention, didn't blink, and replied honorably, "No sir. It is not."

Bama's body slouched at the truthful, but seriously dangerous, reply. Although the rules pertaining to African American soldiers were more than a little loosey-goosey, Bama knew damn well that no soldier was allowed to go absent without leave, or AWOL. And a good case now could be made that his traveling companion, the man he had gotten to know so well and had grown to respect deeply, and the person with perhaps as much innate potential as anyone he ever had met, was a traitorous criminal worthy of years in military prison and a life everlasting of shame and failure.

"If I may, sir," Bama tried to explain.

"NO, *sir*, you may not! I want to know from *this* man exactly what the hell is going on here!"

Sal, still at attention, still unblinking, responded. "Sir, I joined the Army to serve my country and for a better life. I was able to do both, as a medical assistant, at Field Hospital # 4 in Fort Bragg, North Carolina, under my superior officer, Captain David Hodge. Field Hospital # 4 was shut down. Captain Hodge was reassigned to Mojave Anti-Aircraft Range. I was not reassigned or given orders as to my next duty station. Therefore, sir, *on my own*, I abandoned my former post, without leave, and undertook to travel cross-country in hope of resuming my duties under Captain Hodge as he deems fit. We were planning to reach Mojave today, or tomorrow, until we encountered this problem with the tires, sir."

The colonel studied Sal long and hard, staring deeply into his eyes as if reading his soul and gauging the mettle of his manhood, character, and integrity.

"And these people," the colonel said, pointing at Maddie Pearl and Bama without taking his eyes off Sal. "Who are they?"

"Sir. The woman is with me, sir. She came from North Carolina too. She was a patient in Field Hospital # 4 when it was shut down, sir. When she was evicted, sir, she had nowhere else to

go. She has no family any more, no home, no money, and no job. She is acquainted with Captain Hodge, and is hopeful of finding work and a new life in California, sir."

"And the man, the pilot?"

"Sir. Mister John Claxton can answer for himself, sir. For my part, I can attest that he is a good and true American, and a former soldier of respect. The woman—Maddie Pearl—and I met him in Alabama, and he has helped us immensely. Without Mister Claxton, sir, we would have been forced to abandon this... this *mission* long ago, sir."

The colonel backed away from Sallerhead and relaxed his body language, ever so slightly. He walked over to Johnny Bama.

"Captain, now I know you were just trying to protect Private Jefferson, and I can understand that, but are you ready to be square with me now?"

"Sir, yes sir," snapped Bama militarily.

"I feel like I'm a pretty good judge of character... always have been," the colonel said, "and I've got a feeling that each and every word that just came out of that *nigger's* mouth is a damn lie." The colonel nudged ever so closer to Bama. "Now...what do you say to *that?*"

Bama hesitated, with a locked jaw and eyes beadier by the second. With deep resolve, he answered, "Walter Carver Jefferson is a man, sir. An honorable, truthful man. And I don't give a damn who you think you might be, *sir*, don't *ever* call him *that* again!"

The world stopped. The four stood stoically, quietly, motionlessly. The hot wind blew no relief. The road stretched forever in either direction, with no traffic—only sagebrush and tumbleweeds. Seconds passed like hours. Three good men and one strong woman stood at a crossroads, with one man in a starched outfit holding everyone's fate in the palm of his hand.

"As I said..." the colonel broke the séance, "I'm a pretty good judge of character."

Sal, Bama, and Maddie Pearl held their breath waiting what fresh hell was coming now. This scene already had played out at Fort Bragg with the Field Hospital # 4 closure; and in North Carolina when Maddie Pearl lambasted the poor cop to distraction; and in Georgia with the Barney Fife that Maddie Pearl outfoxed; and in Alabama where Sal's own people ripped him off;

and in Mississippi with flyswatter boy; and in Texas with the sundown town; and in New Mexico with Bama's near-death experience; and on the entire trip, from Carolina to California.

"*What fresh hell now?*"

At this point, how could it be any worse?

The colonel eyeballed his captives long and hard, studying each face like a diamond cutter examining the latest South African Randlord find. Then he stuck out his hand—to Sal, then Maddie Pearl and Bama.

"Let me be the first to welcome you to California," he smiled. "Now let's get these damn tires replaced and you folks squared away at your new home!"

"Sir," said Bama, "what the—"

"And by the way..." the colonel cut him off. "My name is Wallace... Colonel Winston Wallace, and I'm the new Commanding Officer at Mojave."

# Chapter 38

All four piled into the Packard for the short drive into Needles, California. Their first ride in an air-conditioned vehicle, Sal, Maddie Pearl and Bama couldn't believe what they'd been missing. It was a whole new world, with no hurricane hot winds, no sweat soaked undies, no salty eye stinging, and no screamed conversation. More than once, they exchanged glances conveying *"can you believe this?"*

The plan was straightforward. Couldn't leave anyone behind to wait in the heat, so all four went along. They would head into Needles, address the tires, get something to eat, and be on their way. If the Plymouth couldn't be towed in, which was likely, the Colonel would take them back and help Sal put on the new tires. But regardless, they considered this a two-hour detour, at worst.

Colonel Winston Wallace, USA, did all the talking during the short ride into Needles. He had been to California many times—mostly San Francisco with short visits to LA and San Diego—but never to Barstow or environs. The soldiers at Mojave Anti-Aircraft Range had been instructed that their new commanding officer would arrive the next day. Wallace wanted to come a day early, to set an example. Although he never said so, it was obvious that he came from wealth. No man this age, in the Army, could afford a car like this. Plus, his travel references made clear that he already had seen much of the world, and it had seen him. He was not arrogant or cocky, but some things just ooze through regardless, like a prodigy's brilliance or gifted musician's talent. And although perhaps not a genius or virtuoso, it was beyond clear that Wallace was very capable indeed.

Despite his obvious attributes, however, Winston had a human side. The fact that he was going out of his way to help was evidence enough. And even before they got into the fancy car, he insisted Sal sit up front and personally apologized for all to hear.

"I hope you understand. I just needed to make sure how things *really* stood between you good folks. And by the way... as far as I'm concerned, and my concern is the only one that matters at Mojave, you're doing an exemplary job carrying out a direct order from a superior officer in getting that vehicle to his new duty station."

As civilization began reappearing on the outskirts of Needles they came upon Kenny's Kountry Kitchen. "Tell you what," said Winston. "Let's go ahead and get something to eat. I bet you're starved, and I'll pay!"

Sal and Bama exchanged knowing glances. "Can't stop there, sir," said Johnny.

"Now come on, Johnny B, quit calling me 'sir' all the time," snapped the Colonel. "You did your time. You don't answer to me."

"I'm sorry, sir... oops... force of habit, I guess," explained Bama. "Anyway... if you don't mind, let's find another place to stop, and you don't need to pay... we've got money."

"No. Now I insist. It's the least I can do. You guys have suffered enough, and I insist!"

"I... I mean... we appreciate that, sir... doggone it, there I go again," said Bama. "But seriously, let's go someplace else, okay?"

"What's the problem? I've been to a couple of these Kenny's on 66, and they're pretty good. Not as good as Kathy's Kountry Kafe, mind you, or Kozy Kottage Kamp, but still pretty good. They're all part of a chain, I think, with those K names. And besides, I thought you southern folks liked country cooking, you know, with lots of vegetables and gravy and red meat and so on."

Colonel Wallace pulled the Packard into the small parking lot, which was half empty with beat up old trucks—Fords particularly. He opened the door and started to get out. "Come on, it'll be good!"

"Sir, I'm sorry, but I'm going to have to insist that we not eat here," said John Claxton, firmly.

Winston stopped abruptly and looked into the back seat at Bama. "Hmmm? Now what in goodness am I missing here?" He looked at Sal. "What do you think, Walter?"

Sal looked back at Bama and Maddie Pearl, and then responded, "Sir, you folks can go ahead. I'll just wait in the car."

"Now what is going on?" asked the frustrated colonel.

"Colonel Wallace," inquired Bama, "did you notice the sign?"

Wallace looked up at the restaurant's marquee and then back at Bama. "Yeah, Kenny's Kountry Kitchen. So?"

Bama glanced at Maddie Pearl and Sal. All three were on a wavelength to which Wallace wasn't tuned. "Don't you think that's kind of... I don't know... *odd* how they spelled country?"

The light above Winston's head clicked on bright and clear. "Ohhhh," said Colonel Wallace, "Well I'll be a son of a bitch... *excuse my language Miss Maddie Pearl.* KKK. I never even gave it a thought. Geez, how could I have been so dense?"

Winston Wallace slid back behind the wheel, turned the ignition, and spun tires leaving the lot. "Let's find a respectable place," he snapped with derision glaring back at the bigot bastion. "My green money will never get into their lily white hands again, that's for God damned sure," he said to himself as they propelled into Needles proper.

*      *      *

From the 1920's to 60's, Needles was a key Route 66 destination, primarily because it was the only civilization for miles around but also since it greeted newcomers to California–the promised land of golden opportunity and green prosperity. Like so many dust bowl immigrants, the Joad family passed through Needles as evidenced by the brief appearance of Carty's Camp in *The Grapes of Wrath.*

By the time Wallace and company were passing through, Carty's had been sold to Howard Carmody who changed its name to Havasu Auto Court and Service Station. It boasted some twenty-eight cabins as well as groceries, a small café, and a gas station with assorted car parts, including tires. Winston figured that they could eat there, get the tires, head back out, fix the Plymouth, and then be on their way to MAAR. The first hitch came when Carty's-now-known-as-Havasu did not have the right sized tires for the Plymouth. The second was that the café was closed. So the intrepid quartet left for better luck elsewhere.

Front Street in Needles was a gauntlet of stores, restaurants, hotels and success. The confluence of the Colorado River running through town, the proximity of both Route 66 and the railroad, and the lack of nearby competition made Needles a place to be, and many chose to be there. Fred Harvey, never one to miss an opportunity, built El Garces in Needles, complete with linen and silver, distinctive china, fresh flowers daily and, of course, the beautiful Harvey Girls. Various service stations likewise found good homes for their gas and parts within the city and, after three stops, Winston et al. found a place with brand new Goodrich tires suitable for the car bought by Doc's parents and given to Doc and now owned by one John Claxton of Alabama, USA.

After consulting the *Green Book*—a "true piece of genius" per Wallace upon seeing it for the first time—they opted for an out-of-the-way Native American diner off Front Street near the river. They could have simply gone to the Harvey House, but this seemed more interesting. They sat outside, ate traditional Indian fare, and had ample opportunity to relax in the shade while watching the Colorado flow toward the Gulf of California and Vermilion Sea.

Their conversation drifted from the heat—Needles often is the hottest spot in America and, some days, the world—to the food to shops and stops they had encountered along Route 66. Winston Wallace brought up the ongoing conflicts across Europe. Sal and Maddie Pearl were oblivious, but learned much from the other two.

Both Bama and Winston thought major war was inevitable, but they disagreed as to whether the United States would get involved. Winston thought it was inescapable. Bama compared the situation to the Great War and emphasized that the US never would have fought then had the Germans not foolishly sunk the Lusitania with Americans aboard. Unless the Germans or even the Japanese did something incredibly reckless, we would have no reason to fight. They agreed to disagree in a friendly manner, and the conversation moved on.

Politics eventually took center stage, with the white men again dominating the discussion. Wallace was liberal; Johnny was conservative. With the election roughly a year away, each had strong opinions about the country's direction. Winston, an FDR

man through-and-through, favored the administration's realistic "stay on the sidelines" approach to the European problem. Bama, knowing what war can do to a people and a country, didn't like "his" candidate's interventionist stance, and even suggested that he "might not vote" this time.

From the day's big issues the tête-à-tête refocused down to each other. Sal and Maddie Pearl finally had a stage, and each expounded at length about where they were from, how they met, their respective home lives, how they ended up here, what they like to do and what they hoped to do—*someday*. Johnny Bama already knew much of their story, but Winston Wallace sat wide-eyed taking in every detail with little comment but great interest. He tuned in particularly to Sal's backstory, and truly seemed impressed with all that this African American man had overcome just to be sitting at this table in this Native American eatery in Needles on this hot day with three white people.

When asked to expound further on his background, Winston initially demurred. "Oh, I've bored you enough already with all that talk while driving into Needles." But they hadn't been bored, not at all, and so like prying out a healthy tooth they finally got him to open up some more. He was raised in New York City, went to boarding school, had no siblings, enjoyed sports, had never dated anyone seriously, and loved his parents but didn't particularly respect them or enjoy his upbringing. In addition to Manhattan, his family had homes in Florida and Georgetown—he liked visiting both—but preferred Europe where he often summered.

Maddie Pearl's eyes glazed over as Wallace talked of so many magical places about which she never had heard and feared never would see. Bama was envious of the travel and wondered why he had not taken more advantage of his resources and lived similarly, particularly before *it* happened. Sal stared at the Colorado River thinking of all the new ideas Aristotle's *Poetics* had instilled and how *"this guy's life is a book unto itself."*

\*     \*     \*

By the time all four tires had been replaced on the Plymouth, with Winston Wallace doing most of the work—"I

insist"—it was after four o'clock. The temperature had dropped to a cool 95° and MAAR remained almost two hundred miles away. With no serious debate, they decided to stay the night and leave early the next morning for their new home. Being *Green Book* approved and a Harvey, the El Garces served them for the night, without incident. However, they respected the expectation that Walter Carver Jefferson would be discreet so as not to upset the other clientele. It was an awful concession, but necessary, and relatively tame considering the alternative.

The overnight stay enabled the four to become even better acquainted. Johnny Bama had encountered his share of rich snobs, but Winston Wallace exhibited absolutely none of the typical traits. Bama likewise had experienced self-superior military officers many times, but the colonel showed no rank as the four talked freely about life, ambitions, "back home," dreams, and everything else that arises when four together have hours to kill and conversation their only weapon.

In fact, nothing about this newfound friend seemed out-of-place or off-putting. He was intelligent, friendly, interesting, and actually somewhat fun to be around. It seemed a little odd that he made no play for Maddie Pearl. After all, she was a stunning beauty with a great personality. But Bama attributed Winston's evident disinterest to Maddie Pearl's age and apparent "relationship" with this David "Doc" Hodge the colonel would meet the next day.

"*He definitely is a gentleman,*" thought Bama. "*And besides, he's probably got more than one or two fine fillies already in the stable back home.*"

Johnny Bama also noticed how tuned-in Wallace seemed to each self-story. He wasn't feigning polite interest; Winston appeared to be genuinely intrigued by every nuance of everyone's life to date, particularly Sal's. It was as if the colonel never had spoken with an African American and desperately wanted to know... well... everything. He shuddered at the various instances of abuse by the likes of even Maddie Pearl's own brother, and he was fascinated by the unfairness of tenant farming.

"Why didn't you just buy the land," he asked naively at one point, displaying just how reality withdrawn rich folk can be—no matter how well meaning. Sal proceeded to tell the family story of

how his grandfather *did* in fact buy the land only to have this "Boss Lee" character get a crooked judge to dispossess the family of it altogether.

Winston Wallace was openly stunned to hear that such dirty dealing could happen here, in America; Johnny Bama advised that "cold like that is just the tip of the iceberg."

Johnny's tragic accident, his continuing love of Jessie Mae and Annabelle, his life-sentence of permanent injury, and his reluctance to be home where haunting memories persist also piqued Winston's interest.

"Your farm sounds magical," Wallace observed at one point.

Bama responded in a faux aristocratic voice dripping with snobbery, "Well actually, my good man, I've many ranches about the estate." Spoken to any other true aristocrat, this would have been insulting; spoken to Winston Wallace, it was hilarious and all joined in the laughter.

Winston also prodded Bama to talk about flying—in great detail. From shear boredom and with afternoons to kill after football season, Wallace had taken flying lessons in college at a small airport outside Cambridge. His father even bought him a Curtiss Robin similar to the model flown by Wrongway Corrigan. It was the Golden Age of aviation with barnstormers, wing walkers, and air shows capturing America's imagination in the wake of the Atlantic crossing by the Nazi sympathizing, eugenics endorsing, anti-Semitic, race baiting American "hero," Charles Augustus Lindbergh.

Winston Wallace was no fan of Lucky Lindy and despised the fact that they shared the colonel rank. Without quoting it directly, Wallace described as "trash" the famed aviator's recent *Readers Digest* piece endorsing the preservation of European blood. [Here is the actual quote: "*We can have peace and security only so long as we band together to preserve that most priceless possession, our inheritance of European blood, only so long as we guard ourselves against attack by foreign armies and dilution by foreign races.*"] Although wholly unexposed to the plight of African Americans, Wallace had a clear sense of right and wrong and unequivocally respected Walter Carver as equal to Johnny Bama

and Maddie Pearl and anybody else... except Lindy, of course who—to Wallace—was less than sub-human.

Winston received Maddie Pearl's personal account differently. It was as if he was trying not to exhibit any attraction whatsoever. By overcompensating, he almost seemed cold and aloof to the point of indifference. He cared that she was poor and seemed concerned about her now-missing family. *("Why don't you contact them?" "Because I don't know where they are or how to get in touch.")* Maddie Pearl did not cover Luke's attack and glossed over her father's KKK ties and propensity to beat Mama. The horrible home life came through nonetheless. Once again, the colonel had no point of reference and couldn't imagine a table without regular food, a home without full flooring, or an existence without medical care, schooling, books, magazines or even daily baths. Despite his outward cool deportment, Winston was developing a deep respect and admiration for Maddie Pearl, with each new tidbit of her difficult life and spunky attitude.

In fact, the more he heard about each of his new friends, the more two truths emerged: first, these truly are very special people; and second, he had so, so much to learn about the *real* America from which he had been sheltered every day of his obnoxiously entitled existence.

His first lessons began the next day.

# Chapter 39

They awoke early the next day, enjoyed a hearty El Garces breakfast served by a genuine Harvey Girl, and piled into their two cars for the final push to a new life in the California wasteland. With 171 miles across the desert and two mountain ranges ahead, they agreed to stay close together. Johnny Bama suggested that Maddie Pearl ride in the colonel's air-conditioned Packard while he and Sal would take the Plymouth.

The five-hour drive provided open opportunity for further conversation, but each pair in each car was *talked out* from the day before. Besides, each was preoccupied with personal thoughts of what may come.

*     *     *

Colonel Winston Wallace slept virtually none the night before. His mind spun with thoughts of Sal and Maddie Pearl, of all they had overcome so far. Compared to these intrepid travelers, life had been a walk in the park for him. Raised literally with a silver spoon in his perfect mouth and his straight, almost too-white teeth, Winston Wallace never had to work for anything. He resented it, deeply.

Even though his boyhood peer group in New York was similarly situated and took their advantages with ease and arrogant expectations, Winston resisted. Escaping his father's powerful sphere was like a rocket struggling to escape Earth's gravity. And like NASA's first missions in the sixties, more than once he crashed and burned in the process.

Running away from home at age twelve proved disastrous when a thunderstorm flooded his impromptu camp in the woods tainting his food and water. At fifteen, he "borrowed" his mother's new Cadillac and made it all the way to Michigan. A random police stop, a check of the luxury car's registration, and the absence of a

driver's license found Winston back east—quickly, and painfully. Summer jobs landed on his own volition quickly were aborted when discovered—no Wallace can be seen working menially.

He was not a bad kid and, in fact, was easily the most conscientious of his contemporaries. Courtesy of purebred genes and boarding school instructors, Winston was highly capable intellectually and physically. At Harvard—to which he gained admission legitimately even though he would have been admitted regardless—Winston captained the Crimson and was a terror among fellow Ivy League footballers. A quick dip in law school, in Cambridge of course, and then it's Wall Street, or perhaps K Street, and the American dream of money, power, influence, wife, kids, a mistress or two, and perfection happily ever after.

To his father's shock and displeasure, Winston eschewed law and privileged order and took a different path: The United States Army.

Like none of his college classmates, all solemnly dedicated to intoxication and skirt chasing, Winston focused on the European conflict. Having spent considerable time abroad, he knew the continent well and recognized the dangers posed by Germany's new dictator, a former wallpaper hanger named Adolf Hitler.

Being a college grad, Winston enlisted as an officer; being a Wallace, he quickly ascended to full colonel; being a man of integrity, he despised the preferential treatment; being a person of character, he vowed to prove himself worthy of the rank.

Considered by far the worst possible assignment to the vilest possible duty station at the most inopportune time in the entire United States Army, Mojave Anti-Aircraft Range prompted every officer to scamper like rats escaping a snake pit. Colonel Winston Wallace stepped up and volunteered, without reservation.

Now he was on the final leg of his cross-country journey to this desert nightmare. He had never managed anything bigger than a huddle and, despite his innate confidence, Winston naturally was concerned. He had read much about leadership, and learned that no one has a damn clue about it. Many say the key is discipline: "the men must fear you." Others say the key is respect: "the men must venerate you." A few say the key is love: "the men must adore you." The Army manual said simply: "the men must follow you,

obediently!" In typical military fashion, however, it neglected to explain *how* precisely one is to *get* followed.

Wallace had thought back to coaches, preachers, professors, and other admired authority figures. They shared no traits whatsoever. Some were honest; some were hypocrites; some were mean; some were kind; some were old; some were young; some were... well... whatever humankind could cough up.

Winston liked the concept of leading by example. Thus he determined to arrive a day early. The effort failed upon his happenstance encounter with three distressed southerners on The Mother Road. Now he would be on time, which still was good, but he'd be riding in with this unexpected posse of non-military personnel. He already had begun formulating ideas as to how each could prove to be an actual asset to MAAR. But still, it would be messy arriving in this manner, and messiness was neither recommended in any of the leadership tomes nor a trait inherent in any of Winston's admired leaders.

But such was his predicament, and he'd make it work—no matter what!

*        *        *

Bama had been in some pain the last couple of days, but strove to hide it from his companions. "*What good will it do them to worry,*" he thought. "*And besides, there's really nothing anyone can do about it.*" The doctor back in Albuquerque had sugarcoated the condition in Maddie Pearl's presence, but Bama knew the *real* story. It was not pretty. Only in his mid-thirties, he'd probably never see fifty, and there was a world of living to do. Until their encounter with Winston Wallace, Bama had managed to suppress his worldly thoughts of travel and adventure but, after hearing of the colonel's exploits from New York to Italy and everywhere in between, his wanderlust had begun creeping back like a scout sneaking up on an enemy campsite.

Although he'd never been there, Johnny Bama knew well what Mojave would entail. It was new, so there would be precious little infrastructure; it was in the desert, so there'd be no local distractions like bars, restaurants, and flophouses; it was Army, so there'd be a lot of young, angry, frustrated, overheated men with

little to do and nothing to do it with. This could be no "home" for Maddie Pearl, and even Sal likely would struggle with African Americans not yet military mainstream. And as to himself, Bama likely would take the first opportunity to leave, probably to Barstow, at least initially, and then to... well... wherever globe skimmers venture.

\*          \*          \*

Sal's thoughts meandered like that Colorado River he had studied the day before while listening to Winston Wallace's magnificent tales of a wonderful life with which the wealthy man seemed so counter-intuitively frustrated. He was worried about Maddie Pearl, deeply, and felt responsible for her impending predicament. He suspected what Bama knew: that this new Mojave Anti-Aircraft Range would be a wild, brutal, inhospitable place at which no naïve, pretty, teenage girl should live. And what would come of her if Mojave failed? Like Sal, she had no fallback, no Plan B.

Sallerhead loved Maddie Pearl—he had from first sight—but suppressed those thoughts, those urges, for obvious reasons. They could never be together, not in this time, not in this country, not in this life. So he didn't hold her even though he so desired, and he didn't pat her back gently or tousle her hair when kidding around. And he didn't whisper cute nothings in private moments.

And he thought often, *"If only."* But only was never to be, and he hated every minute of having to pretend.

Aside from Maddie Pearl, Sal was concerned with those recurring Doc thoughts: what if he doesn't welcome us; what if he won't help; what if he isn't there at all?

Courtesy of Bama's largesse, Sal had money leftover from the sale of the Plymouth. If Mojave were a dead end for Maddie Pearl—better than a fifty-fifty proposition—he'd use most of it to help her get back east. Then he'd do... what?

As evidenced by the white lie that the black man had done an *"exemplary job carrying out a direct order from a superior officer in getting that vehicle to his new duty station,"* Colonel Wallace appeared to like and respect Sal. But even with the new CO's support, Sal's Army prospects seemed dim, at best. Almost

certainly he'd be the only African American at Mojave and destined for menial labor, at best. He'd tough it out and finish his hitch, if necessary, but that would only postpone the inevitable: what was he to do with his life, whether now, or later?

He'd work, but where, doing what, for whom? JB no doubt would offer help, but Sal already felt too beholden to this kind, Alabama man. Could he work on a ranch? Probably. Did he want to continue doing pretty much exactly what he'd done up to now? Definitely not!

The journey from down east swampland to far west wasteland had exposed Walter Carver Jefferson to many new things up close and personally, mostly fresh examples of the stale "man's inhumanity to man" shtick. He'd experienced "sundown towns" with proud signs proclaiming, "WHEN THE SUN GOES DOWN, THE NIGGERS LEAVE TOWN!" He'd been cheated by fellow African Americans, threatened by redneck cops, and even fly-swatted by a pimply little punk. But through the arduous trip's numerous negatives, three positives presented.

The ESSO station in Amarillo, with the black owner so confident and successful, thrilled Sal. He never imagined that possibility—this newly discovered reality, that blacks too can make it in America, on their own, even in the heart of a horrid, backward place like Texas!

When Bama first talked about flying, Sal found it interesting; with Wallace's fine-tuning, Sal was enthralled. He didn't know how or when, but he determined then and there that someday, some way, he was going to fly!

But clearly his most exciting discovery was *The Grapes of Wrath*. He could read and write, having been taught well by his beloved father, but WC Jefferson had no idea just how transformative the written word could be. The book took him places unimaginable to a country farm boy raised on hominy and Jesus, whippings and ploughshares. When he finished the book, he thirsted for more, and next found Aristotle's *Poetics*, the manual for exactly how to do what Steinbeck had done. The possibilities kept Sal up each night since. When Bama or Winston, or even Maddie Pearl, told a story now, Sal's mind filled with ideas and plots and characters and endings.

This whole new world, this literary realm, never existed before, and now it was all Sallerhead could imagine. But again... how? Specifically, how does one become John Steinbeck?

He didn't know, just as he didn't know what was to become of him, or of Maddie Pearl. But Sal knew three things for certain: he loved her, she felt the same, and together they recognized what could have been... *if only.*

*          *          *

While Winston Wallace, Johnny Bama, and Sal were awash in fluid thoughts of what had been and what was to come, Maddie Pearl obsessed over the here and now.

The Packard was cool and very nice, as was sitting beside this handsome, rich, young, evidently available, new colonel. Nevertheless, she missed riding with Sal.

She'd never had a true boyfriend or relations of any sort, other than the two times Sal and she embraced. By day, and especially since Johnny Bama joined the team, she hid her emotions, well. But at night, those encounters dominated her thoughts as she fell asleep with teenage fantasies of love and sex and rapturous joy. But that's all they were, dreamscapes of what never had been and surely never could be, at least not with Sal.

But was David Hodge the answer? In some way she neither understood nor could explain, she *loved* Doc, or at least thought it was love. But why? She barely knew the man. They'd never even dated, much less kissed or uttered breathily "I love you" with passion flowing in full body embrace. Could it have been love at first sight, or mere chemistry, a molecular reaction fully explainable scientifically with charts and graphs?

She'd enjoyed their nights shared within the pages of *National Geographic* comfortably numb to everything and everyone but themselves. Hadn't he felt the same? Or was he just a nice guy, carrying out his duty comforting a patient in need?

And if it were not true love or chemicals amok, then what was it? Were her feelings for him a mere girlish illusion destined to vanish into nothingness like some Mojave mirage? Or even worse... was Doctor Dreamy a second choice, a consolation prize, a convenient alternative...to Sal?

Maddie Pearl didn't know, but she was fed up with *"what if"* and *"if only"* and such similar silliness that con the mind into inaction, unfulfillment, and frustration. She was going to get some answers, once and for all, today.

She had made it a point to wear her Albuquerque outfit all the way down to the new shoes and purse. And she spent extra time brushing her lustrous hair, and fixed her face as well as her limited makeup and experience allowed. Although none of the men that morning had said a word, she knew that Winston, Bama, and Sal noticed, approvingly. And come hell or Armageddon, Captain David "Doc" Hodge was going to notice, too! And if he didn't like it, or if he wasn't even at MAAR, then *that* would be the answer and she'd move on from there.

"You doing okay?" Winston Wallace asked, somewhat out of the blue.

"Huh... oh, yeah. I'm fine."

"You've been kinda quiet. I guess you're not used to the air conditioning. It can kind of lull you to dreamland, I guess."

"No," said Maddie Pearl, "it's not the air conditioning, and I'm not dreaming... not today."

*            *            *

In due course, they traversed Cajon Pass and in the distance it appeared, wavering in the rising heated air like some mystical oasis, their destiny: the United States Army's newest military installation—Mojave Anti-Aircraft Range.

# Chapter 40

The Packard arrived first followed closely by the Plymouth. Before them was a hodgepodge of tents arrayed in no particular order, and sheer nothingness. The place looked abandoned. Except for two small tumbleweed balls passing through on their way to oblivion, there was no movement. Variations of *"is this really it"* clogged the minds of Maddie Pearl, Sal, Johnny Bama, and Winston Wallace as they gawked at the hot, dry, dead desolation.

The new CO emerged from his cool cocoon into the hellish oven and stood, dumbfounded. Had they made a wrong turn somewhere? Had Wallace not been informed of the base's relocation? Could some plague or marauding invaders have overtaken the place?

Wallace called out, "ANYBODY HERE?" After no response, he yelled, "HEY! ANYBODY! THIS IS COLONEL WINSTON WALLACE, THE NEW C-O!"

Maddie Pearl noticed movement some fifty yards away atop a forty-foot tower and what sounded like someone saying "Jesus Christ" in an exasperated tone.

"What's that?" she said, pointing.

Wallace took a few steps in the tower's direction and was about to call out when *CLANG CLANG CLANG* began a bell hanging from a rope fetched at the tower's peak. It reminded Maddie Pearl of the bell back home that Preacher Roe's wife would ring Sunday morning to announce the Lord's Day.

David "Doc" Hodge, dozing in a little tent that served as his medical office, was dreaming of swimming in the Atlantic Ocean off Atlantic Beach near Morehead City. Awakened by the clamor, he mumbled, "What the fuck now?" The medic stretched, straightened his nap-rumpled uniform, and wandered from the hot tent into the blazing world outside.

Squinting at first, then focusing more clearly, he realized this remained a dream and laughed to himself in wonder at the human mind's amazing abilities. There was WC Jefferson and Maddie Pearl, as real as could be, right there in the middle of this godforsaken place, and she wasn't even perspiring, and her clothes looked perfect, as did her hair, and she was more beautiful than he remembered, and "*why is my mind tricking me in such evil fashion?*"

He turned, reentered the tent, stretched back on the cot, closed his eyes, and—

"*Wait a minute! What the hell? JESUS FUCKING CHRIST ALMIGHTY!*"

Doc sprang up, darted outside nearly tripping on a tent stake, and sprinted half dressed to the befuddled quartet standing alone in the middle of the camp compound.

Doc reached the gathering in a cloud of hot desert dust, rudely brushed aside some new guy in his fancy uniform with full bird insignia, grabbed Maddie Pearl by the waist, and kissed her long, hard, and passionately... and she kissed him back—fully.

"Well," said new Commanding Officer Winston Wallace. "I guess you two have met?"

*        *        *

*Beside the once new Plymouth in which Maddie Pearl and he had just completed their epic, cross-country odyssey side-by-side, Walter Carver "Sal" Jefferson stoically stood, stared, and to no one said...*

"If only."

# About the Author

**Jack Jenkins** is a graduate of East Carolina University and the University of North Carolina School of Law. During his legal career, Jenkins practiced in Morehead City, served as General Counsel to the NC Department of Human Resources, was General Counsel to Governor James B. Hunt Jr., and served three terms as a Special Superior Court Judge holding court throughout the Tar Heel state. He is retired and lives with his wife of over forty years, Mary Charles, in their home on Bogue Sound along the North Carolina coast.

Don't miss *MADDIE PEARL - FAR FROM HOME,* the next book in the series by Jack Jenkins chronicling this amazing woman and her incredible life and times. Now available at Amazon in the Book Section.